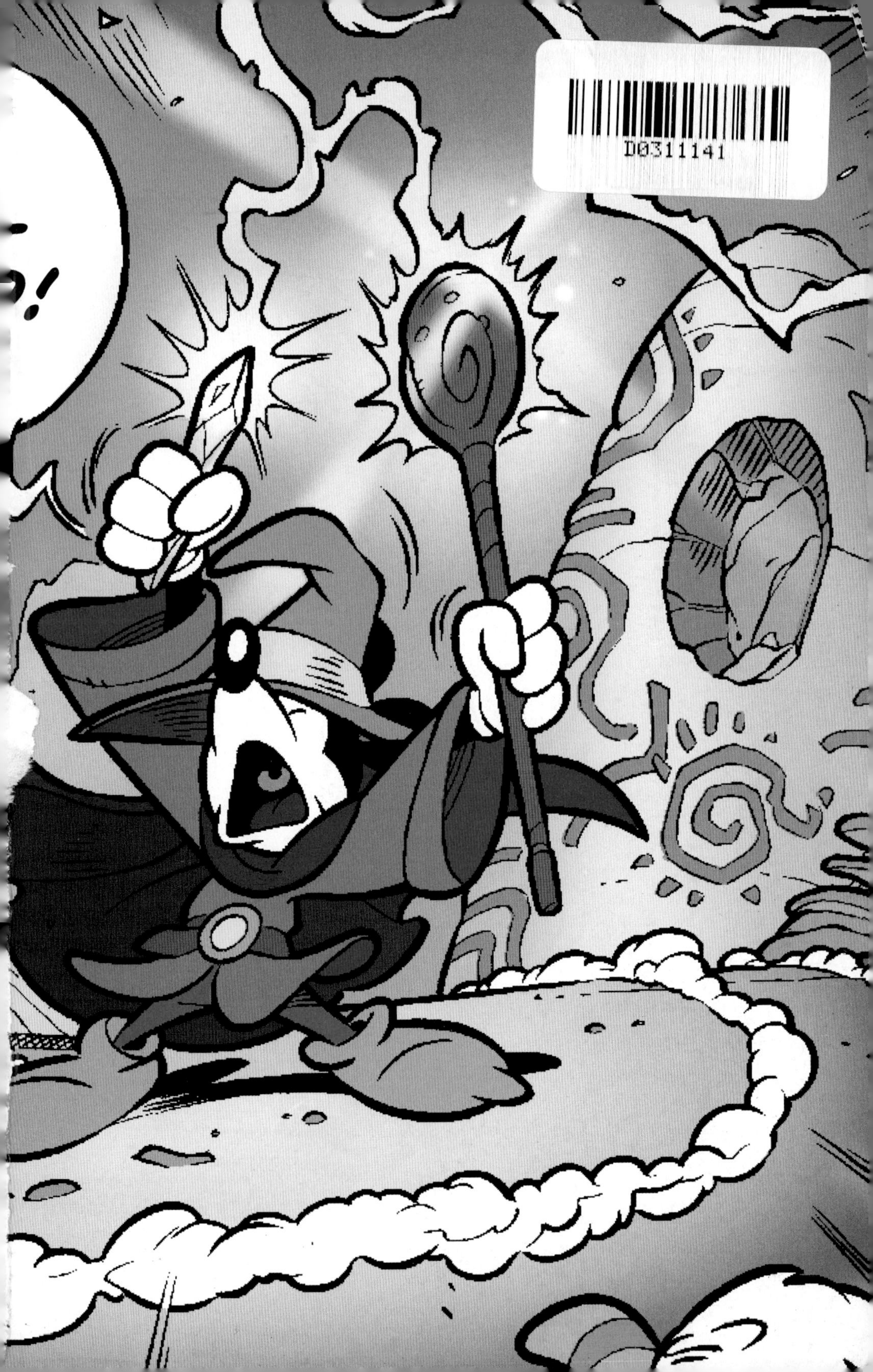

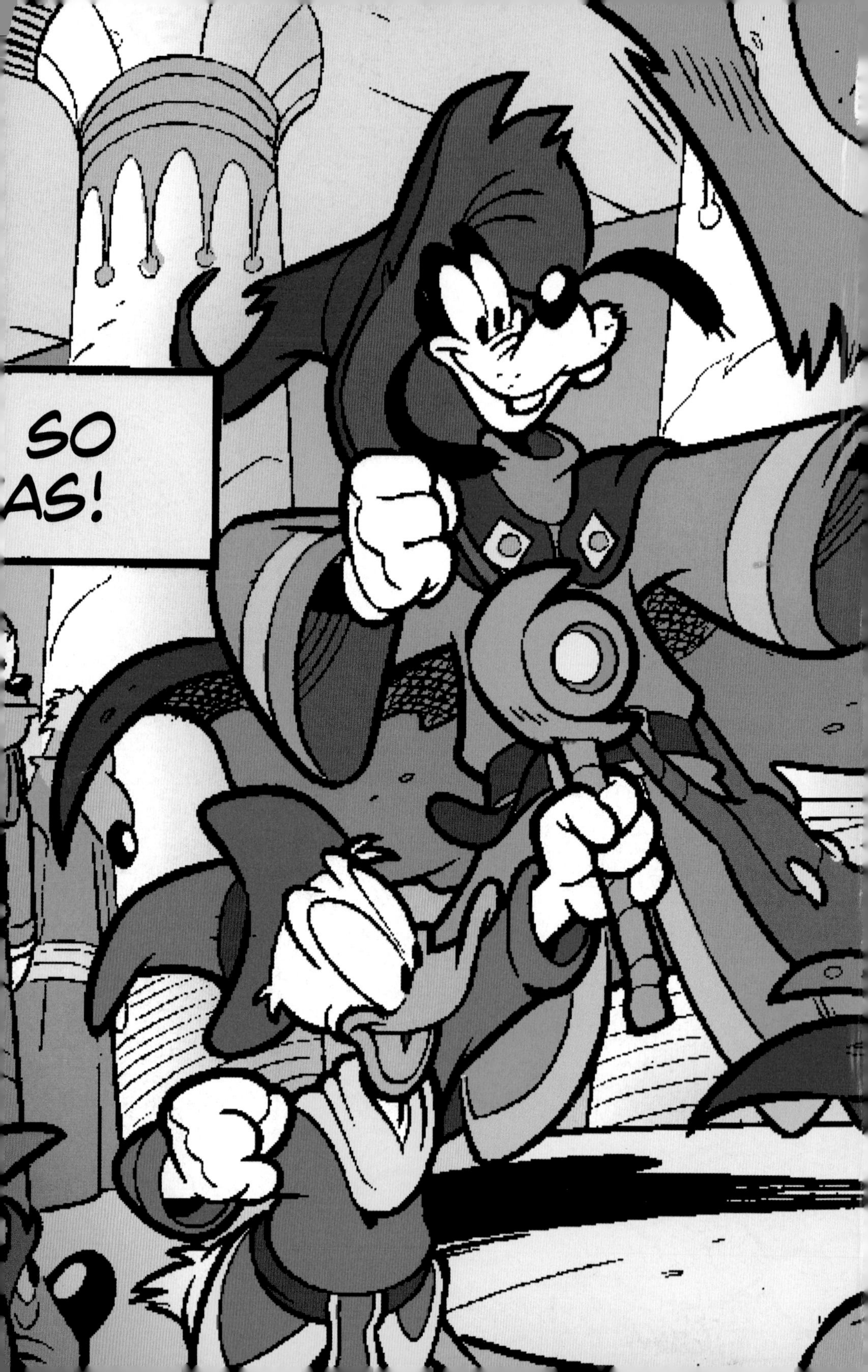
SO
AS!

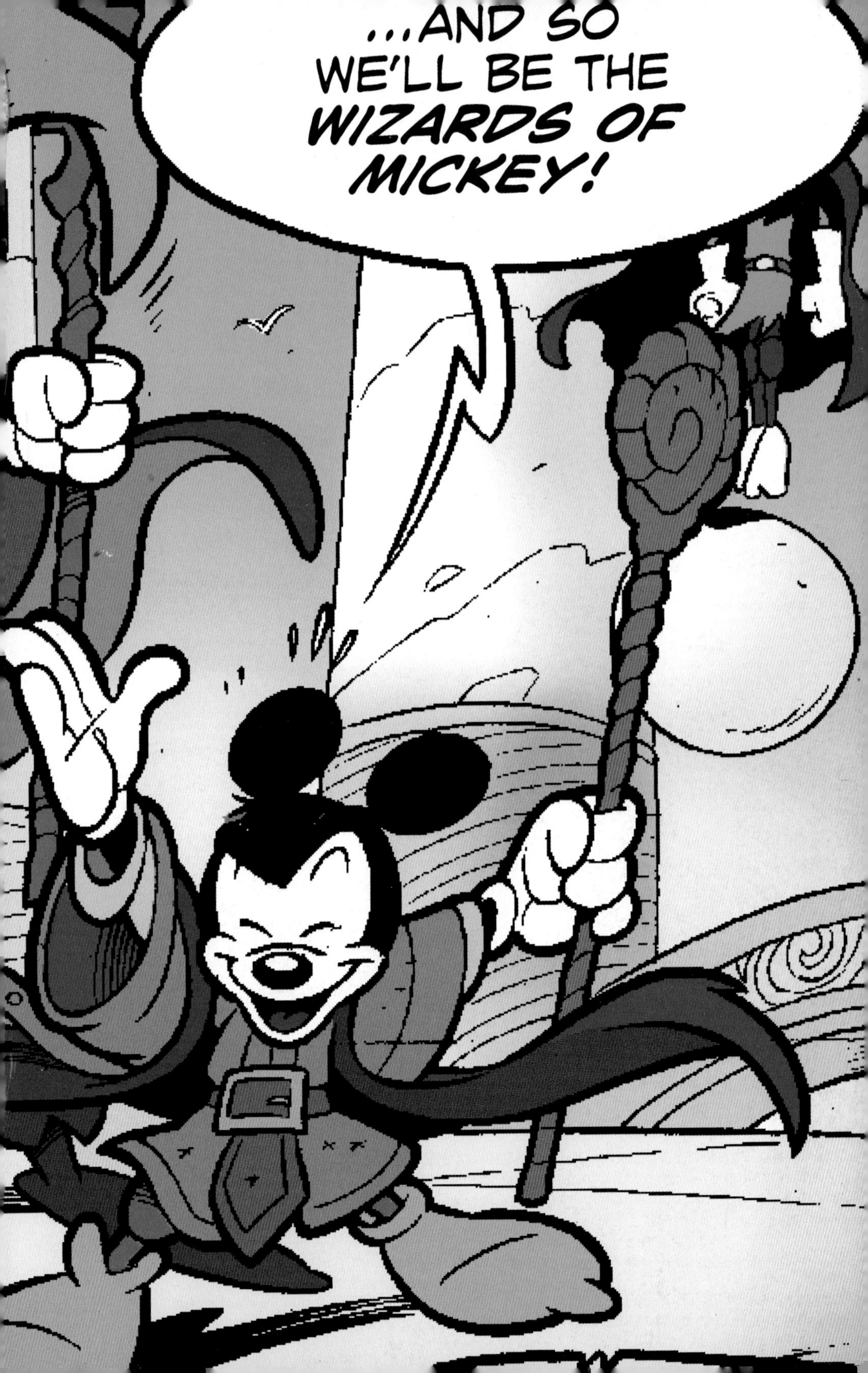
...AND SO WE'LL BE THE *WIZARDS OF MICKEY!*

Walt Disney's Wizards of Mickey
MOUSE MAGIC

ROSS RICHIE
chief executive officer

MARK WAID
editor-in-chief

ADAM FORTIER
vice president,
publishing

CHIP MOSHER
marketing director

MATT GAGNON
managing editor

JENNY CHRISTOPHER
sales director

FIRST EDITION: JANUARY 2010

10 9 8 7 6 5 4 3 2 1
PRINTED BY WORLD COLOR PRESS, INC.,
ST-ROMUALD, QC., CANADA.

Office of publication: 6310 San Vicente Blvd Ste 404, Los Angeles, CA 90048-5457.

A catalog record for this book is available from the Library of Congress and on our website at www.boom-kids.com on the Librarian Resource Page.

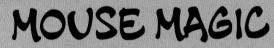

MOUSE MAGIC

COLLECTING ISSUES 296-299

ARTISTS:
LORENZO PASTROVICCHIO
MARCO GERVASIO
MARCO PALAZZI
ALESSANDRO PERINA

WRITER:
STEFANO AMBROSIO

TRADE COVER:
MARCO GHIGLIONE

ASSISTANT EDITOR:
CHRISTOPHER BURNS

TRANSLATION:
SAIDA TEMAFONTE

EDITOR:
AARON SPARROW

LETTERERS:
TROY PETERI
CHAPTER 1
DERON BENNETT
CHAPTER 2-4

DESIGNER:
ERIKA TERRIQUEZ

SPECIAL THANKS TO:
JESSE POST, LAUREN KRESSEL
& ELENA GARBO

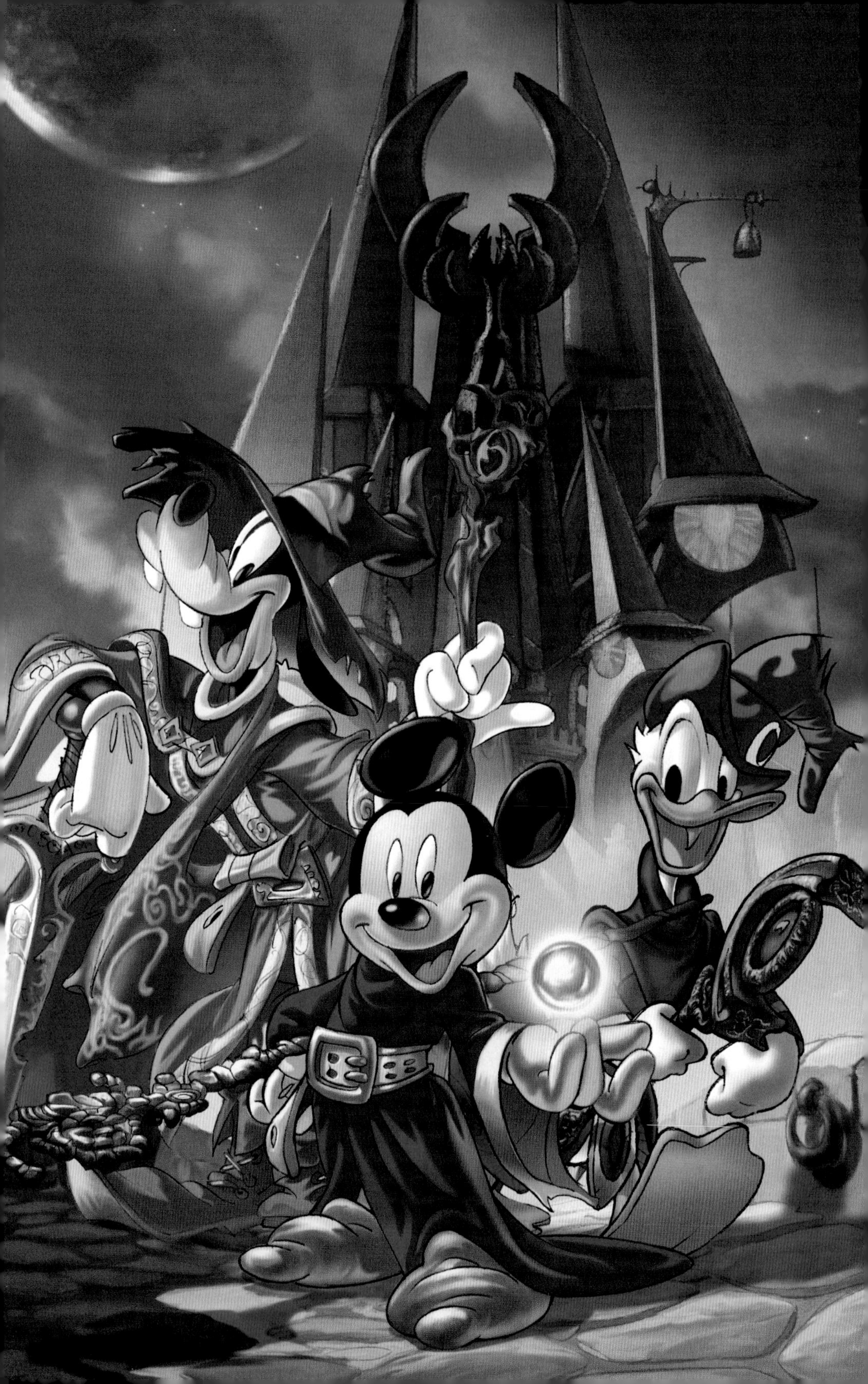

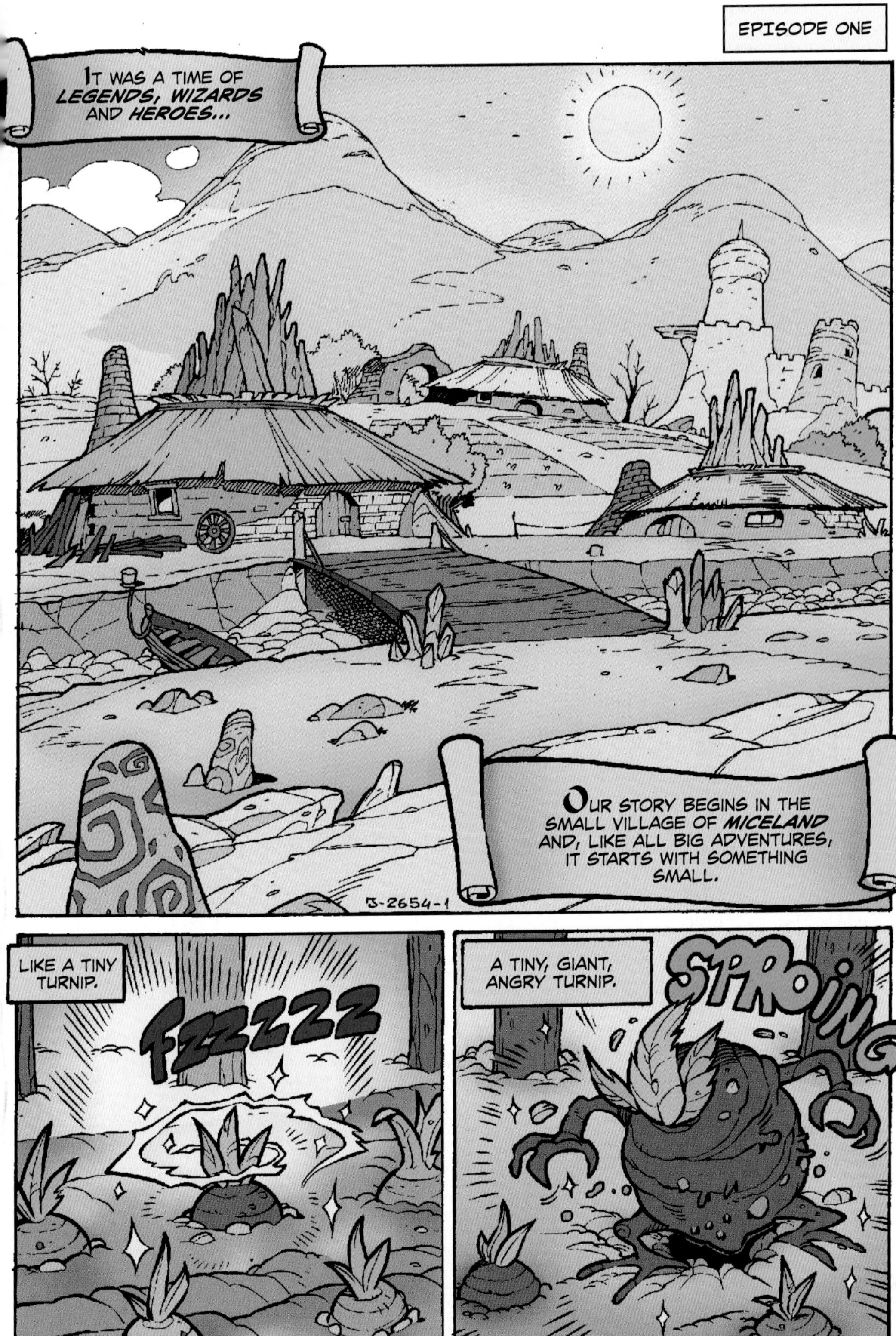
EPISODE ONE
IT WAS A TIME OF LEGENDS, WIZARDS AND HEROES...
OUR STORY BEGINS IN THE SMALL VILLAGE OF MICELAND AND, LIKE ALL BIG ADVENTURES, IT STARTS WITH SOMETHING SMALL.
3-2654-1
LIKE A TINY TURNIP.
FZZZZZ
A TINY, GIANT, ANGRY TURNIP.
SPROING

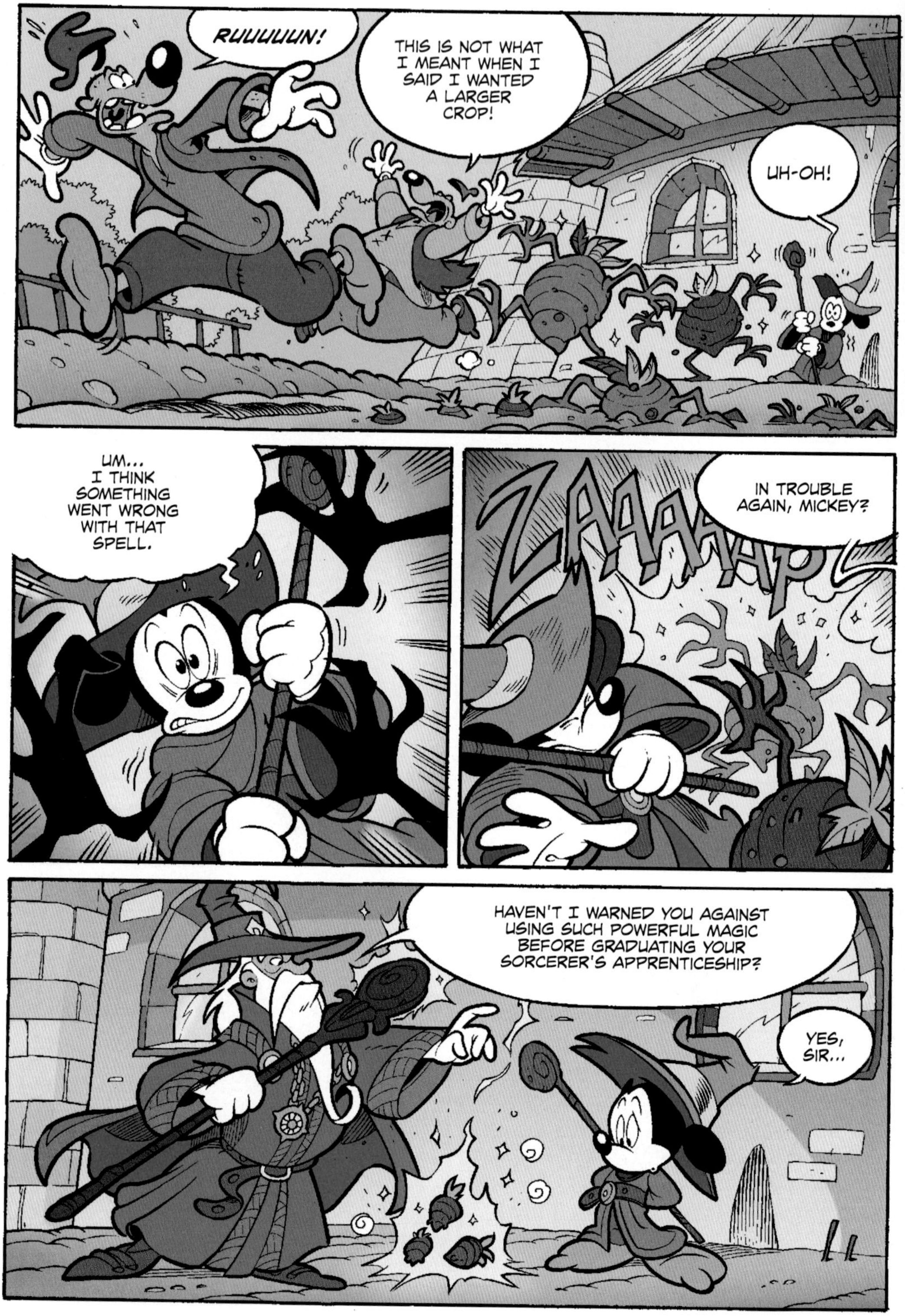
RUUUUUN!
THIS IS NOT WHAT I MEANT WHEN I SAID I WANTED A LARGER CROP!
UH-OH!
UM... I THINK SOMETHING WENT WRONG WITH THAT SPELL.
ZAAAAAP
IN TROUBLE AGAIN, MICKEY?
HAVEN'T I WARNED YOU AGAINST USING SUCH POWERFUL MAGIC BEFORE GRADUATING YOUR SORCERER'S APPRENTICESHIP?
YES, SIR...

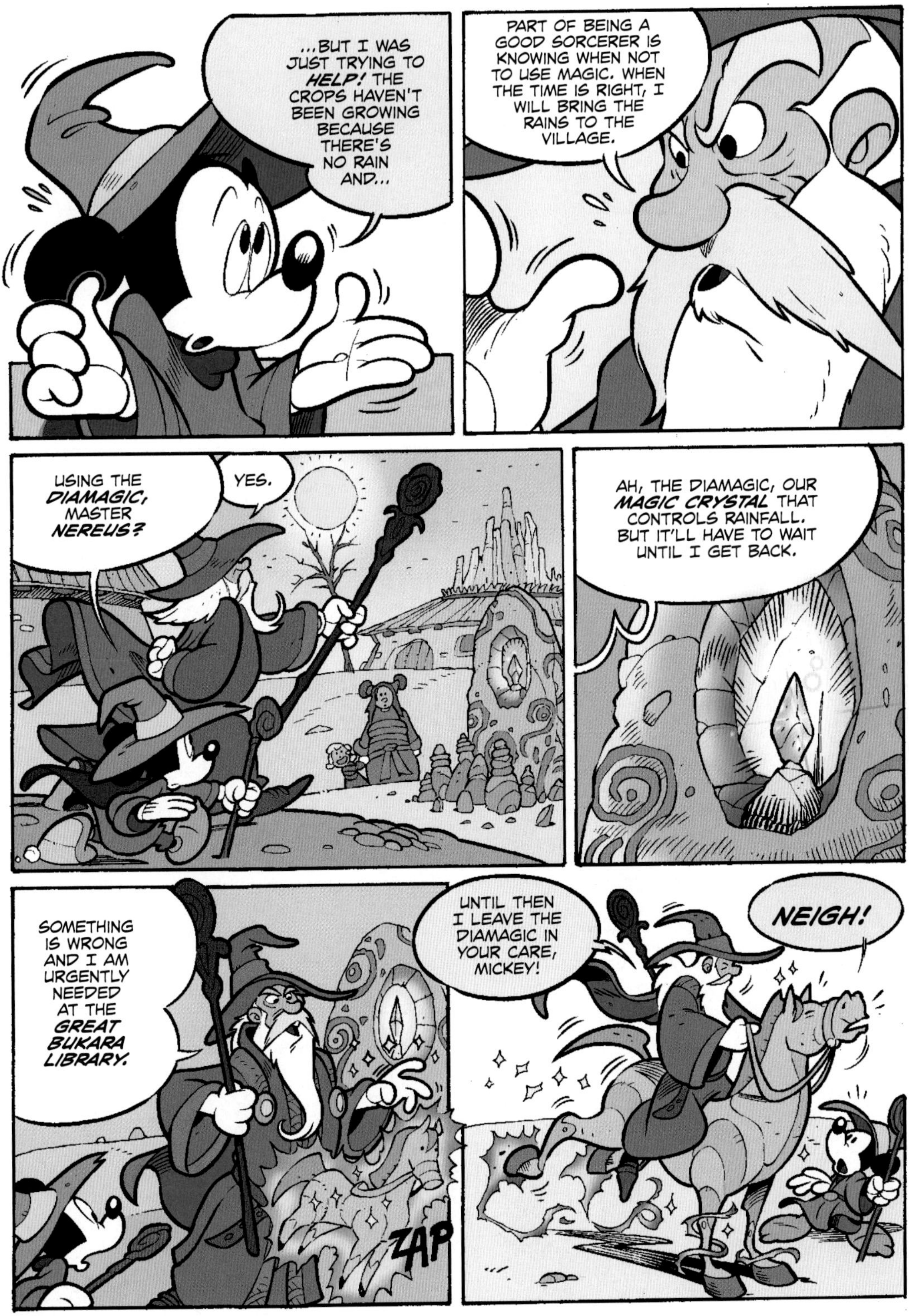

...BUT I WAS JUST TRYING TO *HELP!* THE CROPS HAVEN'T BEEN GROWING BECAUSE THERE'S NO RAIN AND...
PART OF BEING A GOOD SORCERER IS KNOWING WHEN NOT TO USE MAGIC. WHEN THE TIME IS RIGHT, I WILL BRING THE RAINS TO THE VILLAGE.
USING THE *DIAMAGIC,* MASTER *NEREUS?*
YES.
AH, THE DIAMAGIC, OUR *MAGIC CRYSTAL* THAT CONTROLS RAINFALL. BUT IT'LL HAVE TO WAIT UNTIL I GET BACK.
SOMETHING IS WRONG AND I AM URGENTLY NEEDED AT THE *GREAT BUKARA LIBRARY.*
ZAP
UNTIL THEN I LEAVE THE DIAMAGIC IN YOUR CARE, MICKEY!
NEIGH!

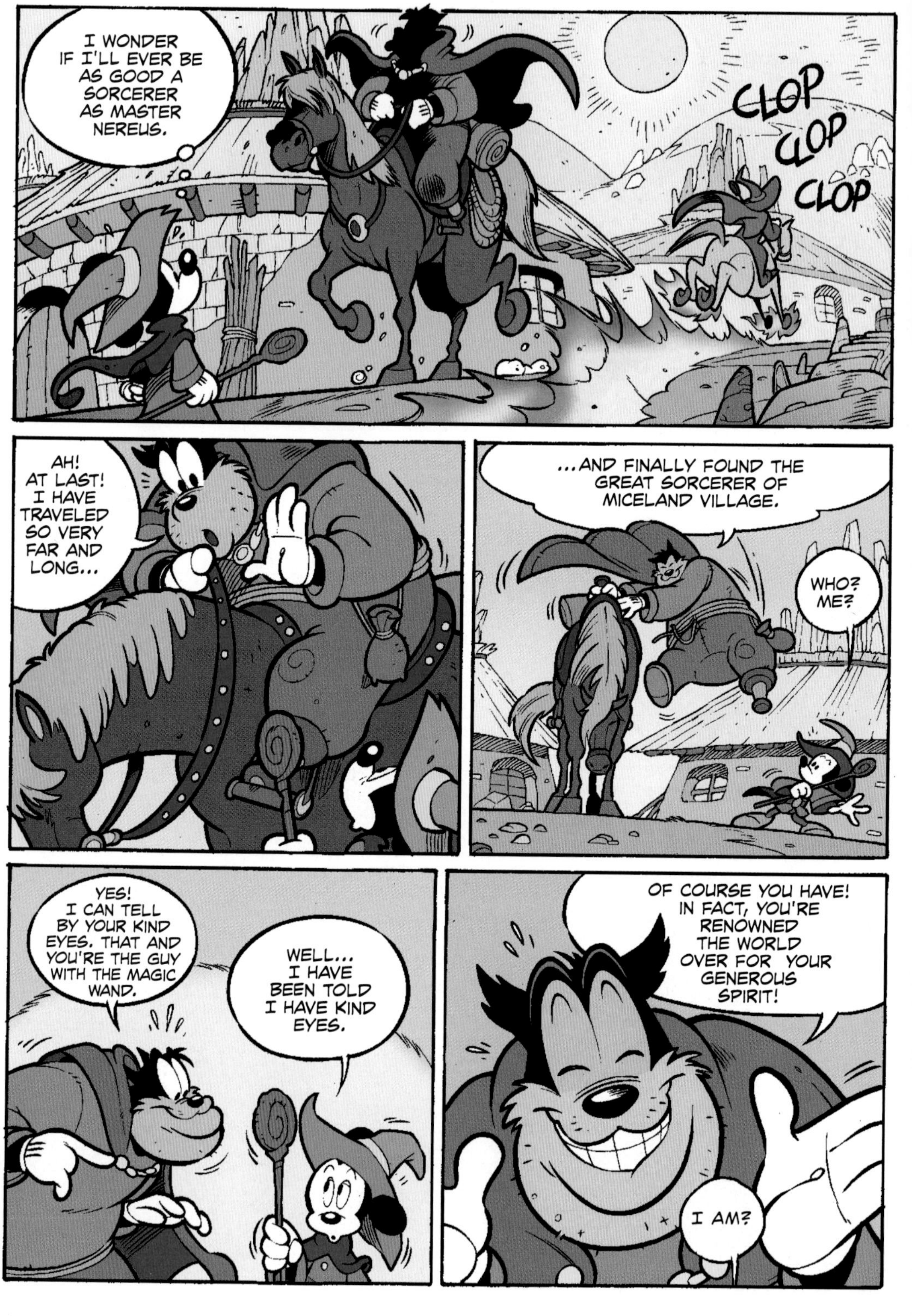
I WONDER IF I'LL EVER BE AS GOOD A SORCERER AS MASTER NEREUS.
CLOP
CLOP
CLOP
AH! AT LAST! I HAVE TRAVELED SO VERY FAR AND LONG...
...AND FINALLY FOUND THE GREAT SORCERER OF MICELAND VILLAGE.
WHO? ME?
YES! I CAN TELL BY YOUR KIND EYES. THAT AND YOU'RE THE GUY WITH THE MAGIC WAND.
WELL... I HAVE BEEN TOLD I HAVE KIND EYES.
OF COURSE YOU HAVE! IN FACT, YOU'RE RENOWNED THE WORLD OVER FOR YOUR GENEROUS SPIRIT!
I AM?

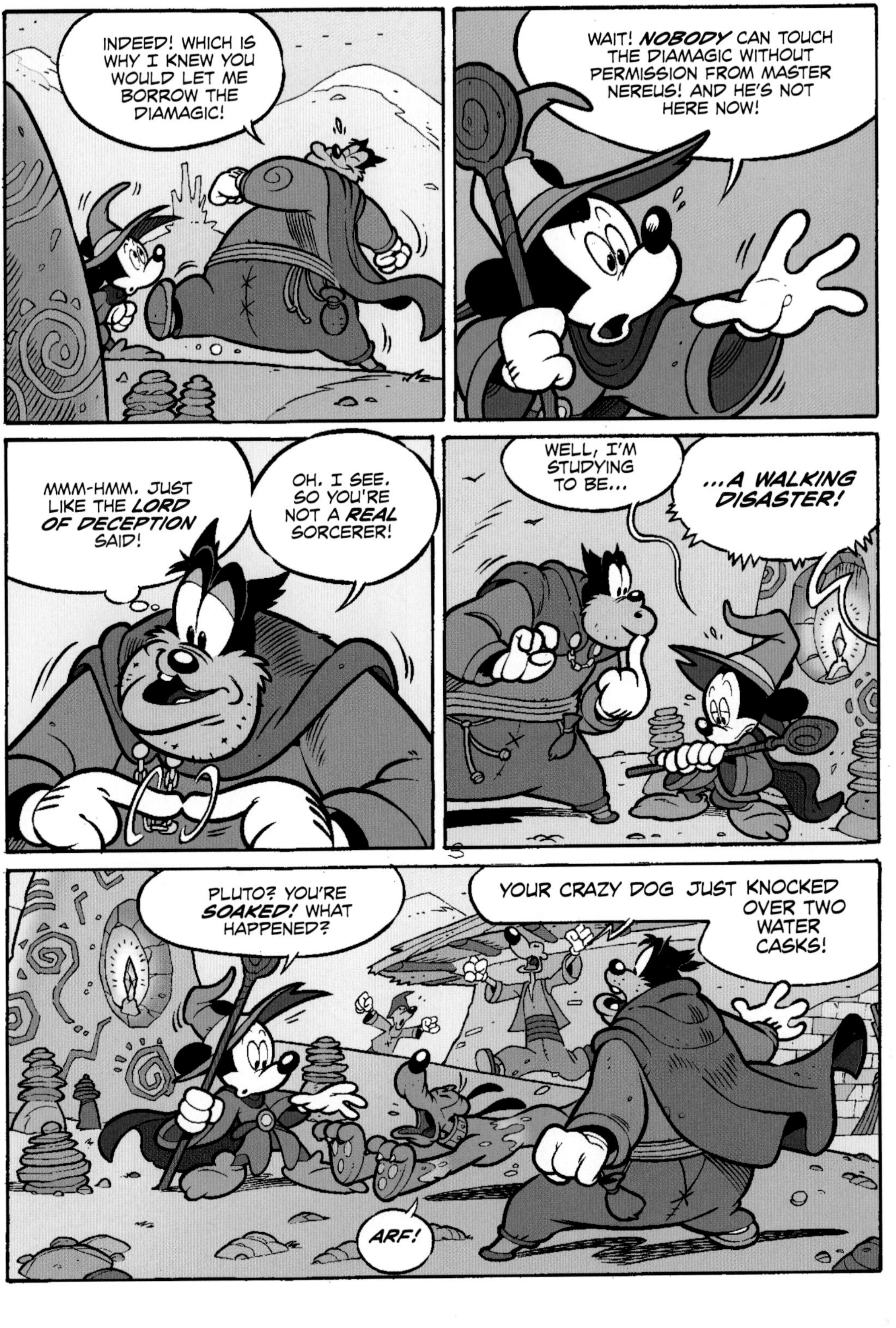
INDEED! WHICH IS WHY I KNEW YOU WOULD LET ME BORROW THE DIAMAGIC!
WAIT! *NOBODY* CAN TOUCH THE DIAMAGIC WITHOUT PERMISSION FROM MASTER NEREUS! AND HE'S NOT HERE NOW!
MMM-HMM. JUST LIKE THE *LORD OF DECEPTION* SAID!
OH. I SEE. SO YOU'RE NOT A *REAL* SORCERER!
WELL, I'M STUDYING TO BE...
...A WALKING DISASTER!
PLUTO? YOU'RE *SOAKED!* WHAT HAPPENED?
YOUR CRAZY DOG JUST KNOCKED OVER TWO WATER CASKS!
ARF!

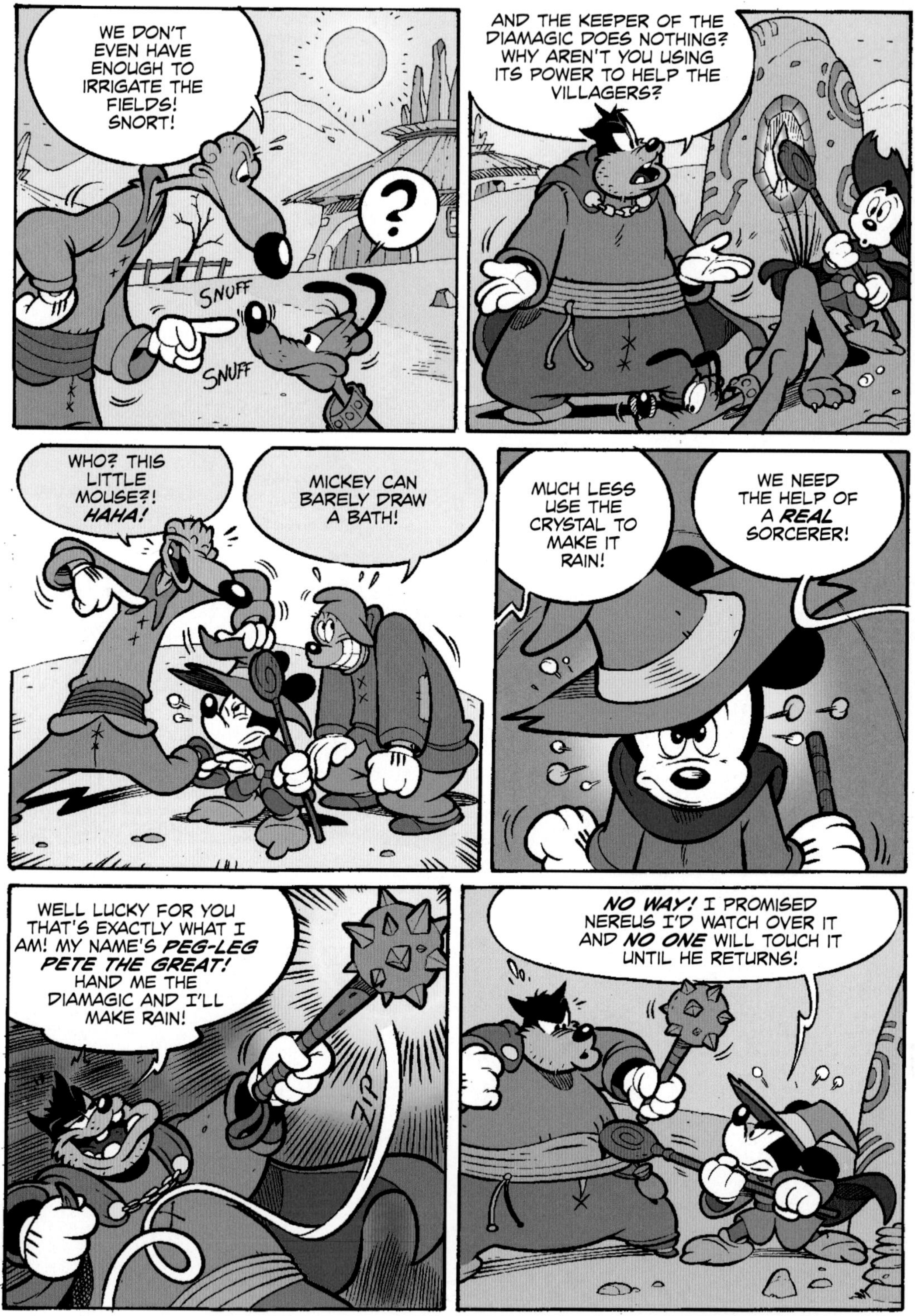
WE DON'T EVEN HAVE ENOUGH TO IRRIGATE THE FIELDS! SNORT!
?
SNUFF
SNUFF
AND THE KEEPER OF THE DIAMAGIC DOES NOTHING? WHY AREN'T YOU USING ITS POWER TO HELP THE VILLAGERS?
WHO? THIS LITTLE MOUSE?! HAHA!
MICKEY CAN BARELY DRAW A BATH!
MUCH LESS USE THE CRYSTAL TO MAKE IT RAIN!
WE NEED THE HELP OF A REAL SORCERER!
WELL LUCKY FOR YOU THAT'S EXACTLY WHAT I AM! MY NAME'S PEG-LEG PETE THE GREAT! HAND ME THE DIAMAGIC AND I'LL MAKE RAIN!
ZIP
NO WAY! I PROMISED NEREUS I'D WATCH OVER IT AND NO ONE WILL TOUCH IT UNTIL HE RETURNS!

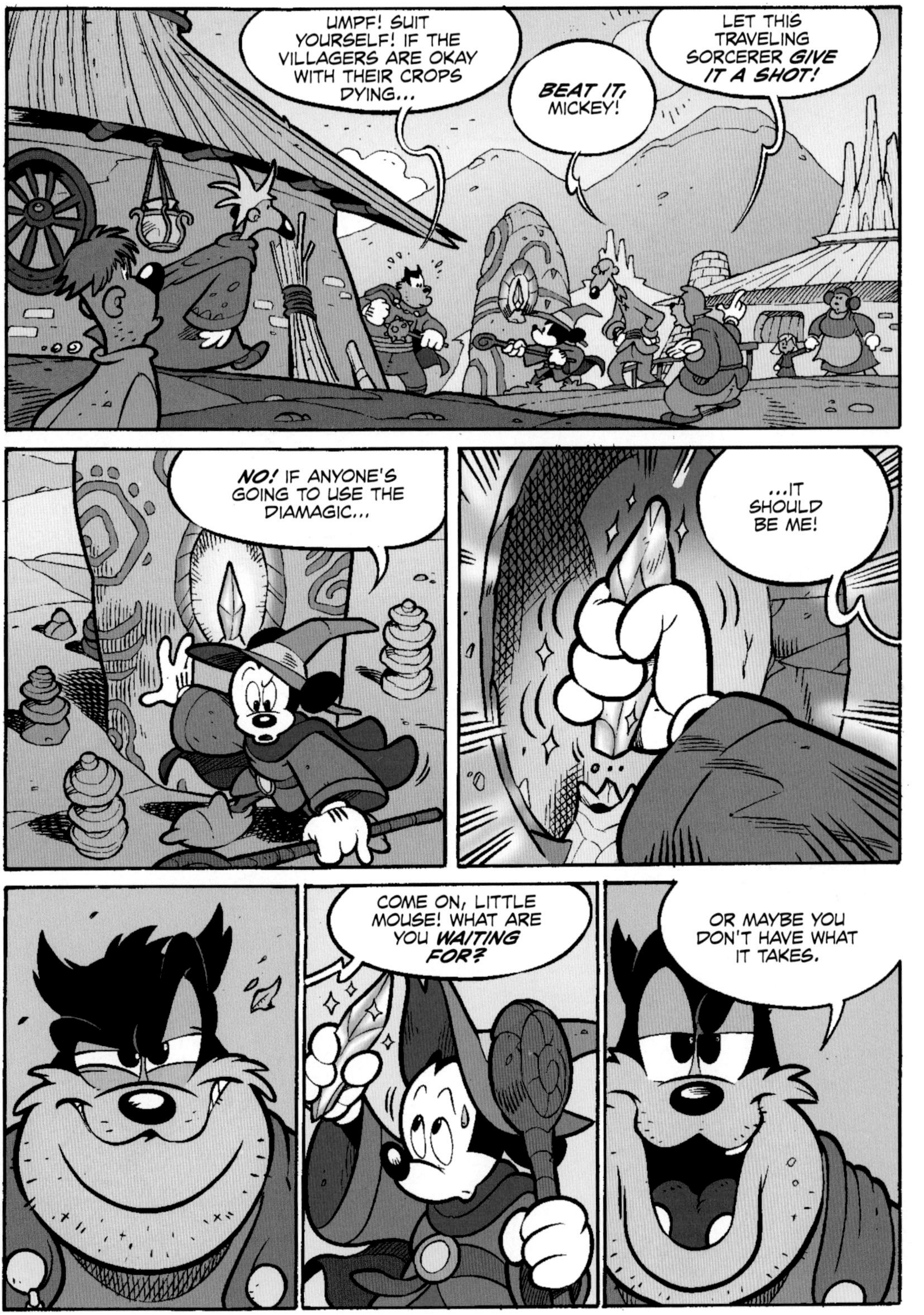
UMPF! SUIT YOURSELF! IF THE VILLAGERS ARE OKAY WITH THEIR CROPS DYING...
BEAT IT, MICKEY!
LET THIS TRAVELING SORCERER GIVE IT A SHOT!
NO! IF ANYONE'S GOING TO USE THE DIAMAGIC...
...IT SHOULD BE ME!
COME ON, LITTLE MOUSE! WHAT ARE YOU WAITING FOR?
OR MAYBE YOU DON'T HAVE WHAT IT TAKES.

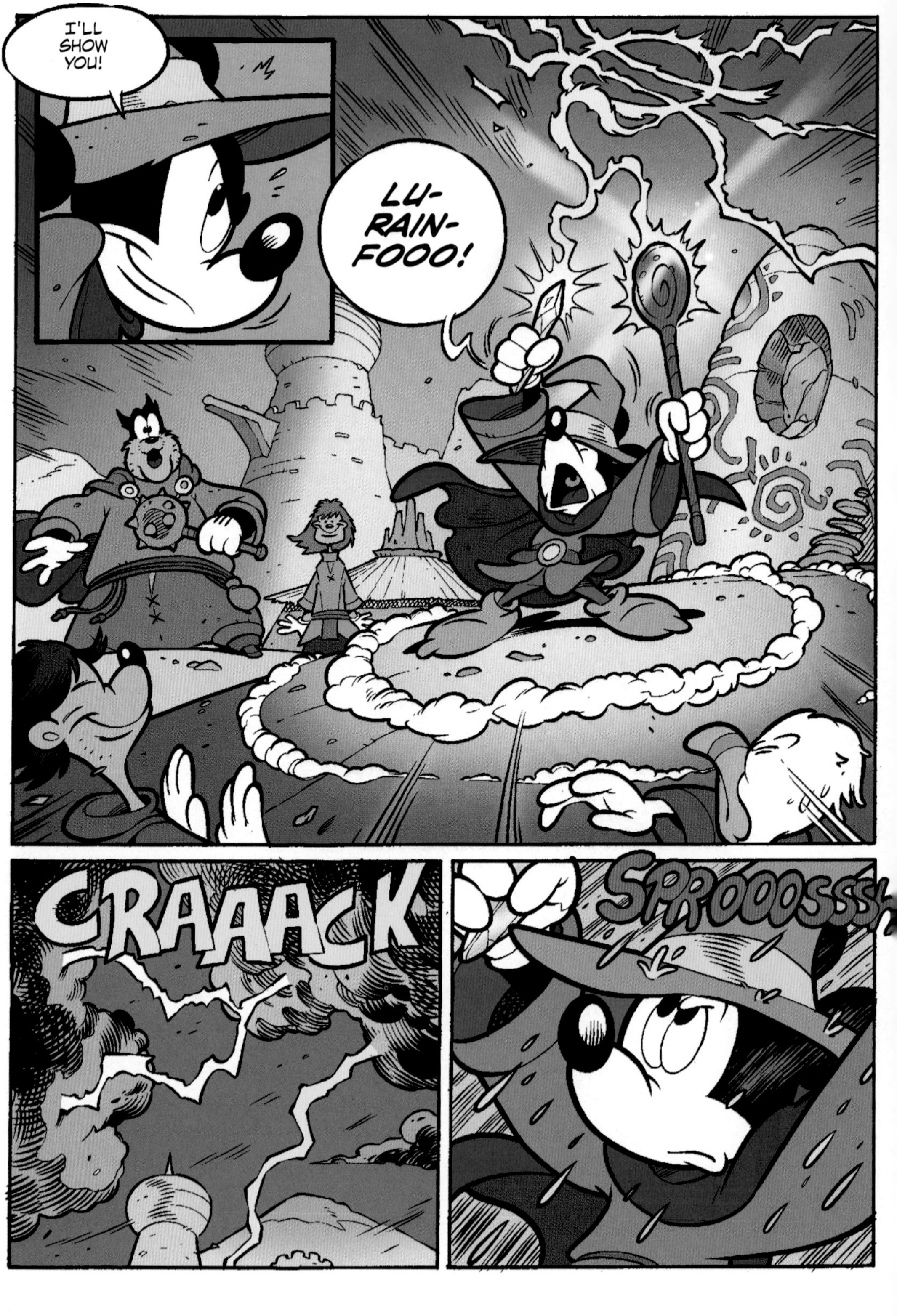
I'LL SHOW YOU!
LU-RAIN-FOOO!
CRAAACK
SPROOOSSSH

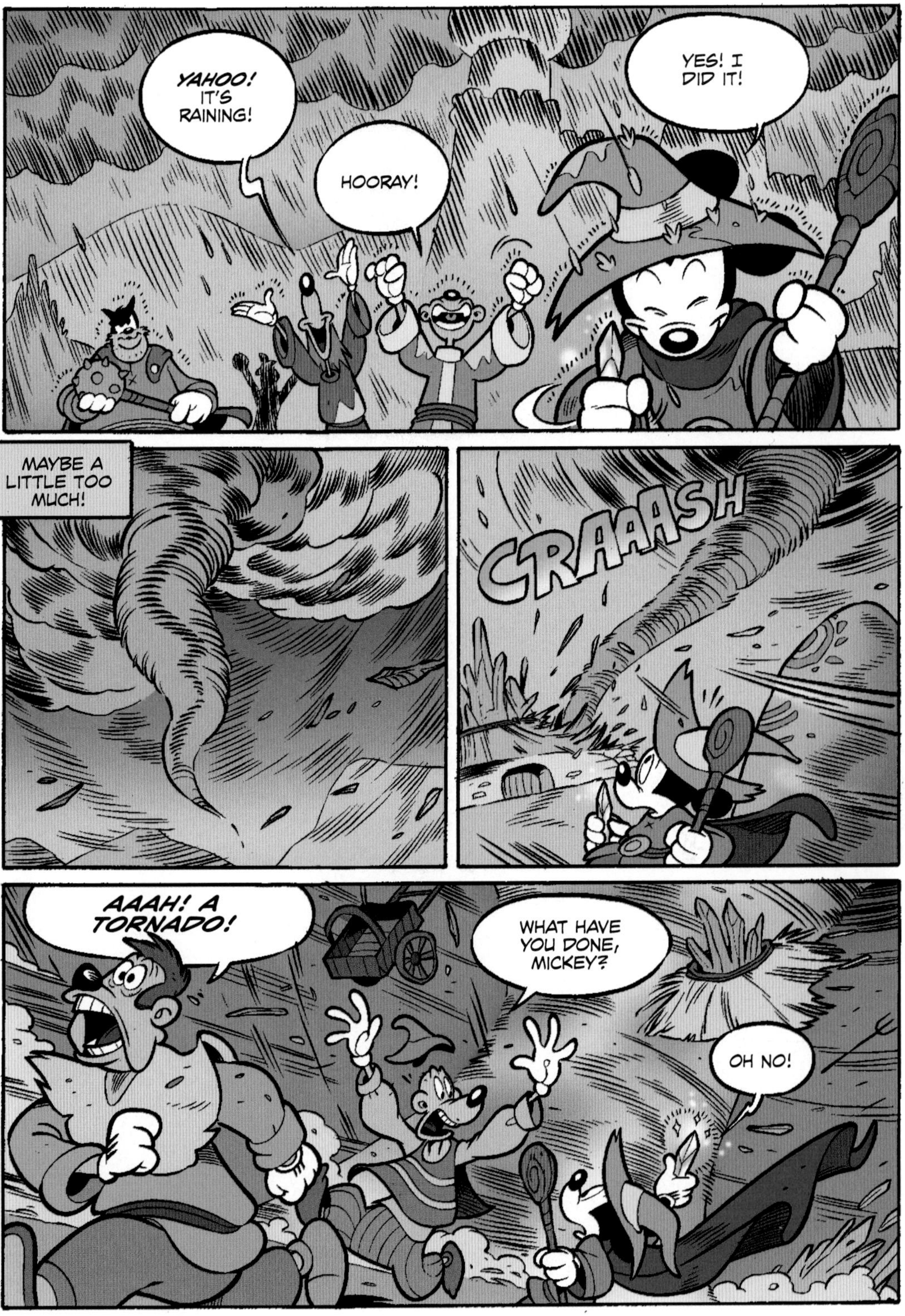

YAHOO! IT'S RAINING!
HOORAY!
YES! I DID IT!
MAYBE A LITTLE TOO MUCH!
CRAAASH
AAAH! A TORNADO!
WHAT HAVE YOU DONE, MICKEY?
OH NO!

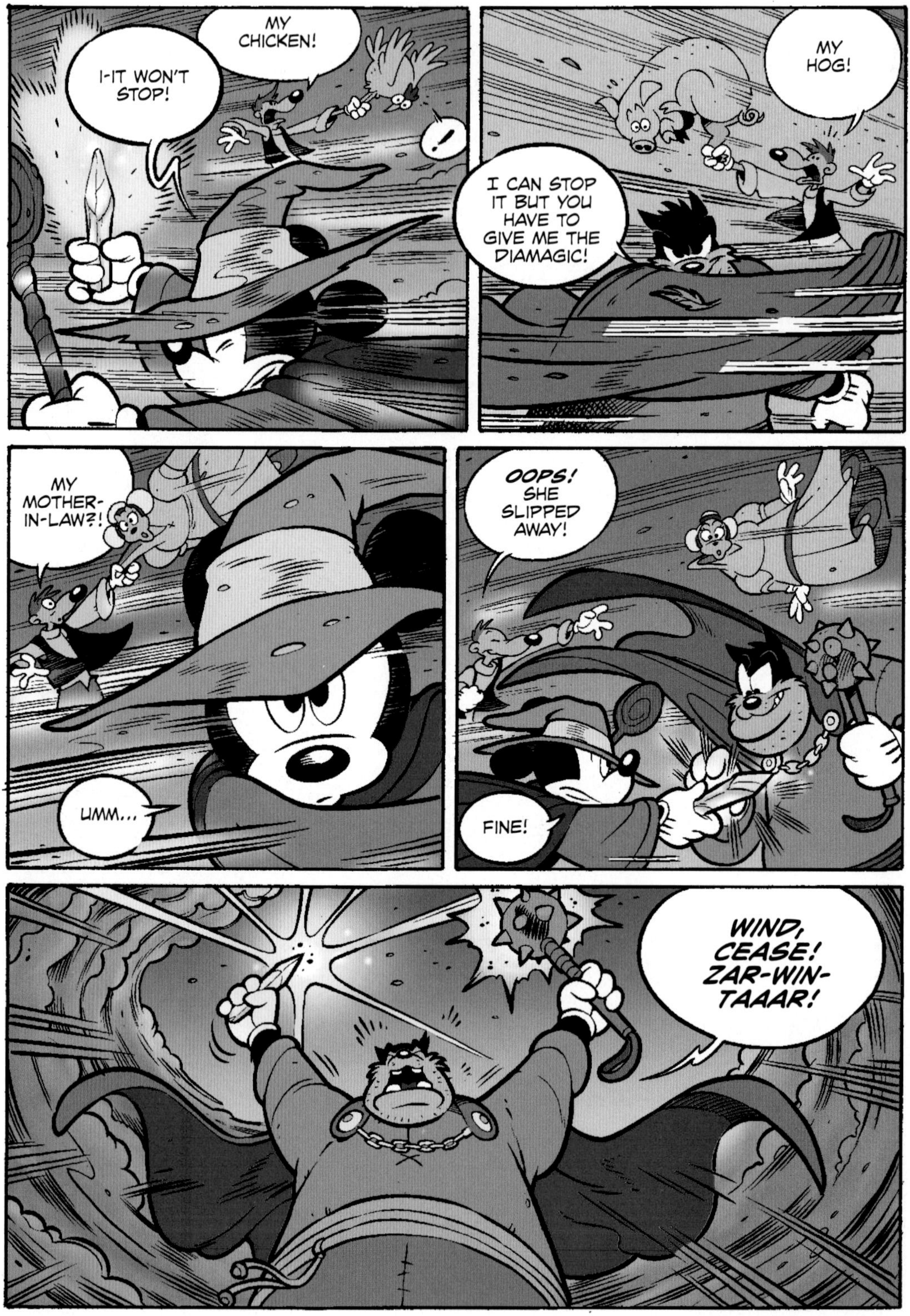
I-IT WON'T STOP!
MY CHICKEN!
!
MY HOG!
I CAN STOP IT BUT YOU HAVE TO GIVE ME THE DIAMAGIC!
MY MOTHER-IN-LAW?!
UMM...
OOPS! SHE SLIPPED AWAY!
FINE!
WIND, CEASE! ZAR-WIN-TAAAR!

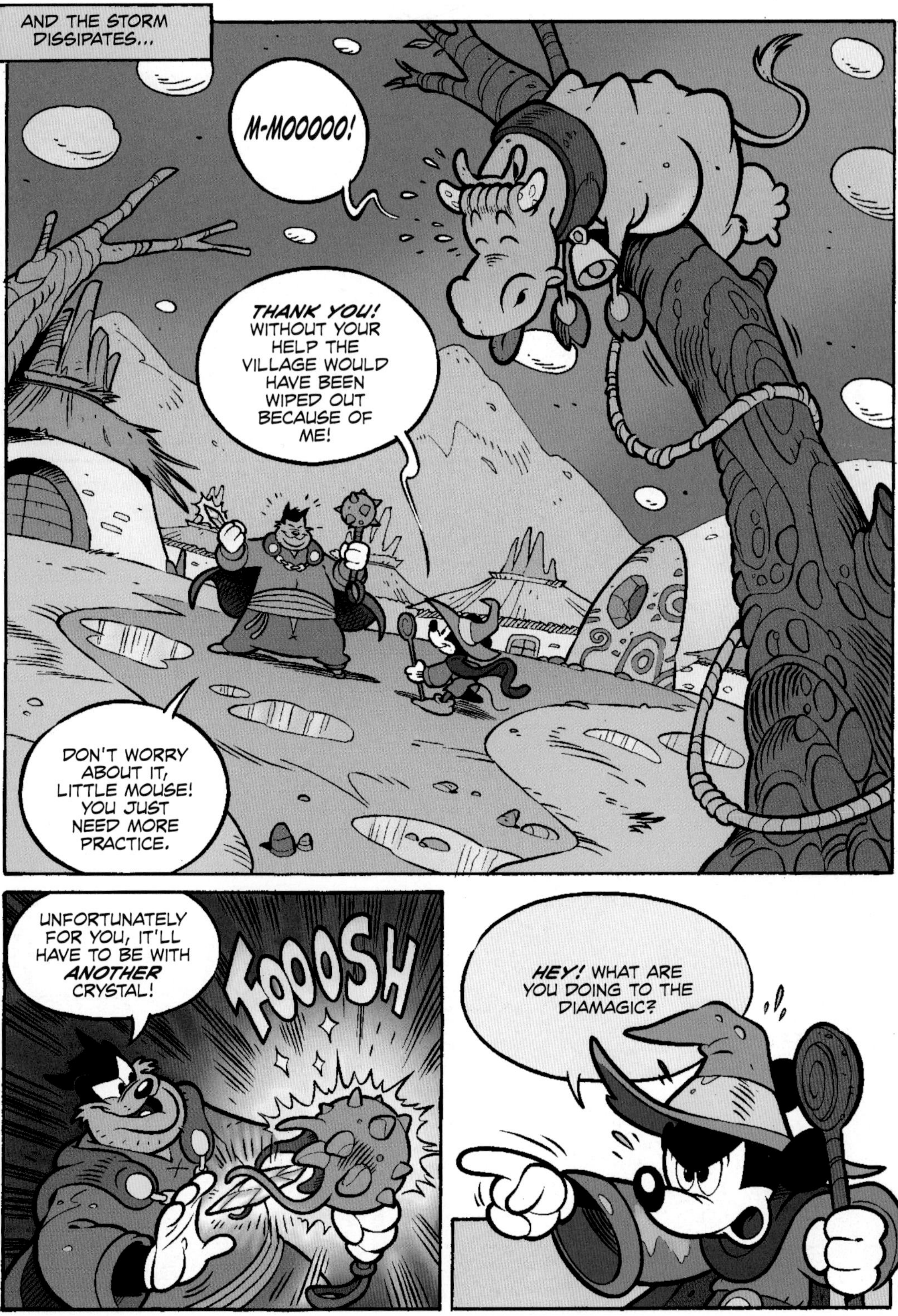
AND THE STORM DISSIPATES...
M-MOOOOO!
THANK YOU! WITHOUT YOUR HELP THE VILLAGE WOULD HAVE BEEN WIPED OUT BECAUSE OF ME!
DON'T WORRY ABOUT IT, LITTLE MOUSE! YOU JUST NEED MORE PRACTICE.
UNFORTUNATELY FOR YOU, IT'LL HAVE TO BE WITH ANOTHER CRYSTAL!
FOOOSH
HEY! WHAT ARE YOU DOING TO THE DIAMAGIC?

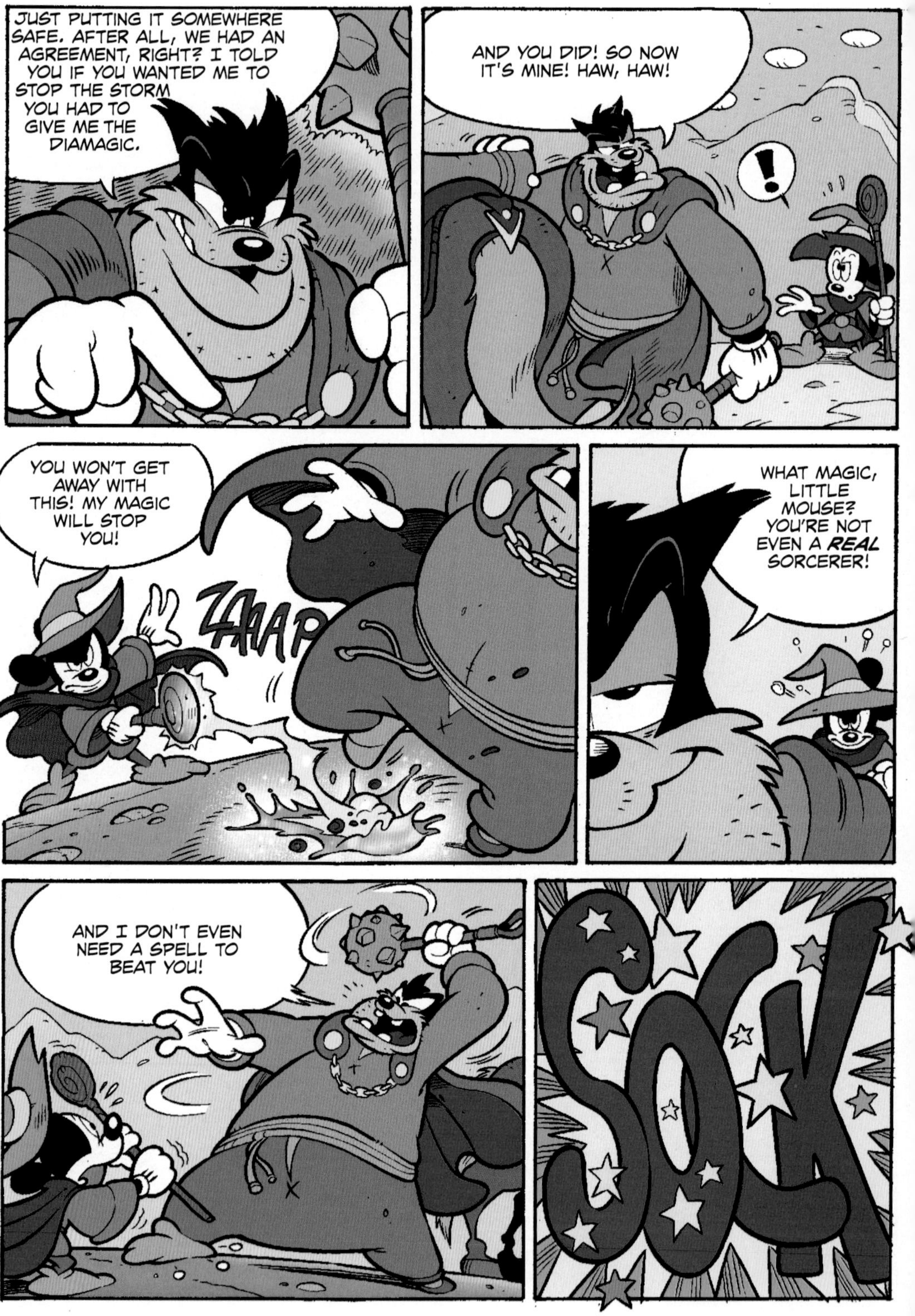

JUST PUTTING IT SOMEWHERE SAFE. AFTER ALL, WE HAD AN AGREEMENT, RIGHT? I TOLD YOU IF YOU WANTED ME TO STOP THE STORM YOU HAD TO GIVE ME THE DIAMAGIC.
AND YOU DID! SO NOW IT'S MINE! HAW, HAW!
!
YOU WON'T GET AWAY WITH THIS! MY MAGIC WILL STOP YOU!
ZAAAP
WHAT MAGIC, LITTLE MOUSE? YOU'RE NOT EVEN A **REAL** SORCERER!
AND I DON'T EVEN NEED A SPELL TO BEAT YOU!
SOCK

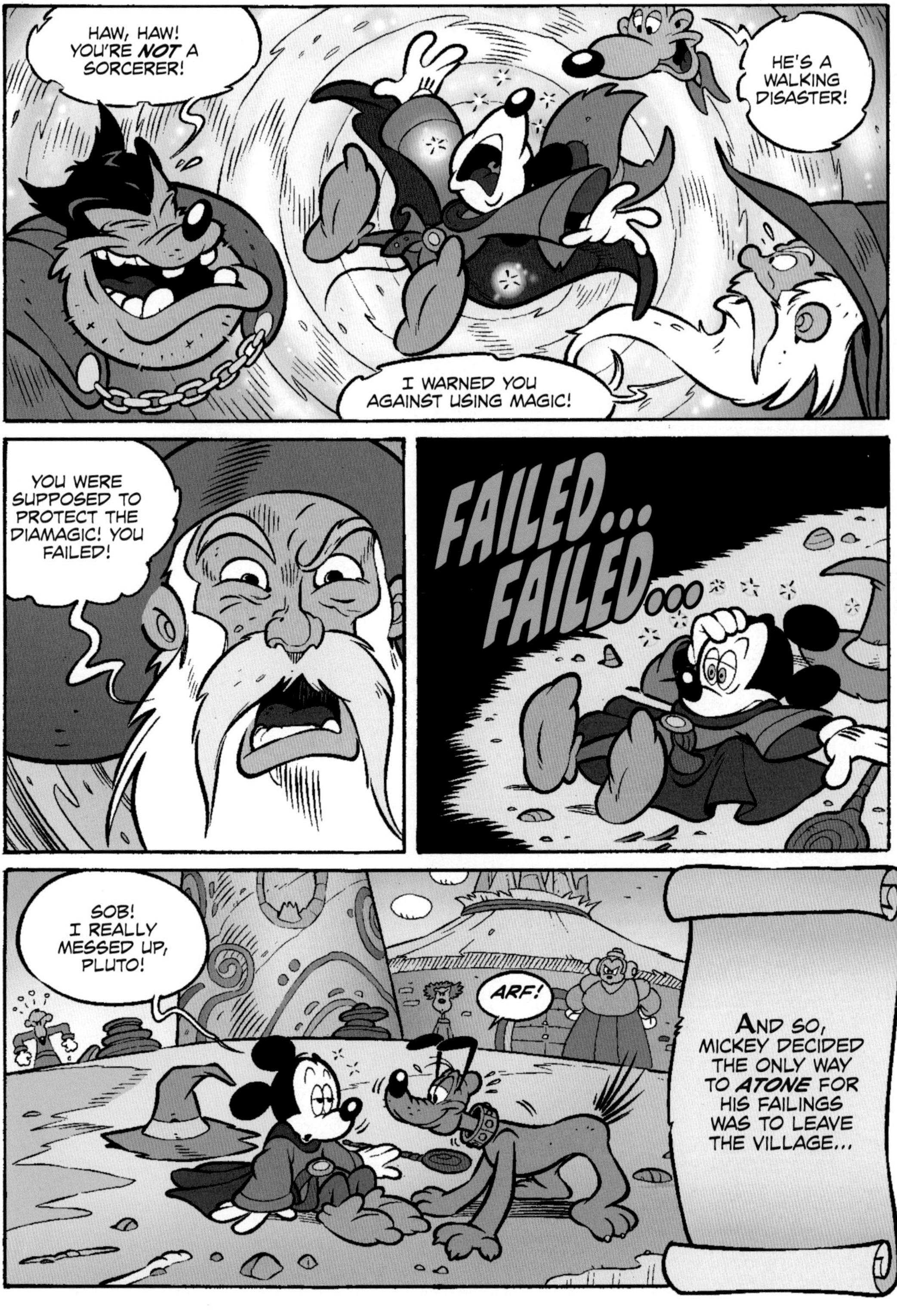
HAW, HAW! YOU'RE *NOT* A SORCERER!
HE'S A WALKING DISASTER!
I WARNED YOU AGAINST USING MAGIC!
YOU WERE SUPPOSED TO PROTECT THE DIAMAGIC! YOU FAILED!
FAILED... FAILED...
SOB! I REALLY MESSED UP, PLUTO!
ARF!
AND SO, MICKEY DECIDED THE ONLY WAY TO *ATONE* FOR HIS FAILINGS WAS TO LEAVE THE VILLAGE...

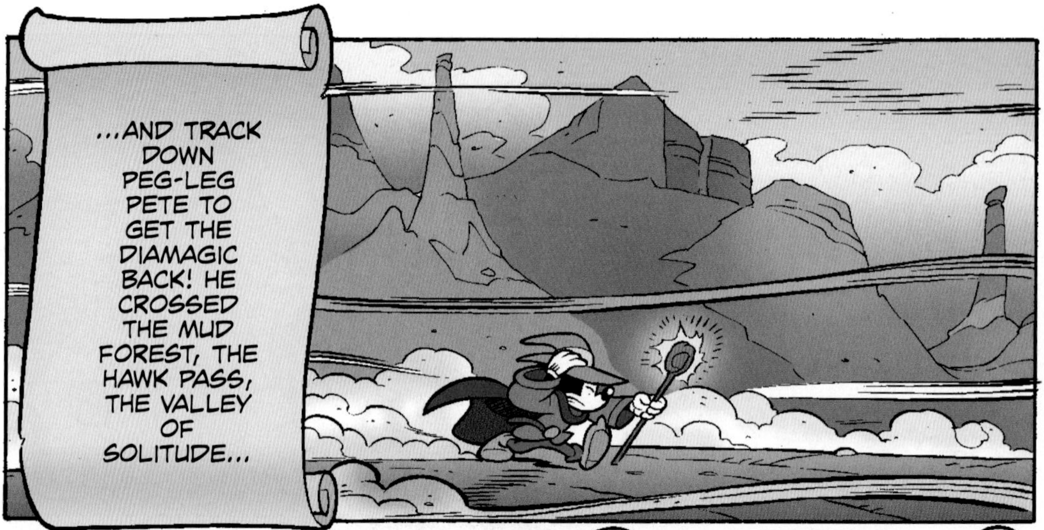
...AND TRACK DOWN PEG-LEG PETE TO GET THE DIAMAGIC BACK! HE CROSSED THE MUD FOREST, THE HAWK PASS, THE VALLEY OF SOLITUDE...

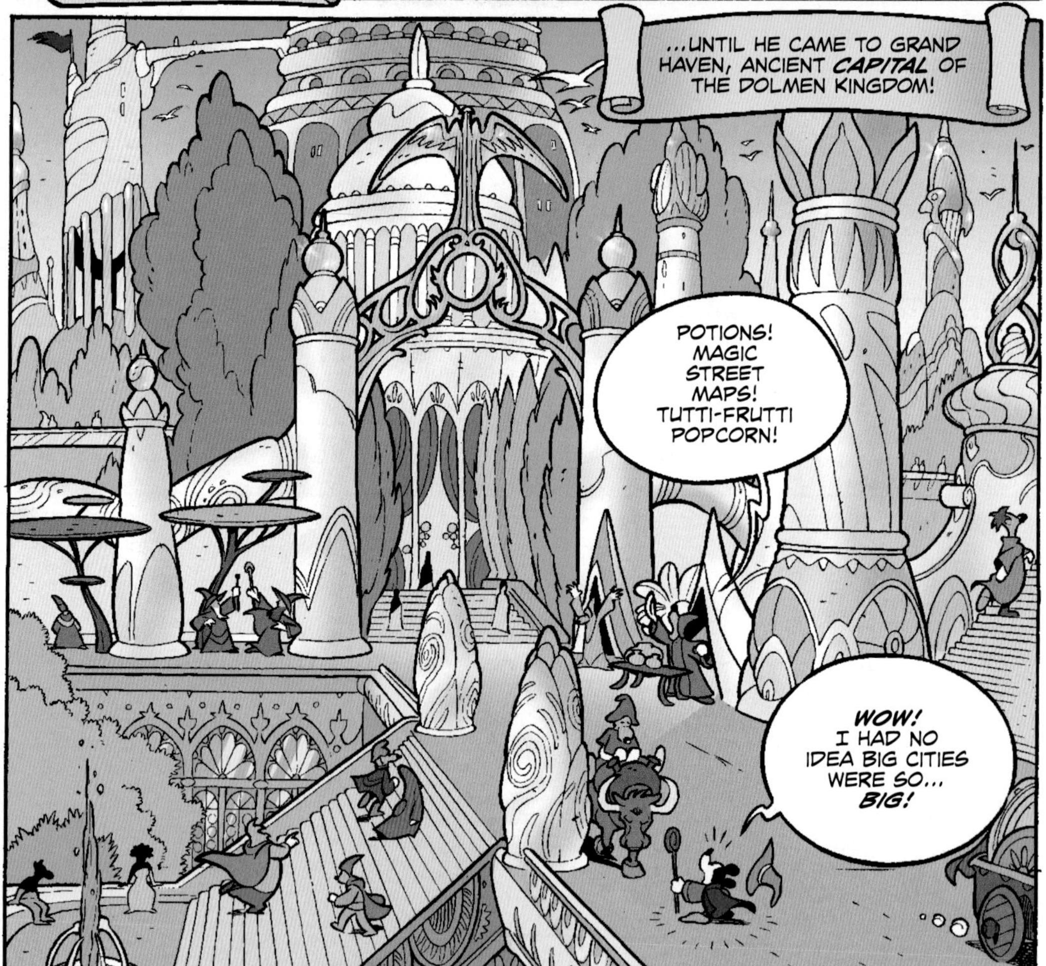
...UNTIL HE CAME TO GRAND HAVEN, ANCIENT *CAPITAL* OF THE DOLMEN KINGDOM!
POTIONS! MAGIC STREET MAPS! TUTTI-FRUTTI POPCORN!
WOW! I HAD NO IDEA BIG CITIES WERE SO... ***BIG!***

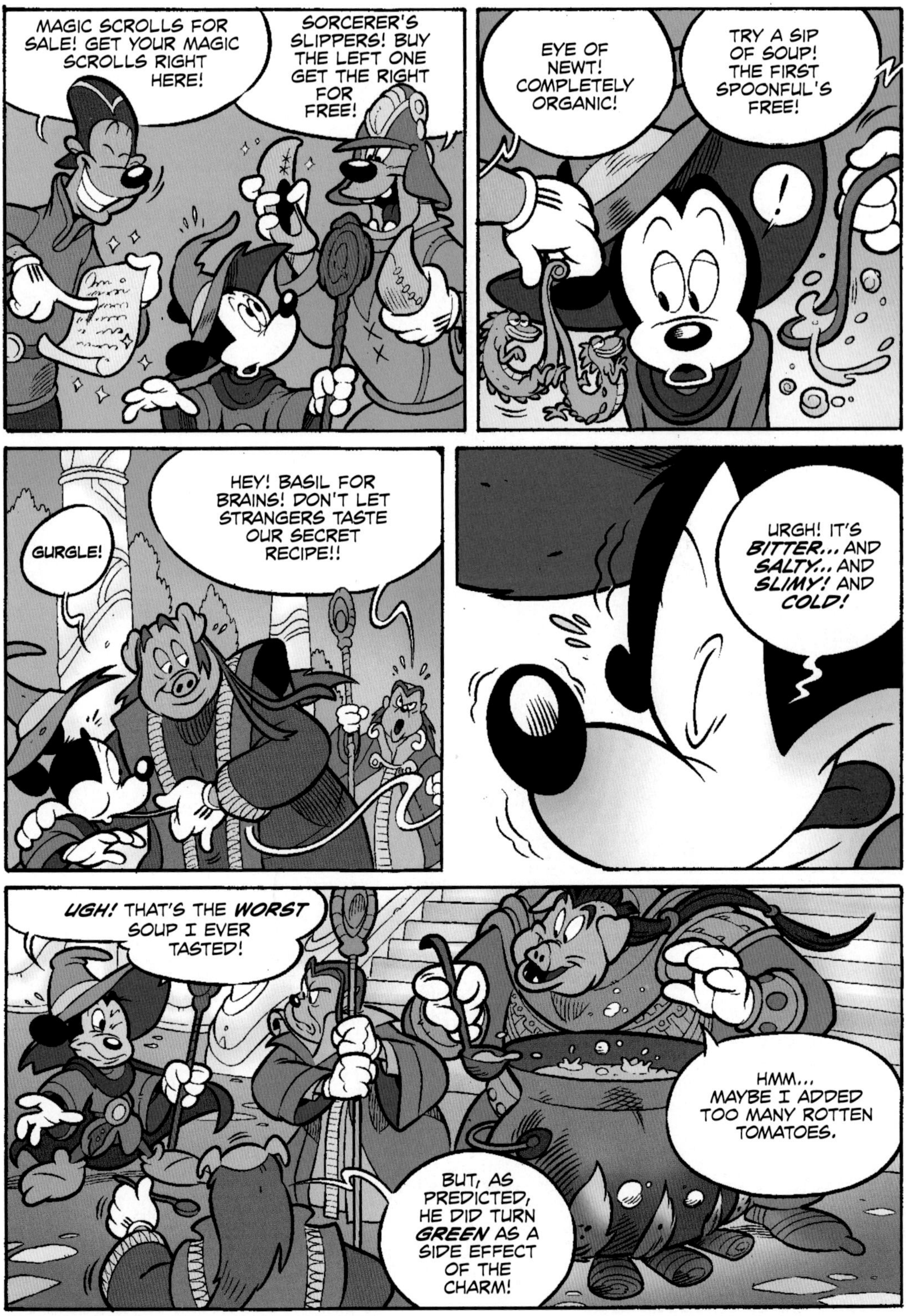
MAGIC SCROLLS FOR SALE! GET YOUR MAGIC SCROLLS RIGHT HERE!
SORCERER'S SLIPPERS! BUY THE LEFT ONE GET THE RIGHT FOR FREE!
EYE OF NEWT! COMPLETELY ORGANIC!
TRY A SIP OF SOUP! THE FIRST SPOONFUL'S FREE!
!
GURGLE!
HEY! BASIL FOR BRAINS! DON'T LET STRANGERS TASTE OUR SECRET RECIPE!!
URGH! IT'S BITTER... AND SALTY... AND SLIMY! AND COLD!
UGH! THAT'S THE WORST SOUP I EVER TASTED!
HMM... MAYBE I ADDED TOO MANY ROTTEN TOMATOES.
BUT, AS PREDICTED, HE DID TURN GREEN AS A SIDE EFFECT OF THE CHARM!

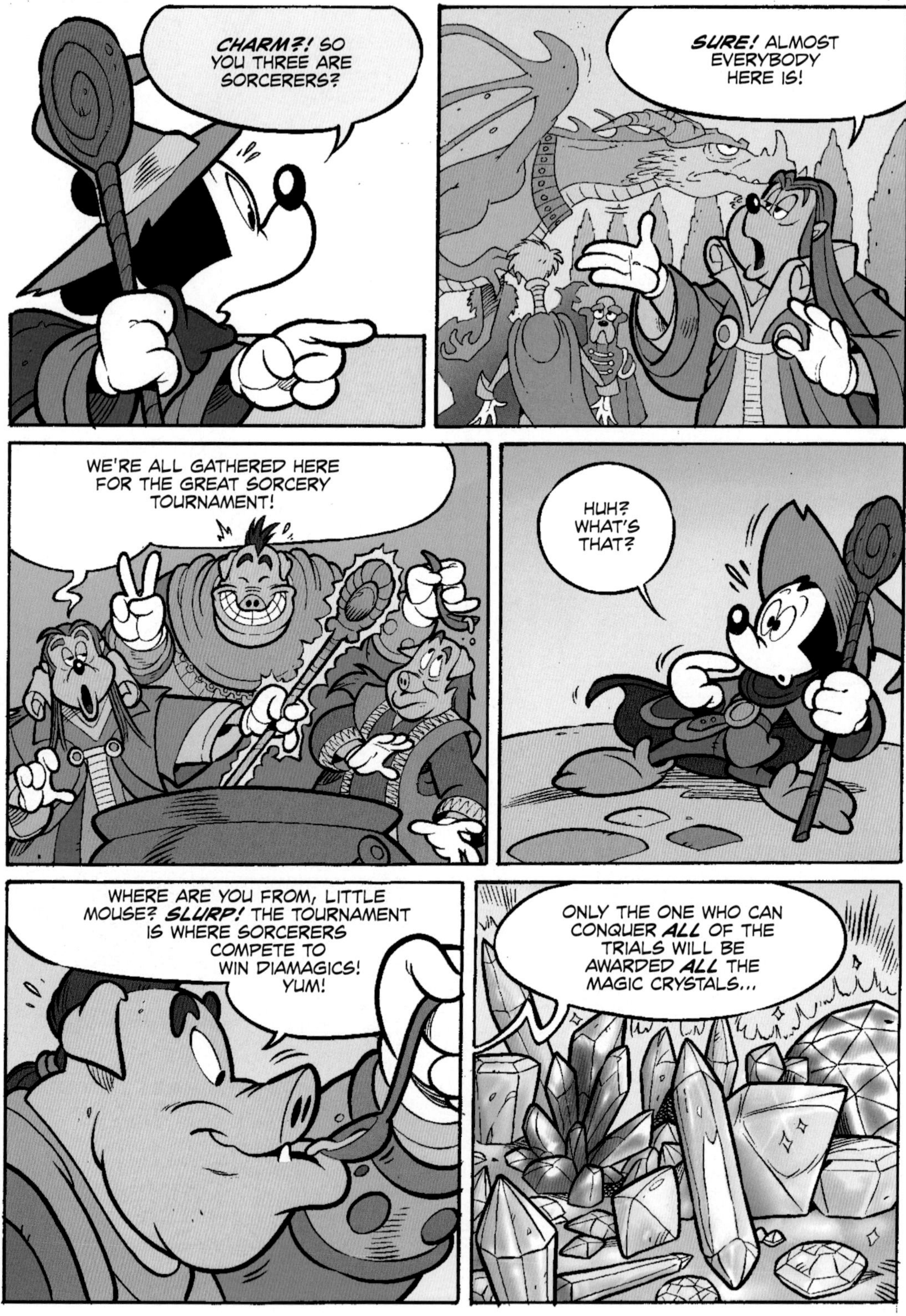
CHARM?! SO YOU THREE ARE SORCERERS?
SURE! ALMOST EVERYBODY HERE IS!
WE'RE ALL GATHERED HERE FOR THE GREAT SORCERY TOURNAMENT!
HUH? WHAT'S THAT?
WHERE ARE YOU FROM, LITTLE MOUSE? SLURP! THE TOURNAMENT IS WHERE SORCERERS COMPETE TO WIN DIAMAGICS! YUM!
ONLY THE ONE WHO CAN CONQUER ALL OF THE TRIALS WILL BE AWARDED ALL THE MAGIC CRYSTALS...

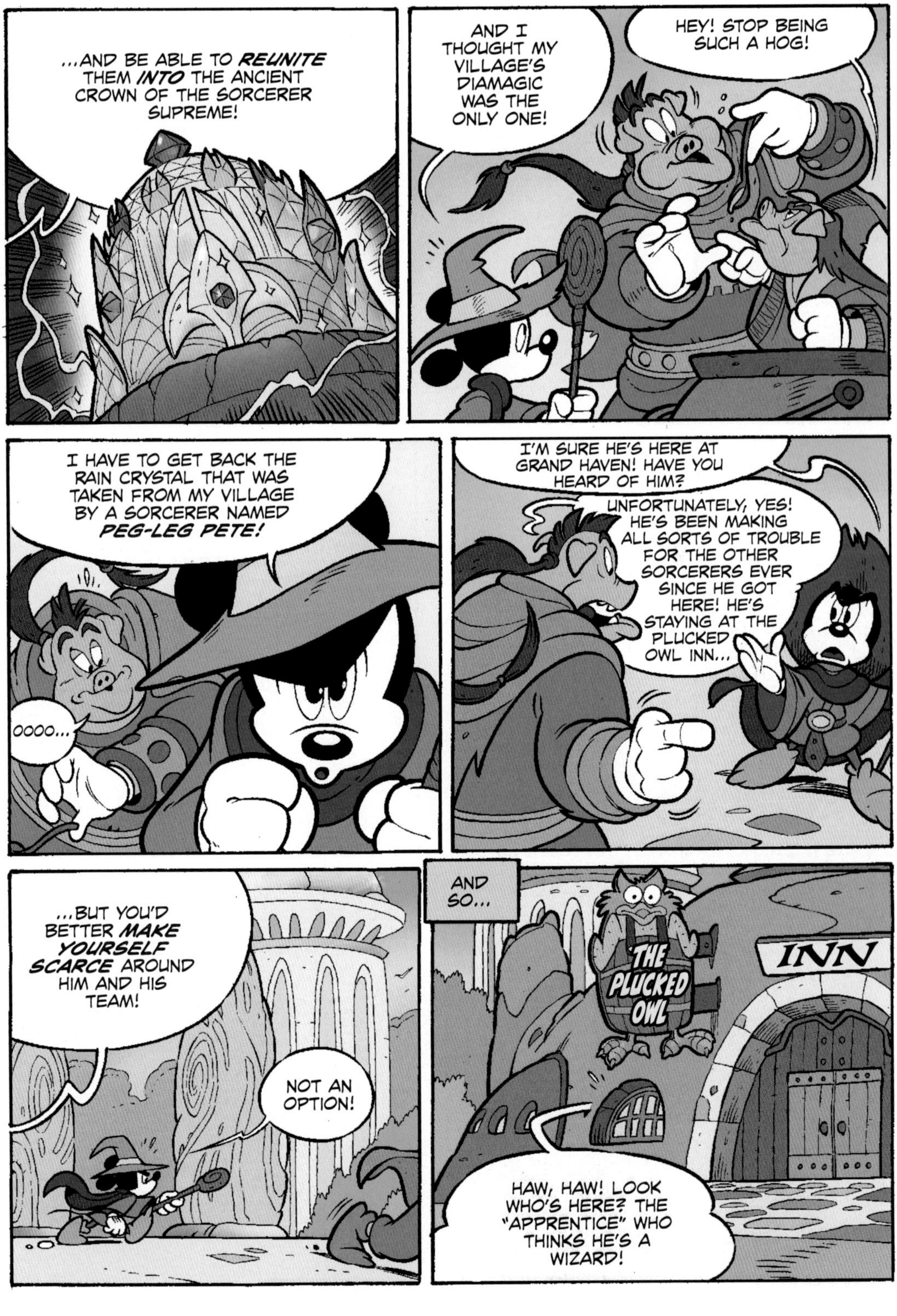
...AND BE ABLE TO REUNITE THEM INTO THE ANCIENT CROWN OF THE SORCERER SUPREME!
AND I THOUGHT MY VILLAGE'S DIAMAGIC WAS THE ONLY ONE!
HEY! STOP BEING SUCH A HOG!
I HAVE TO GET BACK THE RAIN CRYSTAL THAT WAS TAKEN FROM MY VILLAGE BY A SORCERER NAMED PEG-LEG PETE!
OOOO...
I'M SURE HE'S HERE AT GRAND HAVEN! HAVE YOU HEARD OF HIM?
UNFORTUNATELY, YES! HE'S BEEN MAKING ALL SORTS OF TROUBLE FOR THE OTHER SORCERERS EVER SINCE HE GOT HERE! HE'S STAYING AT THE PLUCKED OWL INN...
...BUT YOU'D BETTER MAKE YOURSELF SCARCE AROUND HIM AND HIS TEAM!
NOT AN OPTION!
AND SO...
THE PLUCKED OWL
INN
HAW, HAW! LOOK WHO'S HERE? THE "APPRENTICE" WHO THINKS HE'S A WIZARD!

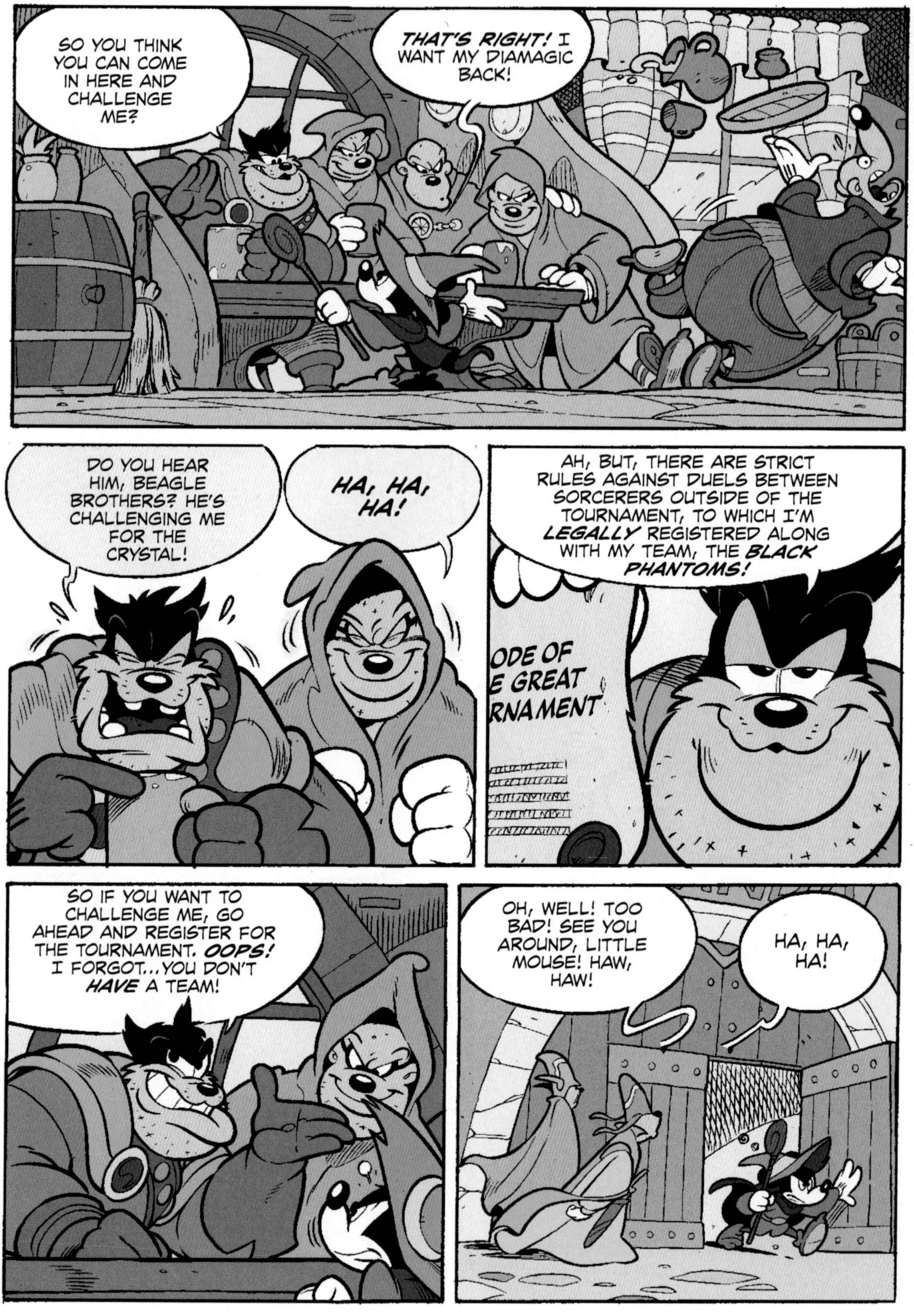
SO YOU THINK YOU CAN COME IN HERE AND CHALLENGE ME?
THAT'S RIGHT! I WANT MY DIAMAGIC BACK!
DO YOU HEAR HIM, BEAGLE BROTHERS? HE'S CHALLENGING ME FOR THE CRYSTAL!
HA, HA, HA!
AH, BUT, THERE ARE STRICT RULES AGAINST DUELS BETWEEN SORCERERS OUTSIDE OF THE TOURNAMENT, TO WHICH I'M LEGALLY REGISTERED ALONG WITH MY TEAM, THE BLACK PHANTOMS!
SO IF YOU WANT TO CHALLENGE ME, GO AHEAD AND REGISTER FOR THE TOURNAMENT. OOPS! I FORGOT...YOU DON'T HAVE A TEAM!
OH, WELL! TOO BAD! SEE YOU AROUND, LITTLE MOUSE! HAW, HAW!
HA, HA, HA!

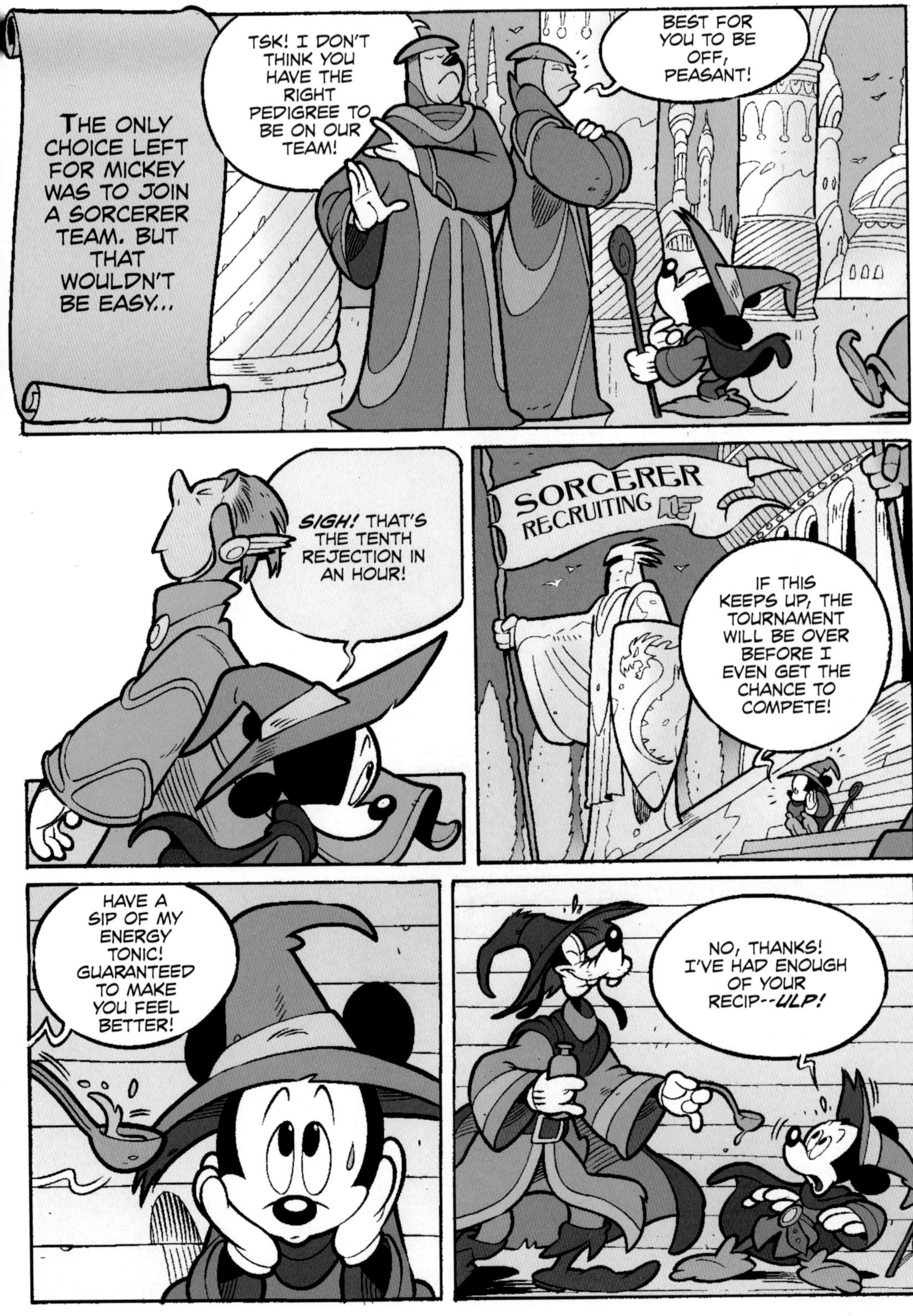
THE ONLY CHOICE LEFT FOR MICKEY WAS TO JOIN A SORCERER TEAM. BUT THAT WOULDN'T BE EASY...
TSK! I DON'T THINK YOU HAVE THE RIGHT PEDIGREE TO BE ON OUR TEAM!
BEST FOR YOU TO BE OFF, PEASANT!
SIGH! THAT'S THE TENTH REJECTION IN AN HOUR!
SORCERER RECRUITING
IF THIS KEEPS UP, THE TOURNAMENT WILL BE OVER BEFORE I EVEN GET THE CHANCE TO COMPETE!
HAVE A SIP OF MY ENERGY TONIC! GUARANTEED TO MAKE YOU FEEL BETTER!
NO, THANKS! I'VE HAD ENOUGH OF YOUR RECIP--ULP!

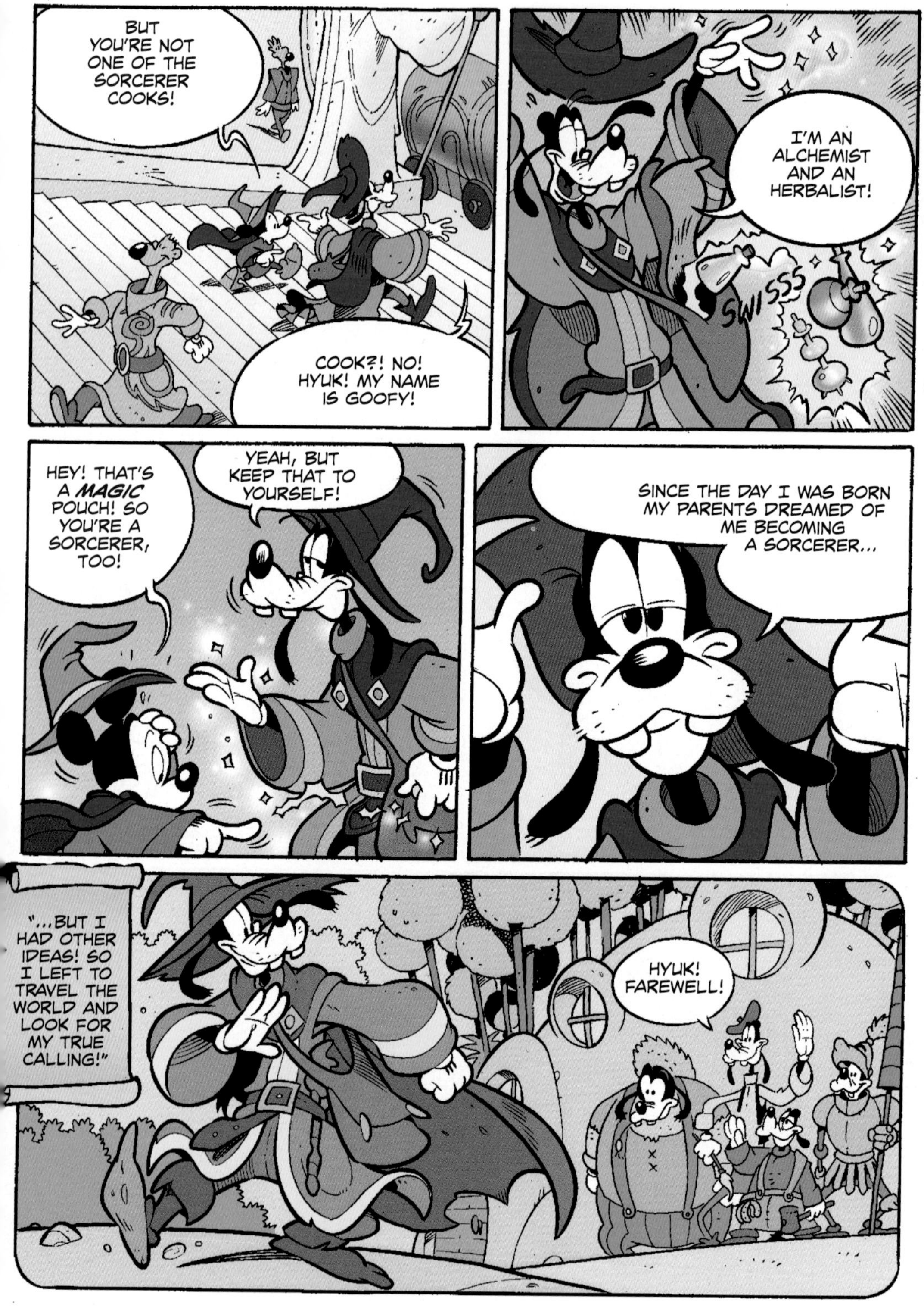

BUT YOU'RE NOT ONE OF THE SORCERER COOKS!
COOK?! NO! HYUK! MY NAME IS GOOFY!
I'M AN ALCHEMIST AND AN HERBALIST!
SWISSS
HEY! THAT'S A MAGIC POUCH! SO YOU'RE A SORCERER, TOO!
YEAH, BUT KEEP THAT TO YOURSELF!
SINCE THE DAY I WAS BORN MY PARENTS DREAMED OF ME BECOMING A SORCERER...
"...BUT I HAD OTHER IDEAS! SO I LEFT TO TRAVEL THE WORLD AND LOOK FOR MY TRUE CALLING!"
HYUK! FAREWELL!

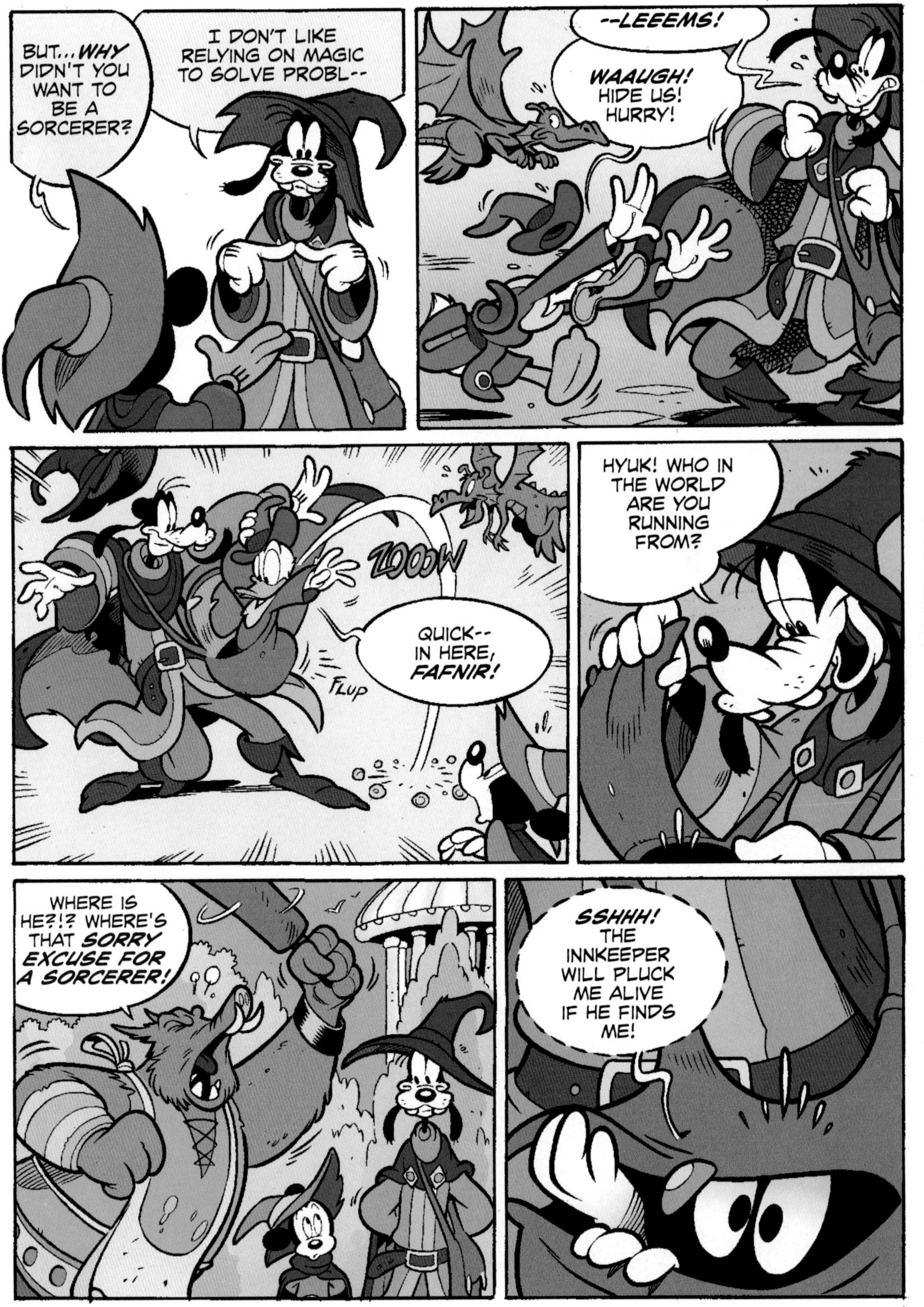
BUT... WHY DIDN'T YOU WANT TO BE A SORCERER?
I DON'T LIKE RELYING ON MAGIC TO SOLVE PROBL--
--LEEEMS!
WAAUGH! HIDE US! HURRY!
ZOOOW
QUICK-- IN HERE, FAFNIR!
FLUP
HYUK! WHO IN THE WORLD ARE YOU RUNNING FROM?
WHERE IS HE?!? WHERE'S THAT SORRY EXCUSE FOR A SORCERER!
SSHHH! THE INNKEEPER WILL PLUCK ME ALIVE IF HE FINDS ME!

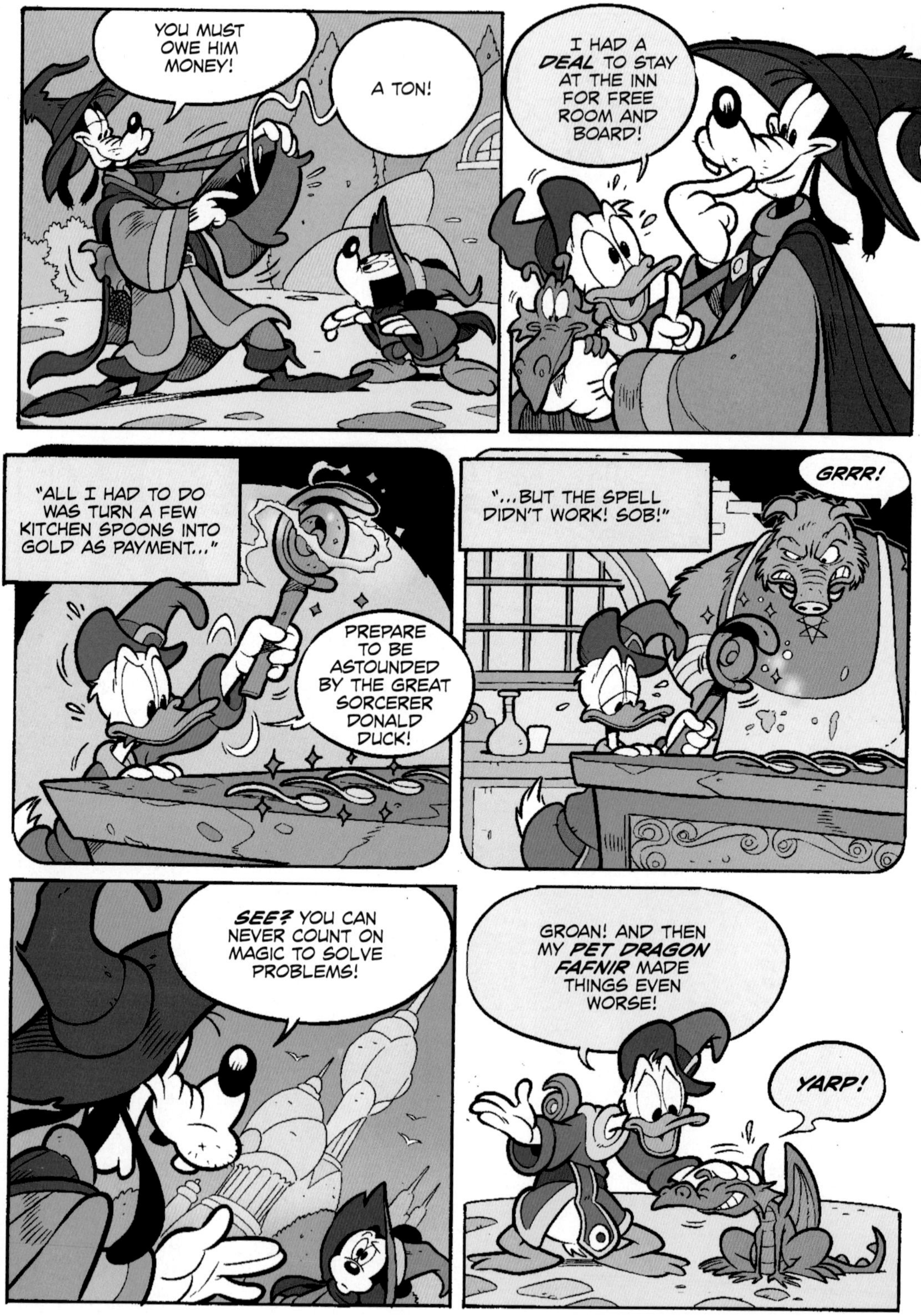
YOU MUST OWE HIM MONEY!
A TON!
I HAD A *DEAL* TO STAY AT THE INN FOR FREE ROOM AND BOARD!
"ALL I HAD TO DO WAS TURN A FEW KITCHEN SPOONS INTO GOLD AS PAYMENT..."
PREPARE TO BE ASTOUNDED BY THE GREAT SORCERER DONALD DUCK!
"...BUT THE SPELL DIDN'T WORK! SOB!"
GRRR!
SEE? YOU CAN NEVER COUNT ON MAGIC TO SOLVE PROBLEMS!
GROAN! AND THEN MY *PET DRAGON FAFNIR* MADE THINGS EVEN WORSE!
YARP!

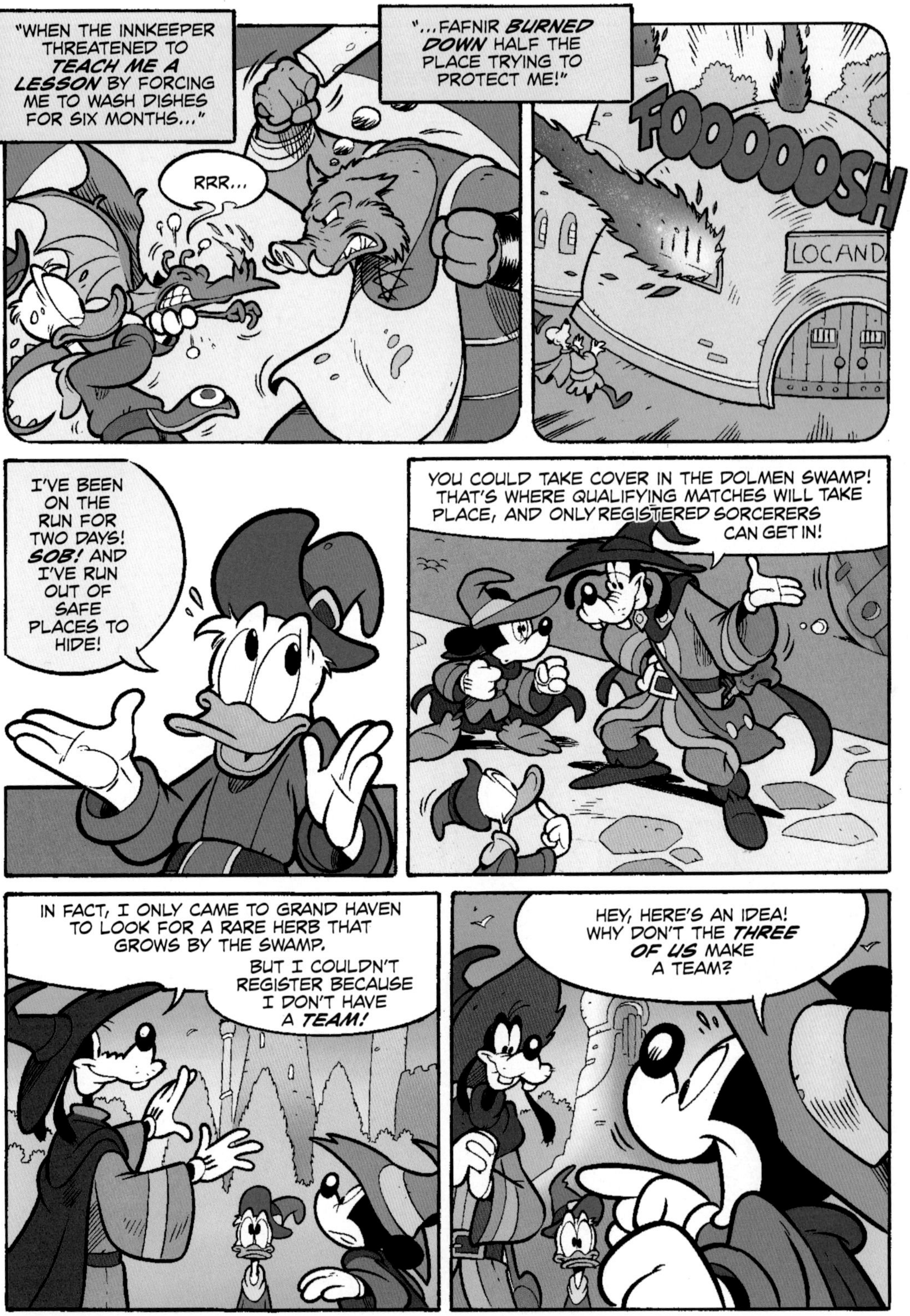
"WHEN THE INNKEEPER THREATENED TO TEACH ME A LESSON BY FORCING ME TO WASH DISHES FOR SIX MONTHS..."
RRR...
"...FAFNIR BURNED DOWN HALF THE PLACE TRYING TO PROTECT ME!"
FOOOOOOSH
LOCAND
I'VE BEEN ON THE RUN FOR TWO DAYS! SOB! AND I'VE RUN OUT OF SAFE PLACES TO HIDE!
YOU COULD TAKE COVER IN THE DOLMEN SWAMP! THAT'S WHERE QUALIFYING MATCHES WILL TAKE PLACE, AND ONLY REGISTERED SORCERERS CAN GET IN!
IN FACT, I ONLY CAME TO GRAND HAVEN TO LOOK FOR A RARE HERB THAT GROWS BY THE SWAMP.
BUT I COULDN'T REGISTER BECAUSE I DON'T HAVE A TEAM!
HEY, HERE'S AN IDEA! WHY DON'T THE THREE OF US MAKE A TEAM?

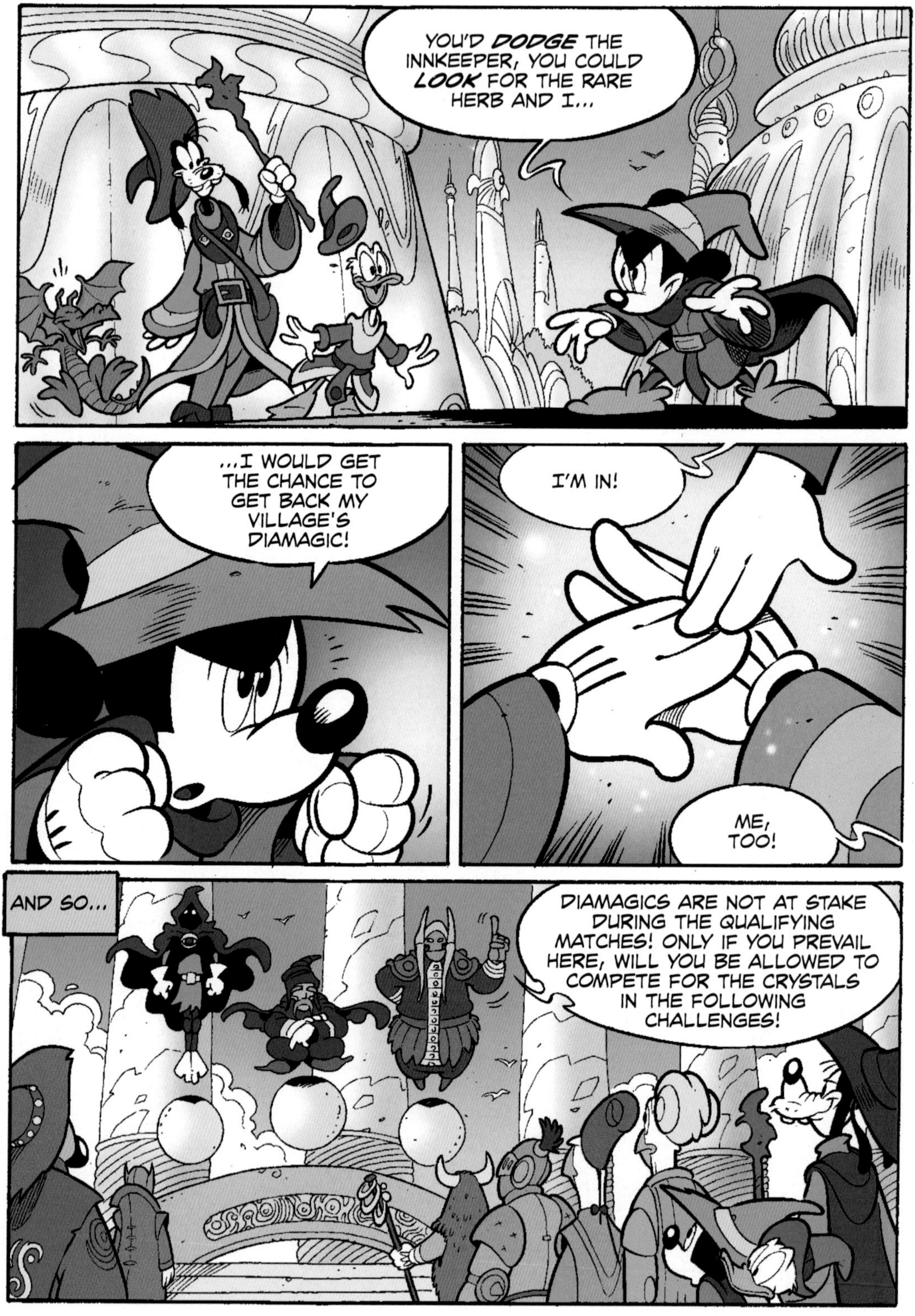
YOU'D DODGE THE INNKEEPER, YOU COULD LOOK FOR THE RARE HERB AND I...
...I WOULD GET THE CHANCE TO GET BACK MY VILLAGE'S DIAMAGIC!
I'M IN!
ME, TOO!
AND SO...
DIAMAGICS ARE NOT AT STAKE DURING THE QUALIFYING MATCHES! ONLY IF YOU PREVAIL HERE, WILL YOU BE ALLOWED TO COMPETE FOR THE CRYSTALS IN THE FOLLOWING CHALLENGES!

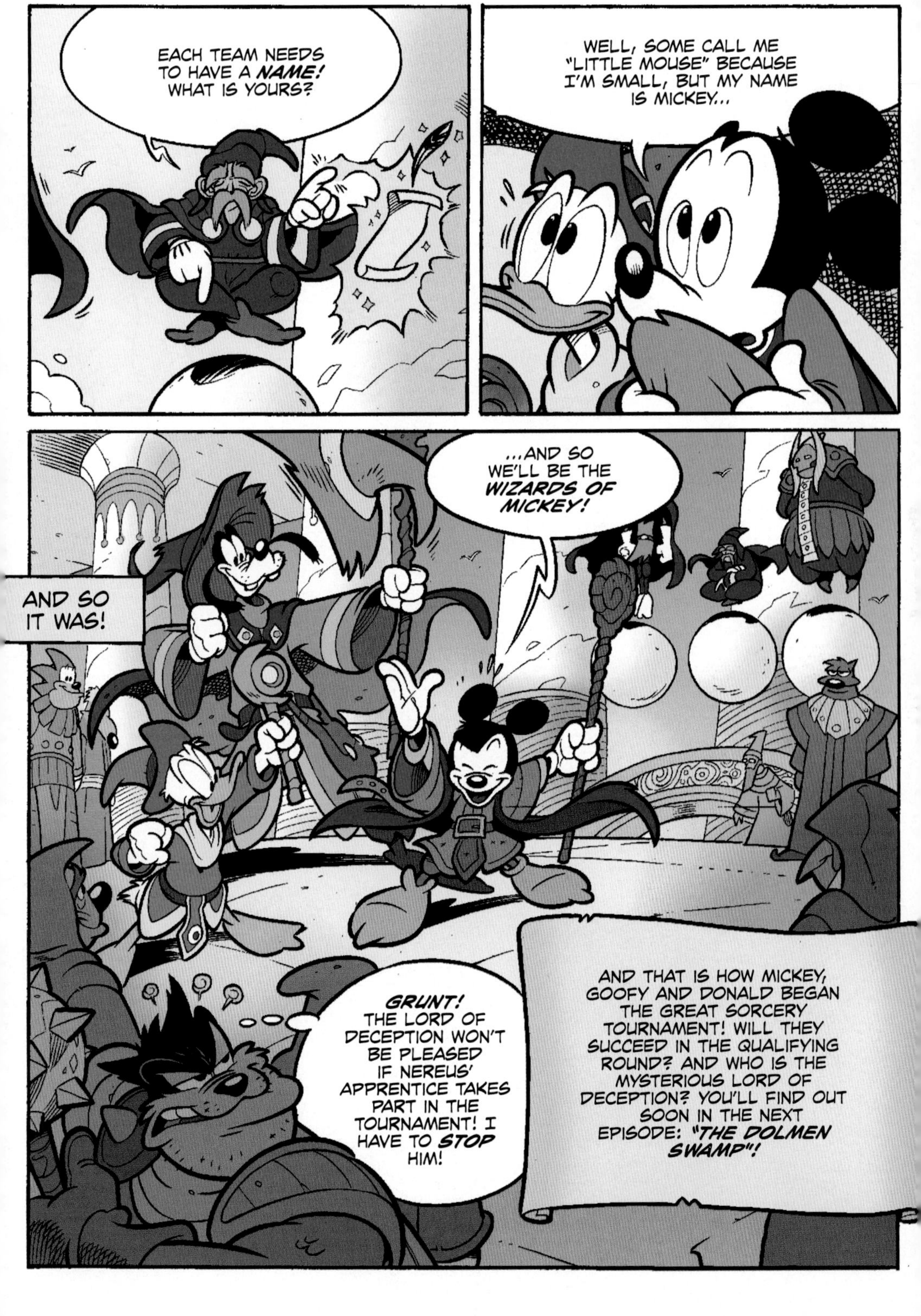

EACH TEAM NEEDS TO HAVE A NAME! WHAT IS YOURS?
WELL, SOME CALL ME "LITTLE MOUSE" BECAUSE I'M SMALL, BUT MY NAME IS MICKEY...
AND SO IT WAS!
...AND SO WE'LL BE THE WIZARDS OF MICKEY!
GRUNT! THE LORD OF DECEPTION WON'T BE PLEASED IF NEREUS' APPRENTICE TAKES PART IN THE TOURNAMENT! I HAVE TO STOP HIM!
AND THAT IS HOW MICKEY, GOOFY AND DONALD BEGAN THE GREAT SORCERY TOURNAMENT! WILL THEY SUCCEED IN THE QUALIFYING ROUND? AND WHO IS THE MYSTERIOUS LORD OF DECEPTION? YOU'LL FIND OUT SOON IN THE NEXT EPISODE: "THE DOLMEN SWAMP"!

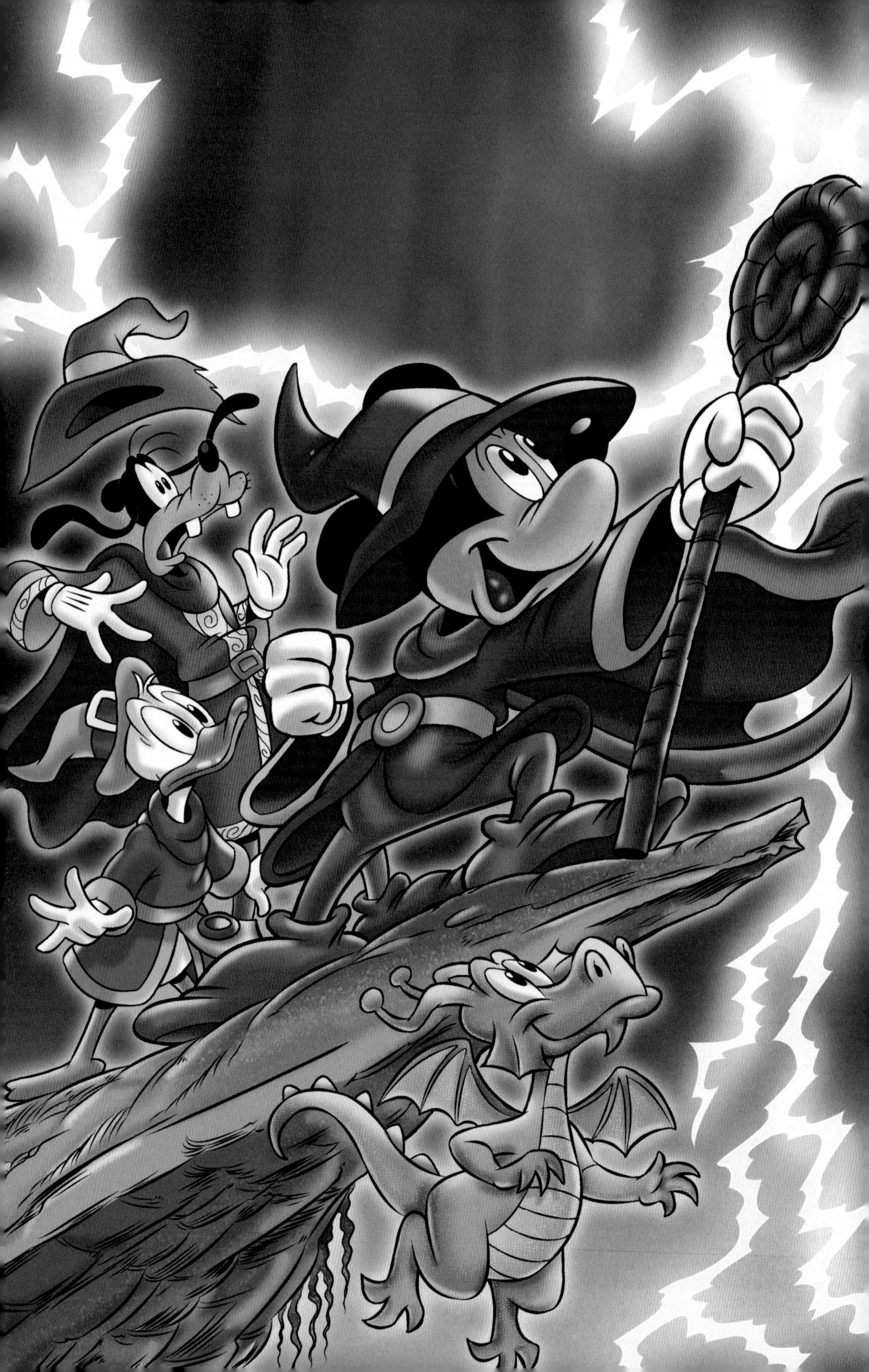

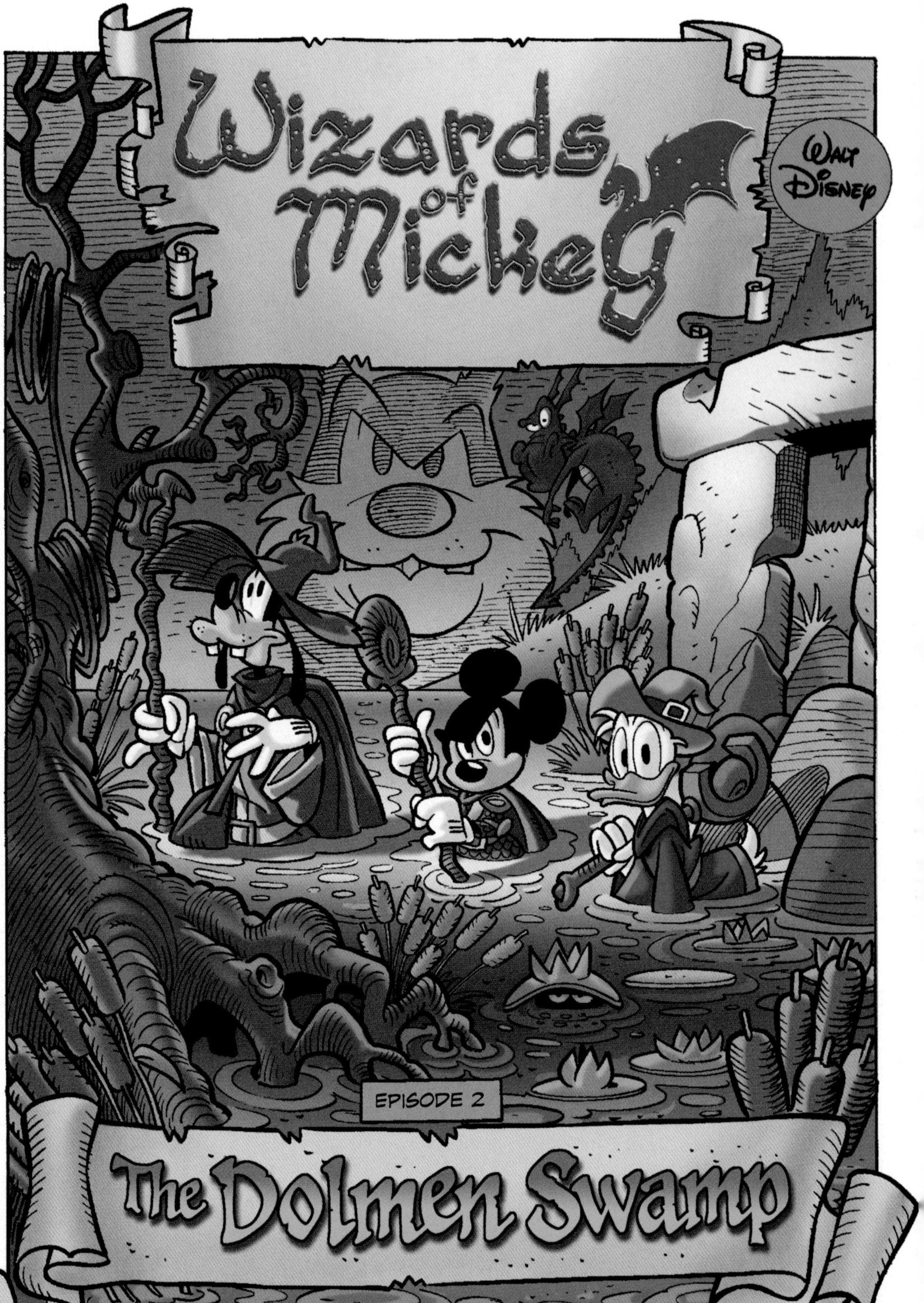
Wizards of Mickey
Walt Disney
EPISODE 2
The Dolmen Swamp
D-2655-6

STORY BY STEFANO AMBROSIO ART BY MARCO GERVASIO

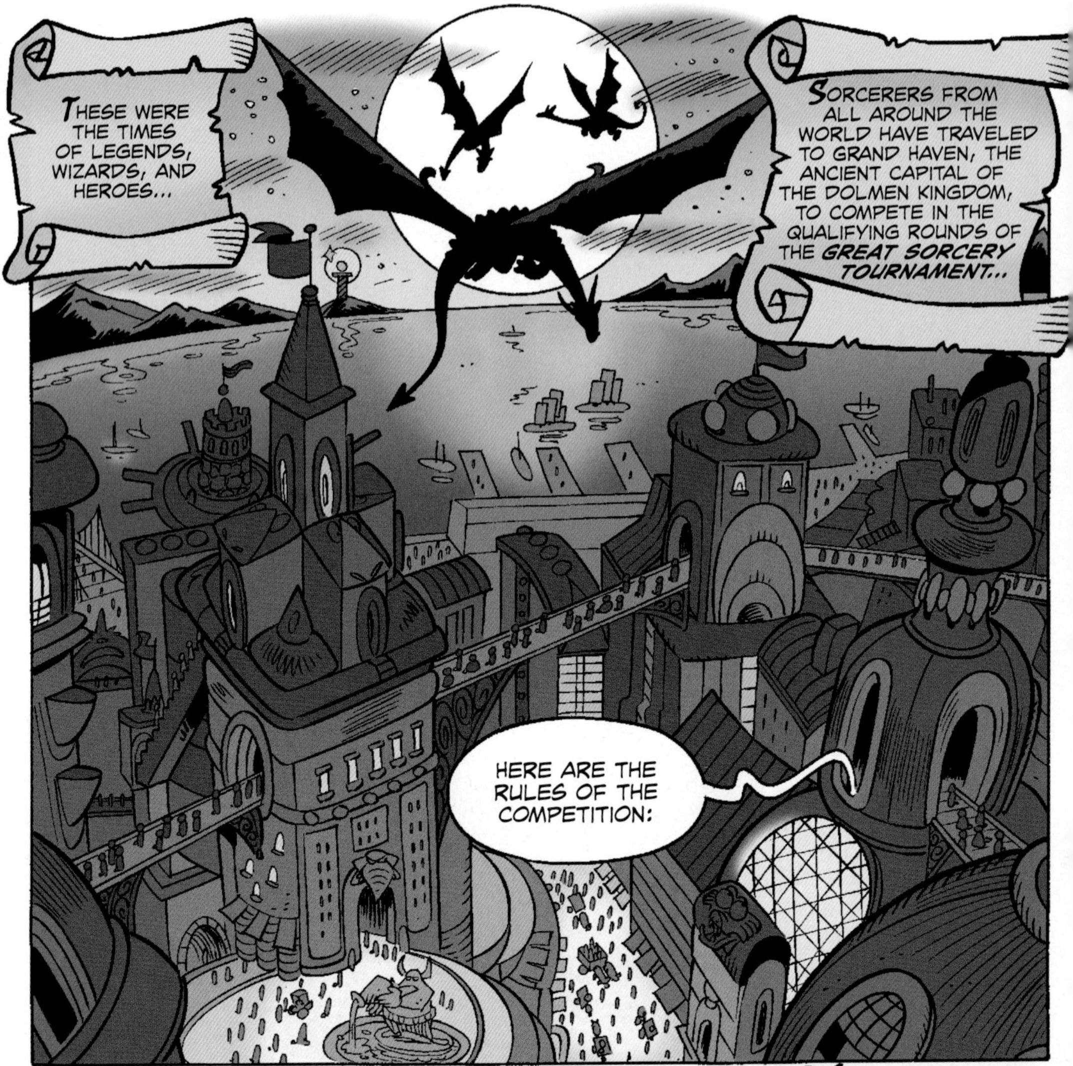
THESE WERE THE TIMES OF LEGENDS, WIZARDS, AND HEROES...
SORCERERS FROM ALL AROUND THE WORLD HAVE TRAVELED TO GRAND HAVEN, THE ANCIENT CAPITAL OF THE DOLMEN KINGDOM, TO COMPETE IN THE QUALIFYING ROUNDS OF THE GREAT SORCERY TOURNAMENT...
HERE ARE THE RULES OF THE COMPETITION:
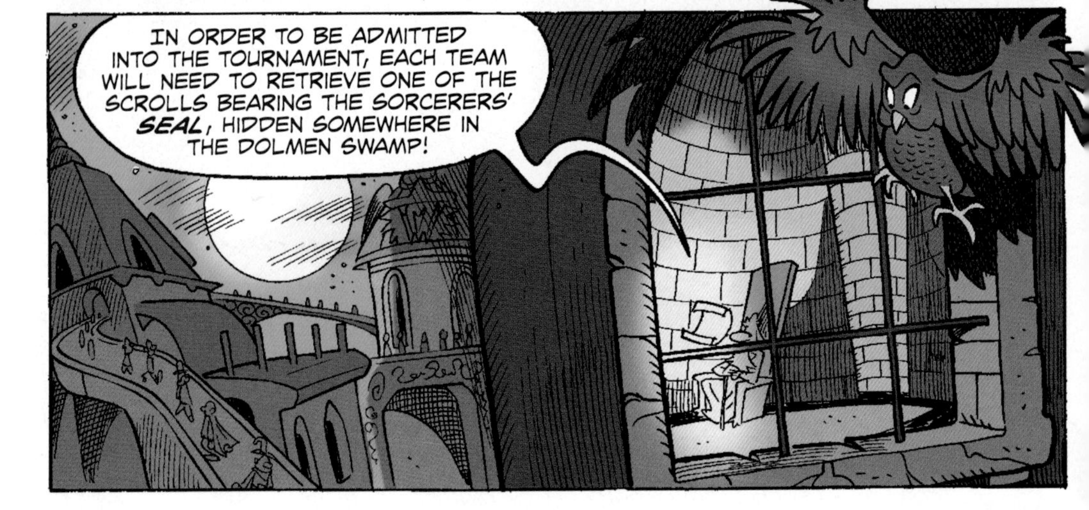
IN ORDER TO BE ADMITTED INTO THE TOURNAMENT, EACH TEAM WILL NEED TO RETRIEVE ONE OF THE SCROLLS BEARING THE SORCERERS' SEAL, HIDDEN SOMEWHERE IN THE DOLMEN SWAMP!

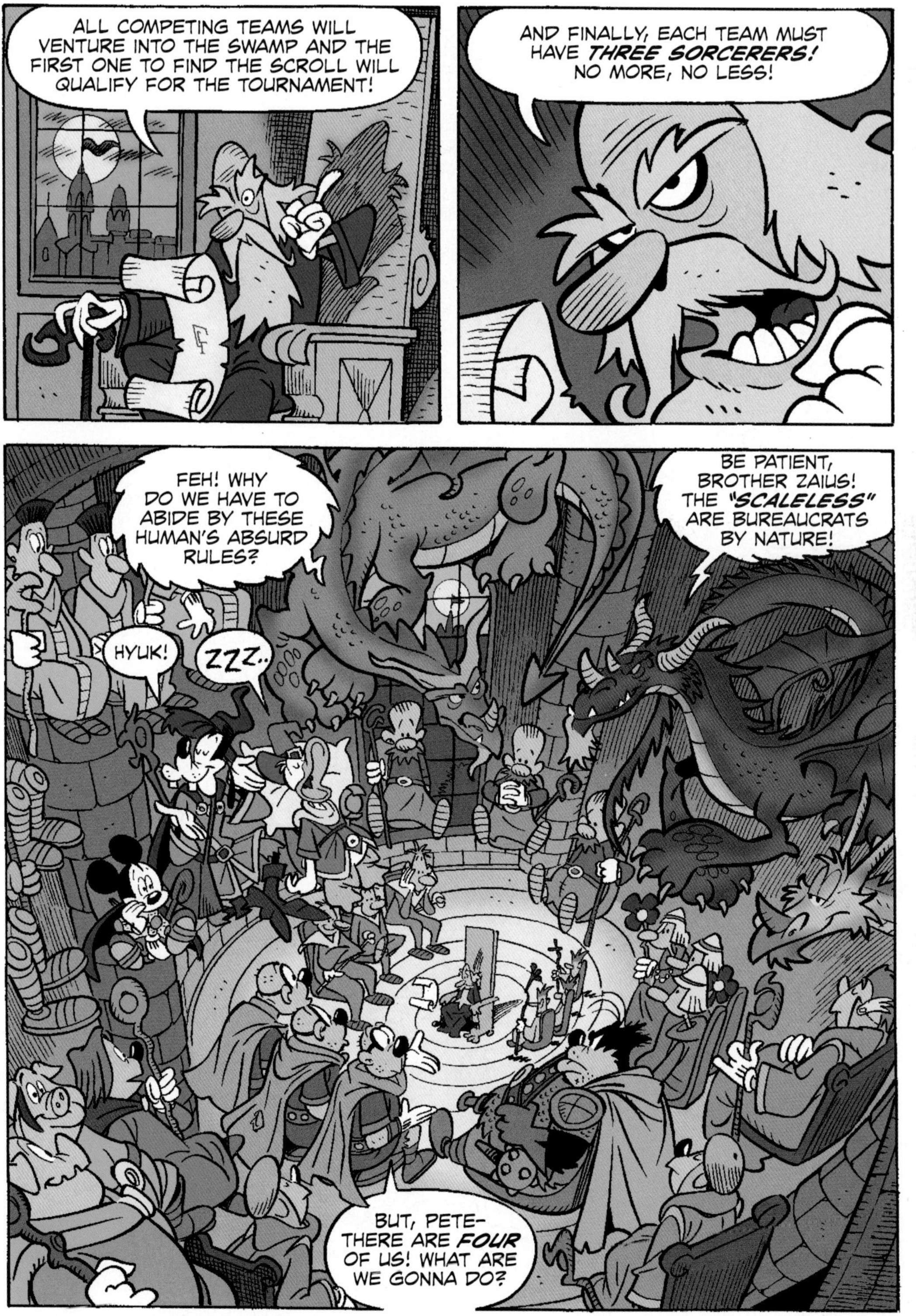
ALL COMPETING TEAMS WILL VENTURE INTO THE SWAMP AND THE FIRST ONE TO FIND THE SCROLL WILL QUALIFY FOR THE TOURNAMENT!
AND FINALLY, EACH TEAM MUST HAVE *THREE SORCERERS!* NO MORE, NO LESS!
FEH! WHY DO WE HAVE TO ABIDE BY THESE HUMAN'S ABSURD RULES?
BE PATIENT, BROTHER ZAIUS! THE *"SCALELESS"* ARE BUREAUCRATS BY NATURE!
HYUK!
ZZZ..
BUT, PETE- THERE ARE *FOUR* OF US! WHAT ARE WE GONNA DO?

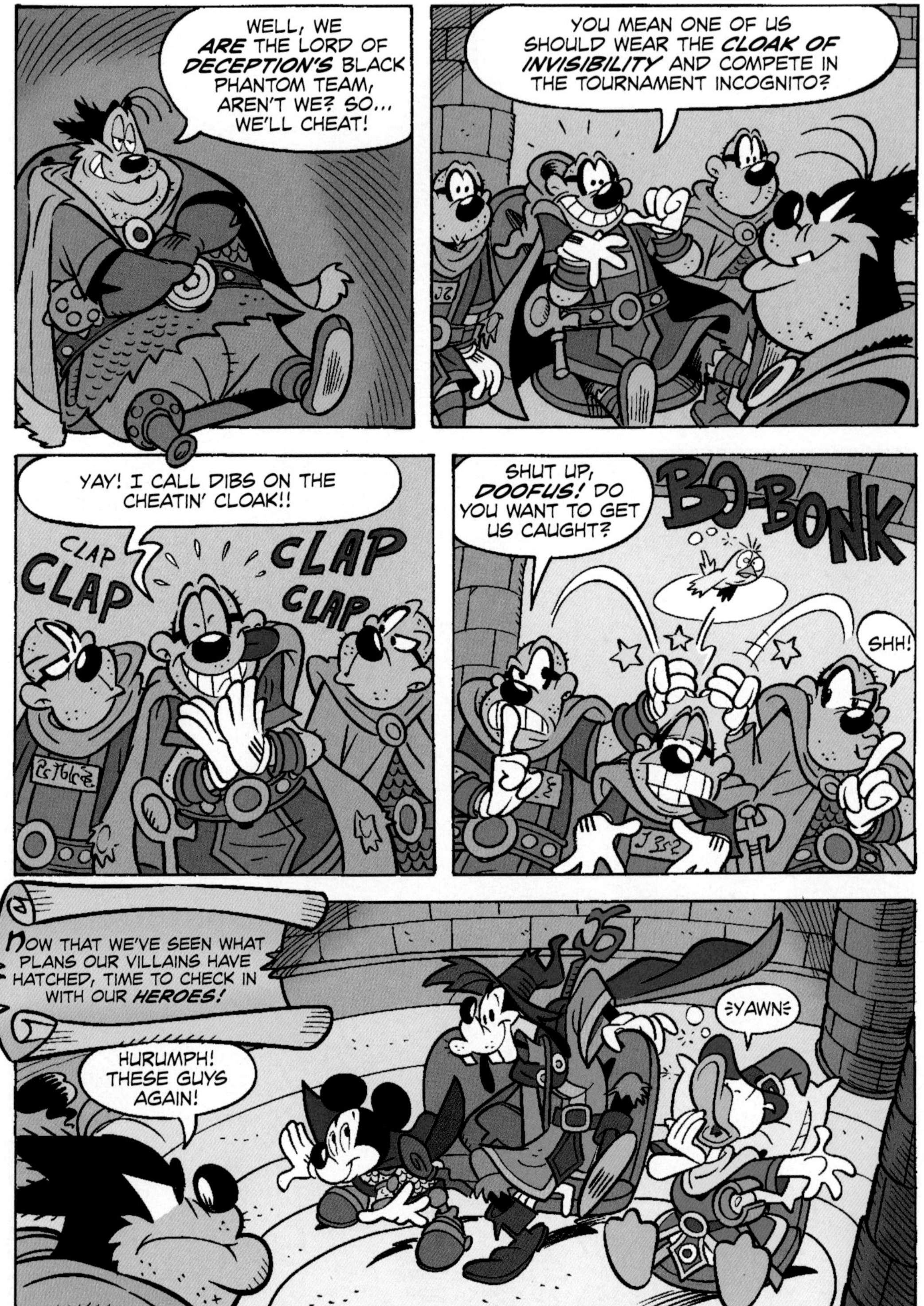
WELL, WE ARE THE LORD OF DECEPTION'S BLACK PHANTOM TEAM, AREN'T WE? SO... WE'LL CHEAT!
YOU MEAN ONE OF US SHOULD WEAR THE CLOAK OF INVISIBILITY AND COMPETE IN THE TOURNAMENT INCOGNITO?
YAY! I CALL DIBS ON THE CHEATIN' CLOAK!!
CLAP CLAP
CLAP CLAP
SHUT UP, DOOFUS! DO YOU WANT TO GET US CAUGHT?
BO-BONK
SHH!
NOW THAT WE'VE SEEN WHAT PLANS OUR VILLAINS HAVE HATCHED, TIME TO CHECK IN WITH OUR HEROES!
HURUMPH! THESE GUYS AGAIN!
YAWN

AND HERE THEY ARE NOW!

HYUK! I WONDER WHO WE'LL BE UP AGAINST FIRST.

IT DOESN'T MATTER TO ME, AS LONG AS WE MAKE IT INTO THE COMPETITION.

THAT'S THE ONLY WAY I'M GOING TO BE ABLE TO AVOID THE INNKEEPER WHOSE BUSINESS FAFNIR BURNED TO THE GROUND!

YARP!

MAYBE YOU SHOULD HAVE JUST PAID FOR THE REPAIRS!

PAID WITH *WHAT?* I'M FLAT BROKE!

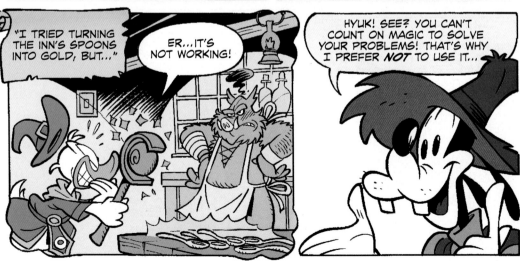

"I TRIED TURNING THE INN'S SPOONS INTO GOLD, BUT..."

ER...IT'S NOT WORKING!

HYUK! SEE? YOU CAN'T COUNT ON MAGIC TO SOLVE YOUR PROBLEMS! THAT'S WHY I PREFER *NOT* TO USE IT...

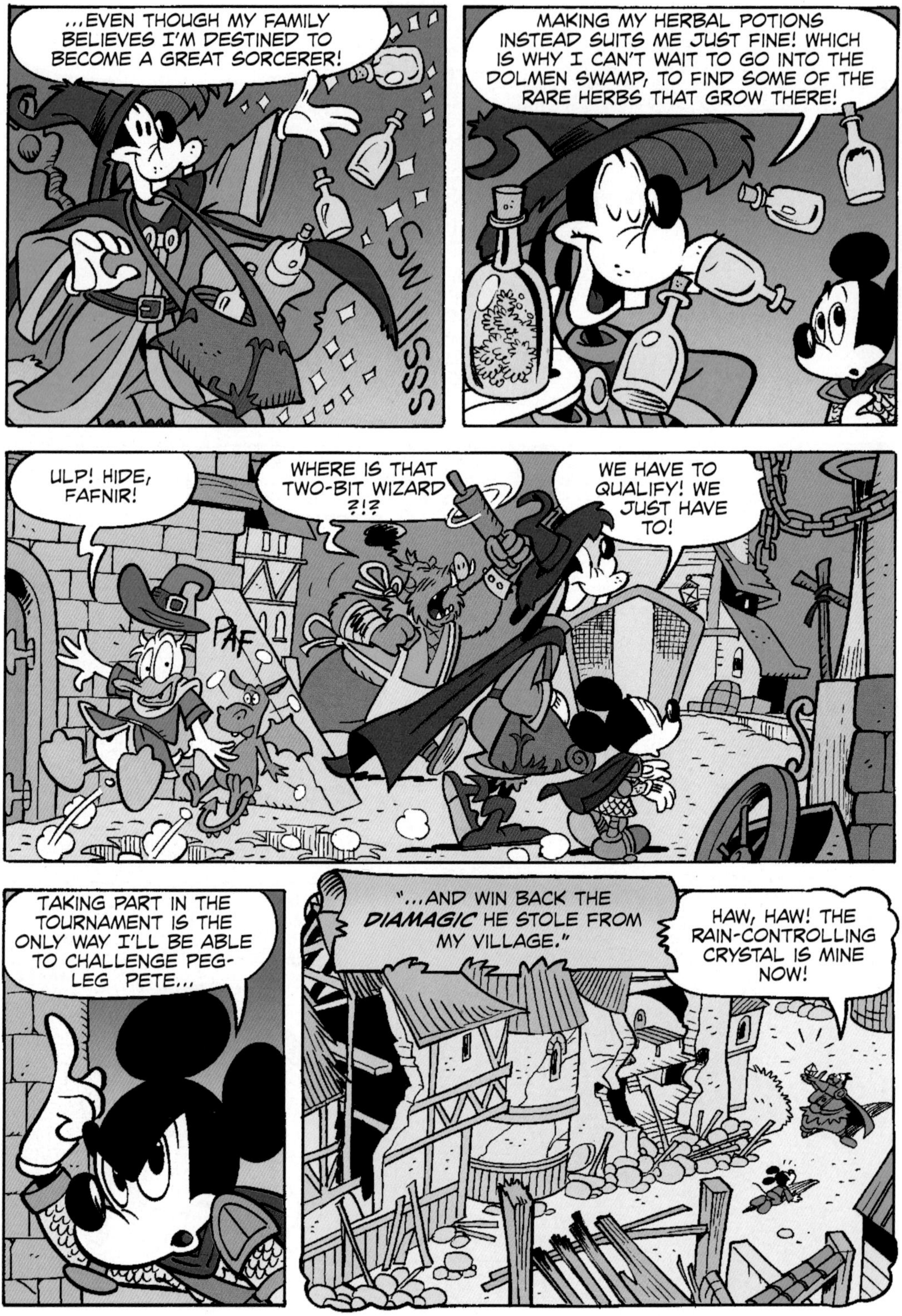
...EVEN THOUGH MY FAMILY BELIEVES I'M DESTINED TO BECOME A GREAT SORCERER!
SWIISSS
MAKING MY HERBAL POTIONS INSTEAD SUITS ME JUST FINE! WHICH IS WHY I CAN'T WAIT TO GO INTO THE DOLMEN SWAMP, TO FIND SOME OF THE RARE HERBS THAT GROW THERE!
ULP! HIDE, FAFNIR!
WHERE IS THAT TWO-BIT WIZARD ?!?
WE HAVE TO QUALIFY! WE JUST HAVE TO!
PAF
TAKING PART IN THE TOURNAMENT IS THE ONLY WAY I'LL BE ABLE TO CHALLENGE PEG-LEG PETE...
"...AND WIN BACK THE *DIAMAGIC* HE STOLE FROM MY VILLAGE."
HAW, HAW! THE RAIN-CONTROLLING CRYSTAL IS MINE NOW!

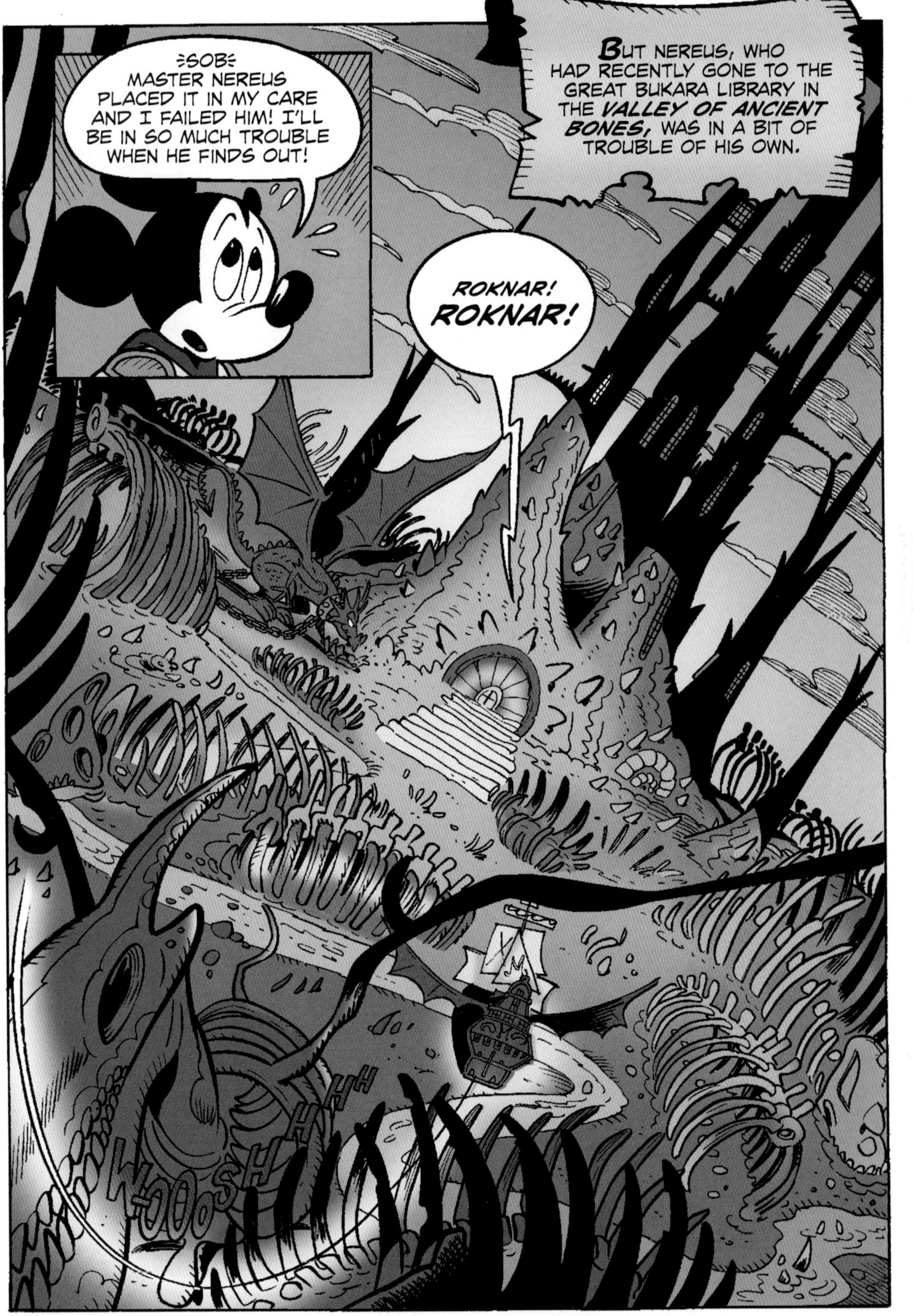

=SOB= MASTER NEREUS PLACED IT IN MY CARE AND I FAILED HIM! I'LL BE IN SO MUCH TROUBLE WHEN HE FINDS OUT!
BUT NEREUS, WHO HAD RECENTLY GONE TO THE GREAT BUKARA LIBRARY IN THE VALLEY OF ANCIENT BONES, WAS IN A BIT OF TROUBLE OF HIS OWN.
ROKNAR! ROKNAR!
WHOOOSHHHHH

NNNGH! LET ME GO! LET ME GO!
STOP PLAYING WITH YOUR FOOD, ROKNAR, AND GET OVER HERE THIS INSTANT!
EHM... S-S-SORRY, M-MASTER!
DID YOU CHAIN UP THE PRISONER?
A-AS YOU C-COMMANDED!
THEN IT'S TIME I GREETED OUR GUEST!
A LITTLE LIGHT PLEASE, YOU OVER-GROWN LIZARD!
F-FOOOSH
A-AT ONCE, MASTER!

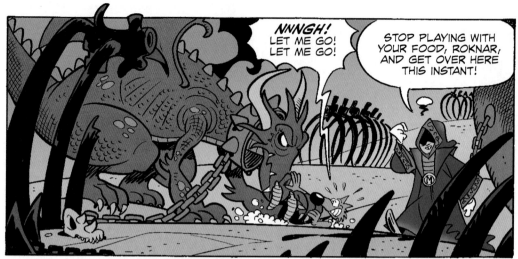

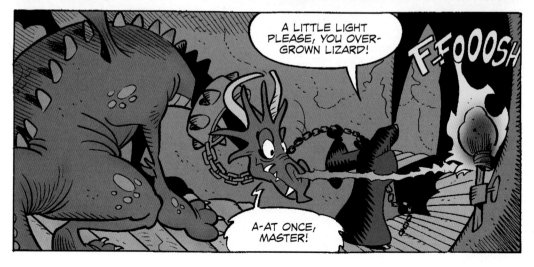

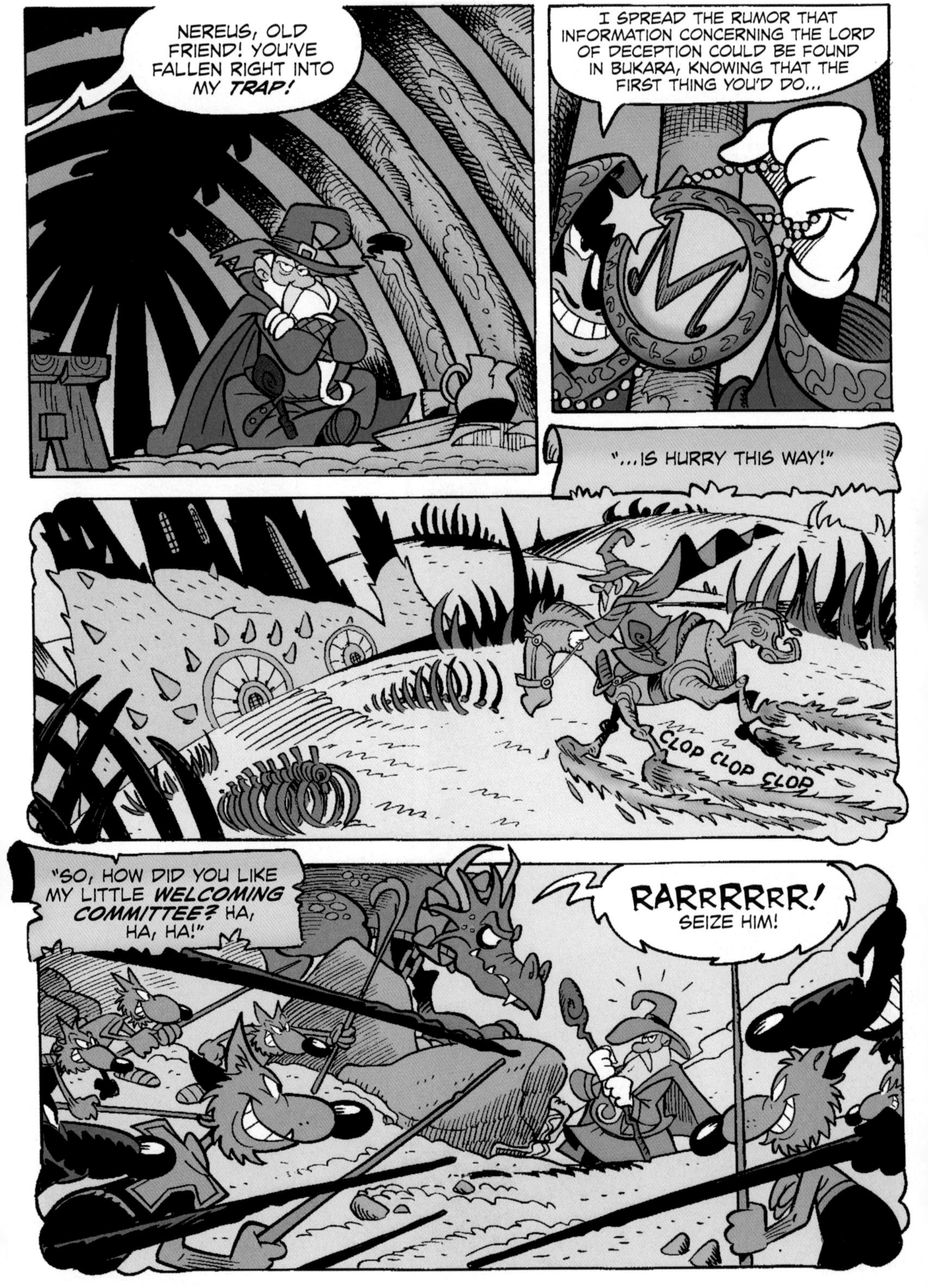
NEREUS, OLD FRIEND! YOU'VE FALLEN RIGHT INTO MY *TRAP!*
I SPREAD THE RUMOR THAT INFORMATION CONCERNING THE LORD OF DECEPTION COULD BE FOUND IN BUKARA, KNOWING THAT THE FIRST THING YOU'D DO...
"...IS HURRY THIS WAY!"
CLOP CLOP CLOP
"SO, HOW DID YOU LIKE MY LITTLE *WELCOMING COMMITTEE?* HA, HA, HA!"
RARRRRRR! SEIZE HIM!

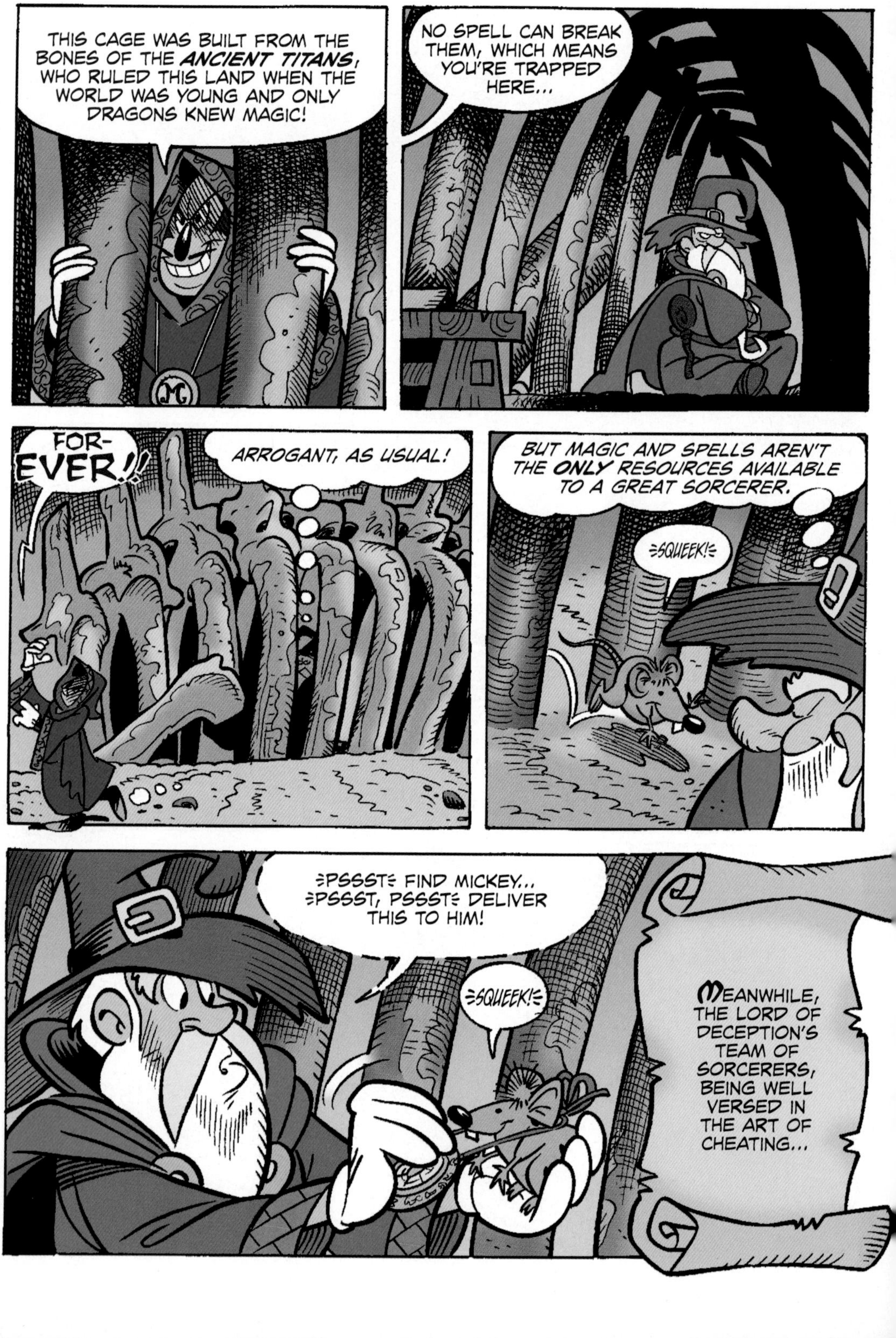
THIS CAGE WAS BUILT FROM THE BONES OF THE *ANCIENT TITANS*, WHO RULED THIS LAND WHEN THE WORLD WAS YOUNG AND ONLY DRAGONS KNEW MAGIC!
NO SPELL CAN BREAK THEM, WHICH MEANS YOU'RE TRAPPED HERE...
FOR-EVER!!
ARROGANT, AS USUAL!
BUT MAGIC AND SPELLS AREN'T THE *ONLY* RESOURCES AVAILABLE TO A GREAT SORCERER.
SQUEEK!
PSSST FIND MICKEY... PSSST, PSSST DELIVER THIS TO HIM!
SQUEEK!
MEANWHILE, THE LORD OF DECEPTION'S TEAM OF SORCERERS, BEING WELL VERSED IN THE ART OF CHEATING...

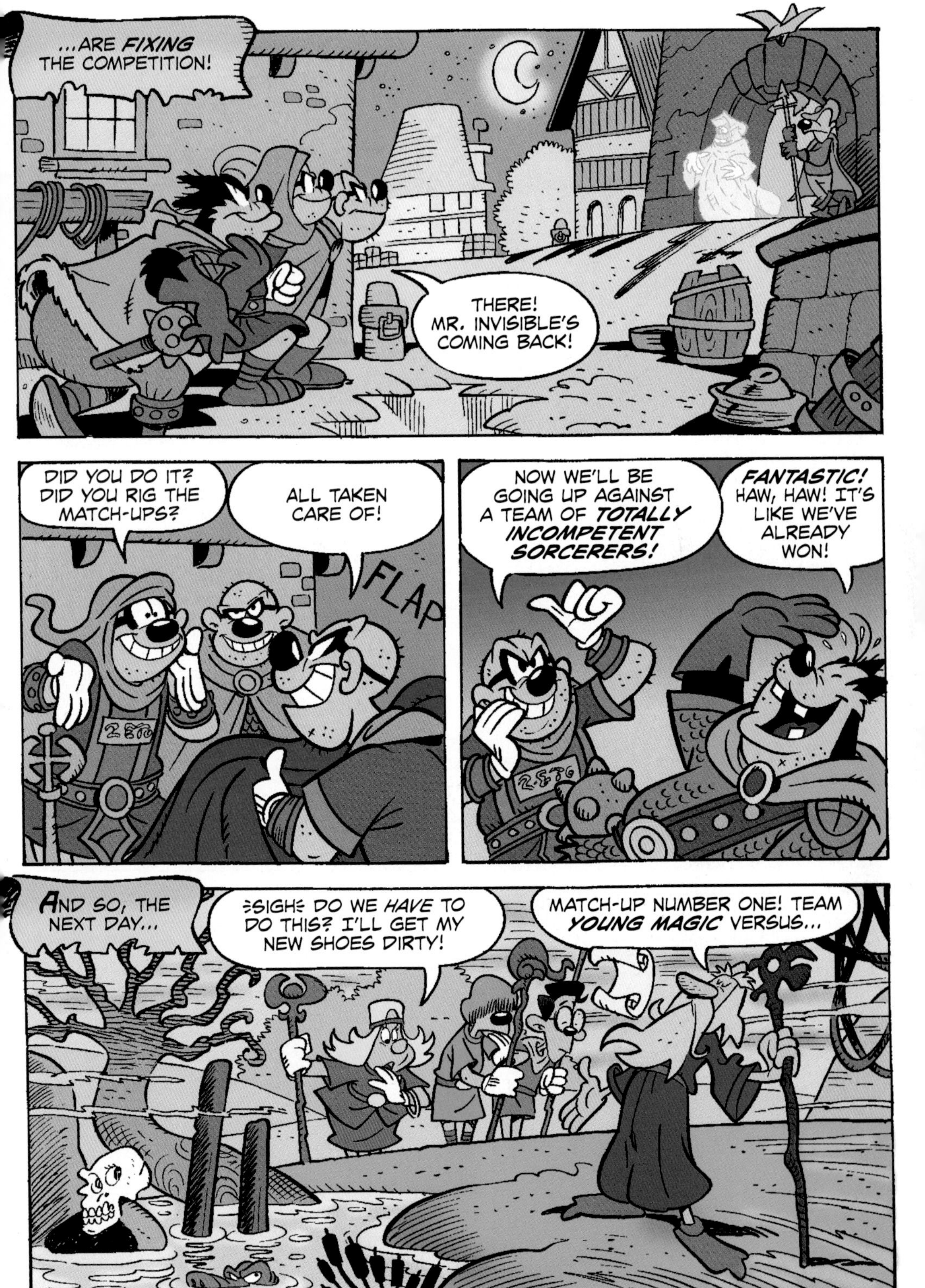

...ARE FIXING THE COMPETITION!
THERE! MR. INVISIBLE'S COMING BACK!
DID YOU DO IT? DID YOU RIG THE MATCH-UPS?
ALL TAKEN CARE OF!
FLAP
NOW WE'LL BE GOING UP AGAINST A TEAM OF TOTALLY INCOMPETENT SORCERERS!
FANTASTIC! HAW, HAW! IT'S LIKE WE'VE ALREADY WON!
AND SO, THE NEXT DAY...
SIGH DO WE HAVE TO DO THIS? I'LL GET MY NEW SHOES DIRTY!
MATCH-UP NUMBER ONE! TEAM YOUNG MAGIC VERSUS...

...TEAM MAGMA FIRE!
!!!
UM... MAYBE WE SHOULD ...
...WITHDRAW FROM THE COMPETITION?
AGREED!
ZO-OOOOWWW
PTUI! THOSE "SCALELESS" ARE A BUNCHA COWARDS!
THE HONOR OF GOING FIRST IS YOURS, BROTHER ZAIUS!

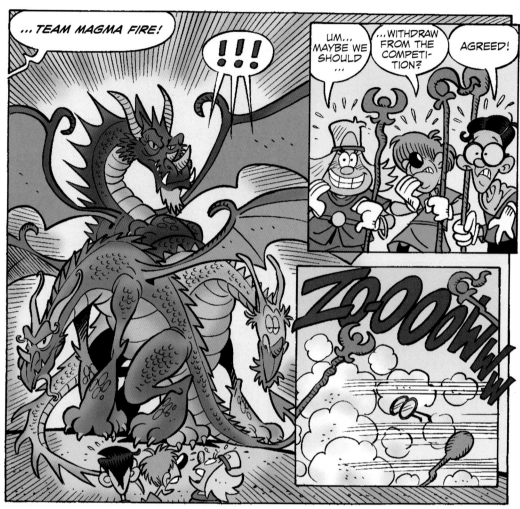

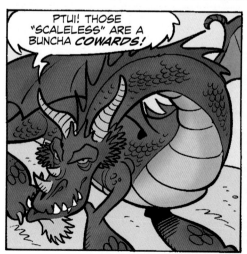

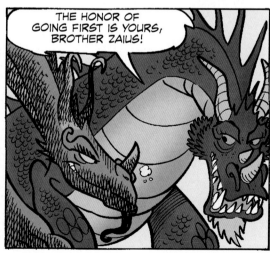

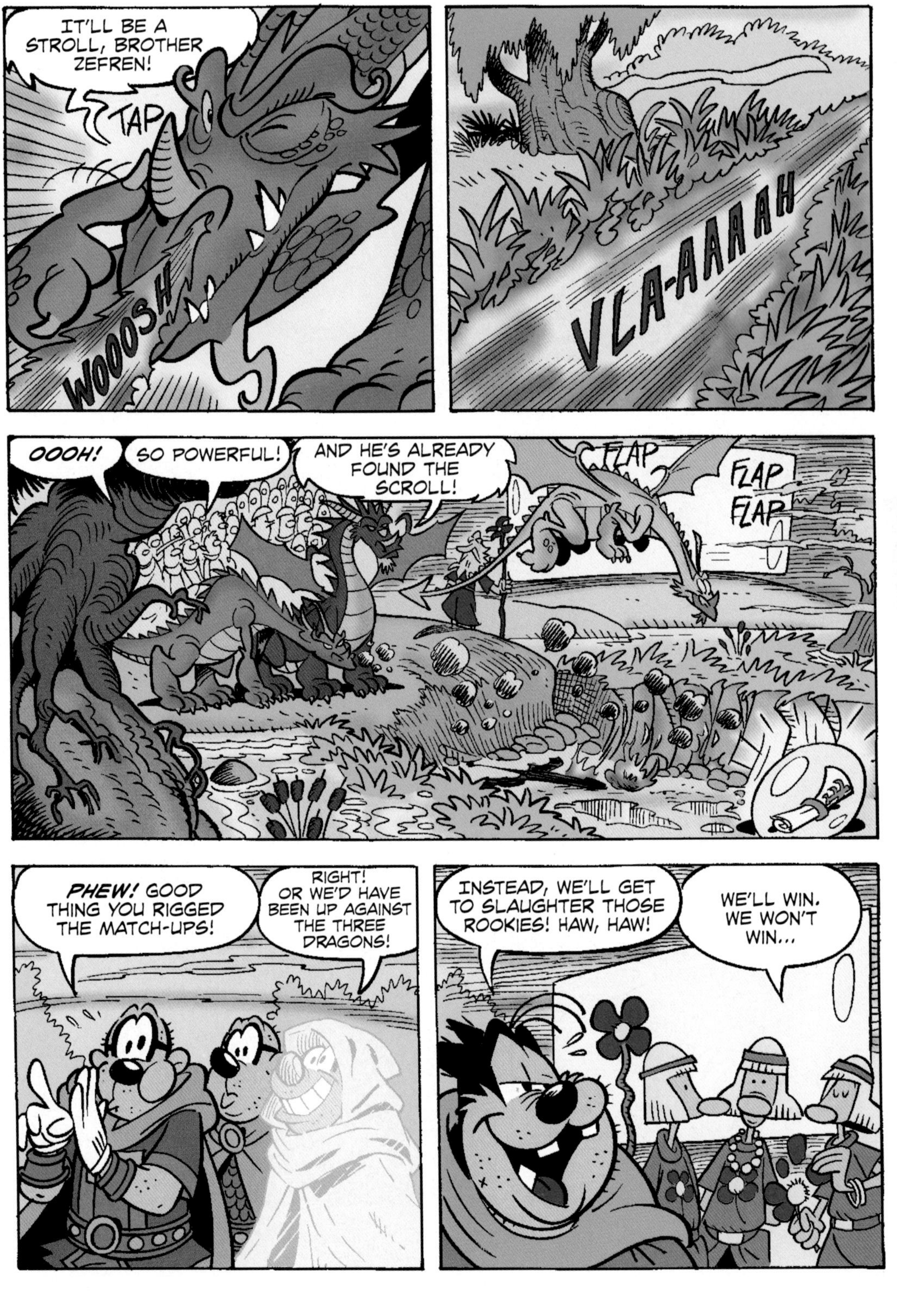
IT'LL BE A STROLL, BROTHER ZEFREN!
TAP
WOOOSH
VLA-AAAAH
OOOH!
SO POWERFUL!
AND HE'S ALREADY FOUND THE SCROLL!
FLAP
FLAP
FLAP
PHEW! GOOD THING YOU RIGGED THE MATCH-UPS!
RIGHT! OR WE'D HAVE BEEN UP AGAINST THE THREE DRAGONS!
INSTEAD, WE'LL GET TO SLAUGHTER THOSE ROOKIES! HAW, HAW!
WE'LL WIN. WE WON'T WIN...

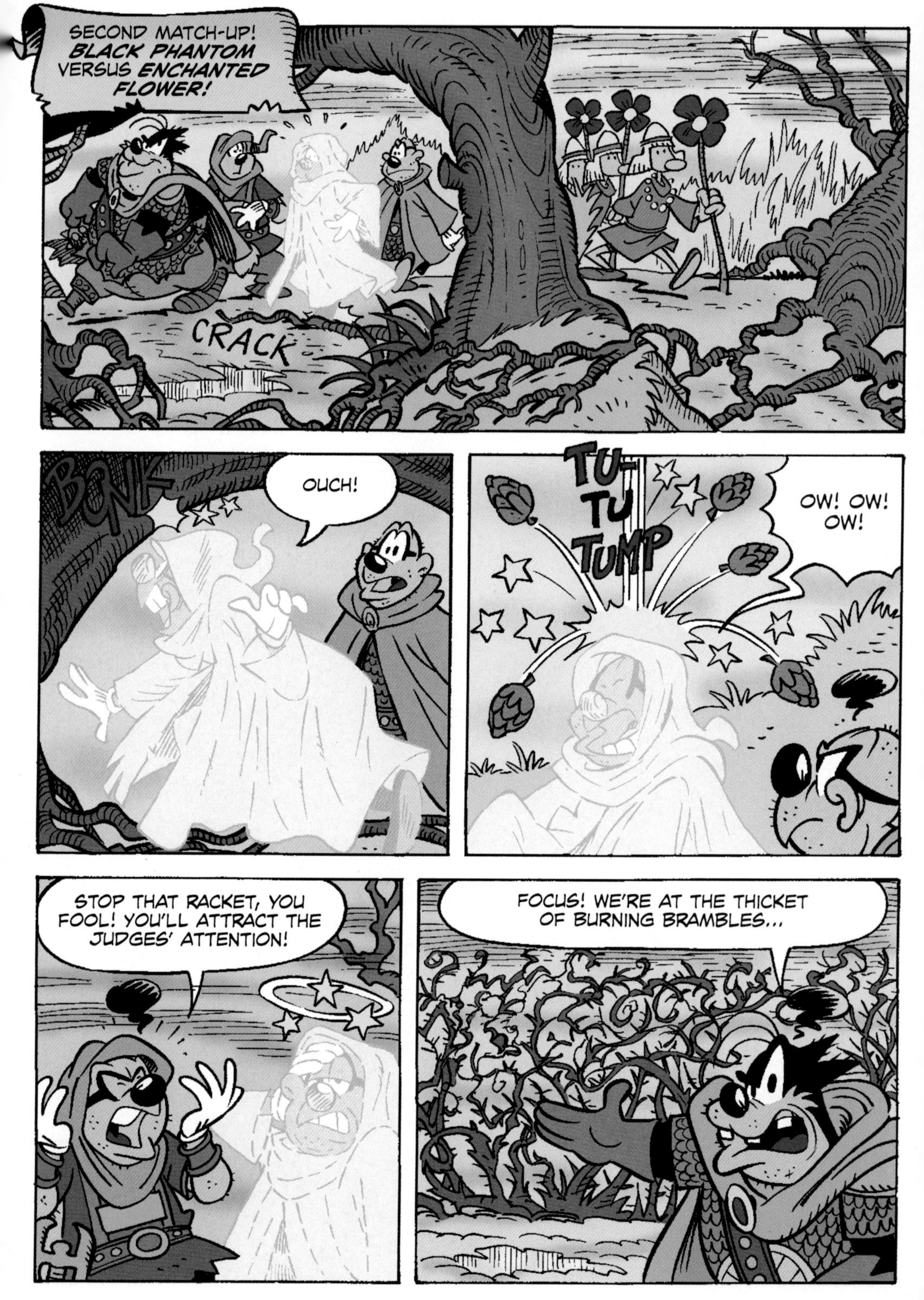
SECOND MATCH-UP! BLACK PHANTOM VERSUS ENCHANTED FLOWER!
CRACK
BONK
OUCH!
TU-TU TUMP
OW! OW! OW!
STOP THAT RACKET, YOU FOOL! YOU'LL ATTRACT THE JUDGES' ATTENTION!
FOCUS! WE'RE AT THE THICKET OF BURNING BRAMBLES...

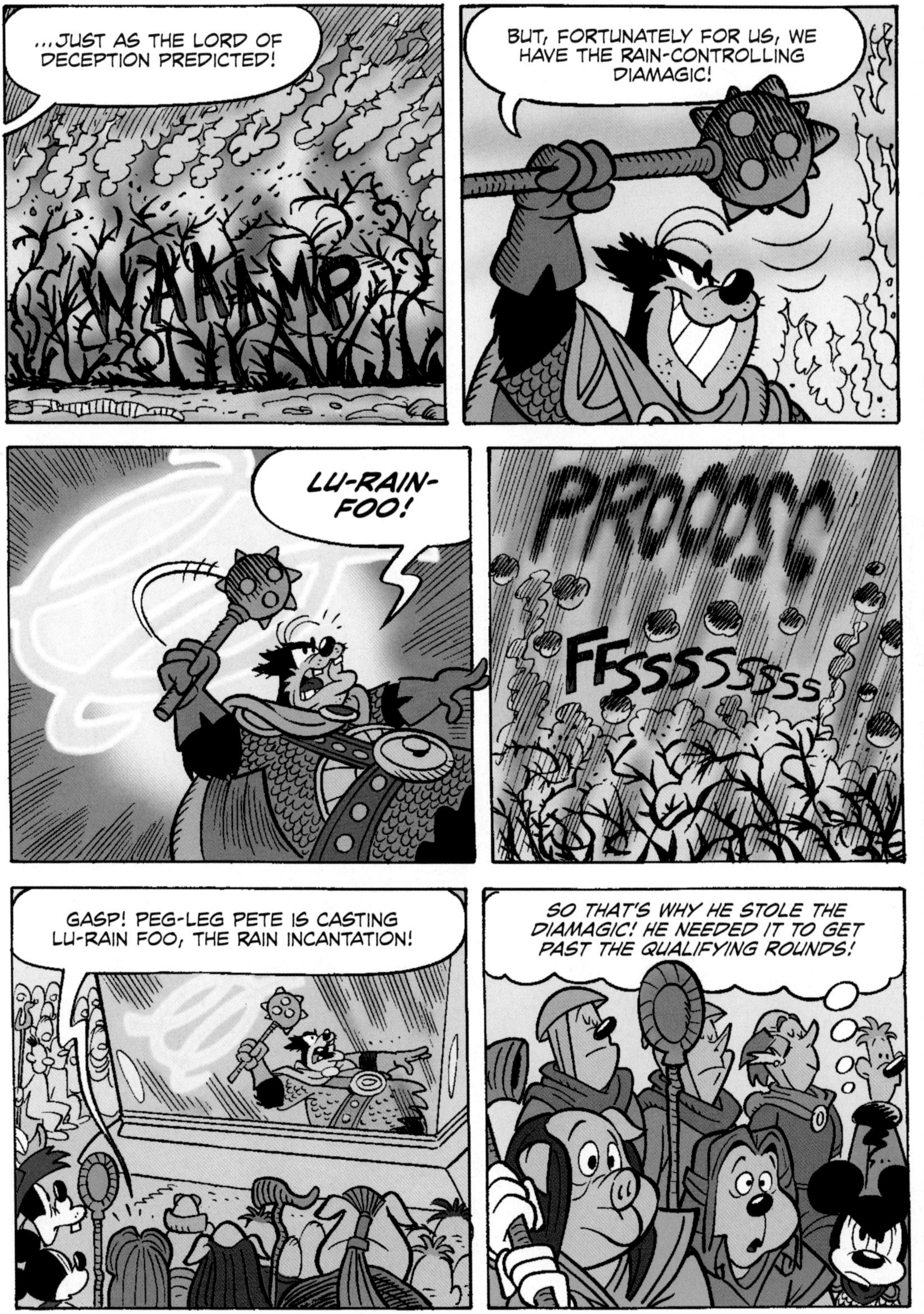
...JUST AS THE LORD OF DECEPTION PREDICTED!
WAAAMP
BUT, FORTUNATELY FOR US, WE HAVE THE RAIN-CONTROLLING DIAMAGIC!
LU-RAIN-FOO!
PROOOSC
FFSSSSSSSS
GASP! PEG-LEG PETE IS CASTING LU-RAIN FOO, THE RAIN INCANTATION!
SO THAT'S WHY HE STOLE THE DIAMAGIC! HE NEEDED IT TO GET PAST THE QUALIFYING ROUNDS!

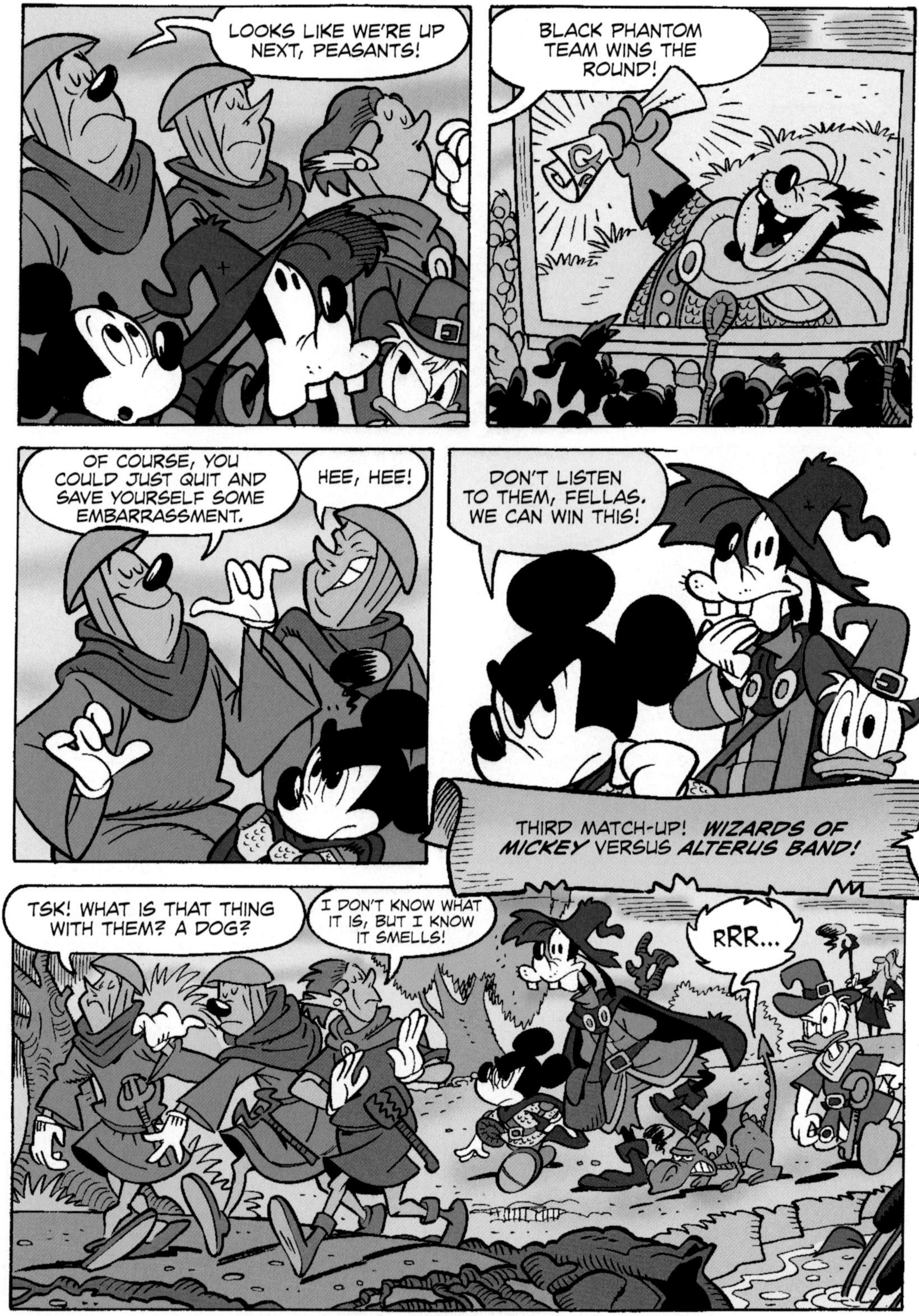

LOOKS LIKE WE'RE UP NEXT, PEASANTS!
BLACK PHANTOM TEAM WINS THE ROUND!
OF COURSE, YOU COULD JUST QUIT AND SAVE YOURSELF SOME EMBARRASSMENT.
HEE, HEE!
DON'T LISTEN TO THEM, FELLAS. WE CAN WIN THIS!
THIRD MATCH-UP! *WIZARDS OF MICKEY* VERSUS *ALTERUS BAND!*
TSK! WHAT IS THAT THING WITH THEM? A DOG?
I DON'T KNOW WHAT IT IS, BUT I KNOW IT SMELLS!
RRR...

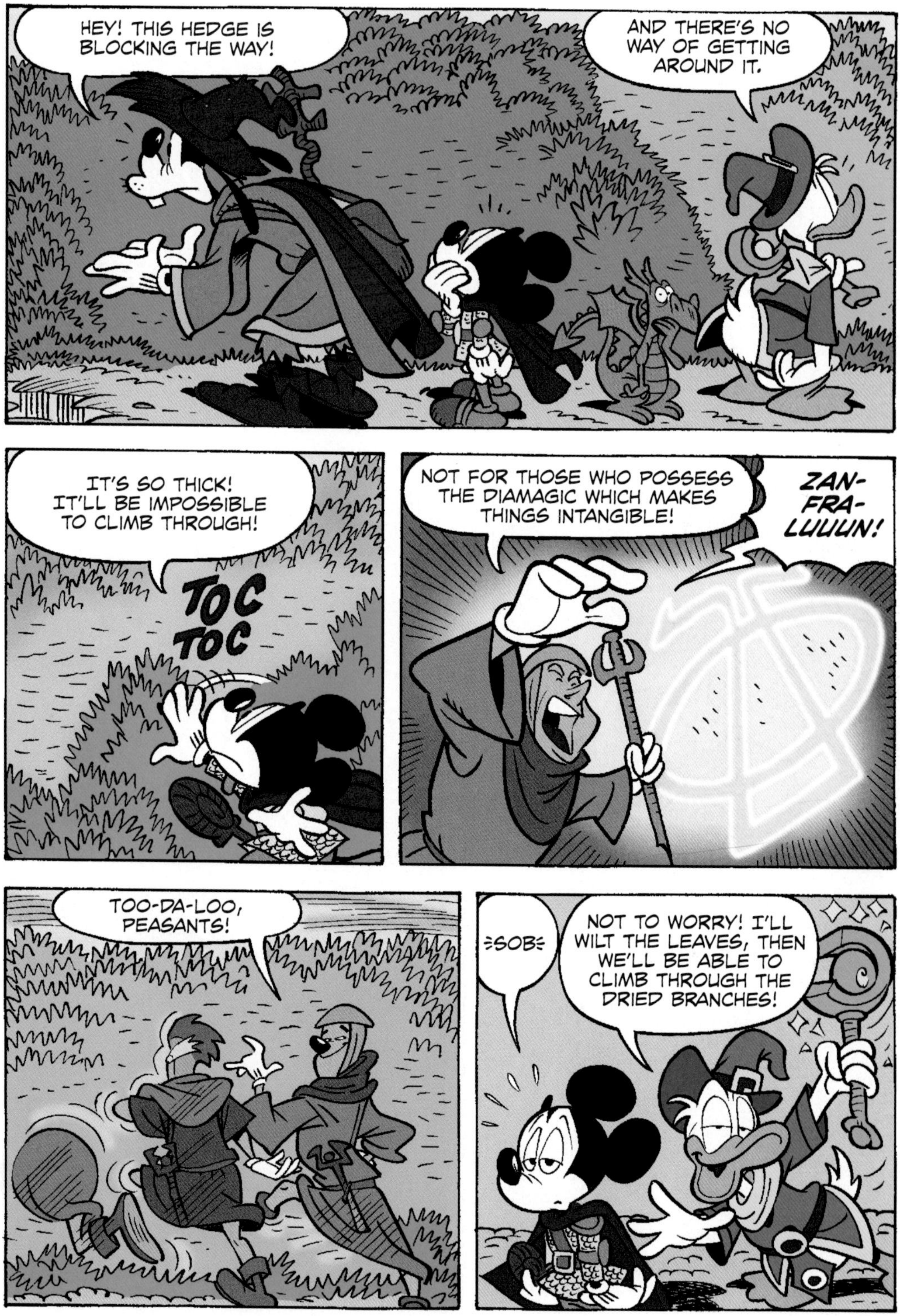
HEY! THIS HEDGE IS BLOCKING THE WAY!
AND THERE'S NO WAY OF GETTING AROUND IT.
IT'S SO THICK! IT'LL BE IMPOSSIBLE TO CLIMB THROUGH!
TOC TOC
NOT FOR THOSE WHO POSSESS THE DIAMAGIC WHICH MAKES THINGS INTANGIBLE!
ZAN-FRA-LUUUN!
TOO-DA-LOO, PEASANTS!
SOB
NOT TO WORRY! I'LL WILT THE LEAVES, THEN WE'LL BE ABLE TO CLIMB THROUGH THE DRIED BRANCHES!

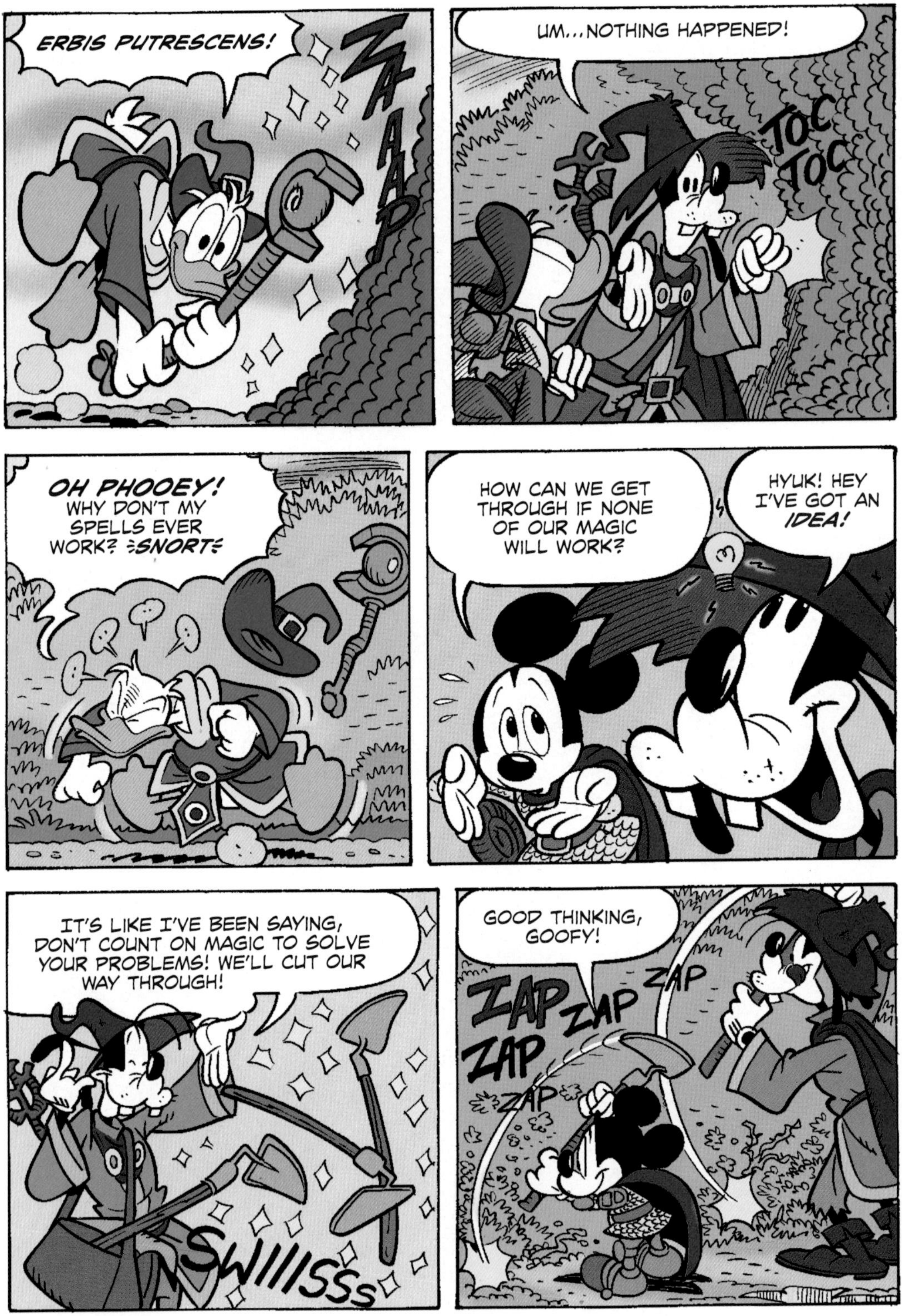

ERBIS PUTRESCENS!
ZAAAP
UM...NOTHING HAPPENED!
TOC TOC
OH PHOOEY! WHY DON'T MY SPELLS EVER WORK? SNORT
HOW CAN WE GET THROUGH IF NONE OF OUR MAGIC WILL WORK?
HYUK! HEY I'VE GOT AN IDEA!
IT'S LIKE I'VE BEEN SAYING, DON'T COUNT ON MAGIC TO SOLVE YOUR PROBLEMS! WE'LL CUT OUR WAY THROUGH!
SWIIIISSSS
GOOD THINKING, GOOFY!
ZAP ZAP ZAP ZAP ZAP

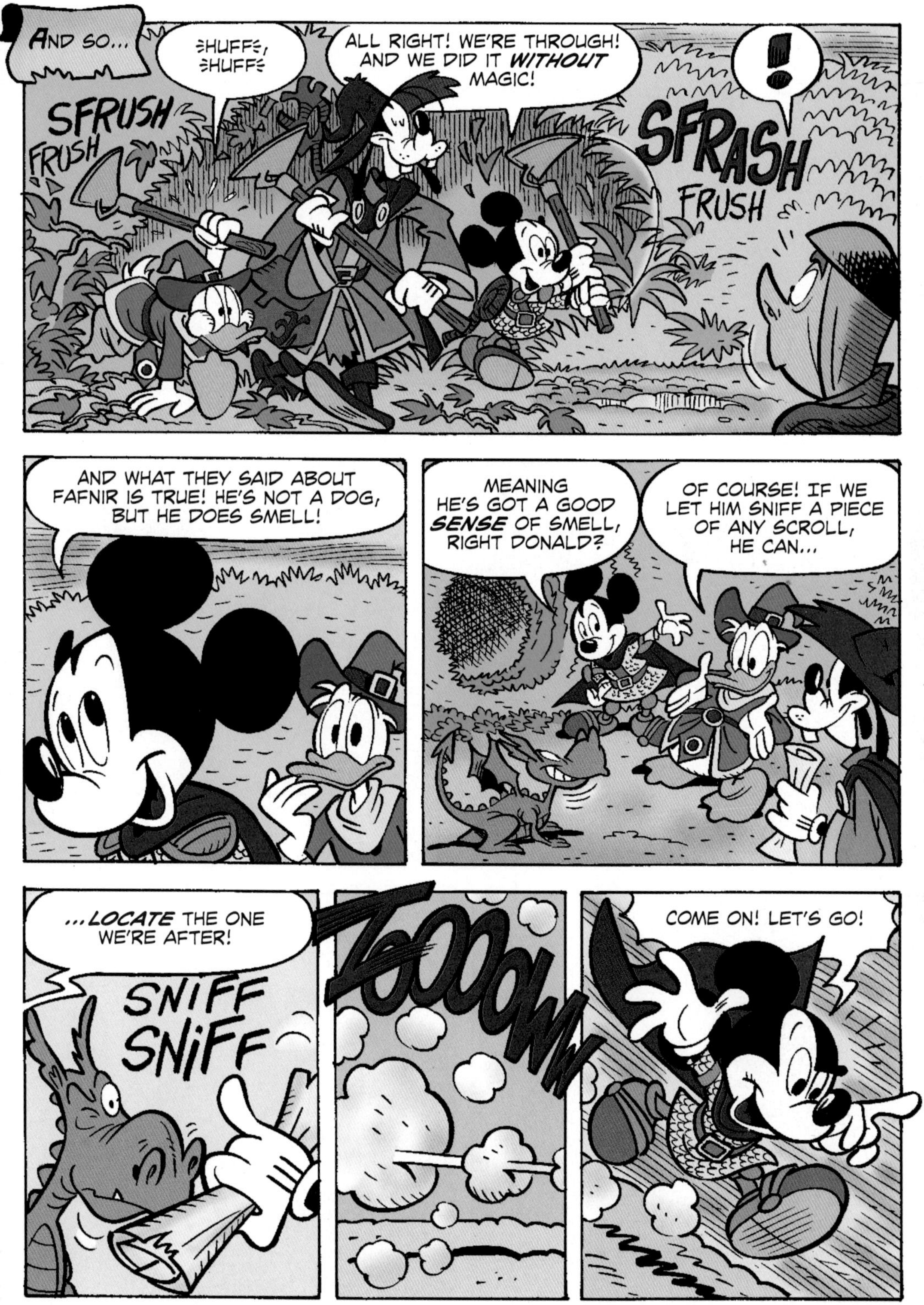
AND SO...
HUFF, HUFF
ALL RIGHT! WE'RE THROUGH! AND WE DID IT WITHOUT MAGIC!
!
SFRUSH
FRUSH
SFRASH
FRUSH
AND WHAT THEY SAID ABOUT FAFNIR IS TRUE! HE'S NOT A DOG, BUT HE DOES SMELL!
MEANING HE'S GOT A GOOD SENSE OF SMELL, RIGHT DONALD?
OF COURSE! IF WE LET HIM SNIFF A PIECE OF ANY SCROLL, HE CAN...
...LOCATE THE ONE WE'RE AFTER!
SNIFF SNIFF
ZOOOOM
COME ON! LET'S GO!

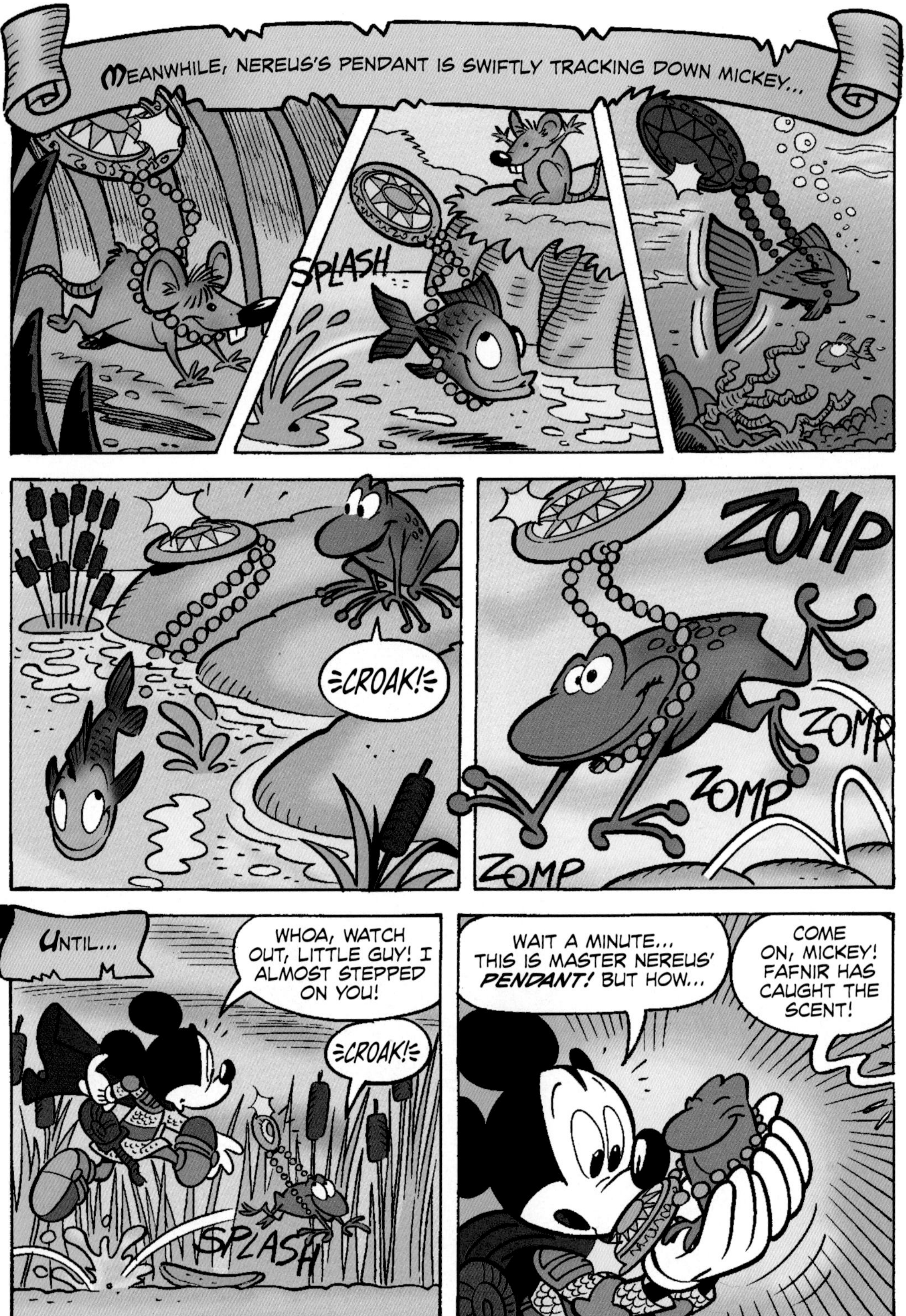
MEANWHILE, NEREUS'S PENDANT IS SWIFTLY TRACKING DOWN MICKEY...
SPLASH
ZOMP
ZOMP
ZOMP
ZOMP
CROAK!
UNTIL...
WHOA, WATCH OUT, LITTLE GUY! I ALMOST STEPPED ON YOU!
CROAK!
SPLASH
WAIT A MINUTE... THIS IS MASTER NEREUS' PENDANT! BUT HOW...
COME ON, MICKEY! FAFNIR HAS CAUGHT THE SCENT!

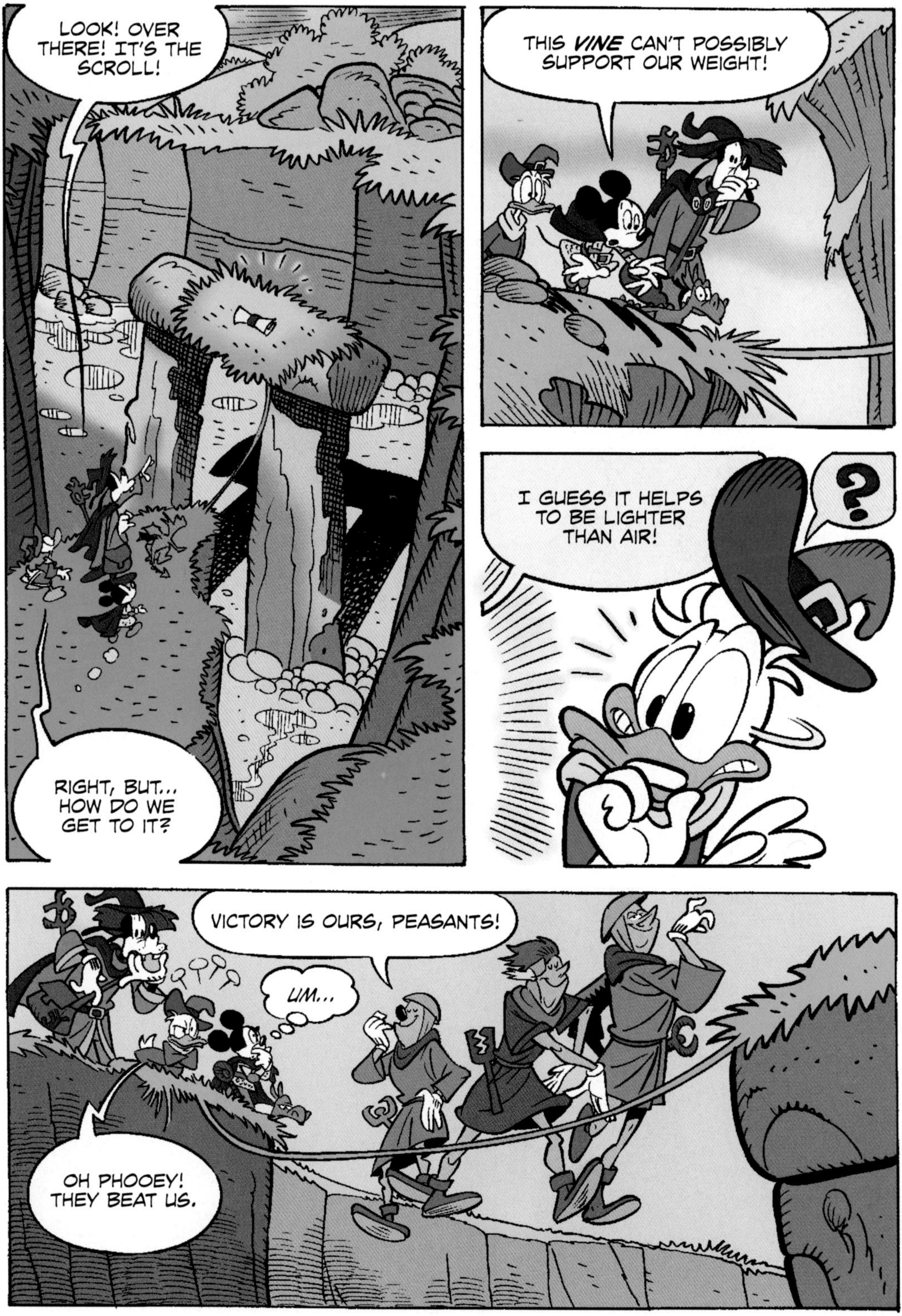
LOOK! OVER THERE! IT'S THE SCROLL!
RIGHT, BUT... HOW DO WE GET TO IT?
THIS VINE CAN'T POSSIBLY SUPPORT OUR WEIGHT!
I GUESS IT HELPS TO BE LIGHTER THAN AIR!
?
VICTORY IS OURS, PEASANTS!
UM...
OH PHOOEY! THEY BEAT US.

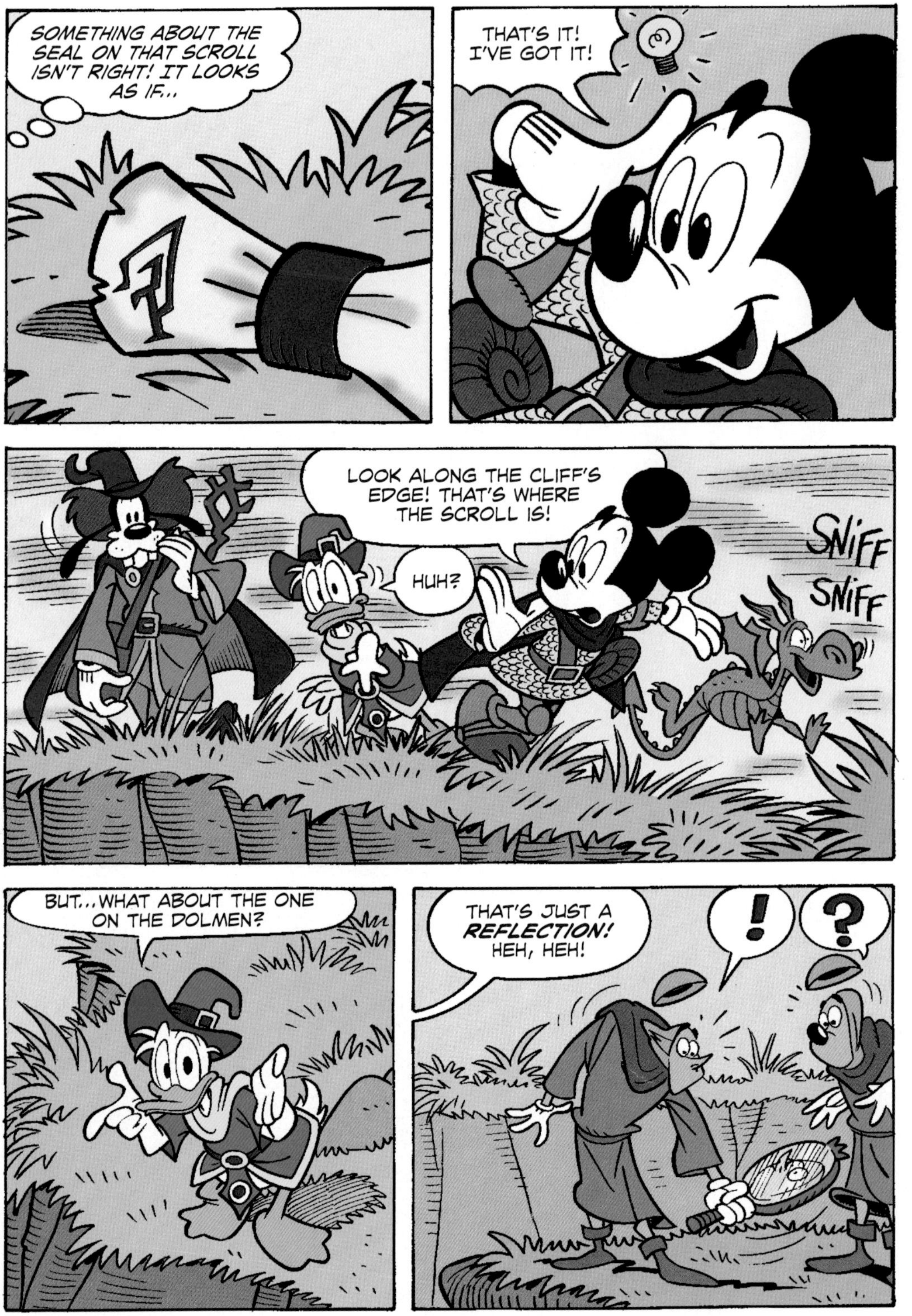

SOMETHING ABOUT THE SEAL ON THAT SCROLL ISN'T RIGHT! IT LOOKS AS IF...
THAT'S IT! I'VE GOT IT!
LOOK ALONG THE CLIFF'S EDGE! THAT'S WHERE THE SCROLL IS!
HUH?
SNIFF SNIFF
BUT...WHAT ABOUT THE ONE ON THE DOLMEN?
THAT'S JUST A *REFLECTION!* HEH, HEH!
!
?

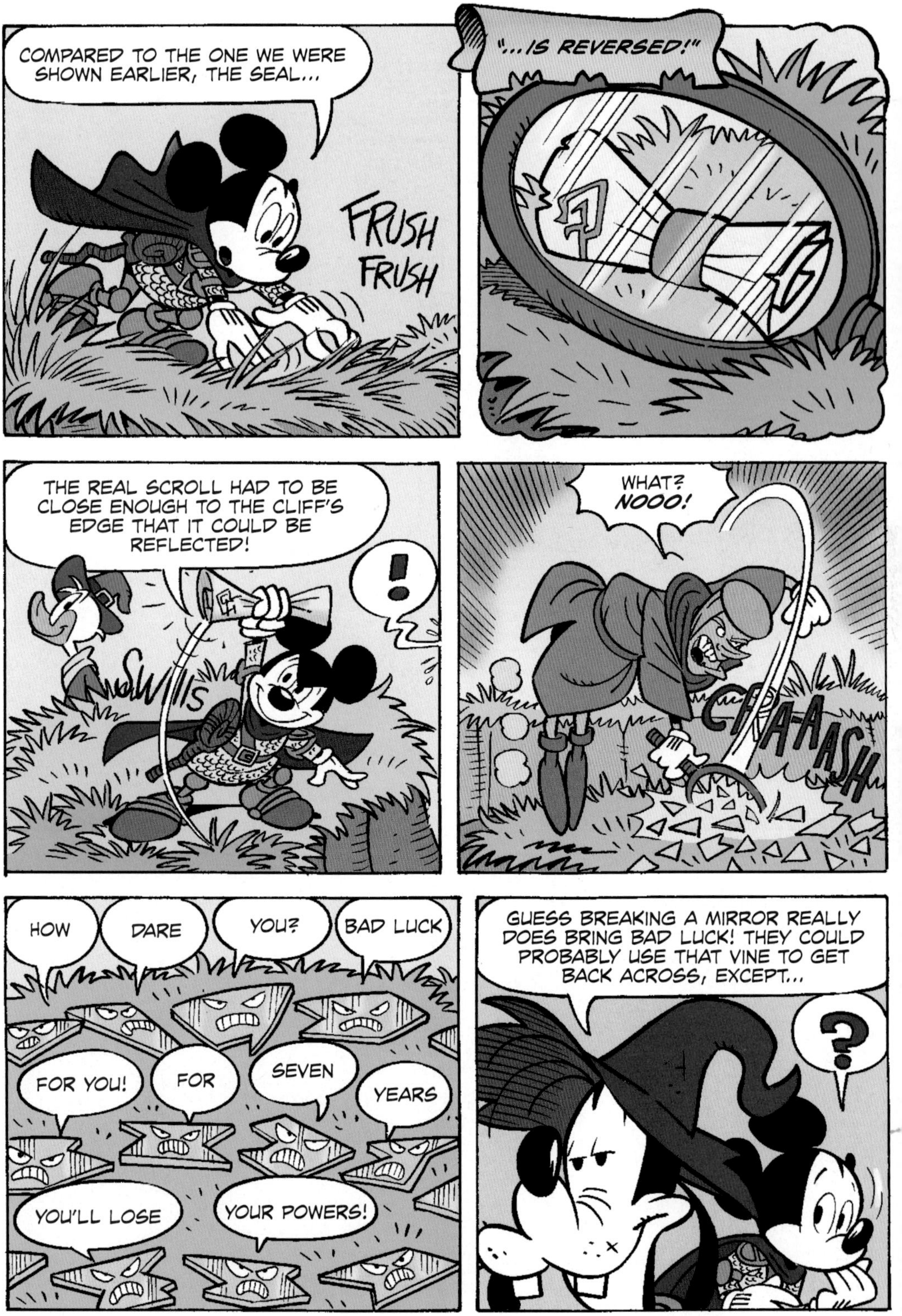

COMPARED TO THE ONE WE WERE SHOWN EARLIER, THE SEAL...
FRUSH FRUSH
"...IS REVERSED!"
THE REAL SCROLL HAD TO BE CLOSE ENOUGH TO THE CLIFF'S EDGE THAT IT COULD BE REFLECTED!
SWISS
!
WHAT? NOOO!
CRA-AASH
HOW
DARE
YOU?
BAD LUCK
FOR YOU!
FOR
SEVEN
YEARS
YOU'LL LOSE
YOUR POWERS!
GUESS BREAKING A MIRROR REALLY DOES BRING BAD LUCK! THEY COULD PROBABLY USE THAT VINE TO GET BACK ACROSS, EXCEPT...
?

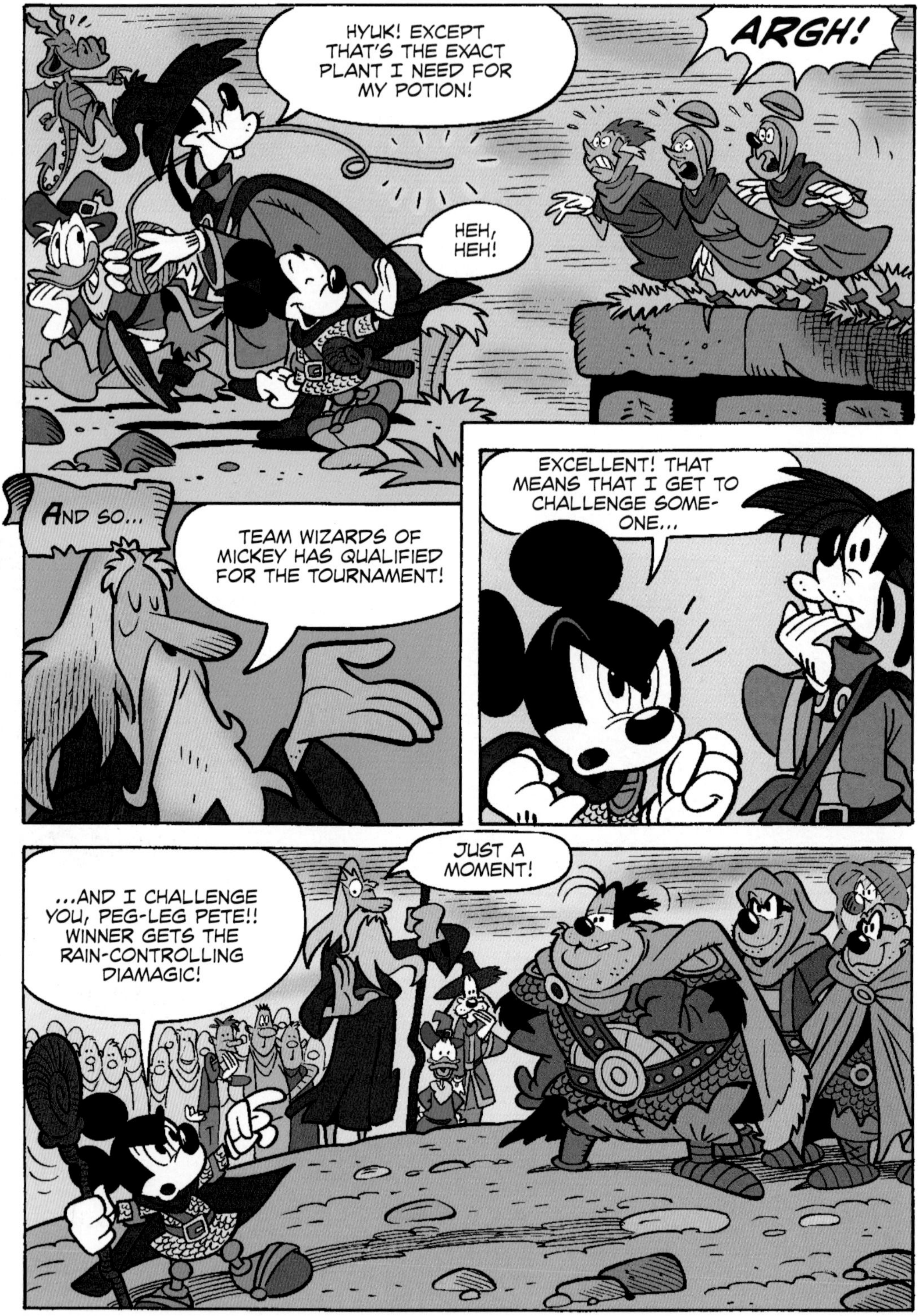
HYUK! EXCEPT THAT'S THE EXACT PLANT I NEED FOR MY POTION!
ARGH!
HEH, HEH!
AND SO...
TEAM WIZARDS OF MICKEY HAS QUALIFIED FOR THE TOURNAMENT!
EXCELLENT! THAT MEANS THAT I GET TO CHALLENGE SOME-ONE...
...AND I CHALLENGE YOU, PEG-LEG PETE!! WINNER GETS THE RAIN-CONTROLLING DIAMAGIC!
JUST A MOMENT!

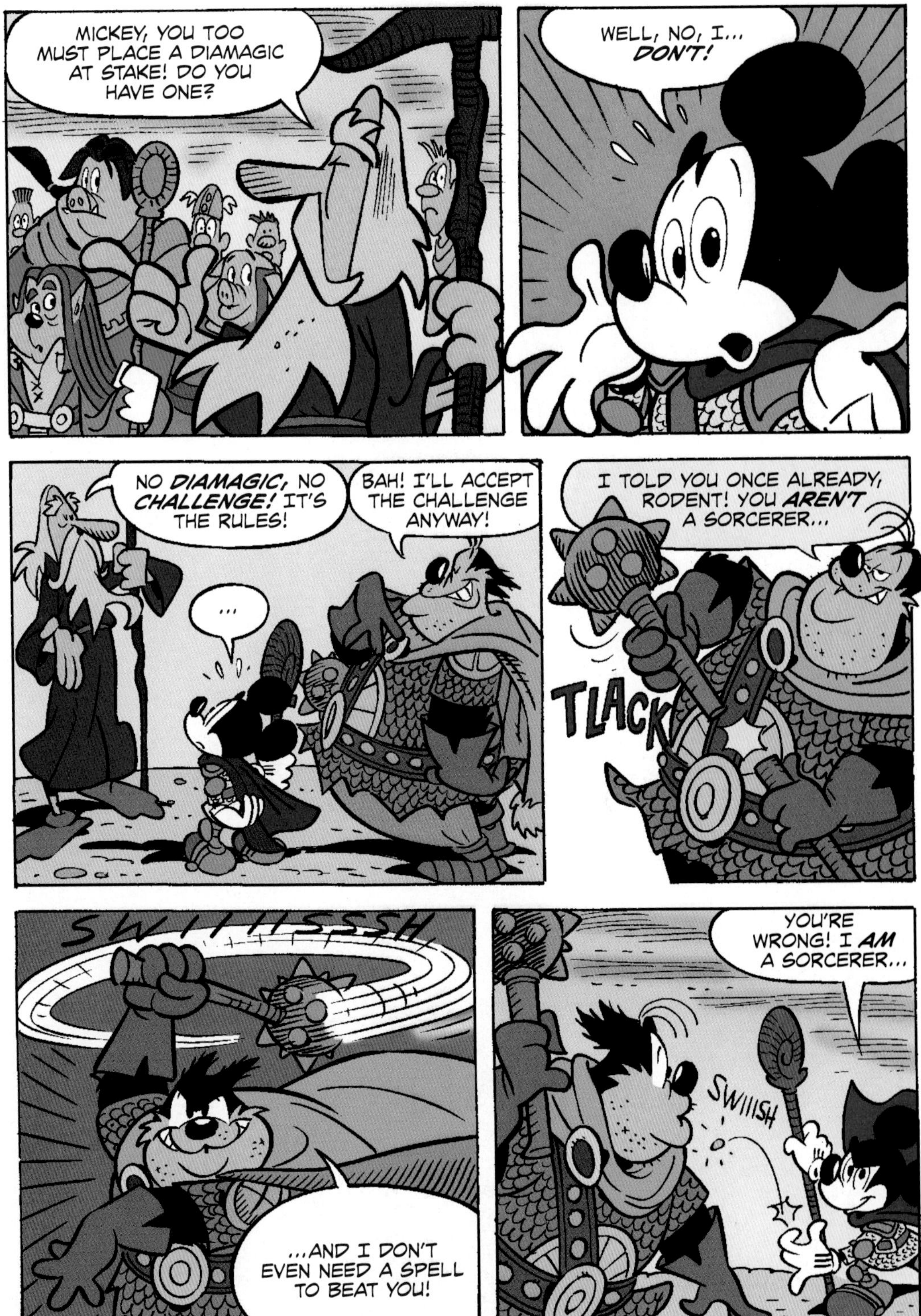
MICKEY, YOU TOO MUST PLACE A DIAMAGIC AT STAKE! DO YOU HAVE ONE?
WELL, NO, I... DON'T!
NO DIAMAGIC, NO CHALLENGE! IT'S THE RULES!
...
BAH! I'LL ACCEPT THE CHALLENGE ANYWAY!
I TOLD YOU ONCE ALREADY, RODENT! YOU AREN'T A SORCERER...
TLACK
SWIIIISSSSH
...AND I DON'T EVEN NEED A SPELL TO BEAT YOU!
YOU'RE WRONG! I AM A SORCERER...
SWIIISH

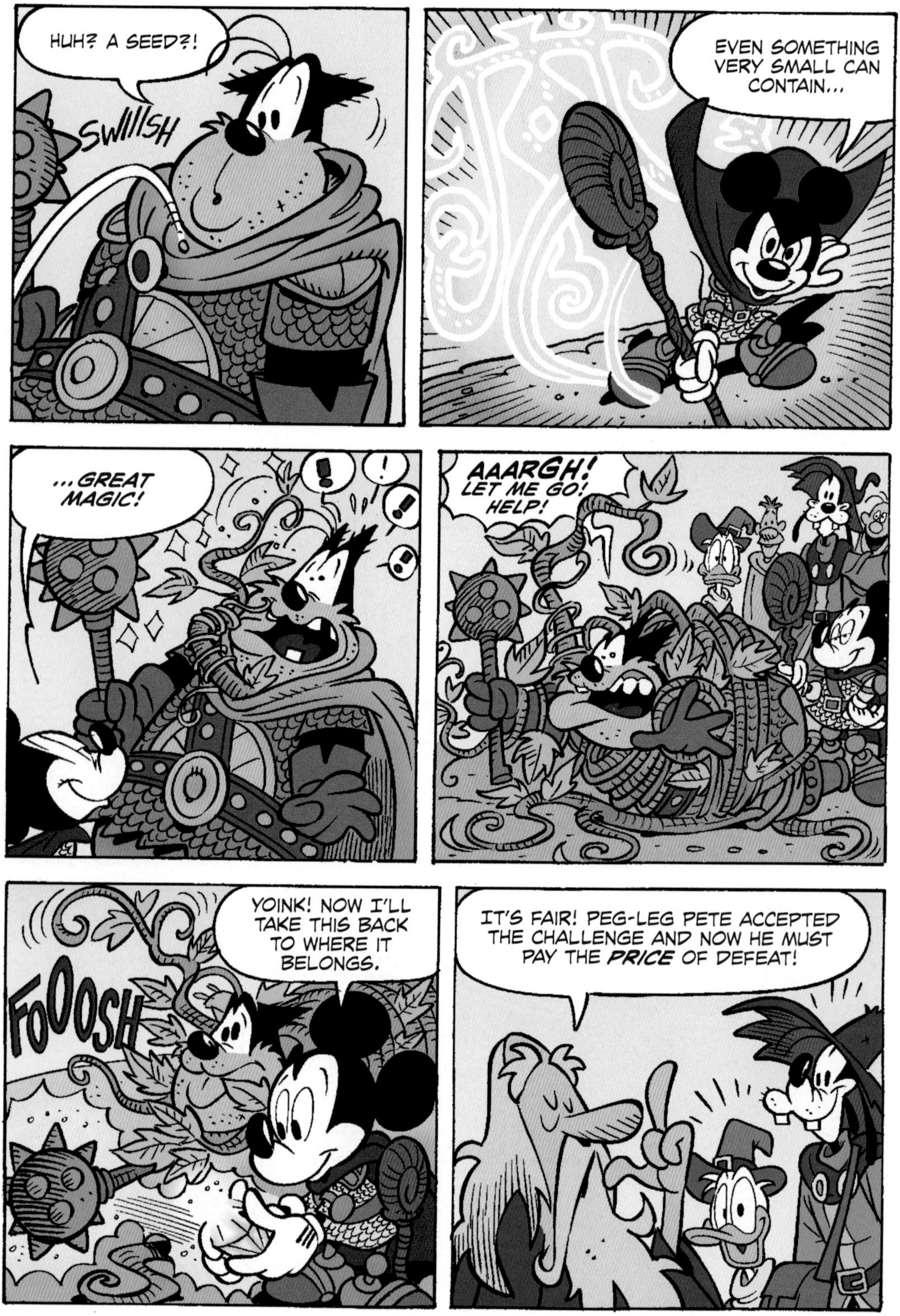
HUH? A SEED?!
SWIIISH
EVEN SOMETHING VERY SMALL CAN CONTAIN...
...GREAT MAGIC!
!
!
!
!
AAARGH! LET ME GO! HELP!
YOINK! NOW I'LL TAKE THIS BACK TO WHERE IT BELONGS.
FOOOSH
IT'S FAIR! PEG-LEG PETE ACCEPTED THE CHALLENGE AND NOW HE MUST PAY THE *PRICE* OF DEFEAT!

I DID IT! I'LL BE ABLE TO RETURN THE CRYSTAL AND SAVE MY VILLAGE FROM THE DROUGHT!

AND YOU WILL ALL BE MY GUESTS!

HYUK! MAYBE I CAN FIND ANOTHER PROFESSION BESIDES BEING AN HERBALIST...

...CONSIDERING I JUST FOUND OUT I'M *ALLERGIC* TO RARE HERBS!

AND MAYBE YOUR MASTER WILL BE ABLE TO EXPLAIN *WHY* MY SPELLS DON'T WORK!

SCRATCH
SCRATCH
SCRATCH
SCRATCH

*P*OOR DONALD! IF ONLY HE HADN'T LEFT SO QUICKLY, HE WOULD HAVE LEARNED THE TRUTH!

GOLD! MY SPOONS HAVE TURNED TO GOLD! THAT DUCK'S MAGIC WORKED...IT WAS JUST *A DELAYED REACTION!*

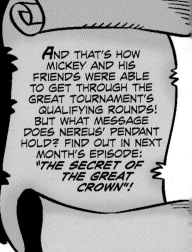

*A*ND THAT'S HOW MICKEY AND HIS FRIENDS WERE ABLE TO GET THROUGH THE GREAT TOURNAMENT'S QUALIFYING ROUNDS! BUT WHAT MESSAGE DOES NEREUS' PENDANT HOLD? FIND OUT IN NEXT MONTH'S EPISODE: *"THE SECRET OF THE GREAT CROWN"!*

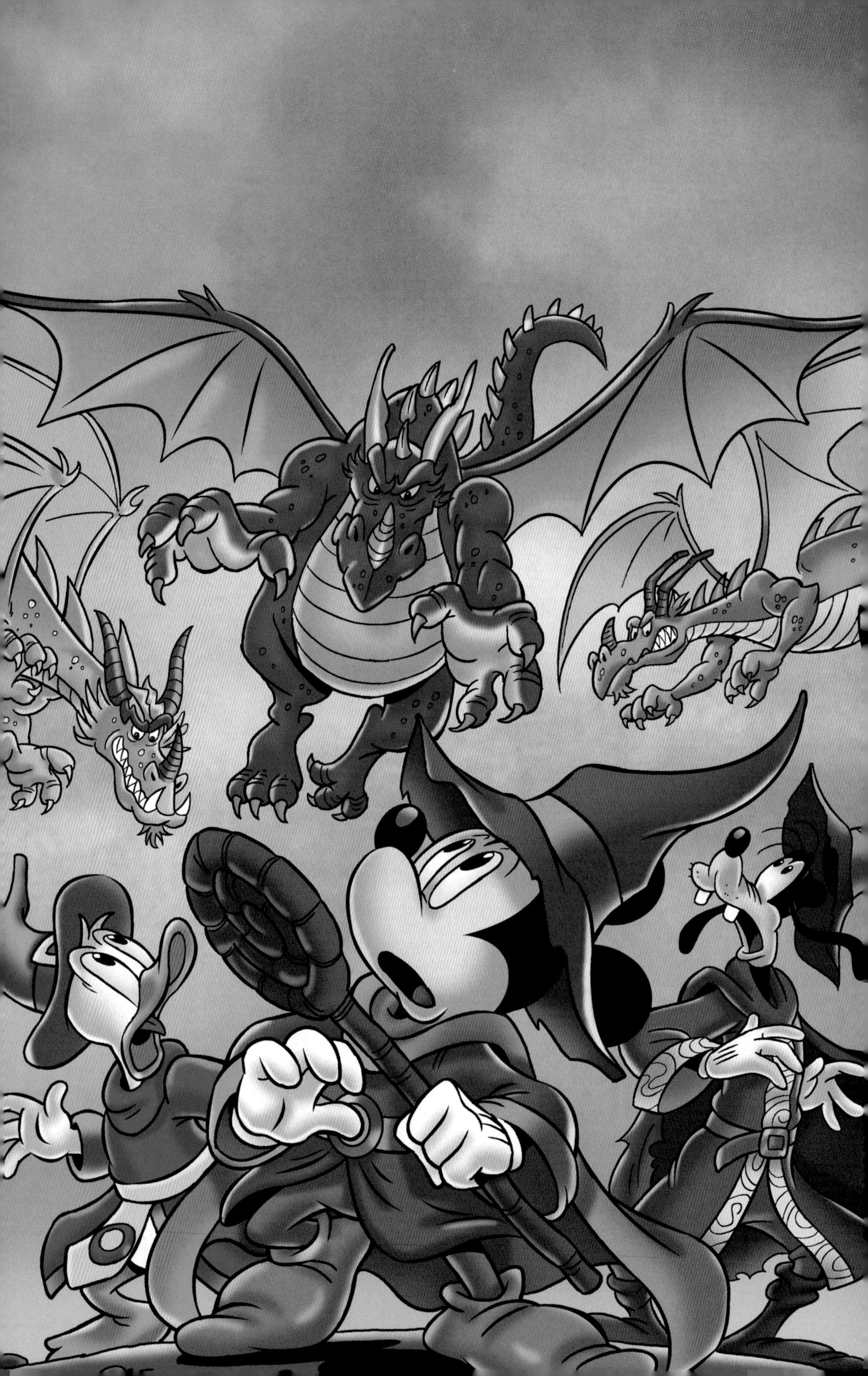

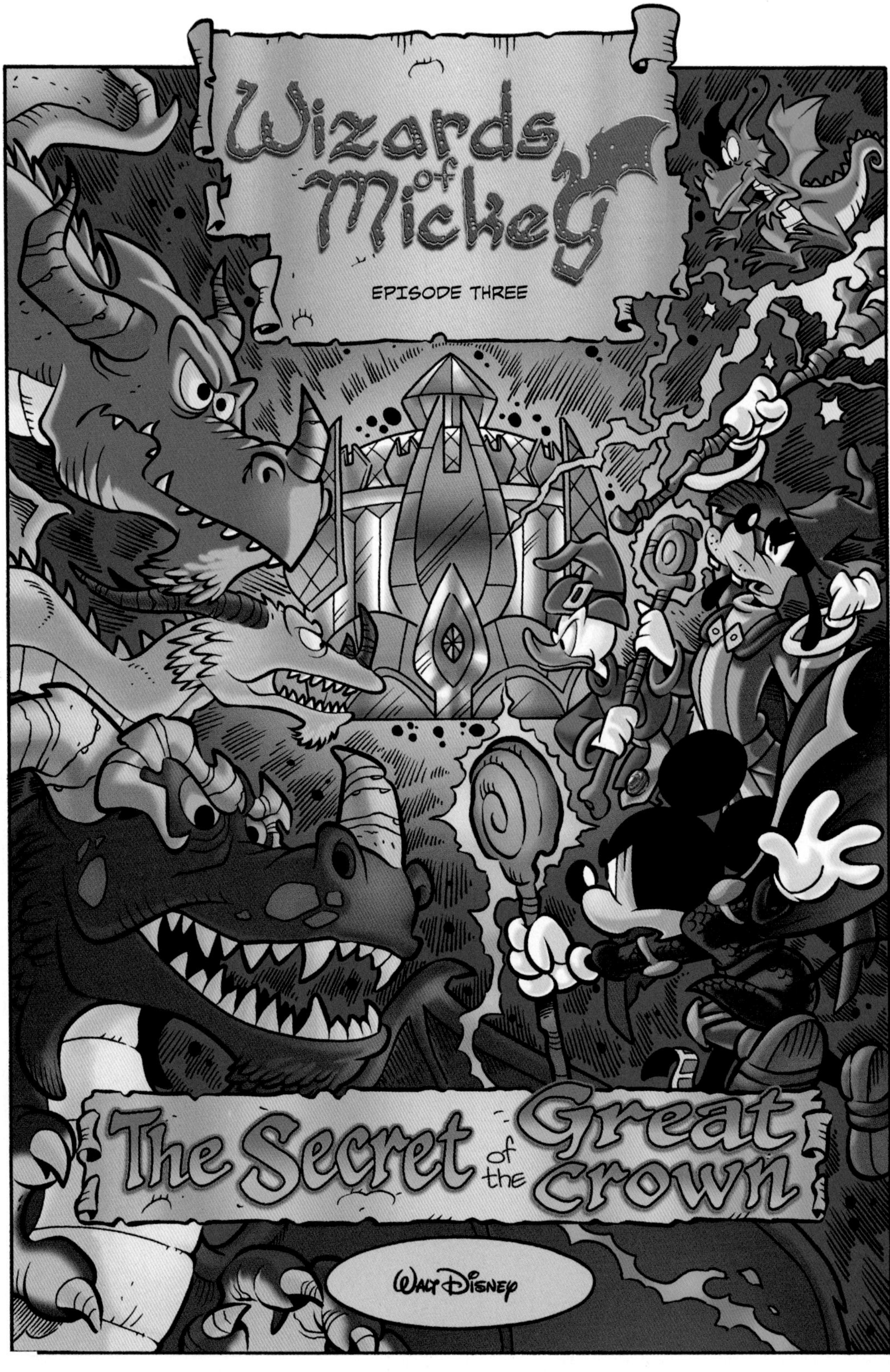

Wizards of Mickey
EPISODE THREE
The Secret of the Great Crown
Walt Disney

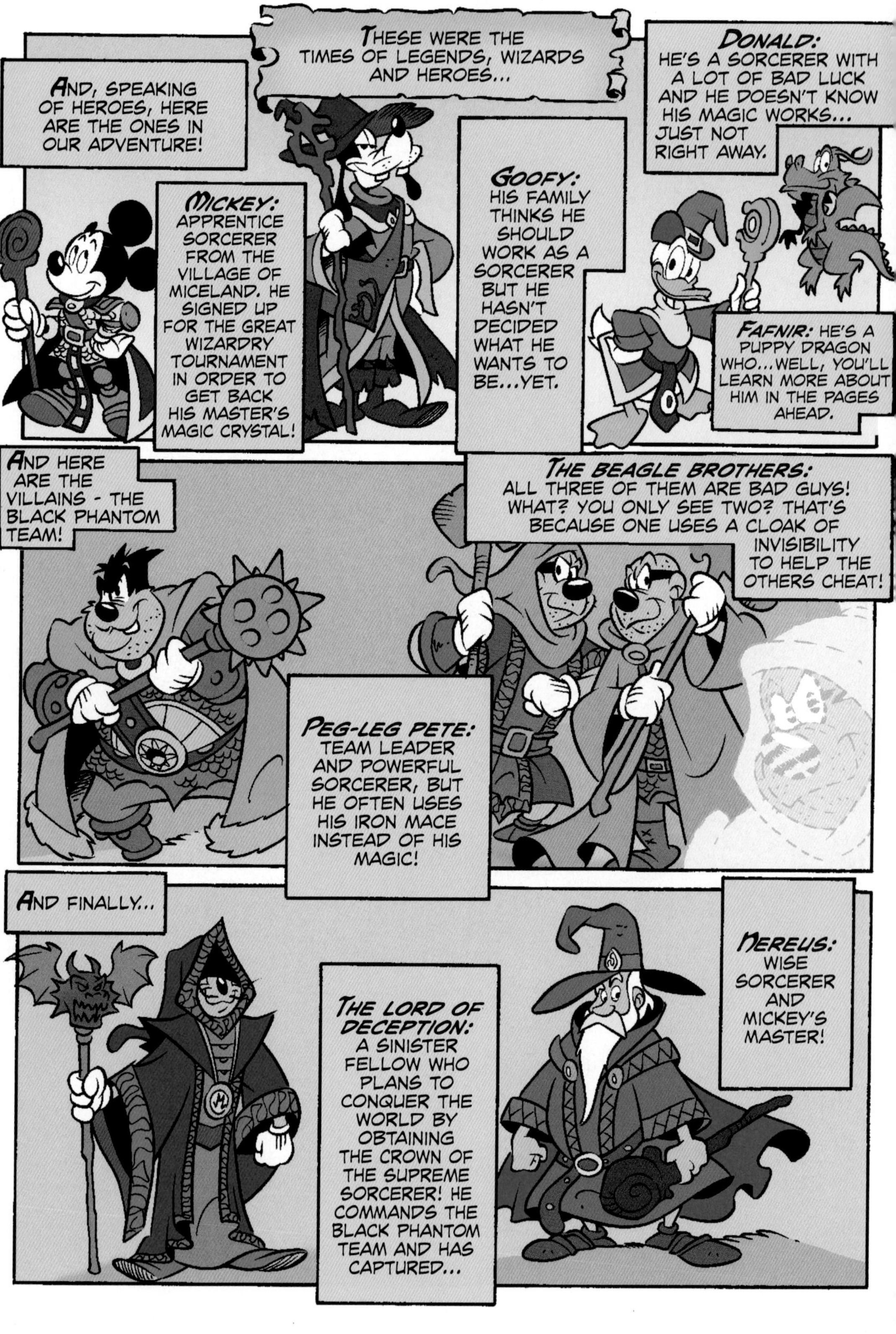

THESE WERE THE TIMES OF LEGENDS, WIZARDS AND HEROES...
AND, SPEAKING OF HEROES, HERE ARE THE ONES IN OUR ADVENTURE!
MICKEY: APPRENTICE SORCERER FROM THE VILLAGE OF MICELAND. HE SIGNED UP FOR THE GREAT WIZARDRY TOURNAMENT IN ORDER TO GET BACK HIS MASTER'S MAGIC CRYSTAL!
GOOFY: HIS FAMILY THINKS HE SHOULD WORK AS A SORCERER BUT HE HASN'T DECIDED WHAT HE WANTS TO BE...YET.
DONALD: HE'S A SORCERER WITH A LOT OF BAD LUCK AND HE DOESN'T KNOW HIS MAGIC WORKS... JUST NOT RIGHT AWAY.
FAFNIR: HE'S A PUPPY DRAGON WHO...WELL, YOU'LL LEARN MORE ABOUT HIM IN THE PAGES AHEAD.
AND HERE ARE THE VILLAINS - THE BLACK PHANTOM TEAM!
THE BEAGLE BROTHERS: ALL THREE OF THEM ARE BAD GUYS! WHAT? YOU ONLY SEE TWO? THAT'S BECAUSE ONE USES A CLOAK OF INVISIBILITY TO HELP THE OTHERS CHEAT!
PEG-LEG PETE: TEAM LEADER AND POWERFUL SORCERER, BUT HE OFTEN USES HIS IRON MACE INSTEAD OF HIS MAGIC!
AND FINALLY...
THE LORD OF DECEPTION: A SINISTER FELLOW WHO PLANS TO CONQUER THE WORLD BY OBTAINING THE CROWN OF THE SUPREME SORCERER! HE COMMANDS THE BLACK PHANTOM TEAM AND HAS CAPTURED...
NEREUS: WISE SORCERER AND MICKEY'S MASTER!

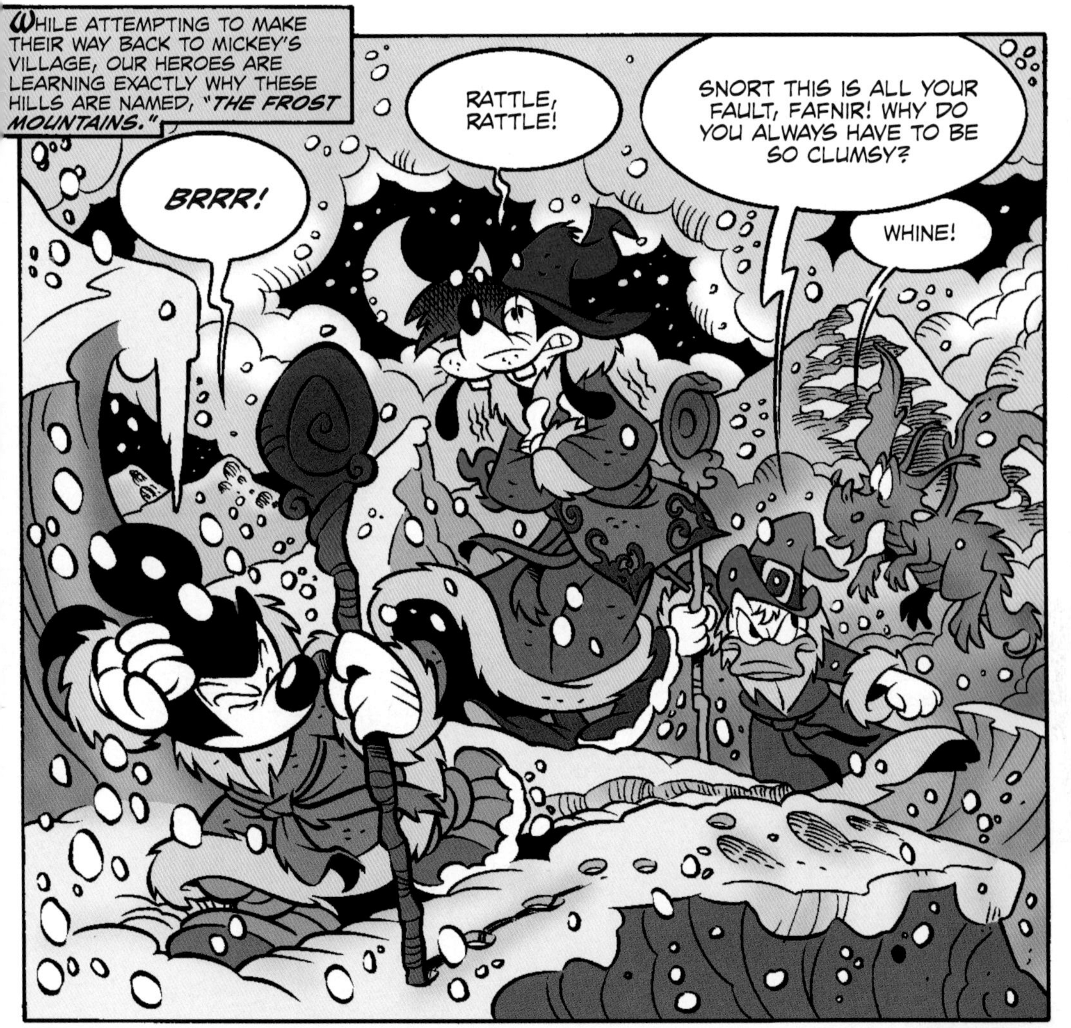
WHILE ATTEMPTING TO MAKE THEIR WAY BACK TO MICKEY'S VILLAGE, OUR HEROES ARE LEARNING EXACTLY WHY THESE HILLS ARE NAMED, "THE FROST MOUNTAINS."
BRRR!
RATTLE, RATTLE!
SNORT THIS IS ALL YOUR FAULT, FAFNIR! WHY DO YOU ALWAYS HAVE TO BE SO CLUMSY?
WHINE!

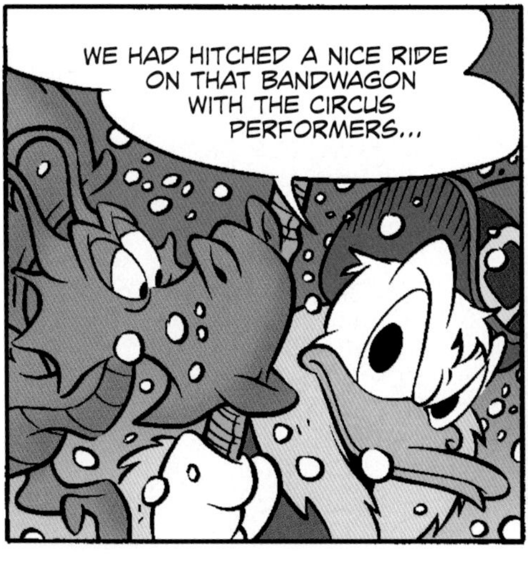
WE HAD HITCHED A NICE RIDE ON THAT BANDWAGON WITH THE CIRCUS PERFORMERS...

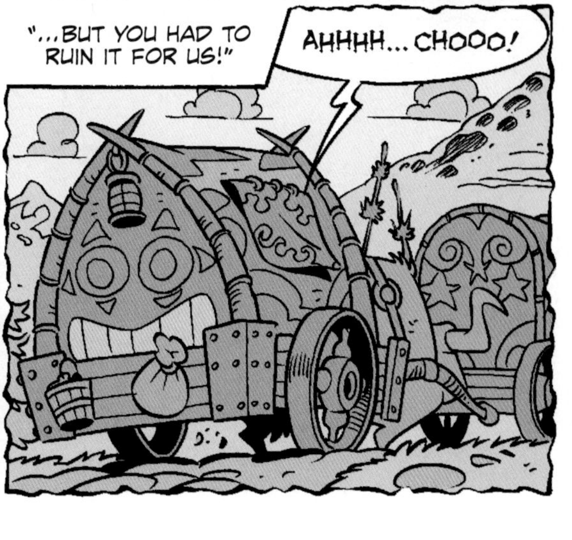
"...BUT YOU HAD TO RUIN IT FOR US!"
AHHHH... CHOOO!

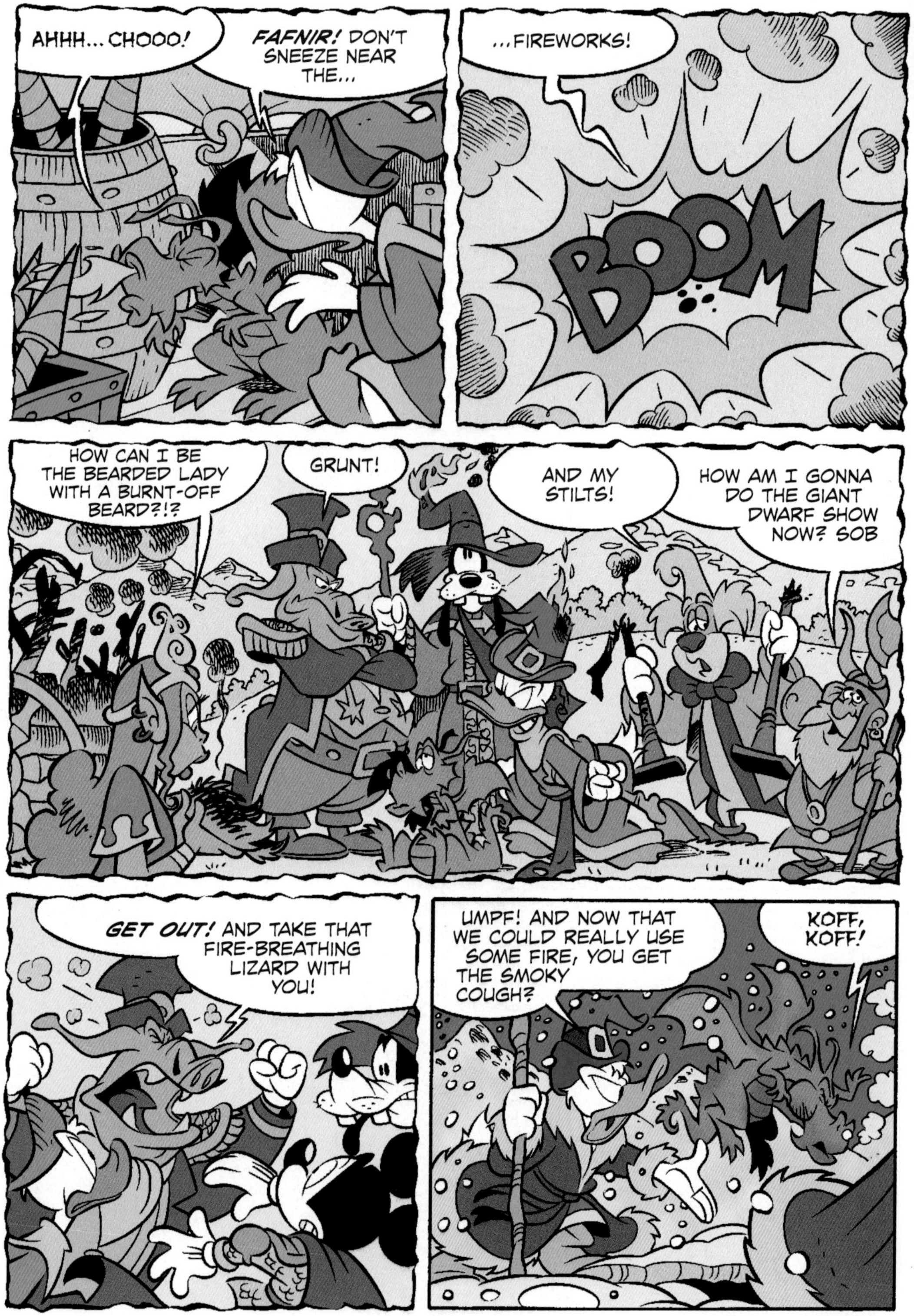
AHHH... CHOOO!
FAFNIR! DON'T SNEEZE NEAR THE...
...FIREWORKS!
BOOM
HOW CAN I BE THE BEARDED LADY WITH A BURNT-OFF BEARD?!?
GRUNT!
AND MY STILTS!
HOW AM I GONNA DO THE GIANT DWARF SHOW NOW? SOB
GET OUT! AND TAKE THAT FIRE-BREATHING LIZARD WITH YOU!
UMPF! AND NOW THAT WE COULD REALLY USE SOME FIRE, YOU GET THE SMOKY COUGH?
KOFF, KOFF!

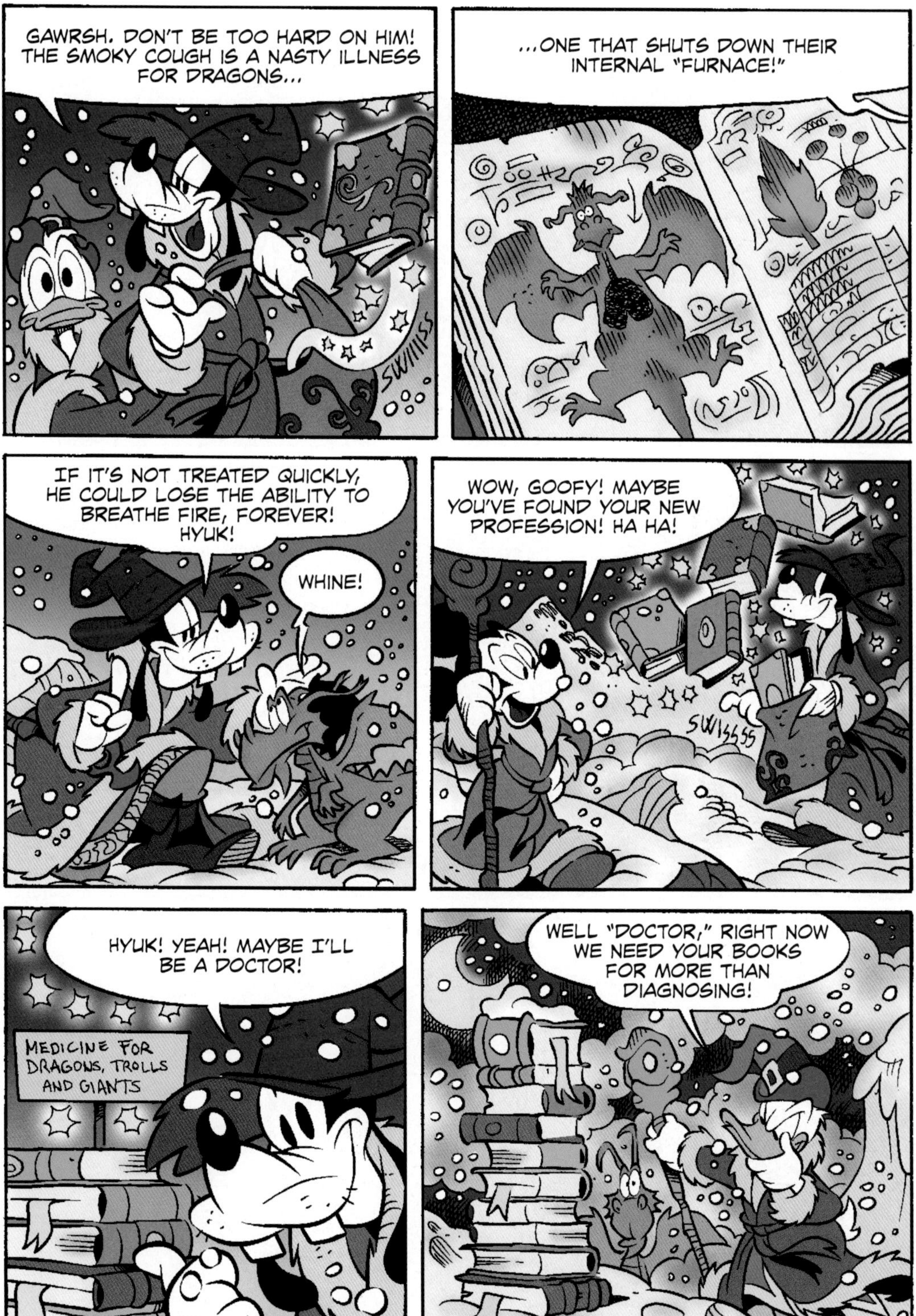
GAWRSH. DON'T BE TOO HARD ON HIM! THE SMOKY COUGH IS A NASTY ILLNESS FOR DRAGONS...
SWIIIISS
...ONE THAT SHUTS DOWN THEIR INTERNAL "FURNACE!"
IF IT'S NOT TREATED QUICKLY, HE COULD LOSE THE ABILITY TO BREATHE FIRE, FOREVER! HYUK!
WHINE!
WOW, GOOFY! MAYBE YOU'VE FOUND YOUR NEW PROFESSION! HA HA!
SWISSSS
HYUK! YEAH! MAYBE I'LL BE A DOCTOR!
MEDICINE FOR DRAGONS, TROLLS AND GIANTS
WELL "DOCTOR," RIGHT NOW WE NEED YOUR BOOKS FOR MORE THAN DIAGNOSING!

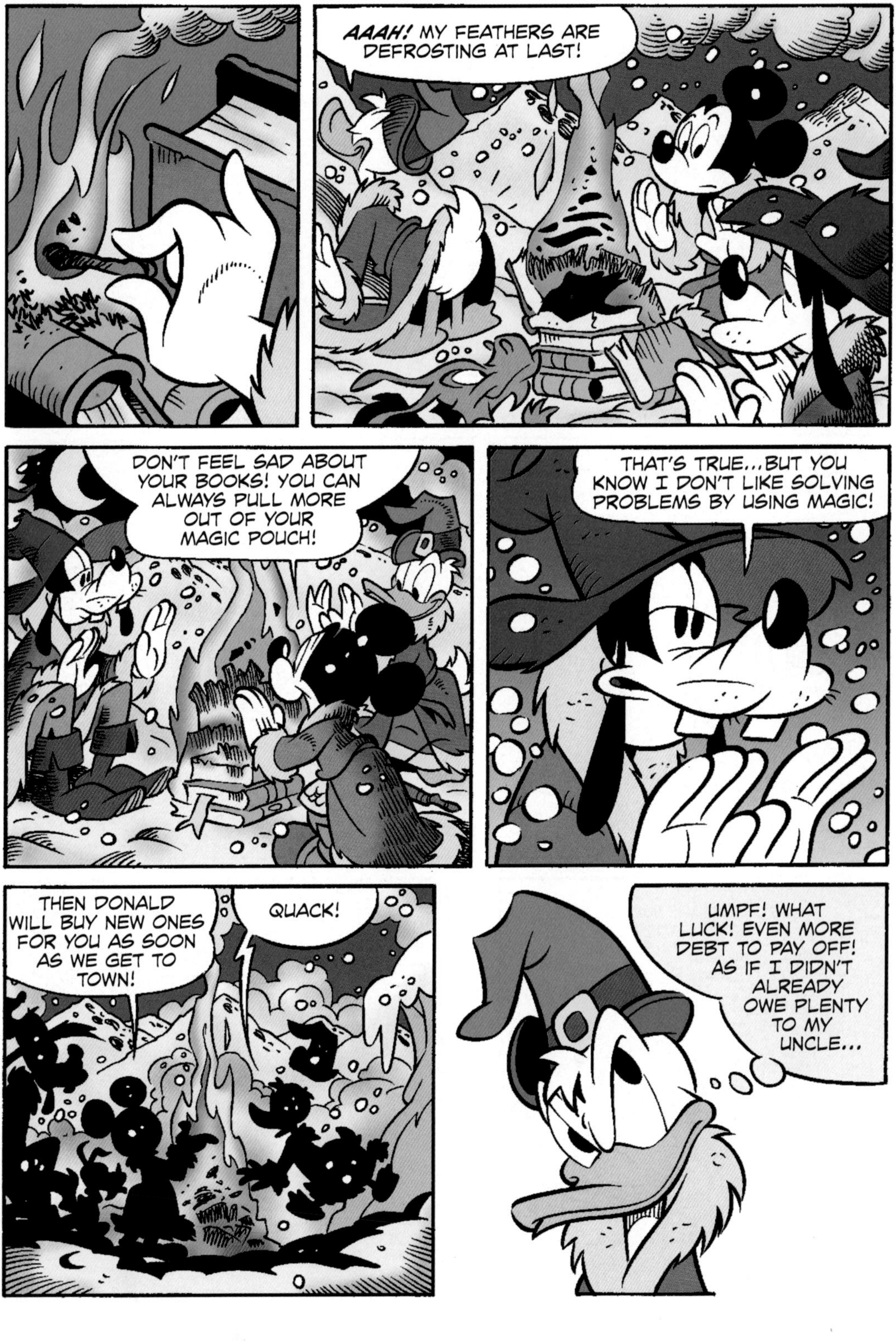
AAAH! MY FEATHERS ARE DEFROSTING AT LAST!
DON'T FEEL SAD ABOUT YOUR BOOKS! YOU CAN ALWAYS PULL MORE OUT OF YOUR MAGIC POUCH!
THAT'S TRUE...BUT YOU KNOW I DON'T LIKE SOLVING PROBLEMS BY USING MAGIC!
THEN DONALD WILL BUY NEW ONES FOR YOU AS SOON AS WE GET TO TOWN!
QUACK!
UMPF! WHAT LUCK! EVEN MORE DEBT TO PAY OFF! AS IF I DIDN'T ALREADY OWE PLENTY TO MY UNCLE...

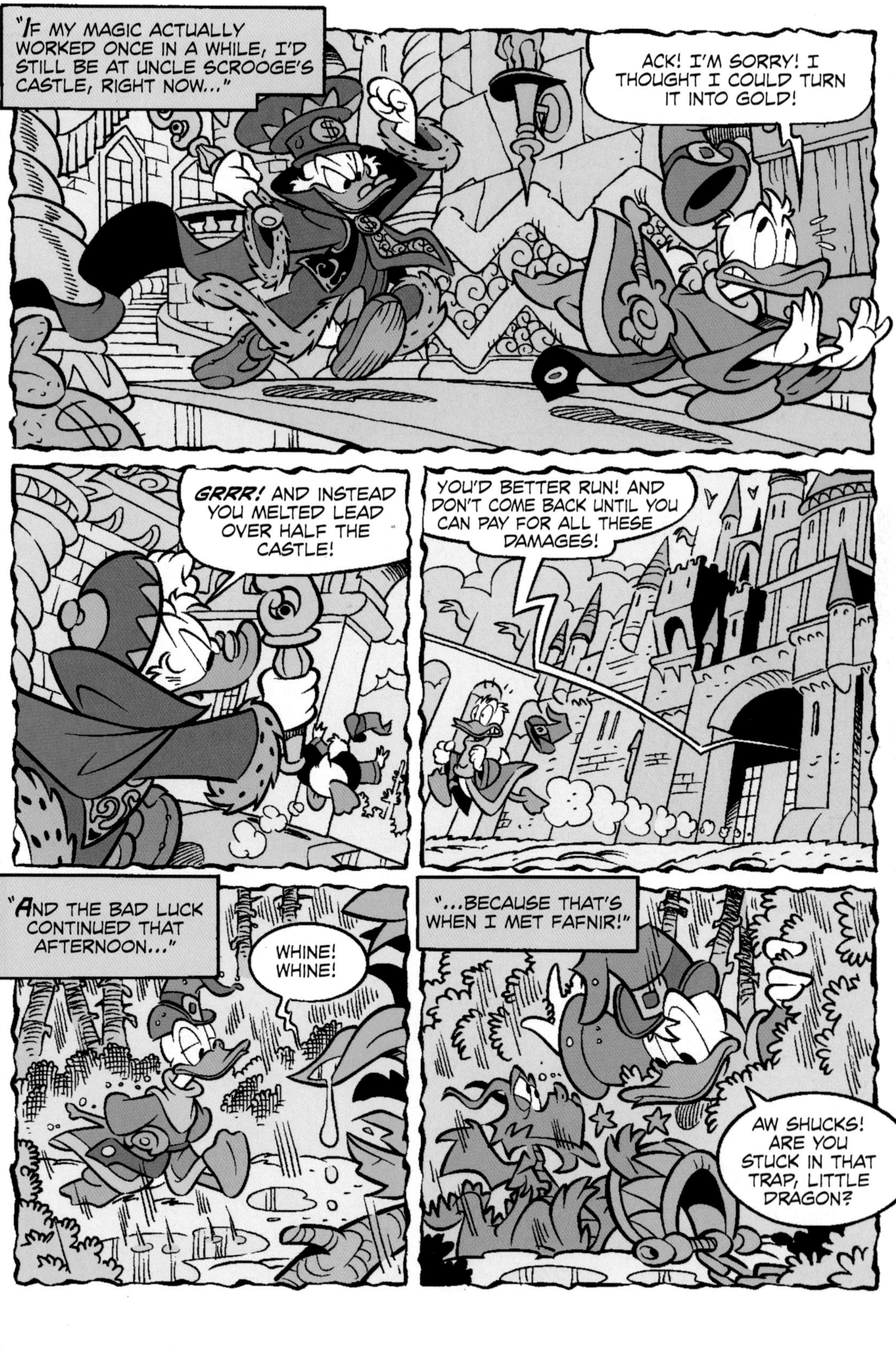
"IF MY MAGIC ACTUALLY WORKED ONCE IN A WHILE, I'D STILL BE AT UNCLE SCROOGE'S CASTLE, RIGHT NOW..."
ACK! I'M SORRY! I THOUGHT I COULD TURN IT INTO GOLD!
GRRR! AND INSTEAD YOU MELTED LEAD OVER HALF THE CASTLE!
YOU'D BETTER RUN! AND DON'T COME BACK UNTIL YOU CAN PAY FOR ALL THESE DAMAGES!
"AND THE BAD LUCK CONTINUED THAT AFTERNOON..."
WHINE! WHINE!
"...BECAUSE THAT'S WHEN I MET FAFNIR!"
AW SHUCKS! ARE YOU STUCK IN THAT TRAP, LITTLE DRAGON?

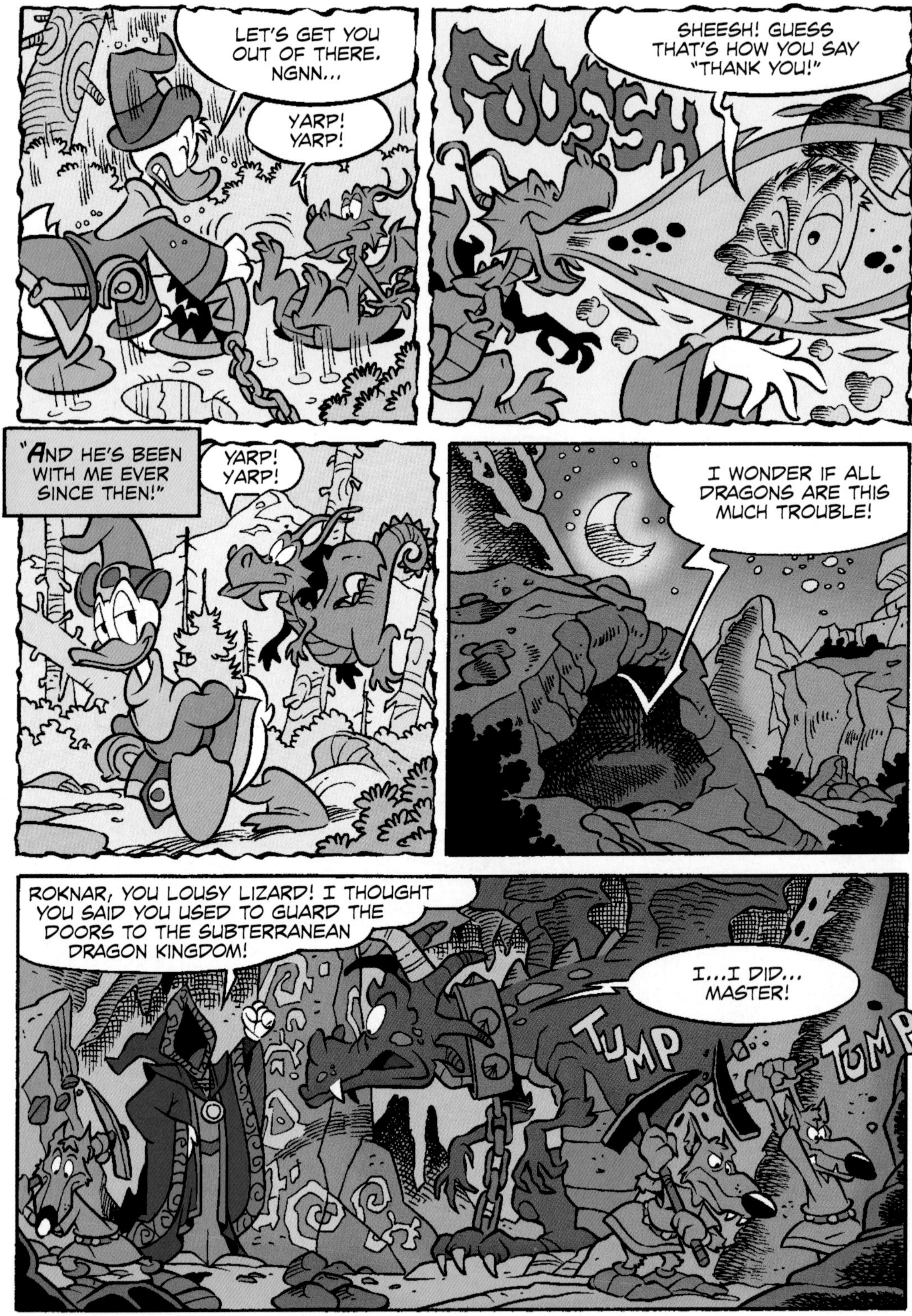
LET'S GET YOU OUT OF THERE. NGNN...
YARP! YARP!
FOOSSH
SHEESH! GUESS THAT'S HOW YOU SAY "THANK YOU!"
"AND HE'S BEEN WITH ME EVER SINCE THEN!"
YARP! YARP!
I WONDER IF ALL DRAGONS ARE THIS MUCH TROUBLE!
ROKNAR, YOU LOUSY LIZARD! I THOUGHT YOU SAID YOU USED TO GUARD THE DOORS TO THE SUBTERRANEAN DRAGON KINGDOM!
I...I DID... MASTER!
TUMP
TUMP

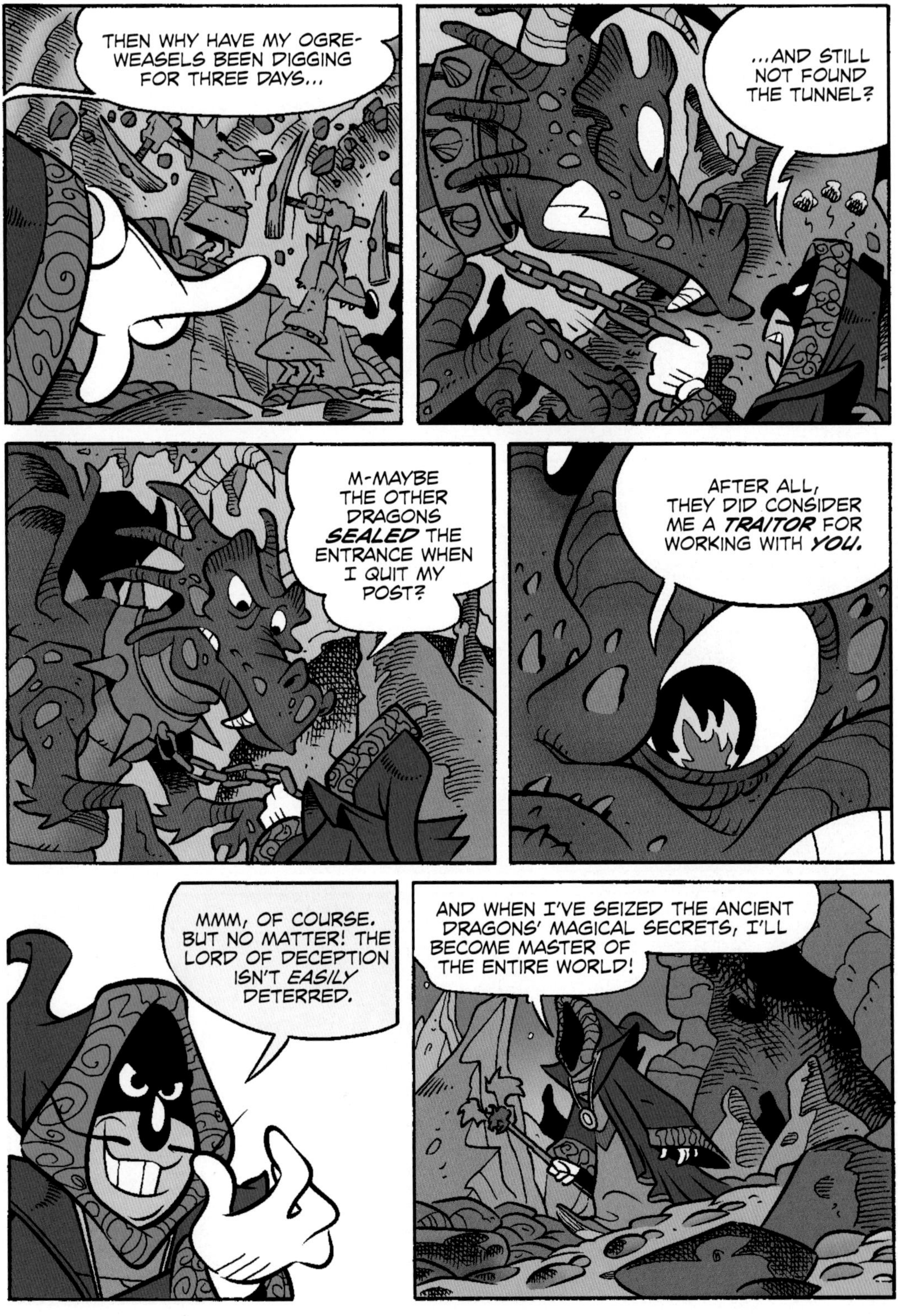
THEN WHY HAVE MY OGRE-WEASELS BEEN DIGGING FOR THREE DAYS...
...AND STILL NOT FOUND THE TUNNEL?
M-MAYBE THE OTHER DRAGONS SEALED THE ENTRANCE WHEN I QUIT MY POST?
AFTER ALL, THEY DID CONSIDER ME A TRAITOR FOR WORKING WITH YOU.
MMM, OF COURSE. BUT NO MATTER! THE LORD OF DECEPTION ISN'T EASILY DETERRED.
AND WHEN I'VE SEIZED THE ANCIENT DRAGONS' MAGICAL SECRETS, I'LL BECOME MASTER OF THE ENTIRE WORLD!

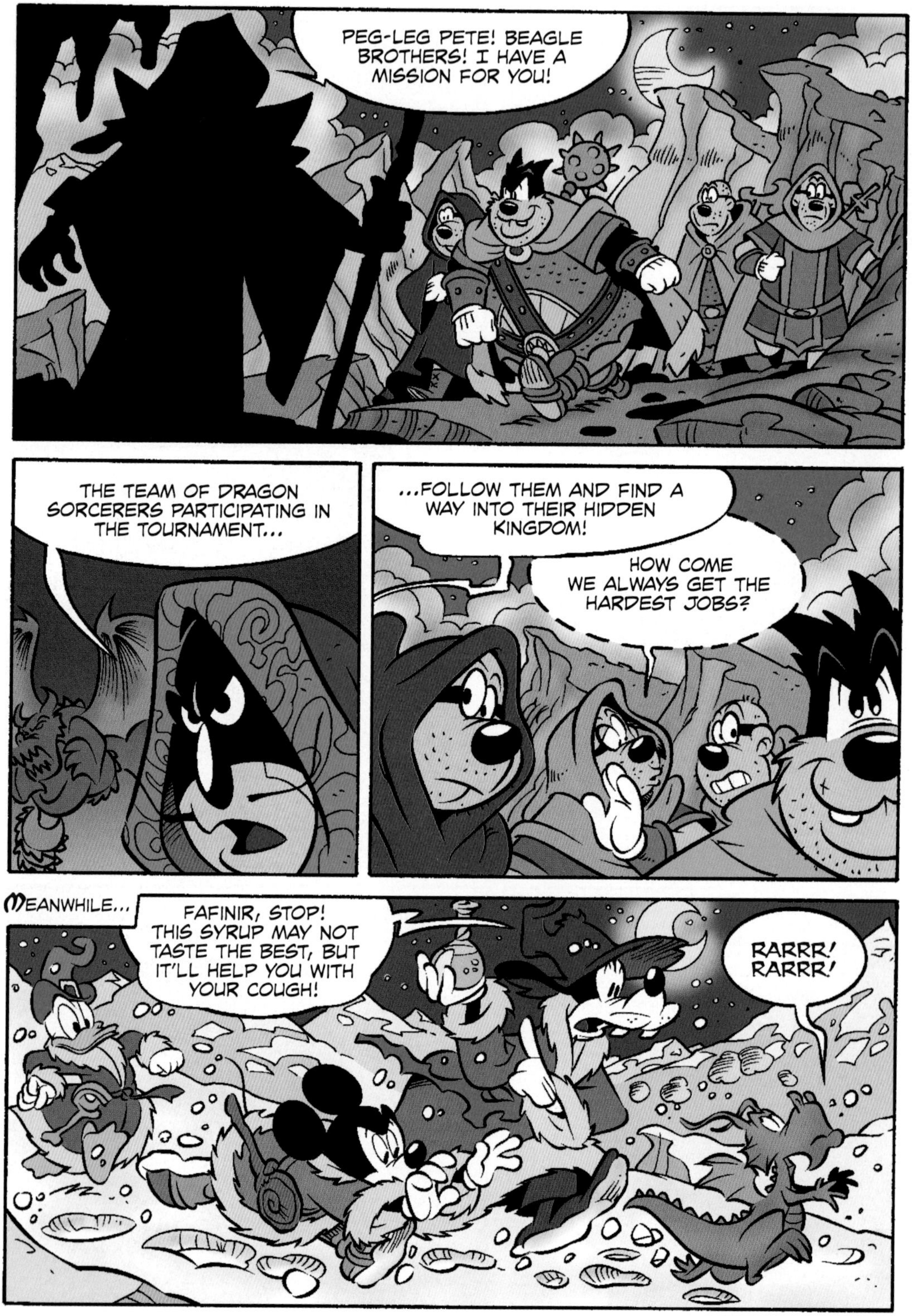
PEG-LEG PETE! BEAGLE BROTHERS! I HAVE A MISSION FOR YOU!
THE TEAM OF DRAGON SORCERERS PARTICIPATING IN THE TOURNAMENT...
...FOLLOW THEM AND FIND A WAY INTO THEIR HIDDEN KINGDOM!
HOW COME WE ALWAYS GET THE HARDEST JOBS?
MEANWHILE...
FAFINIR, STOP! THIS SYRUP MAY NOT TASTE THE BEST, BUT IT'LL HELP YOU WITH YOUR COUGH!
RARRR! RARRR!

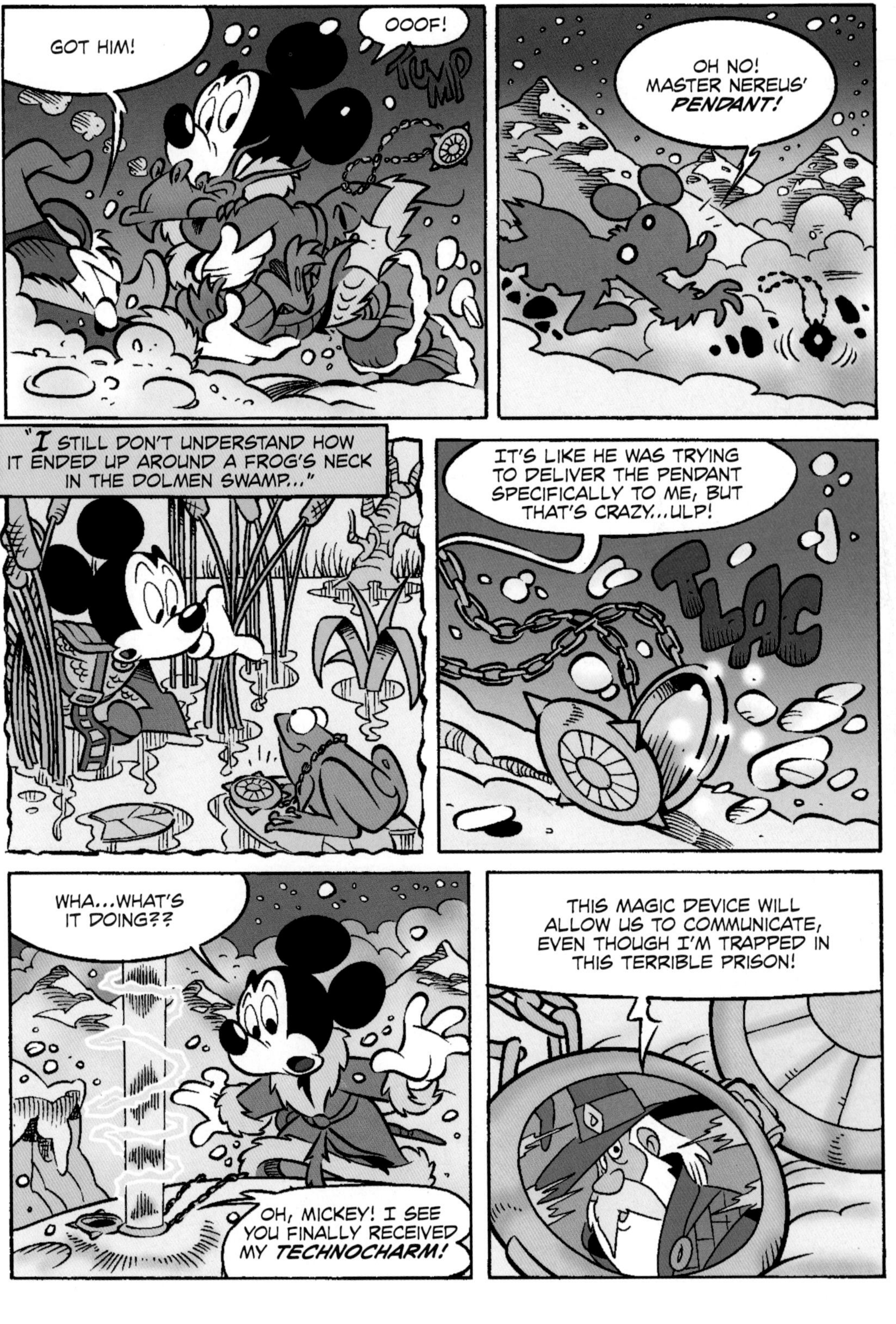
GOT HIM!
OOOF!
TUMP
OH NO! MASTER NEREUS' PENDANT!
"I STILL DON'T UNDERSTAND HOW IT ENDED UP AROUND A FROG'S NECK IN THE DOLMEN SWAMP..."
IT'S LIKE HE WAS TRYING TO DELIVER THE PENDANT SPECIFICALLY TO ME, BUT THAT'S CRAZY...ULP!
TLAC
WHA...WHAT'S IT DOING??
OH, MICKEY! I SEE YOU FINALLY RECEIVED MY TECHNOCHARM!
THIS MAGIC DEVICE WILL ALLOW US TO COMMUNICATE, EVEN THOUGH I'M TRAPPED IN THIS TERRIBLE PRISON!

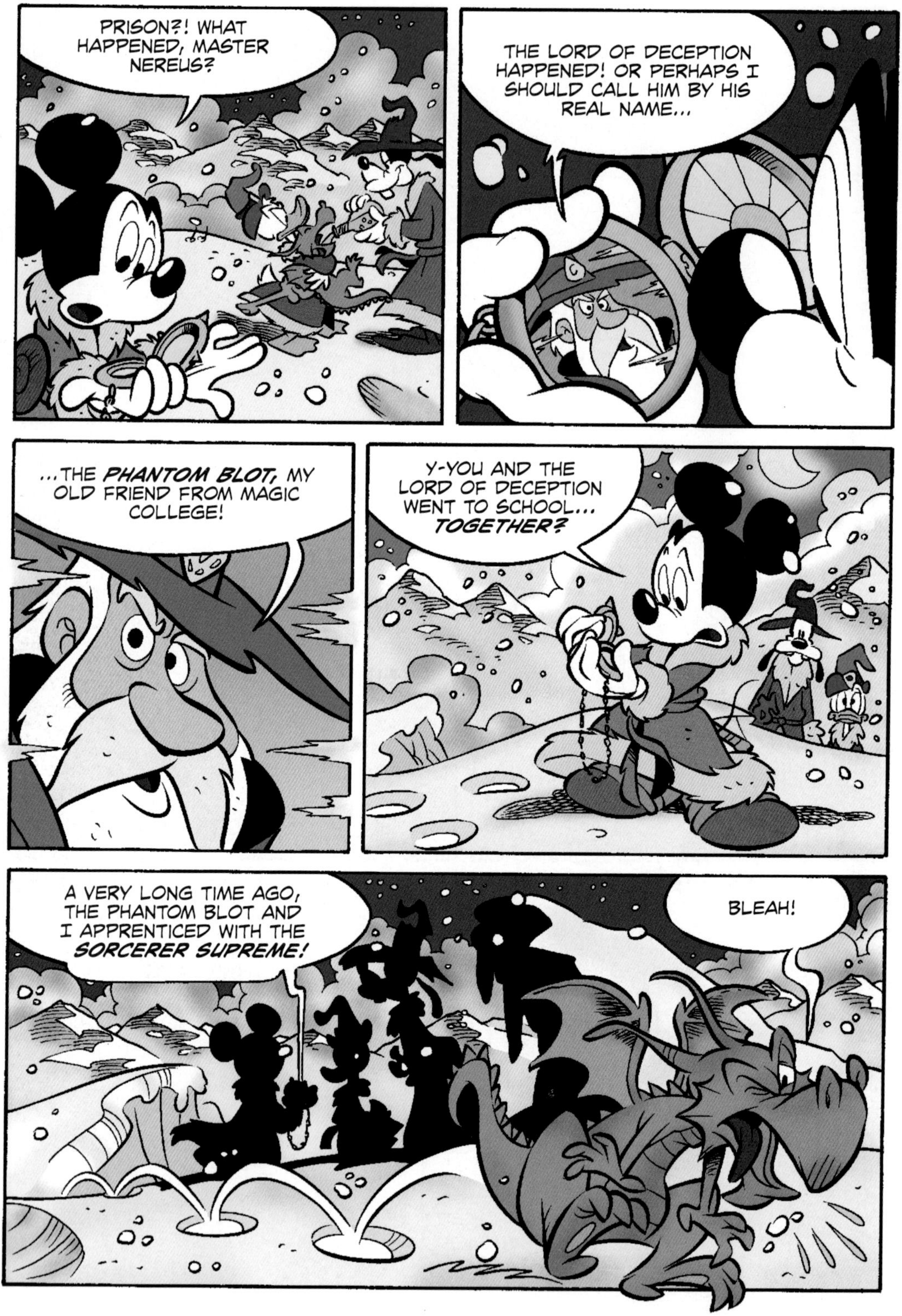
PRISON?! WHAT HAPPENED, MASTER NEREUS?
THE LORD OF DECEPTION HAPPENED! OR PERHAPS I SHOULD CALL HIM BY HIS REAL NAME...
...THE *PHANTOM BLOT,* MY OLD FRIEND FROM MAGIC COLLEGE!
Y-YOU AND THE LORD OF DECEPTION WENT TO SCHOOL... *TOGETHER?*
A VERY LONG TIME AGO, THE PHANTOM BLOT AND I APPRENTICED WITH THE *SORCERER SUPREME!*
BLEAH!

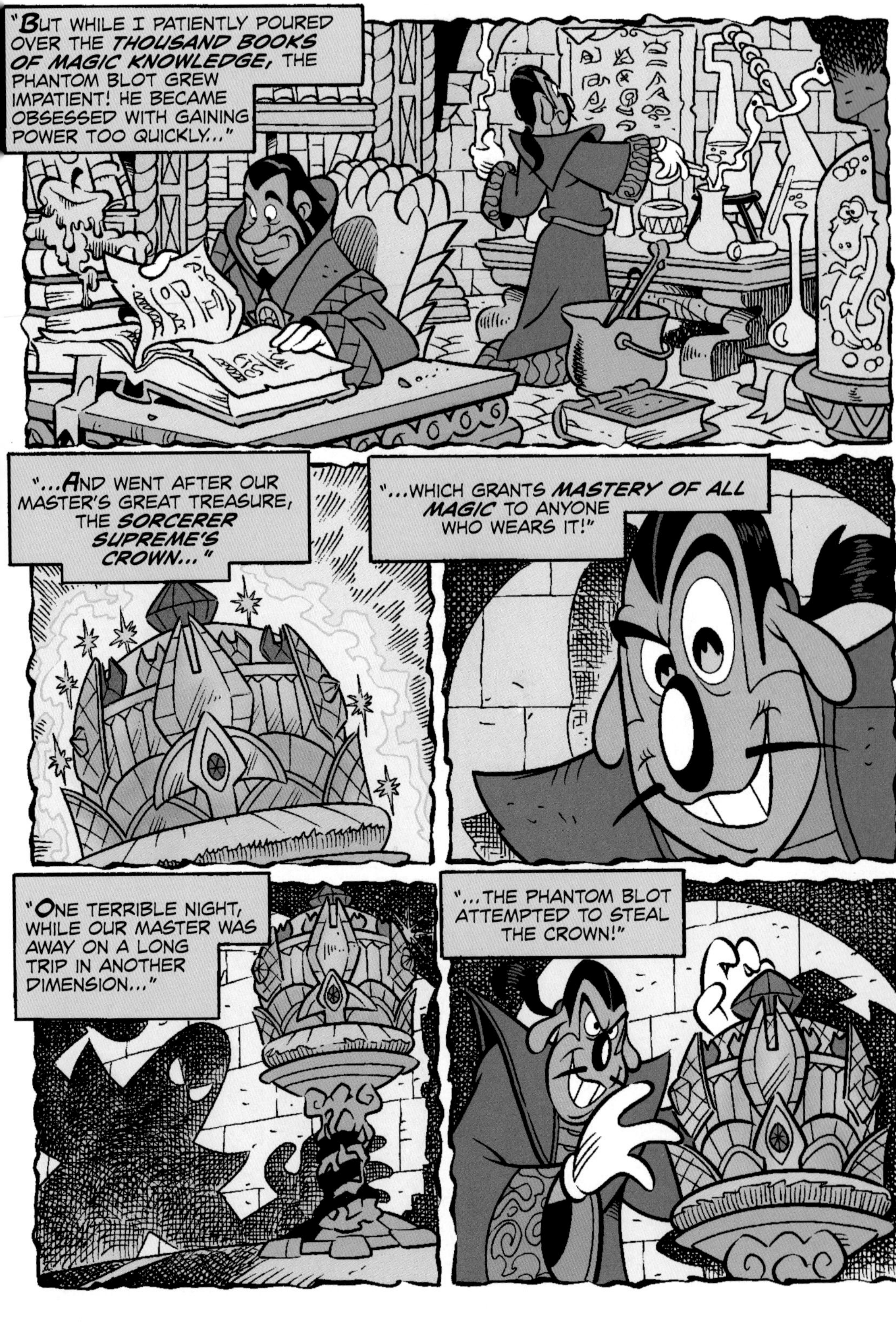
"BUT WHILE I PATIENTLY POURED OVER THE THOUSAND BOOKS OF MAGIC KNOWLEDGE, THE PHANTOM BLOT GREW IMPATIENT! HE BECAME OBSESSED WITH GAINING POWER TOO QUICKLY..."
"...AND WENT AFTER OUR MASTER'S GREAT TREASURE, THE SORCERER SUPREME'S CROWN..."
"...WHICH GRANTS MASTERY OF ALL MAGIC TO ANYONE WHO WEARS IT!"
"ONE TERRIBLE NIGHT, WHILE OUR MASTER WAS AWAY ON A LONG TRIP IN ANOTHER DIMENSION..."
"...THE PHANTOM BLOT ATTEMPTED TO STEAL THE CROWN!"

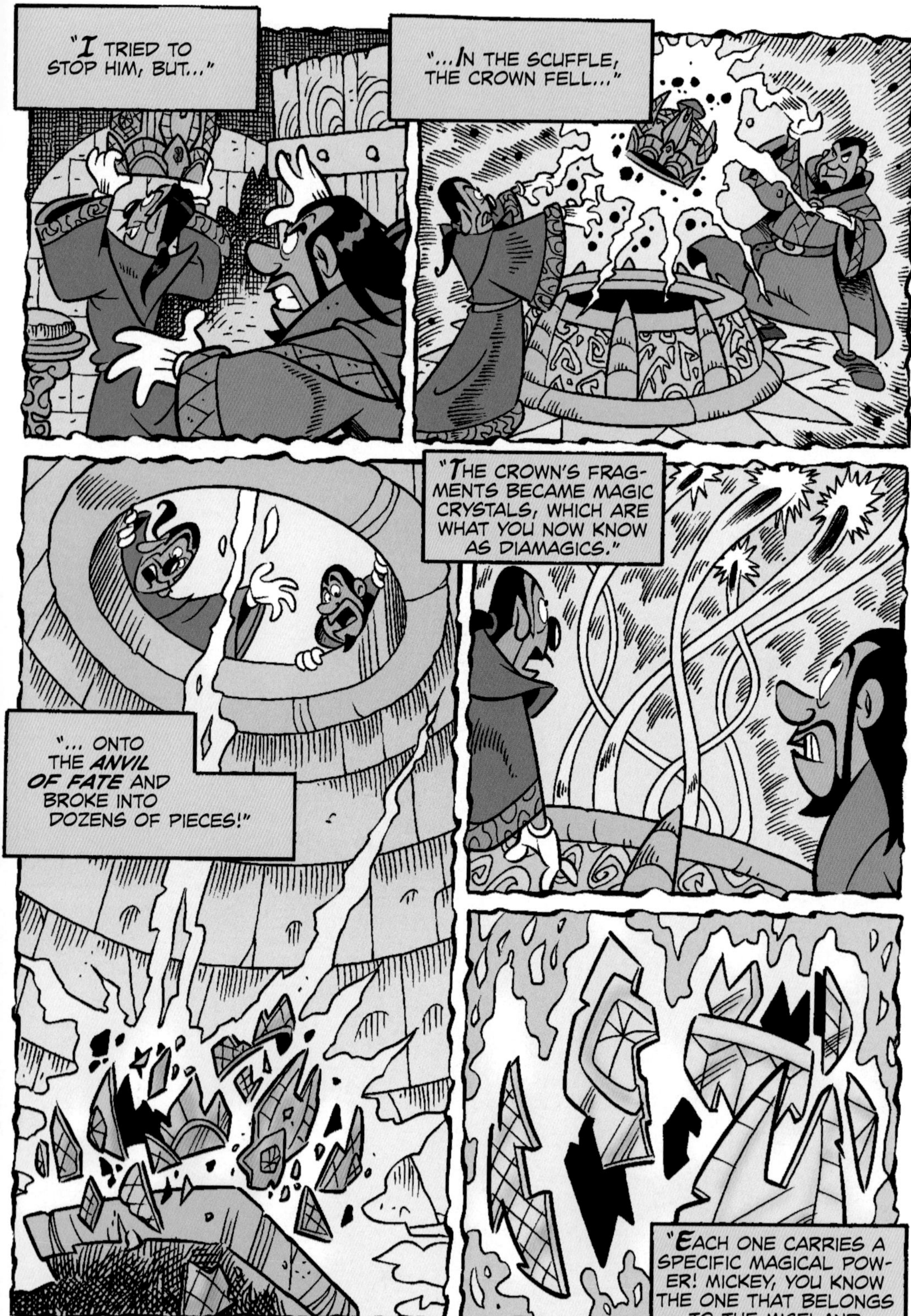
"I TRIED TO STOP HIM, BUT..."
"...IN THE SCUFFLE, THE CROWN FELL..."
"THE CROWN'S FRAGMENTS BECAME MAGIC CRYSTALS, WHICH ARE WHAT YOU NOW KNOW AS DIAMAGICS."
"... ONTO THE ANVIL OF FATE AND BROKE INTO DOZENS OF PIECES!"
"EACH ONE CARRIES A SPECIFIC MAGICAL POWER! MICKEY, YOU KNOW THE ONE THAT BELONGS TO THE MICELAND VILLAGE..."

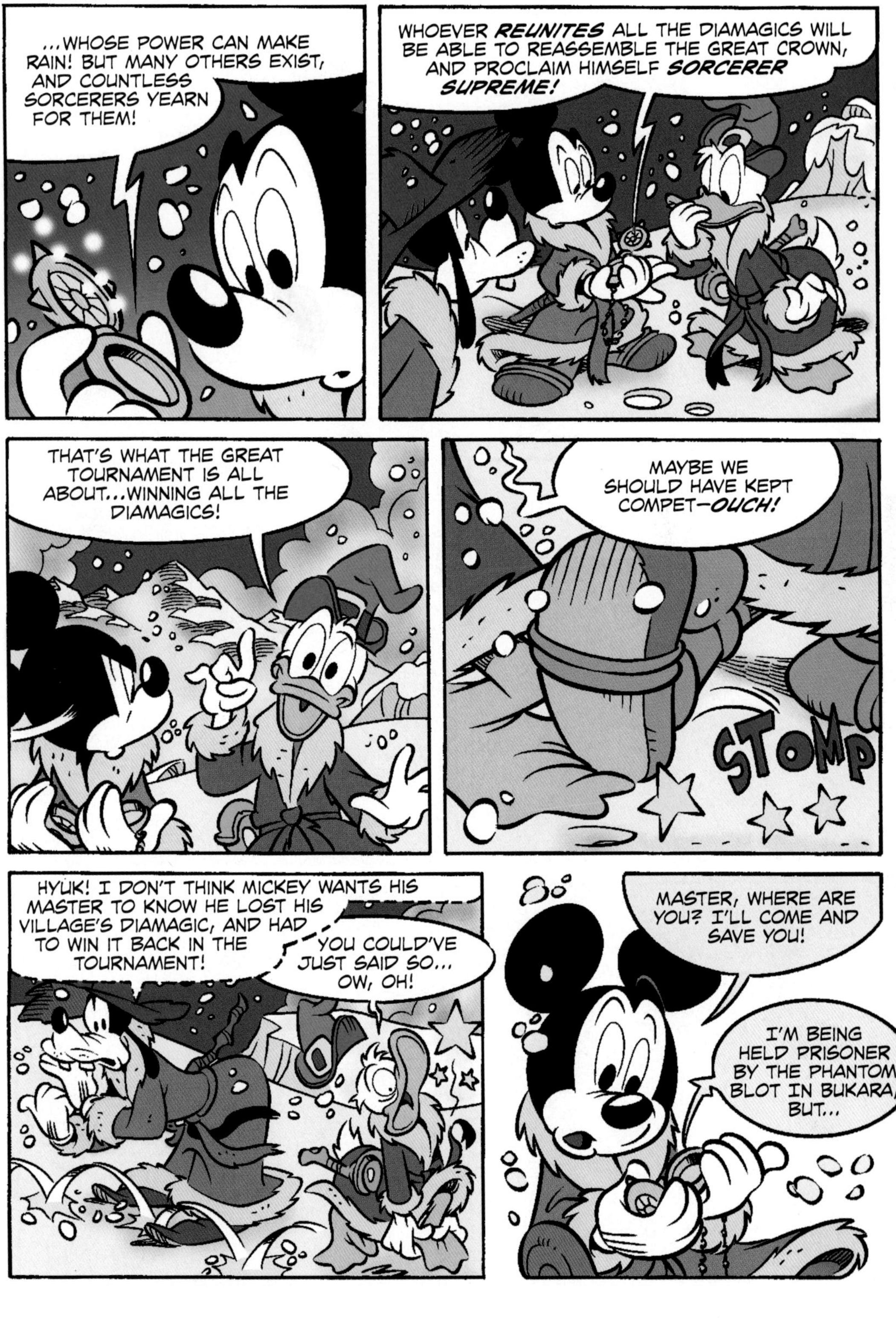
...WHOSE POWER CAN MAKE RAIN! BUT MANY OTHERS EXIST, AND COUNTLESS SORCERERS YEARN FOR THEM!
WHOEVER REUNITES ALL THE DIAMAGICS WILL BE ABLE TO REASSEMBLE THE GREAT CROWN, AND PROCLAIM HIMSELF SORCERER SUPREME!
THAT'S WHAT THE GREAT TOURNAMENT IS ALL ABOUT...WINNING ALL THE DIAMAGICS!
MAYBE WE SHOULD HAVE KEPT COMPET—OUCH!
STOMP
HYUK! I DON'T THINK MICKEY WANTS HIS MASTER TO KNOW HE LOST HIS VILLAGE'S DIAMAGIC, AND HAD TO WIN IT BACK IN THE TOURNAMENT!
YOU COULD'VE JUST SAID SO... OW, OH!
MASTER, WHERE ARE YOU? I'LL COME AND SAVE YOU!
I'M BEING HELD PRISONER BY THE PHANTOM BLOT IN BUKARA, BUT...

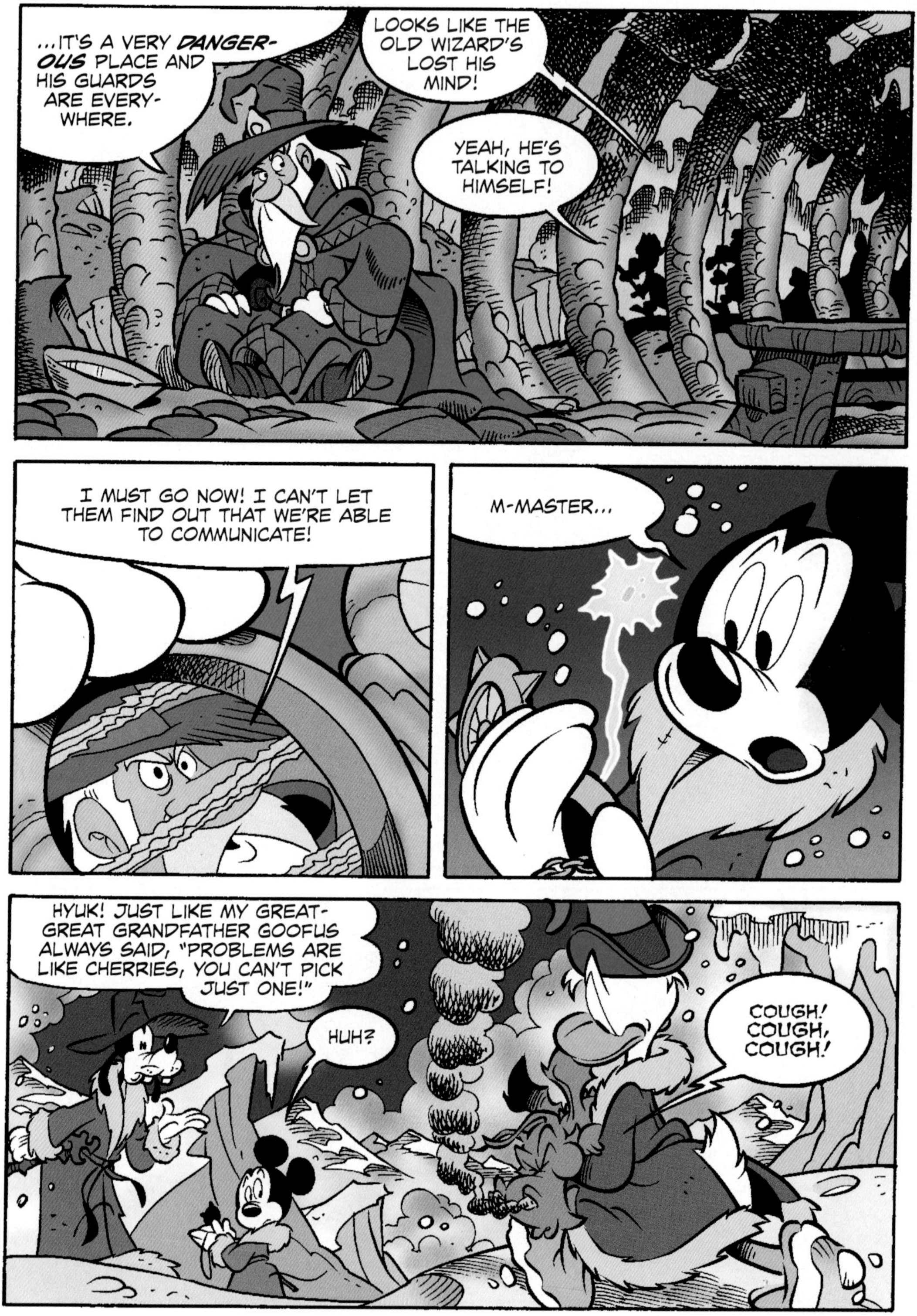
...IT'S A VERY DANGER-OUS PLACE AND HIS GUARDS ARE EVERY-WHERE.
LOOKS LIKE THE OLD WIZARD'S LOST HIS MIND!
YEAH, HE'S TALKING TO HIMSELF!
I MUST GO NOW! I CAN'T LET THEM FIND OUT THAT WE'RE ABLE TO COMMUNICATE!
M-MASTER...
HYUK! JUST LIKE MY GREAT-GREAT GRANDFATHER GOOFUS ALWAYS SAID, "PROBLEMS ARE LIKE CHERRIES, YOU CAN'T PICK JUST ONE!"
HUH?
COUGH! COUGH, COUGH!

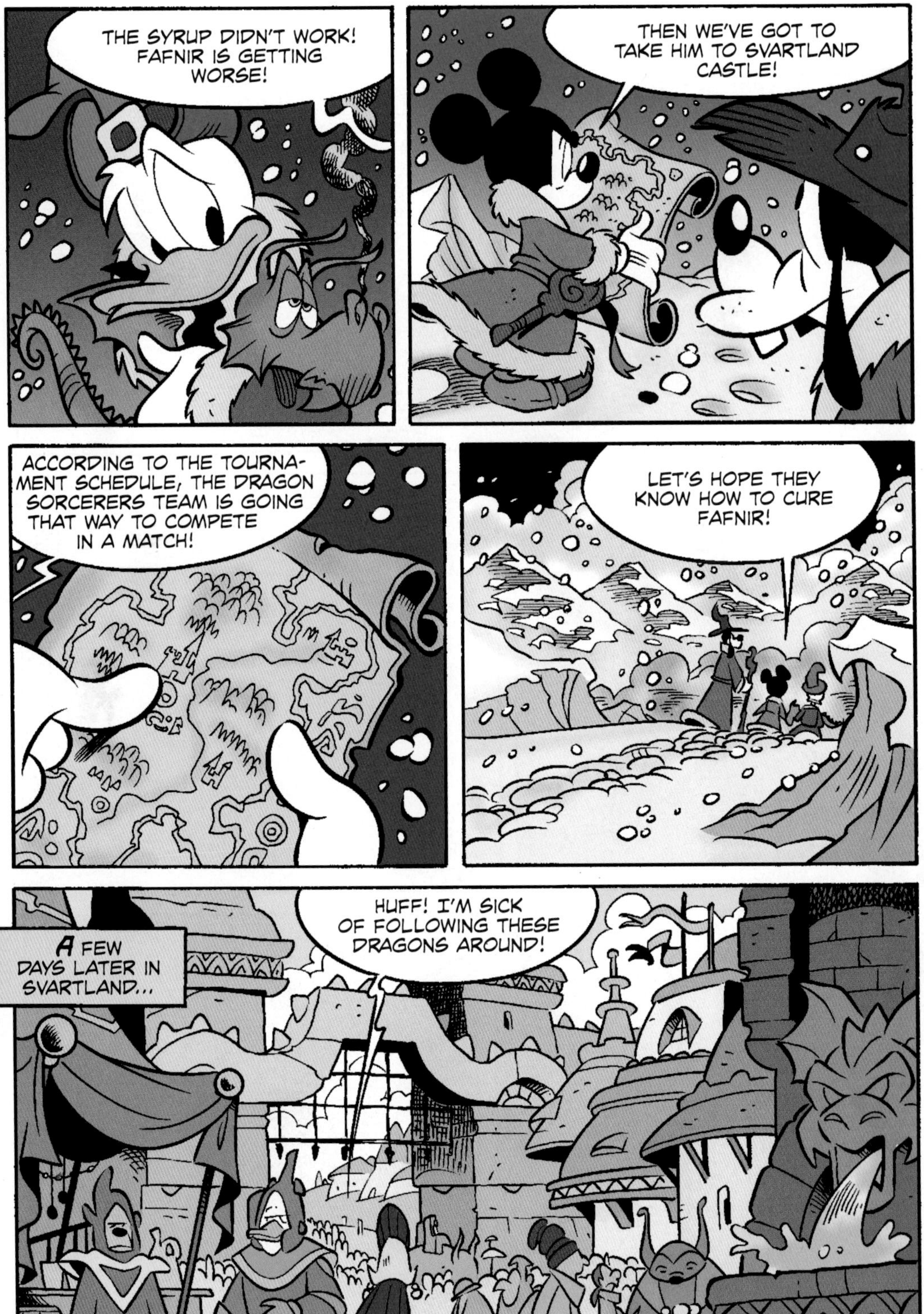
THE SYRUP DIDN'T WORK! FAFNIR IS GETTING WORSE!
THEN WE'VE GOT TO TAKE HIM TO SVARTLAND CASTLE!
ACCORDING TO THE TOURNAMENT SCHEDULE, THE DRAGON SORCERERS TEAM IS GOING THAT WAY TO COMPETE IN A MATCH!
LET'S HOPE THEY KNOW HOW TO CURE FAFNIR!
A FEW DAYS LATER IN SVARTLAND...
HUFF! I'M SICK OF FOLLOWING THESE DRAGONS AROUND!

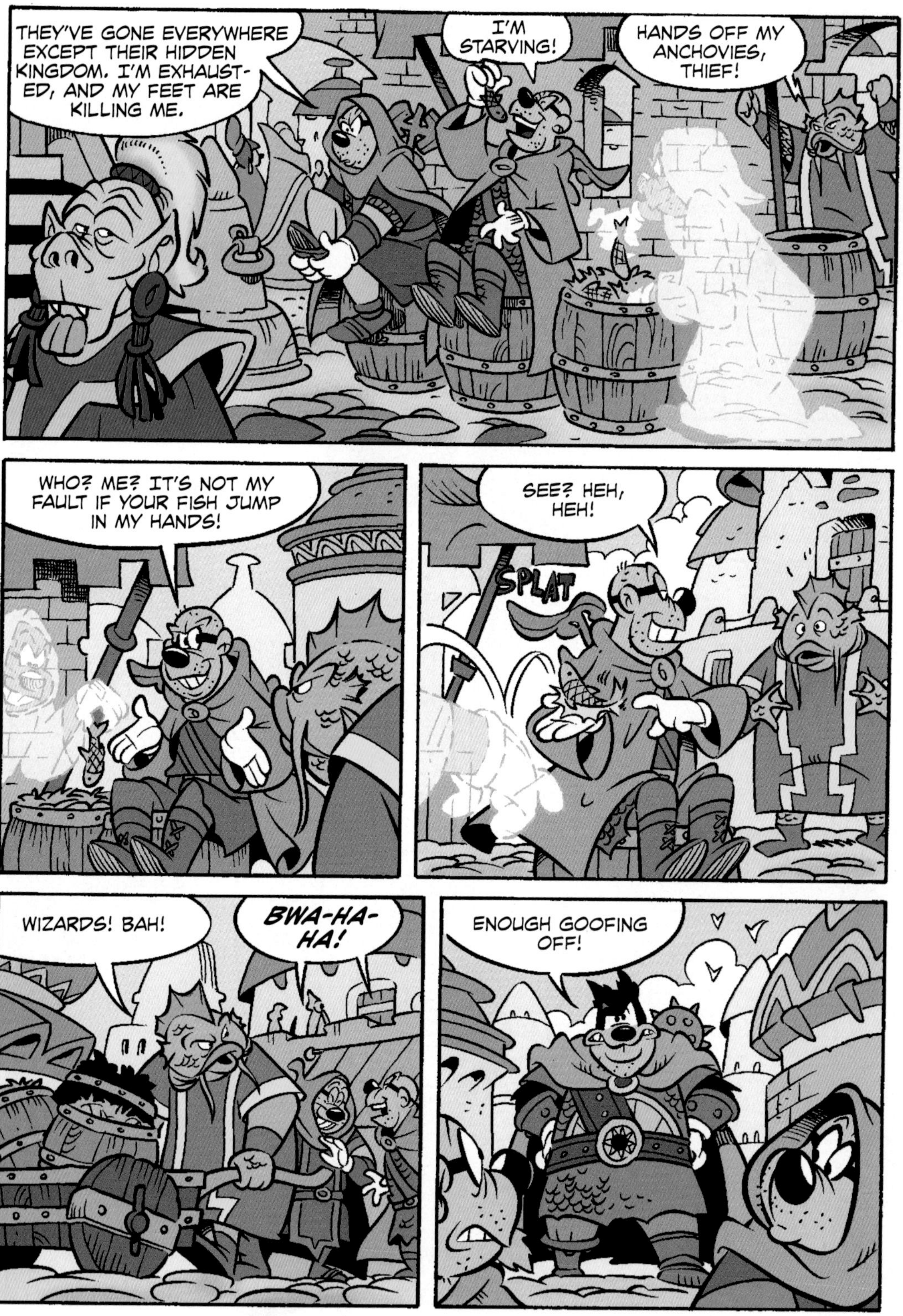
THEY'VE GONE EVERYWHERE EXCEPT THEIR HIDDEN KINGDOM. I'M EXHAUST-ED, AND MY FEET ARE KILLING ME.
I'M STARVING!
HANDS OFF MY ANCHOVIES, THIEF!
WHO? ME? IT'S NOT MY FAULT IF YOUR FISH JUMP IN MY HANDS!
SEE? HEH, HEH!
SPLAT
WIZARDS! BAH!
BWA-HA-HA!
ENOUGH GOOFING OFF!

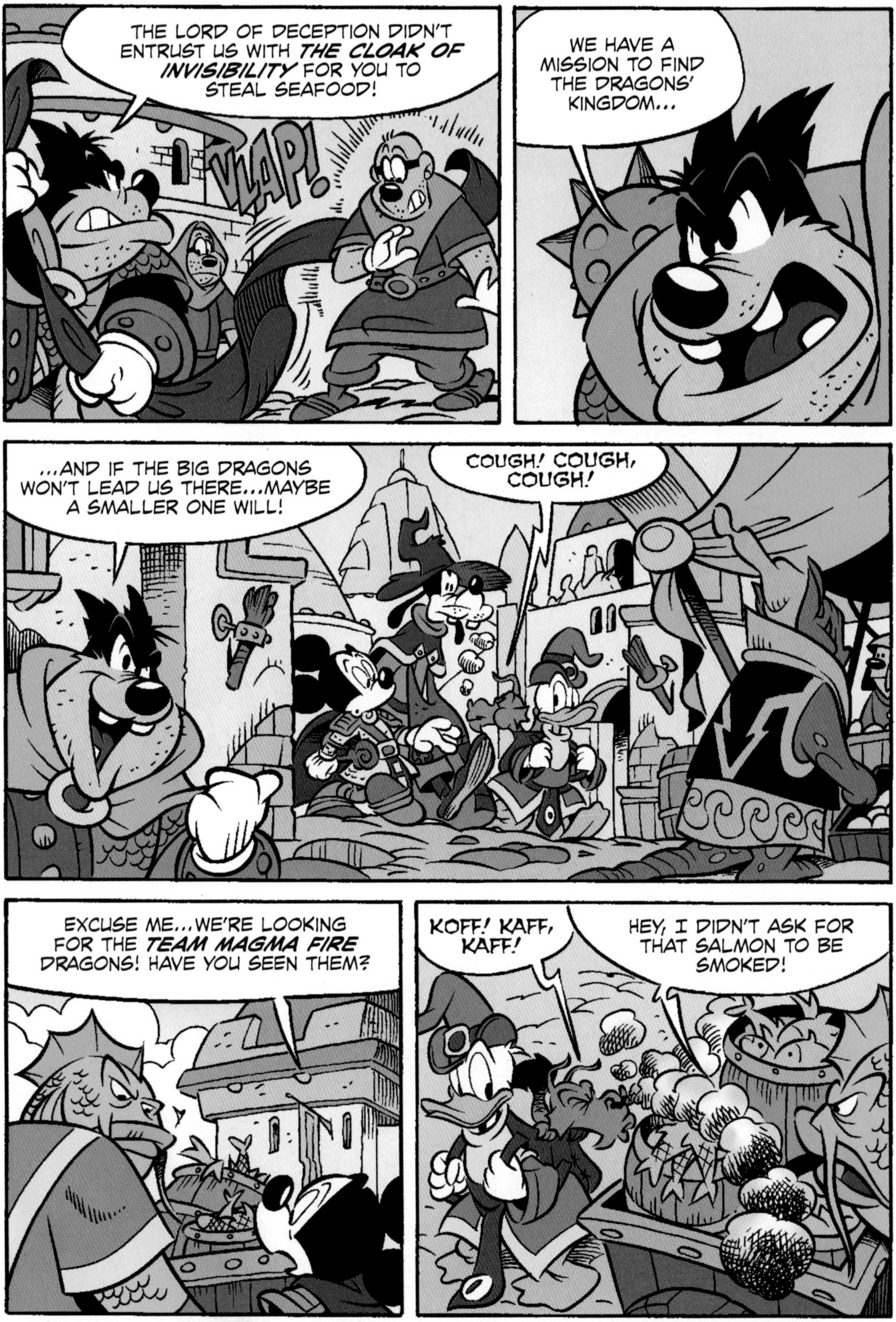
THE LORD OF DECEPTION DIDN'T ENTRUST US WITH THE CLOAK OF INVISIBILITY FOR YOU TO STEAL SEAFOOD!
VLAP!
WE HAVE A MISSION TO FIND THE DRAGONS' KINGDOM...
...AND IF THE BIG DRAGONS WON'T LEAD US THERE...MAYBE A SMALLER ONE WILL!
COUGH! COUGH, COUGH!
EXCUSE ME...WE'RE LOOKING FOR THE TEAM MAGMA FIRE DRAGONS! HAVE YOU SEEN THEM?
KOFF! KAFF, KAFF!
HEY, I DIDN'T ASK FOR THAT SALMON TO BE SMOKED!

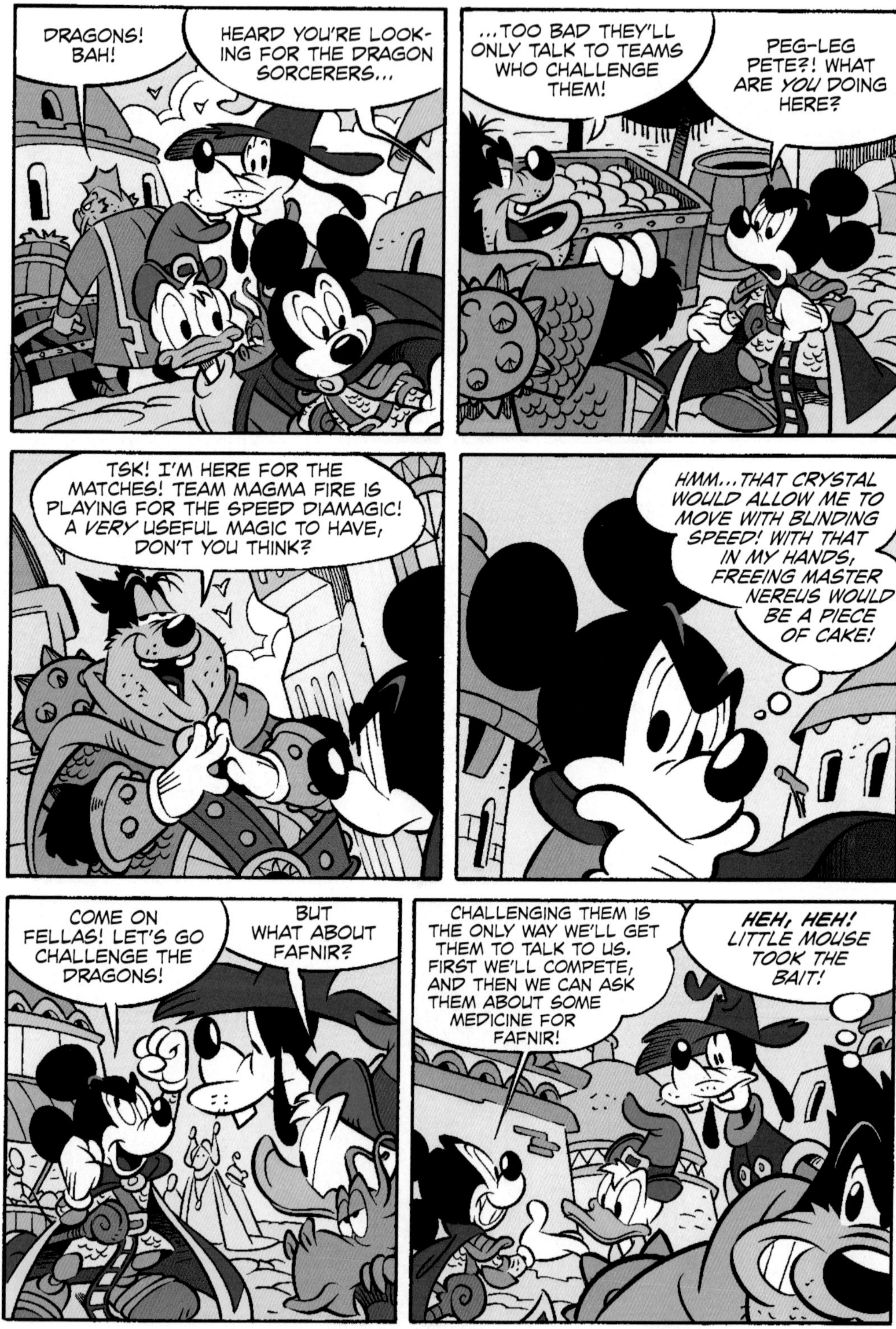
DRAGONS! BAH!
HEARD YOU'RE LOOKING FOR THE DRAGON SORCERERS...
...TOO BAD THEY'LL ONLY TALK TO TEAMS WHO CHALLENGE THEM!
PEG-LEG PETE?! WHAT ARE *YOU* DOING HERE?
TSK! I'M HERE FOR THE MATCHES! TEAM MAGMA FIRE IS PLAYING FOR THE SPEED DIAMAGIC! A *VERY* USEFUL MAGIC TO HAVE, DON'T YOU THINK?
HMM...THAT CRYSTAL WOULD ALLOW ME TO MOVE WITH BLINDING SPEED! WITH THAT IN MY HANDS, FREEING MASTER NEREUS WOULD BE A PIECE OF CAKE!
COME ON FELLAS! LET'S GO CHALLENGE THE DRAGONS!
BUT WHAT ABOUT FAFNIR?
CHALLENGING THEM IS THE ONLY WAY WE'LL GET THEM TO TALK TO US. FIRST WE'LL COMPETE, AND THEN WE CAN ASK THEM ABOUT SOME MEDICINE FOR FAFNIR!
HEH, HEH! *LITTLE MOUSE TOOK THE BAIT!*

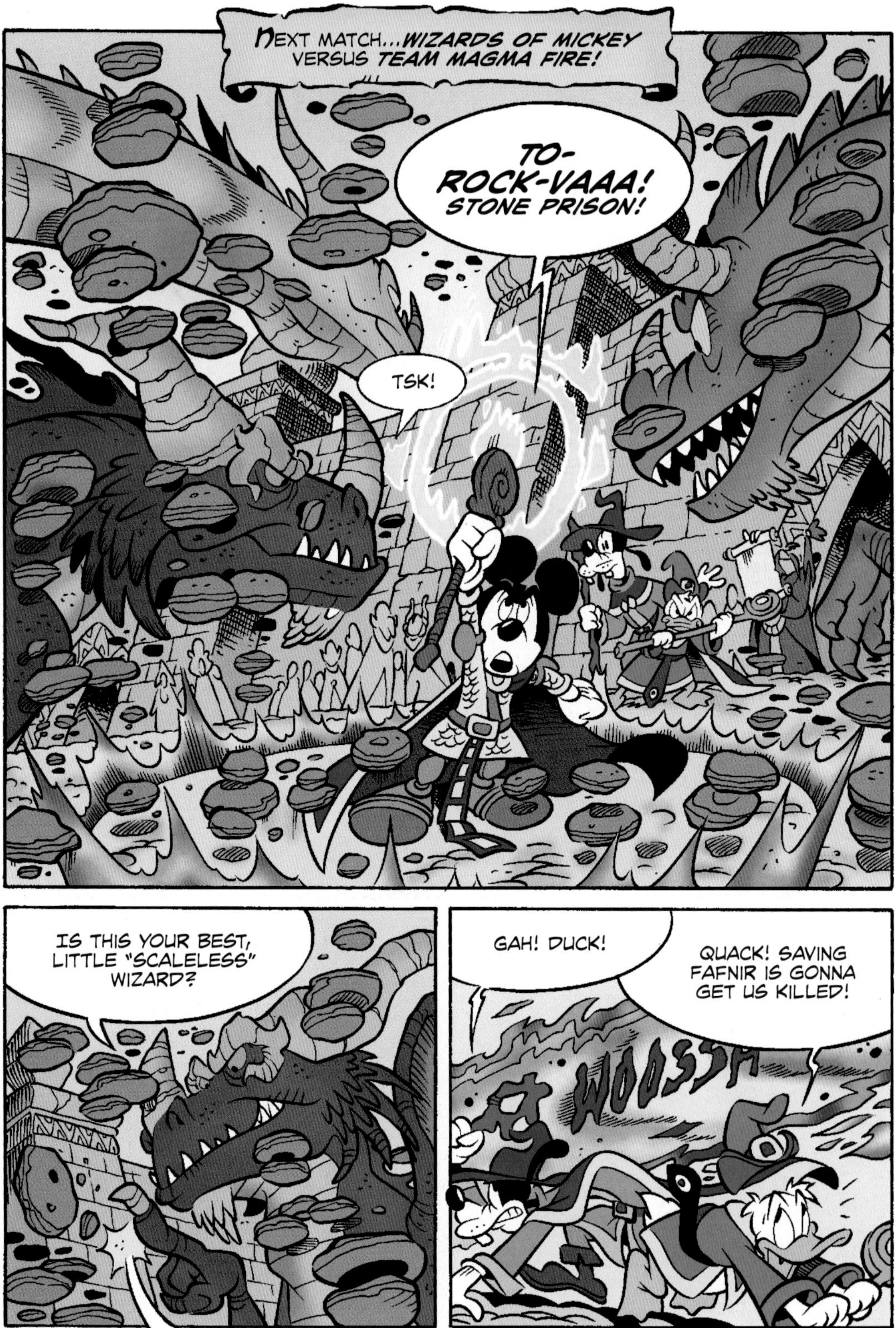
NEXT MATCH... WIZARDS OF MICKEY VERSUS TEAM MAGMA FIRE!
TO-ROCK-VAAA! STONE PRISON!
TSK!
IS THIS YOUR BEST, LITTLE "SCALELESS" WIZARD?
GAH! DUCK!
QUACK! SAVING FAFNIR IS GONNA GET US KILLED!
WOOSSH

MEANWHILE... A-HA! HERE'S THE PUPPY DRAGON, JUST LIKE PETE SAID!

NOW WE'LL FIND THE DRAGONS' KINGDOM FOR SURE! AND WITH THE DRAGONS' MAGIC, THE LORD OF DECEPTION WILL BE UNSTOPPABLE! HEE, HEE!

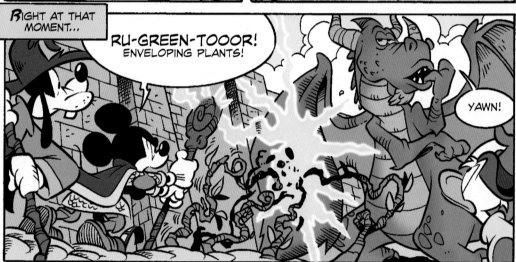

RIGHT AT THAT MOMENT...

RU-GREEN-TOOOR! ENVELOPING PLANTS!

YAWN!

IF THESE GUYS DECIDE TO BREATHE FIRE, I'M GONNA BE ONE CRISPY DUCK!

HYUK! SPEAKING OF FIRE, LOOK AT THAT SMOKE OVER THERE!

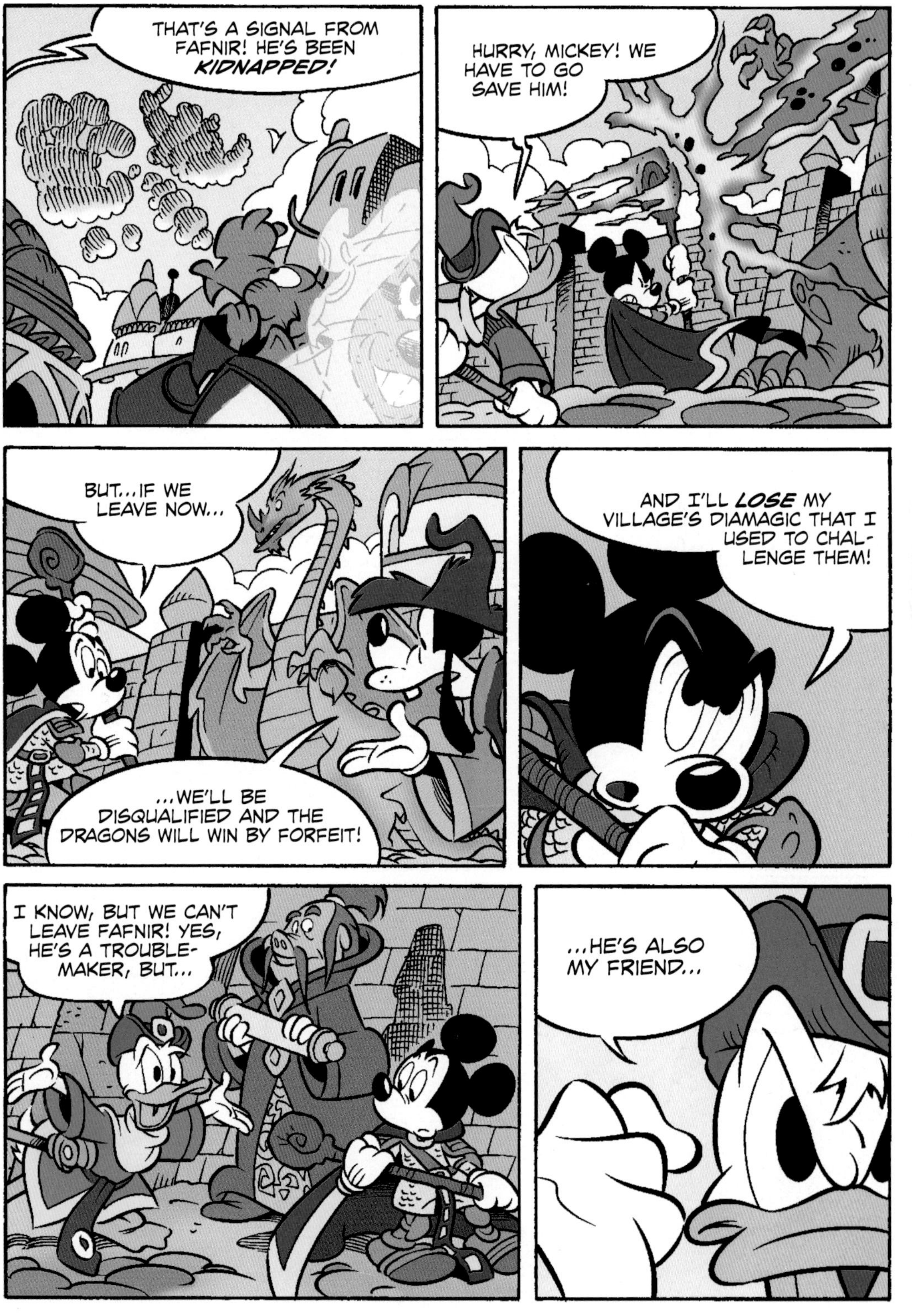
THAT'S A SIGNAL FROM FAFNIR! HE'S BEEN KIDNAPPED!
HURRY, MICKEY! WE HAVE TO GO SAVE HIM!
BUT...IF WE LEAVE NOW...
...WE'LL BE DISQUALIFIED AND THE DRAGONS WILL WIN BY FORFEIT!
AND I'LL LOSE MY VILLAGE'S DIAMAGIC THAT I USED TO CHAL-LENGE THEM!
I KNOW, BUT WE CAN'T LEAVE FAFNIR! YES, HE'S A TROUBLE-MAKER, BUT...
...HE'S ALSO MY FRIEND...

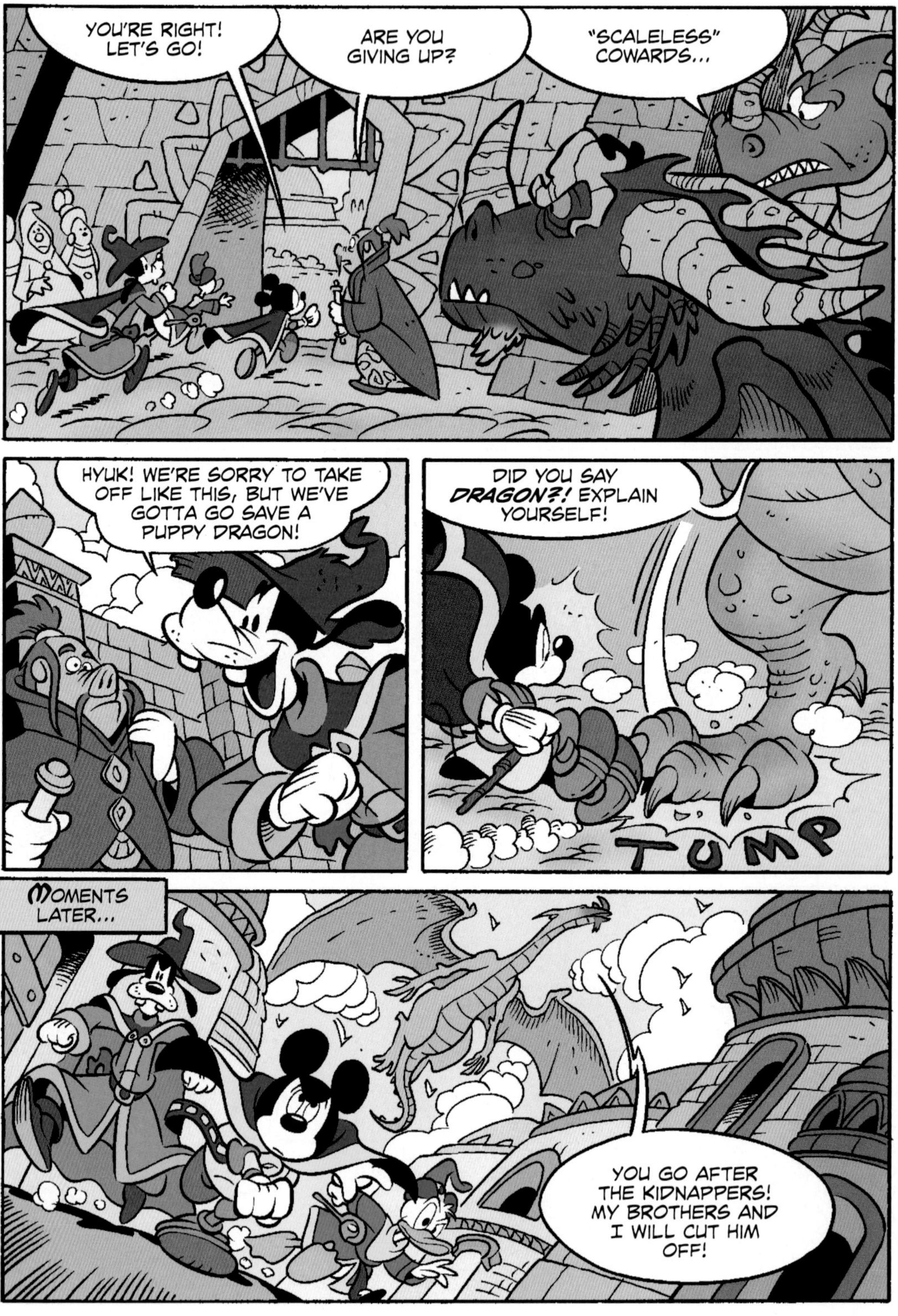
YOU'RE RIGHT! LET'S GO!
ARE YOU GIVING UP?
"SCALELESS" COWARDS...
HYUK! WE'RE SORRY TO TAKE OFF LIKE THIS, BUT WE'VE GOTTA GO SAVE A PUPPY DRAGON!
DID YOU SAY DRAGON?! EXPLAIN YOURSELF!
TUMP
MOMENTS LATER...
YOU GO AFTER THE KIDNAPPERS! MY BROTHERS AND I WILL CUT HIM OFF!

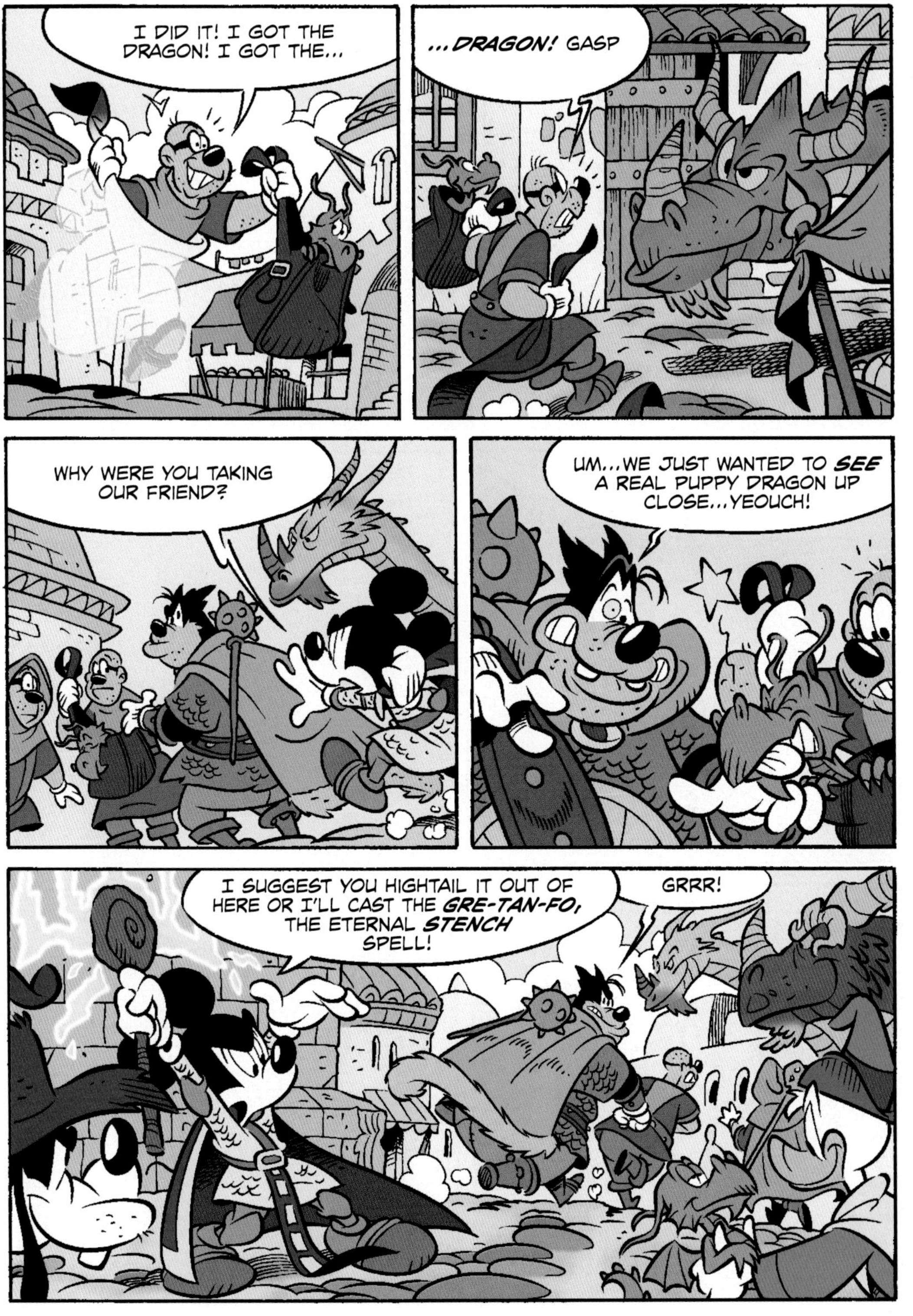
I DID IT! I GOT THE DRAGON! I GOT THE...
...DRAGON! GASP
WHY WERE YOU TAKING OUR FRIEND?
UM...WE JUST WANTED TO SEE A REAL PUPPY DRAGON UP CLOSE...YEOUCH!
I SUGGEST YOU HIGHTAIL IT OUT OF HERE OR I'LL CAST THE GRE-TAN-FO, THE ETERNAL STENCH SPELL!
GRRR!

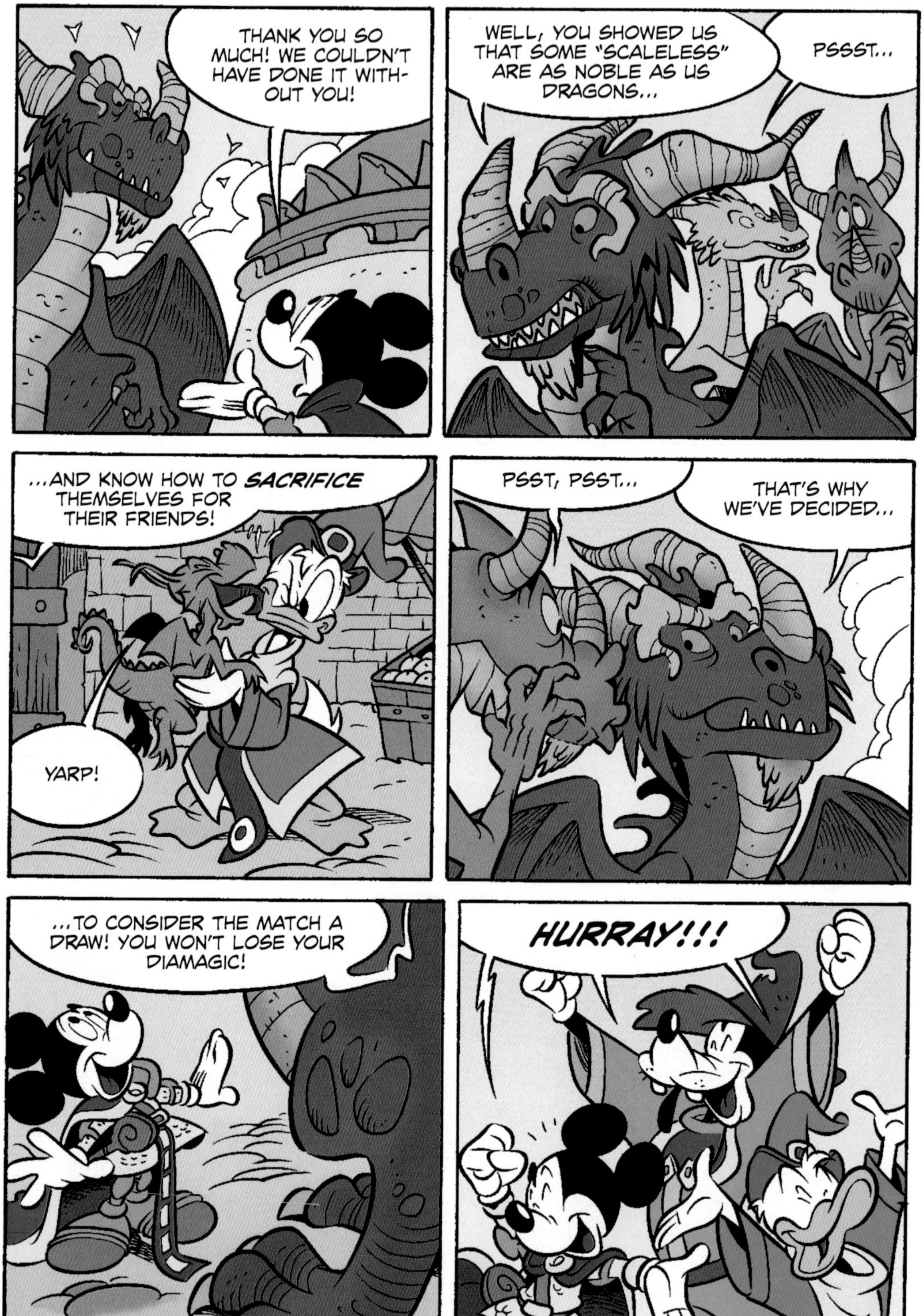
THANK YOU SO MUCH! WE COULDN'T HAVE DONE IT WITH-OUT YOU!
WELL, YOU SHOWED US THAT SOME "SCALELESS" ARE AS NOBLE AS US DRAGONS...
PSSST...
...AND KNOW HOW TO SACRIFICE THEMSELVES FOR THEIR FRIENDS!
YARP!
PSST, PSST...
THAT'S WHY WE'VE DECIDED...
...TO CONSIDER THE MATCH A DRAW! YOU WON'T LOSE YOUR DIAMAGIC!
HURRAY!!!

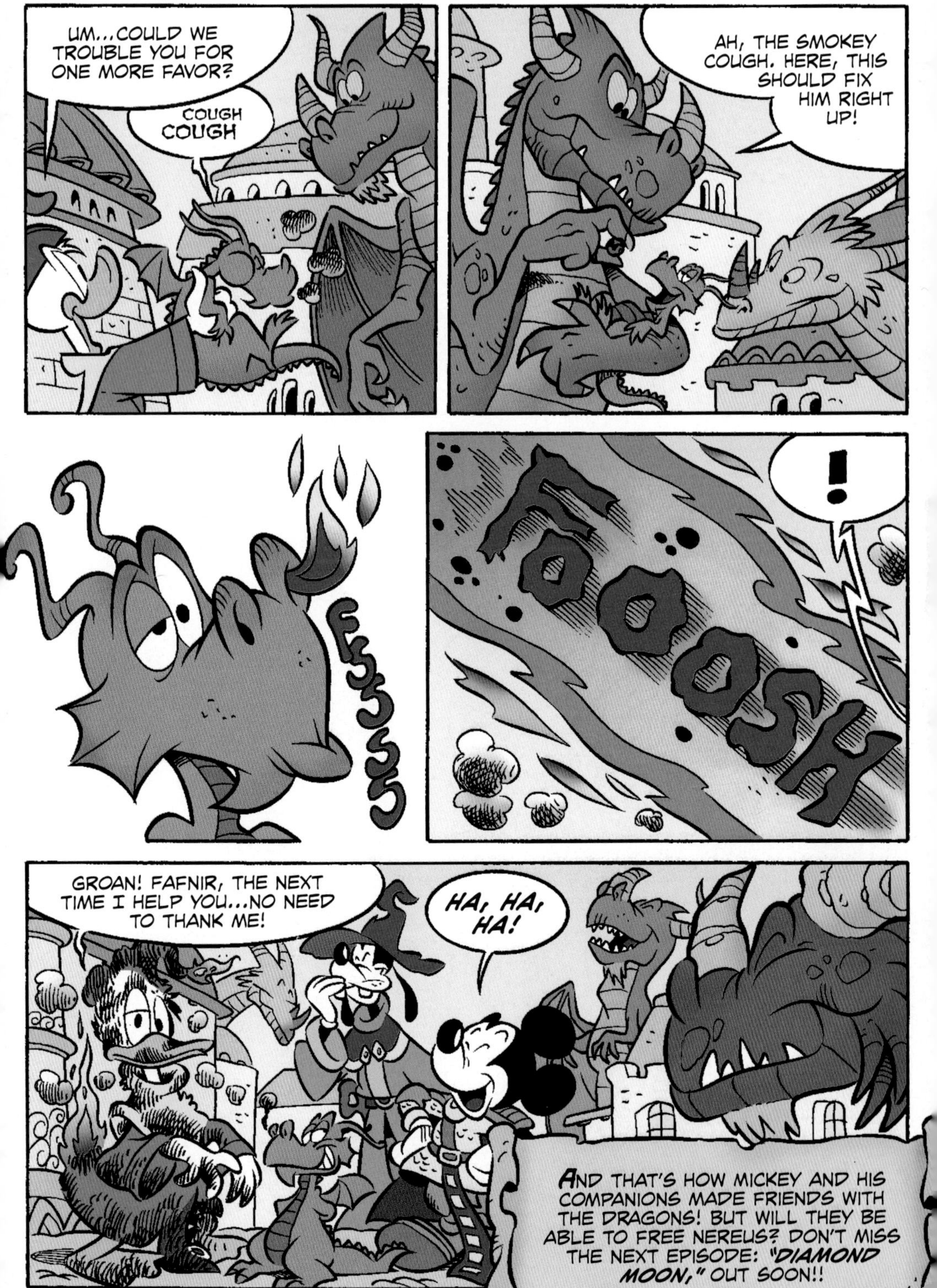
UM...COULD WE TROUBLE YOU FOR ONE MORE FAVOR?
COUGH COUGH
AH, THE SMOKEY COUGH. HERE, THIS SHOULD FIX HIM RIGHT UP!
FSSSS
!
FOOOSH
GROAN! FAFNIR, THE NEXT TIME I HELP YOU...NO NEED TO THANK ME!
HA, HA, HA!
AND THAT'S HOW MICKEY AND HIS COMPANIONS MADE FRIENDS WITH THE DRAGONS! BUT WILL THEY BE ABLE TO FREE NEREUS? DON'T MISS THE NEXT EPISODE: "DIAMOND MOON," OUT SOON!!

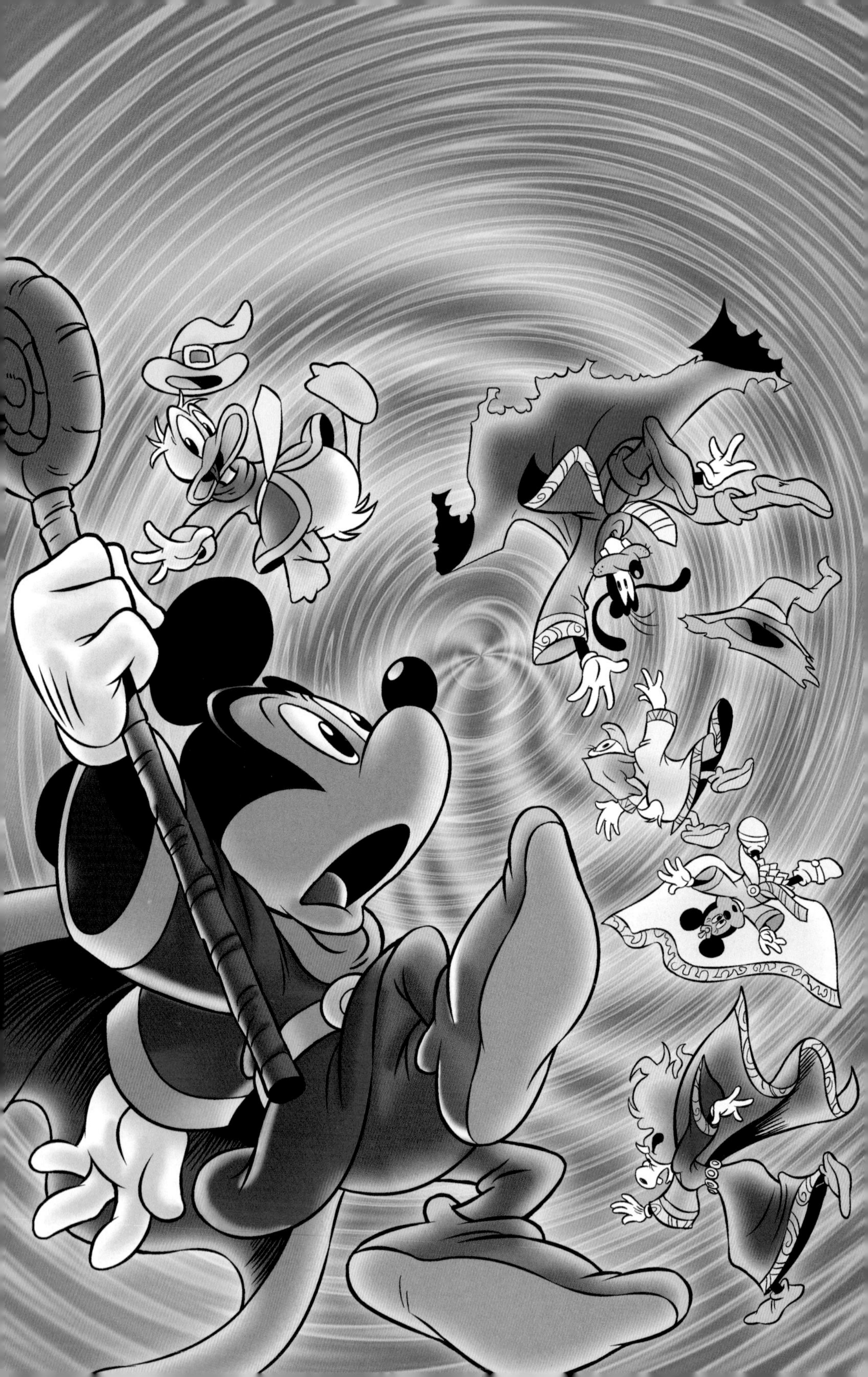

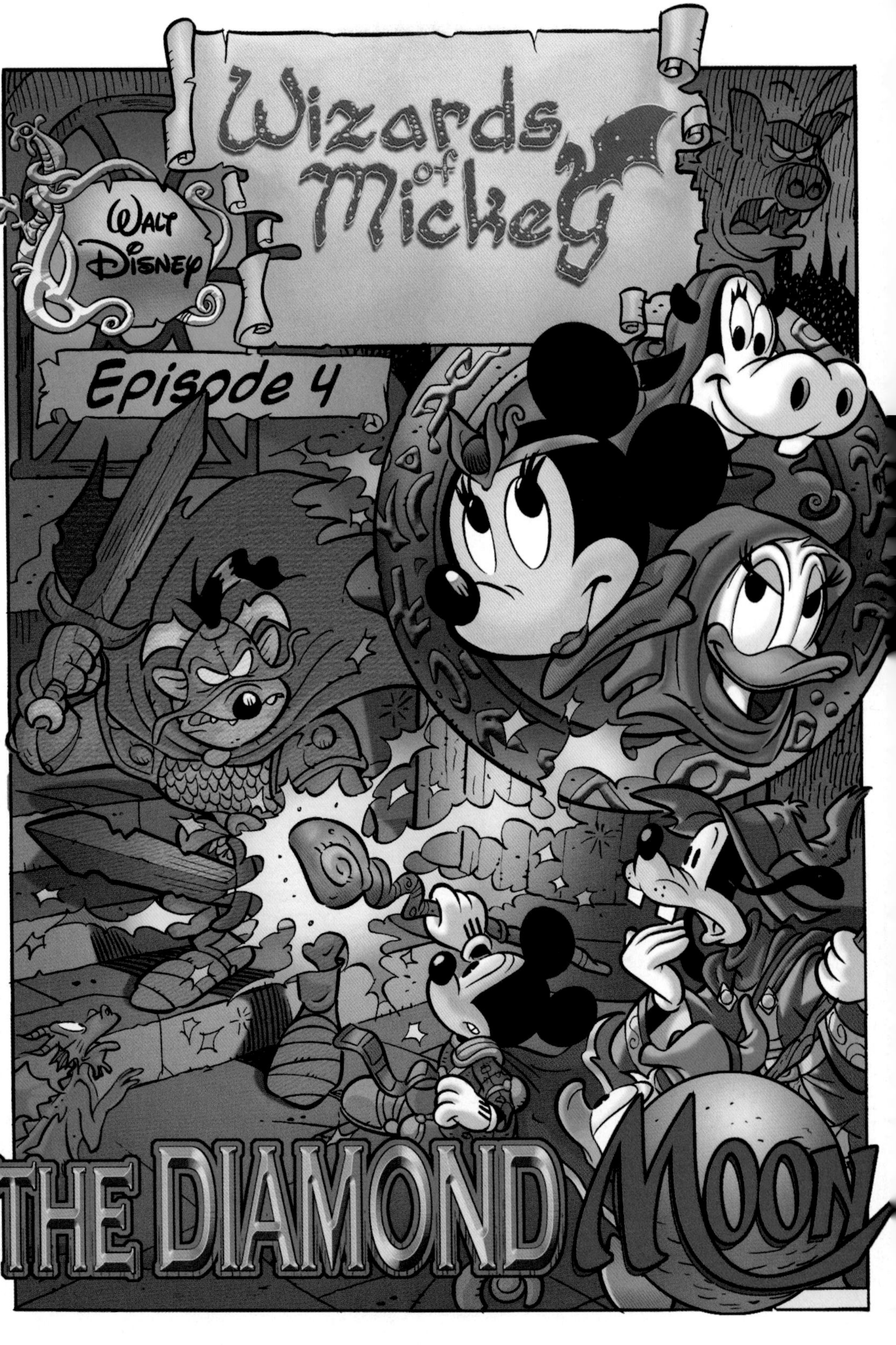
Wizards of Mickey
Walt Disney
Episode 4
THE DIAMOND MOON

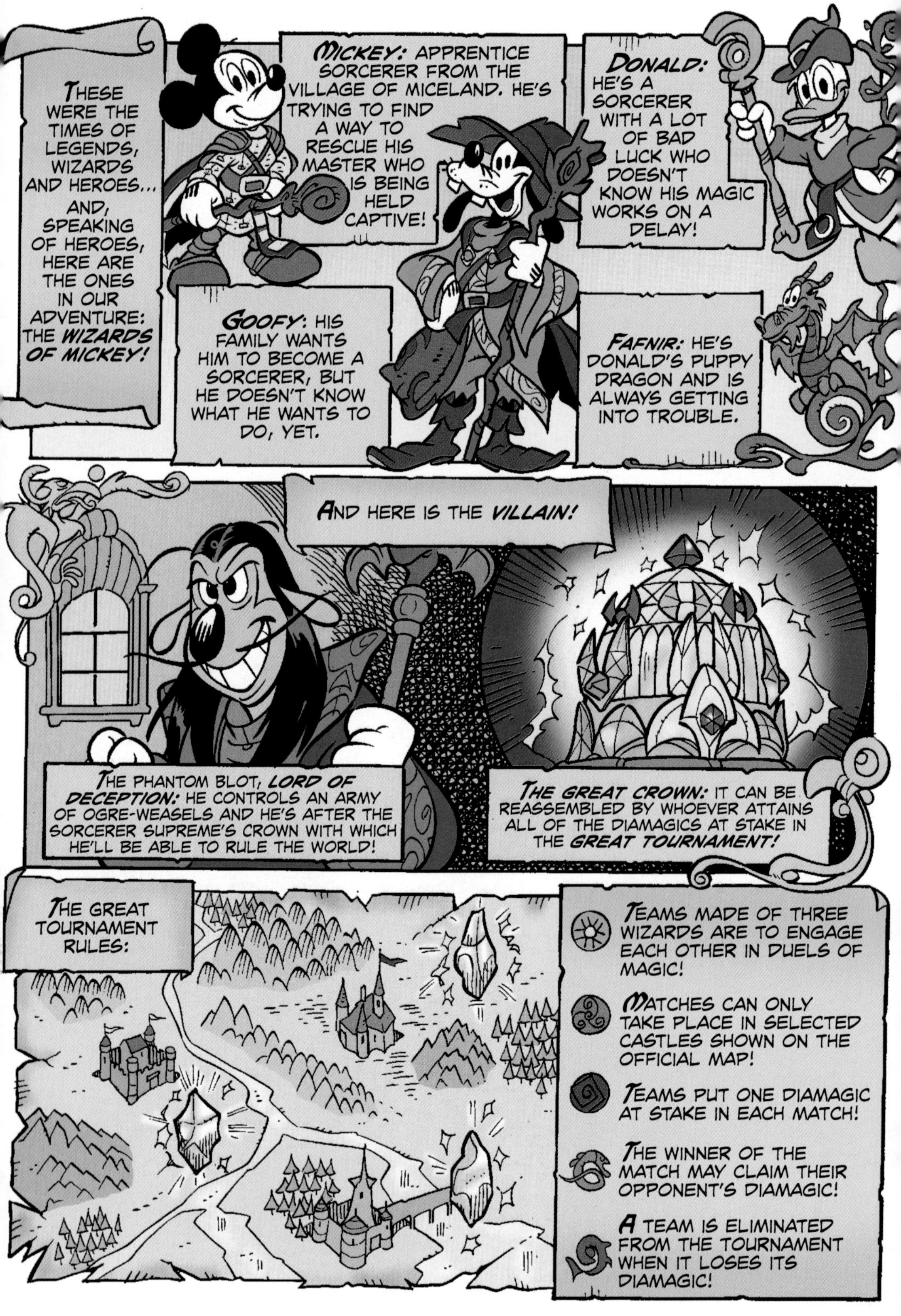
THESE WERE THE TIMES OF LEGENDS, WIZARDS AND HEROES... AND, SPEAKING OF HEROES, HERE ARE THE ONES IN OUR ADVENTURE: THE WIZARDS OF MICKEY!
MICKEY: APPRENTICE SORCERER FROM THE VILLAGE OF MICELAND. HE'S TRYING TO FIND A WAY TO RESCUE HIS MASTER WHO IS BEING HELD CAPTIVE!
DONALD: HE'S A SORCERER WITH A LOT OF BAD LUCK WHO DOESN'T KNOW HIS MAGIC WORKS ON A DELAY!
GOOFY: HIS FAMILY WANTS HIM TO BECOME A SORCERER, BUT HE DOESN'T KNOW WHAT HE WANTS TO DO, YET.
FAFNIR: HE'S DONALD'S PUPPY DRAGON AND IS ALWAYS GETTING INTO TROUBLE.
AND HERE IS THE VILLAIN!
THE PHANTOM BLOT, LORD OF DECEPTION: HE CONTROLS AN ARMY OF OGRE-WEASELS AND HE'S AFTER THE SORCERER SUPREME'S CROWN WITH WHICH HE'LL BE ABLE TO RULE THE WORLD!
THE GREAT CROWN: IT CAN BE REASSEMBLED BY WHOEVER ATTAINS ALL OF THE DIAMAGICS AT STAKE IN THE GREAT TOURNAMENT!
THE GREAT TOURNAMENT RULES:
TEAMS MADE OF THREE WIZARDS ARE TO ENGAGE EACH OTHER IN DUELS OF MAGIC!
MATCHES CAN ONLY TAKE PLACE IN SELECTED CASTLES SHOWN ON THE OFFICIAL MAP!
TEAMS PUT ONE DIAMAGIC AT STAKE IN EACH MATCH!
THE WINNER OF THE MATCH MAY CLAIM THEIR OPPONENT'S DIAMAGIC!
A TEAM IS ELIMINATED FROM THE TOURNAMENT WHEN IT LOSES ITS DIAMAGIC!

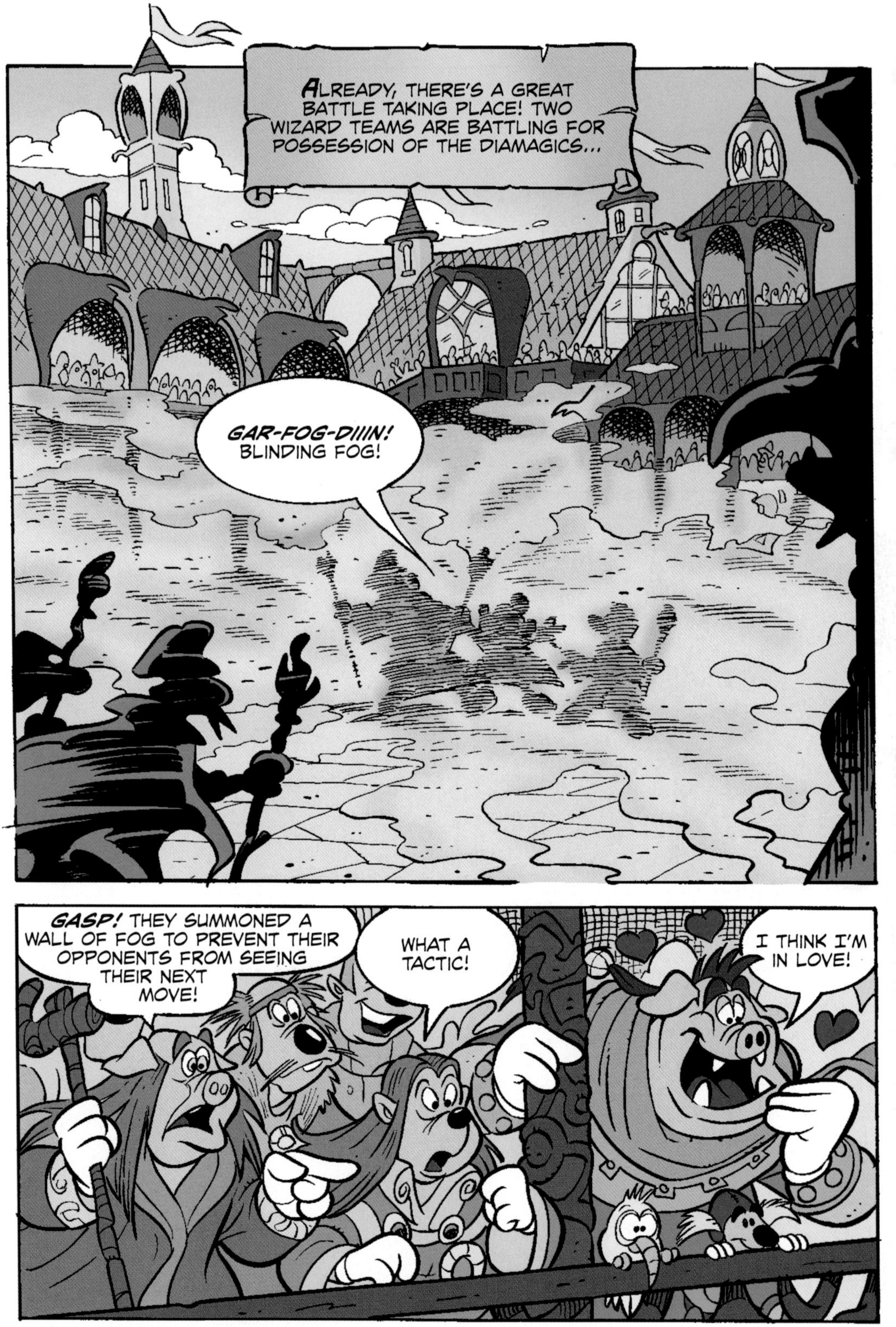
ALREADY, THERE'S A GREAT BATTLE TAKING PLACE! TWO WIZARD TEAMS ARE BATTLING FOR POSSESSION OF THE DIAMAGICS...
GAR-FOG-DIIIN! BLINDING FOG!
GASP! THEY SUMMONED A WALL OF FOG TO PREVENT THEIR OPPONENTS FROM SEEING THEIR NEXT MOVE!
WHAT A TACTIC!
I THINK I'M IN LOVE!

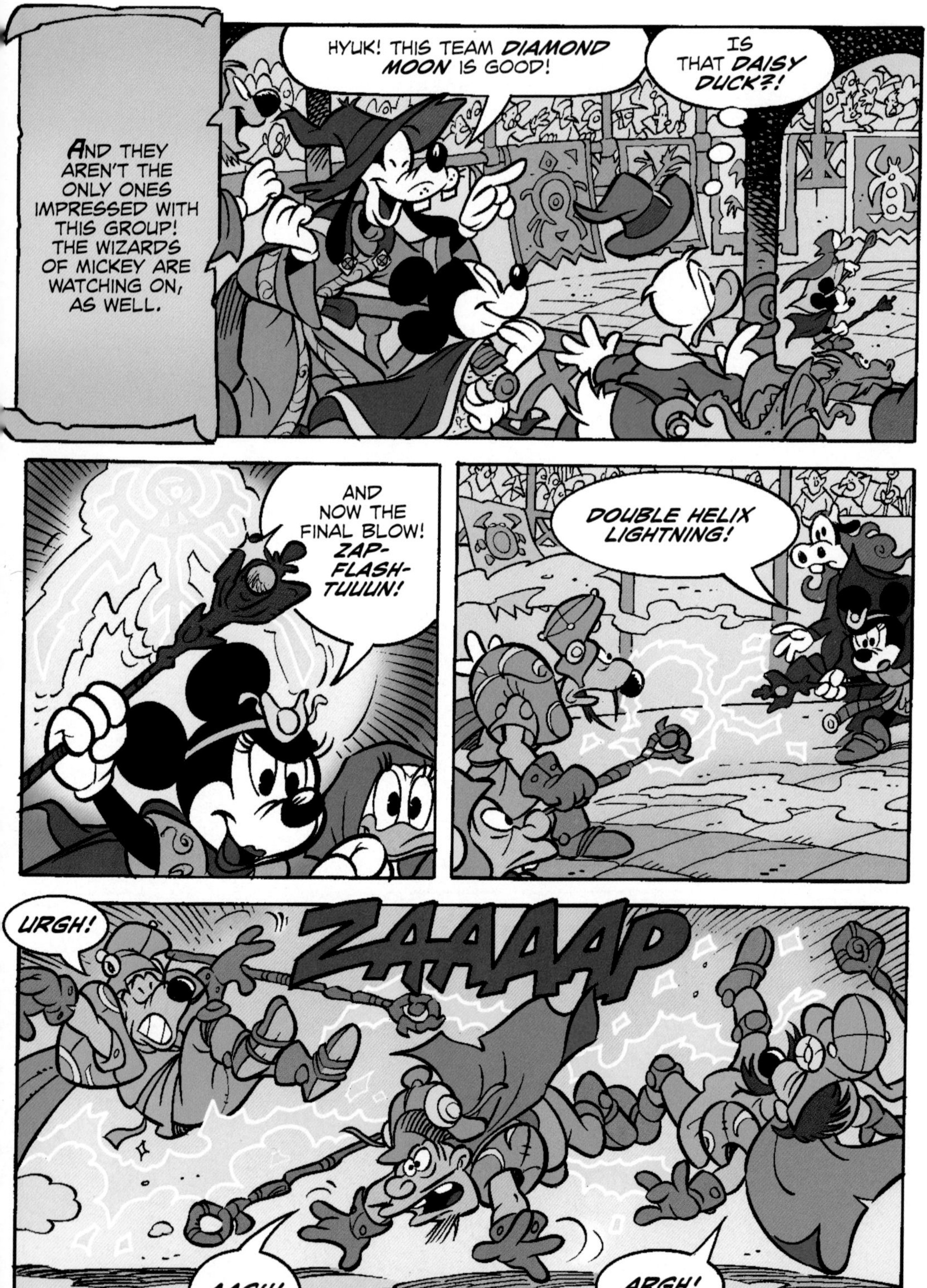
AND THEY AREN'T THE ONLY ONES IMPRESSED WITH THIS GROUP! THE WIZARDS OF MICKEY ARE WATCHING ON, AS WELL.
HYUK! THIS TEAM DIAMOND MOON IS GOOD!
IS THAT DAISY DUCK?!
AND NOW THE FINAL BLOW! ZAP-FLASH-TUUUN!
DOUBLE HELIX LIGHTNING!
URGH!
ZAAAAP
AAGH!
ARGH!

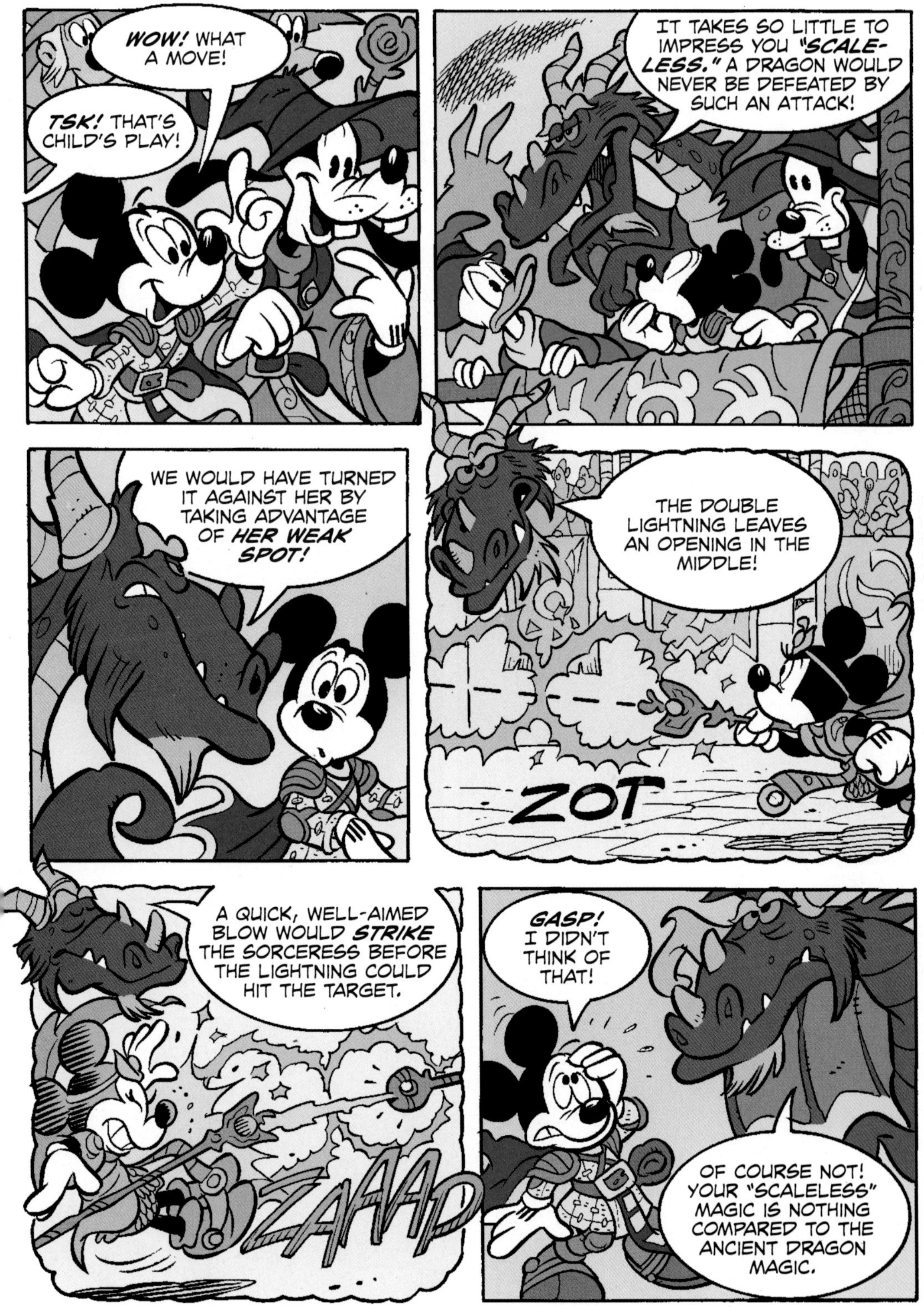
WOW! WHAT A MOVE!
TSK! THAT'S CHILD'S PLAY!
IT TAKES SO LITTLE TO IMPRESS YOU "SCALE-LESS." A DRAGON WOULD NEVER BE DEFEATED BY SUCH AN ATTACK!
WE WOULD HAVE TURNED IT AGAINST HER BY TAKING ADVANTAGE OF HER WEAK SPOT!
THE DOUBLE LIGHTNING LEAVES AN OPENING IN THE MIDDLE!
ZOT
A QUICK, WELL-AIMED BLOW WOULD STRIKE THE SORCERESS BEFORE THE LIGHTNING COULD HIT THE TARGET.
ZAAAP
GASP! I DIDN'T THINK OF THAT!
OF COURSE NOT! YOUR "SCALELESS" MAGIC IS NOTHING COMPARED TO THE ANCIENT DRAGON MAGIC.

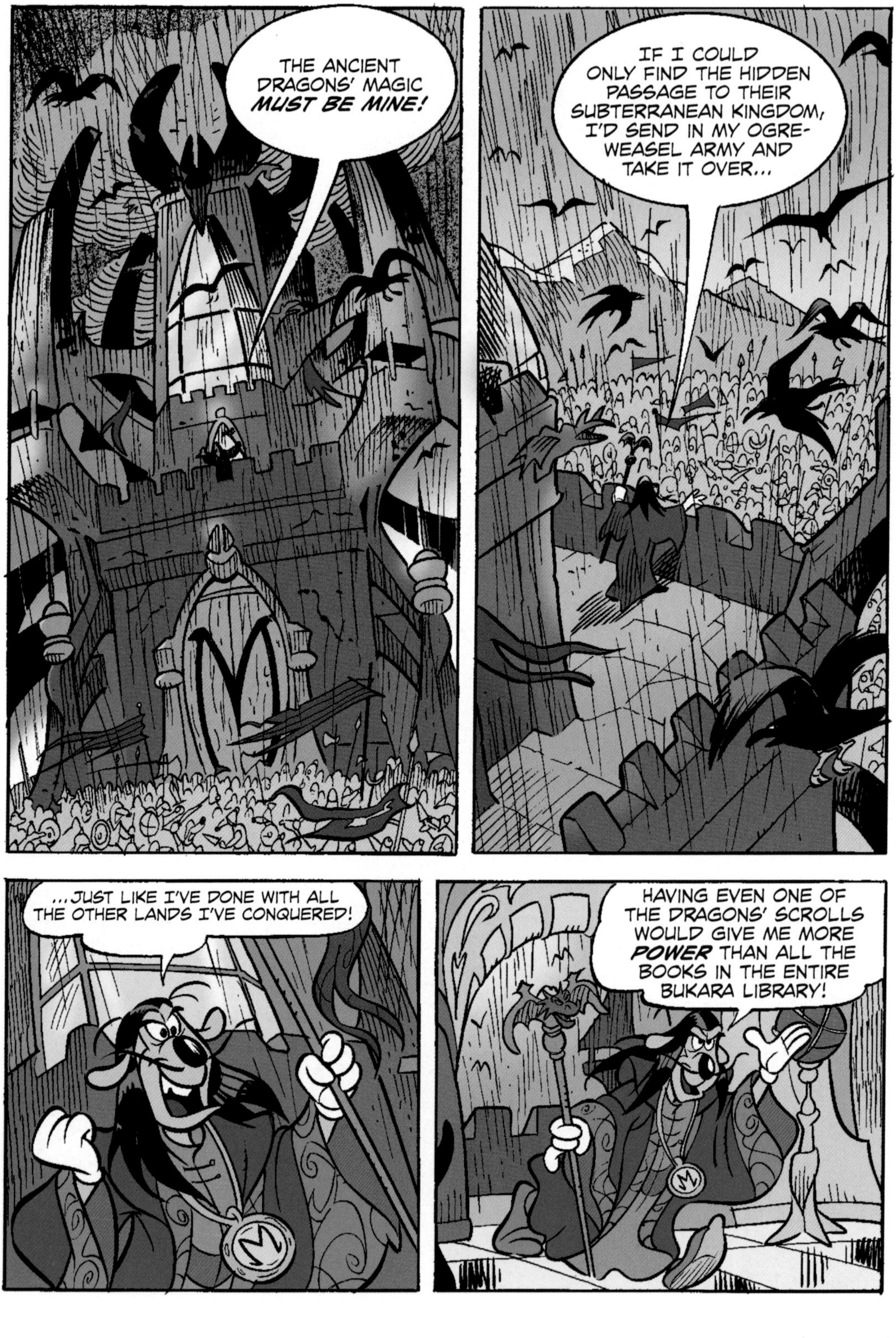
THE ANCIENT DRAGONS' MAGIC MUST BE MINE!
IF I COULD ONLY FIND THE HIDDEN PASSAGE TO THEIR SUBTERRANEAN KINGDOM, I'D SEND IN MY OGRE-WEASEL ARMY AND TAKE IT OVER...
...JUST LIKE I'VE DONE WITH ALL THE OTHER LANDS I'VE CONQUERED!
HAVING EVEN ONE OF THE DRAGONS' SCROLLS WOULD GIVE ME MORE POWER THAN ALL THE BOOKS IN THE ENTIRE BUKARA LIBRARY!

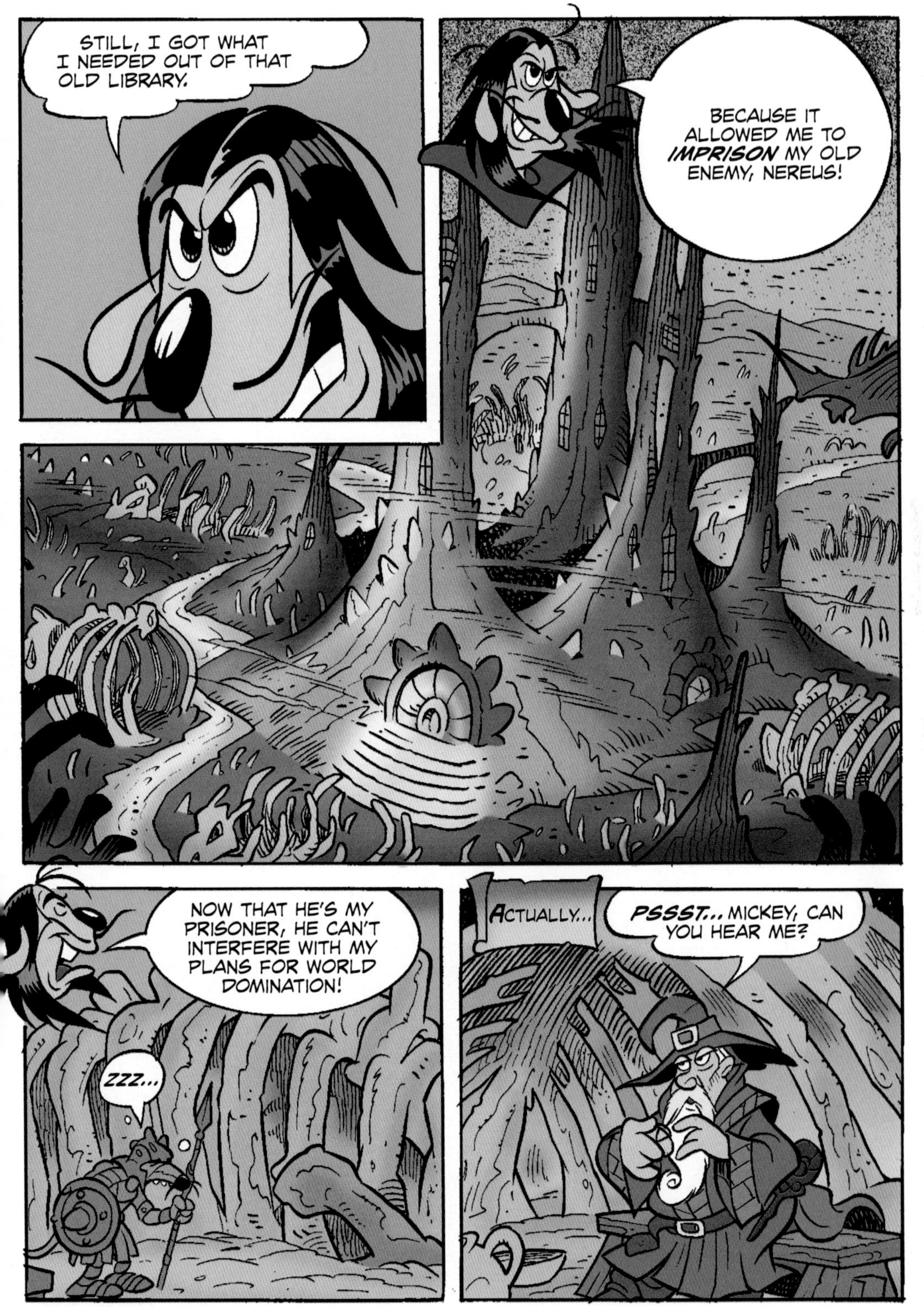
STILL, I GOT WHAT I NEEDED OUT OF THAT OLD LIBRARY.
BECAUSE IT ALLOWED ME TO IMPRISON MY OLD ENEMY, NEREUS!
NOW THAT HE'S MY PRISONER, HE CAN'T INTERFERE WITH MY PLANS FOR WORLD DOMINATION!
ZZZ...
ACTUALLY...
PSSST... MICKEY, CAN YOU HEAR ME?

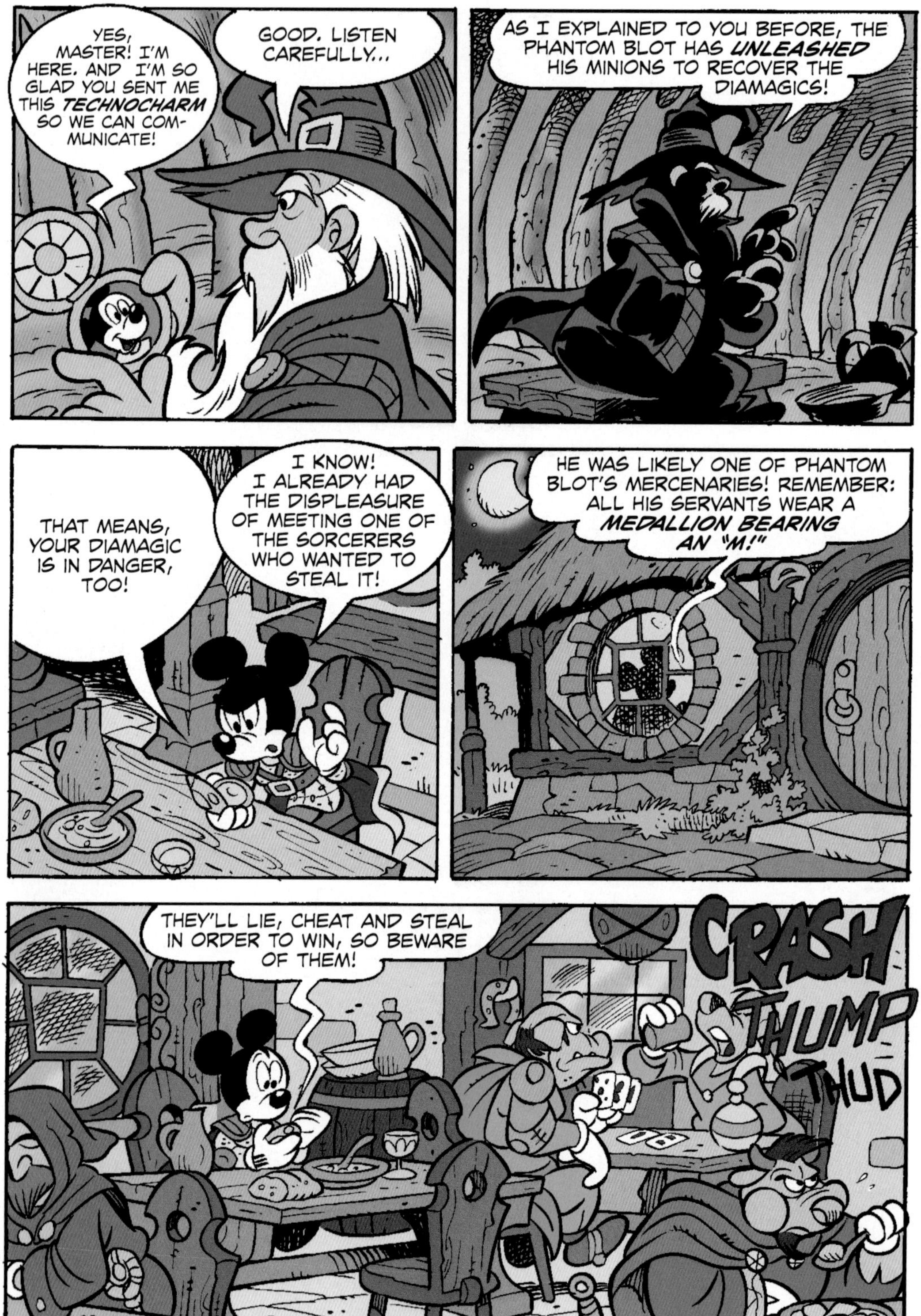
YES, MASTER! I'M HERE. AND I'M SO GLAD YOU SENT ME THIS TECHNOCHARM SO WE CAN COMMUNICATE!
GOOD. LISTEN CAREFULLY...
AS I EXPLAINED TO YOU BEFORE, THE PHANTOM BLOT HAS UNLEASHED HIS MINIONS TO RECOVER THE DIAMAGICS!
THAT MEANS, YOUR DIAMAGIC IS IN DANGER, TOO!
I KNOW! I ALREADY HAD THE DISPLEASURE OF MEETING ONE OF THE SORCERERS WHO WANTED TO STEAL IT!
HE WAS LIKELY ONE OF PHANTOM BLOT'S MERCENARIES! REMEMBER: ALL HIS SERVANTS WEAR A MEDALLION BEARING AN "M!"
THEY'LL LIE, CHEAT AND STEAL IN ORDER TO WIN, SO BEWARE OF THEM!
CRASH
THUMP
THUD

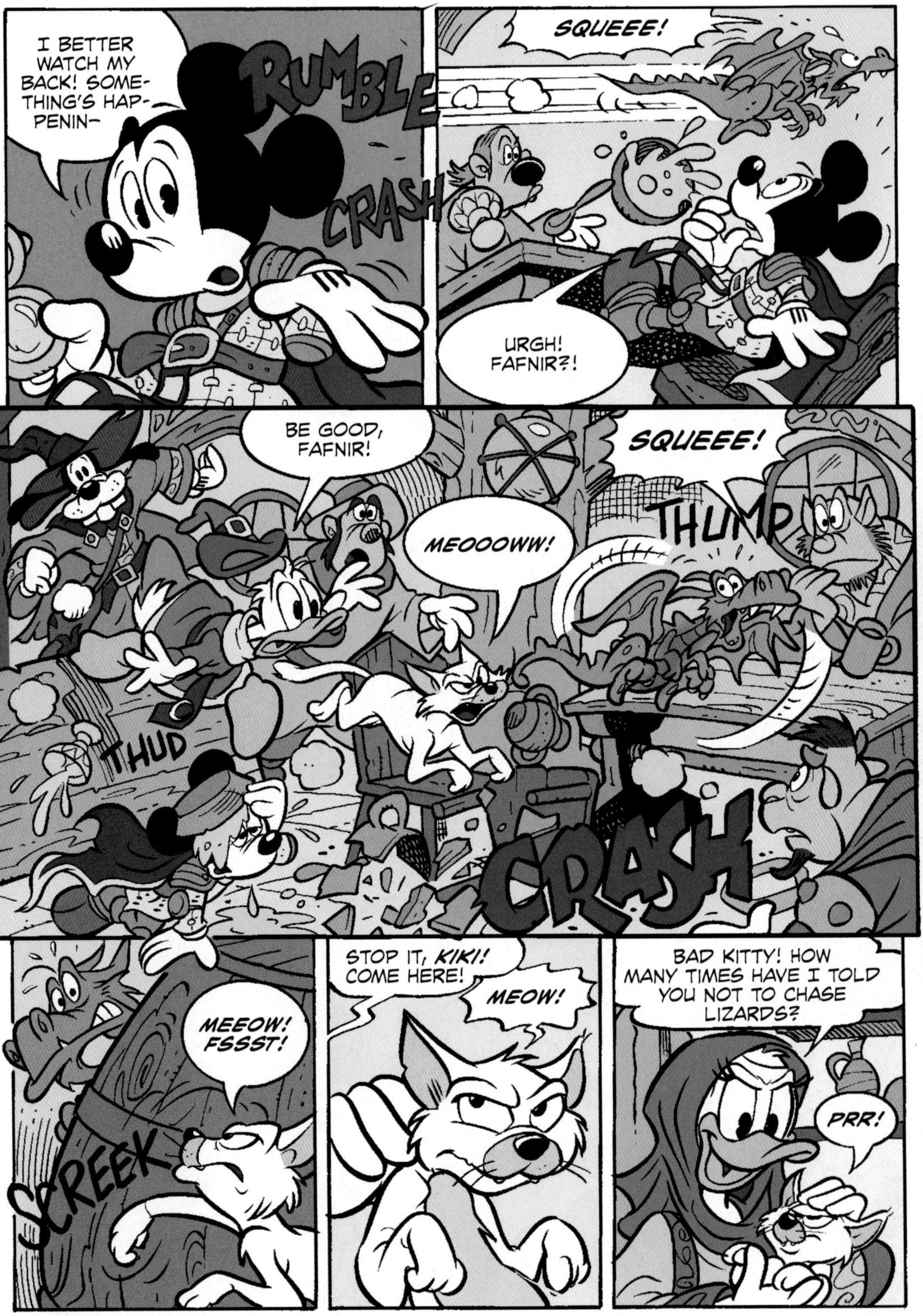
I BETTER WATCH MY BACK! SOME-THING'S HAP-PENIN—
RUMBLE
CRASH
SQUEEE!
URGH! FAFNIR?!
BE GOOD, FAFNIR!
SQUEEE!
MEOOOWW!
THUMP
THUD
CRASH
MEEOW! FSSST!
SCREEK
STOP IT, KIKI! COME HERE!
MEOW!
BAD KITTY! HOW MANY TIMES HAVE I TOLD YOU NOT TO CHASE LIZARDS?
PRR!

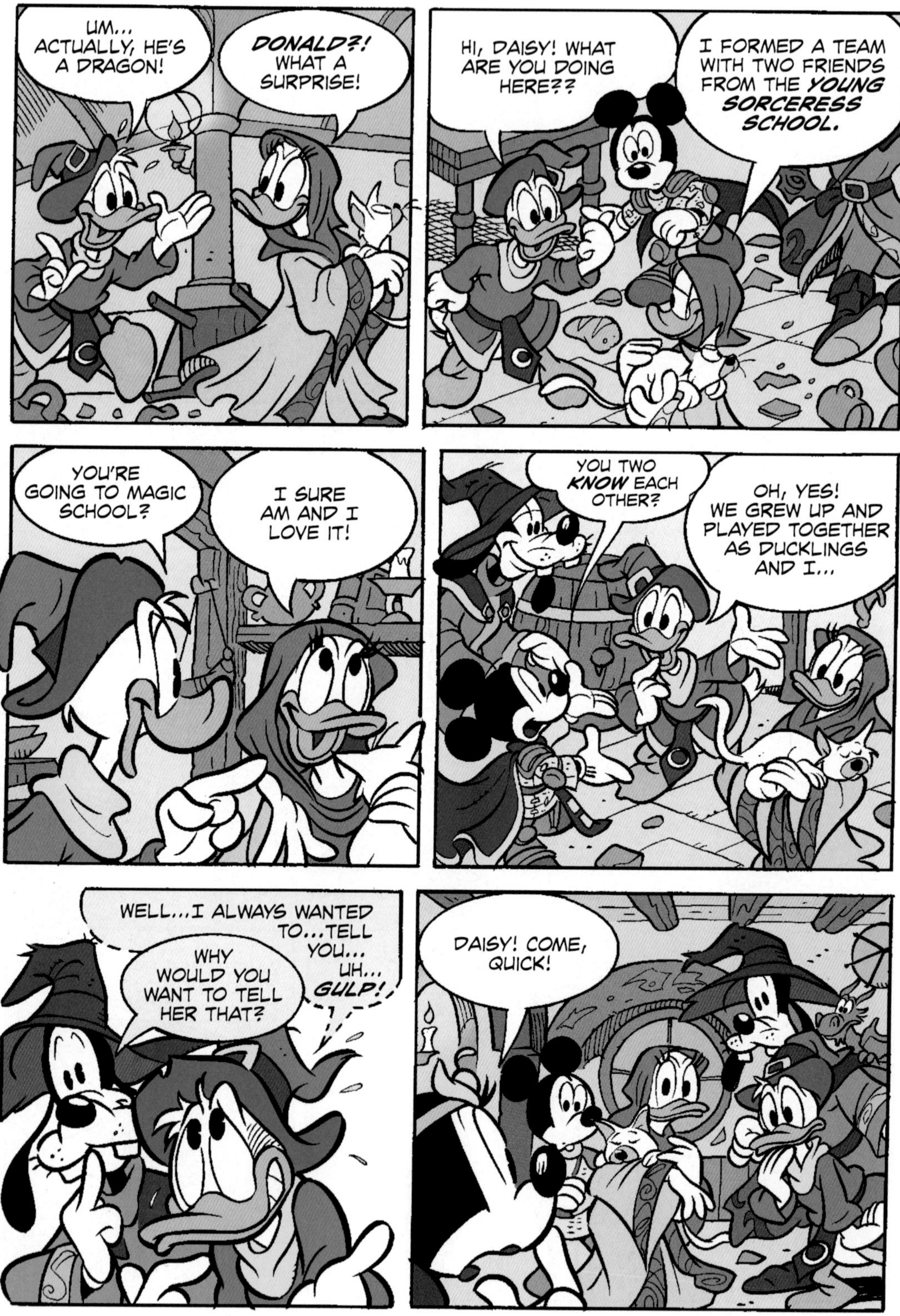

UM... ACTUALLY, HE'S A DRAGON!
DONALD?! WHAT A SURPRISE!
HI, DAISY! WHAT ARE YOU DOING HERE??
I FORMED A TEAM WITH TWO FRIENDS FROM THE YOUNG SORCERESS SCHOOL.
YOU'RE GOING TO MAGIC SCHOOL?
I SURE AM AND I LOVE IT!
YOU TWO KNOW EACH OTHER?
OH, YES! WE GREW UP AND PLAYED TOGETHER AS DUCKLINGS AND I...
WELL...I ALWAYS WANTED TO...TELL YOU... UH... GULP!
WHY WOULD YOU WANT TO TELL HER THAT?
DAISY! COME, QUICK!

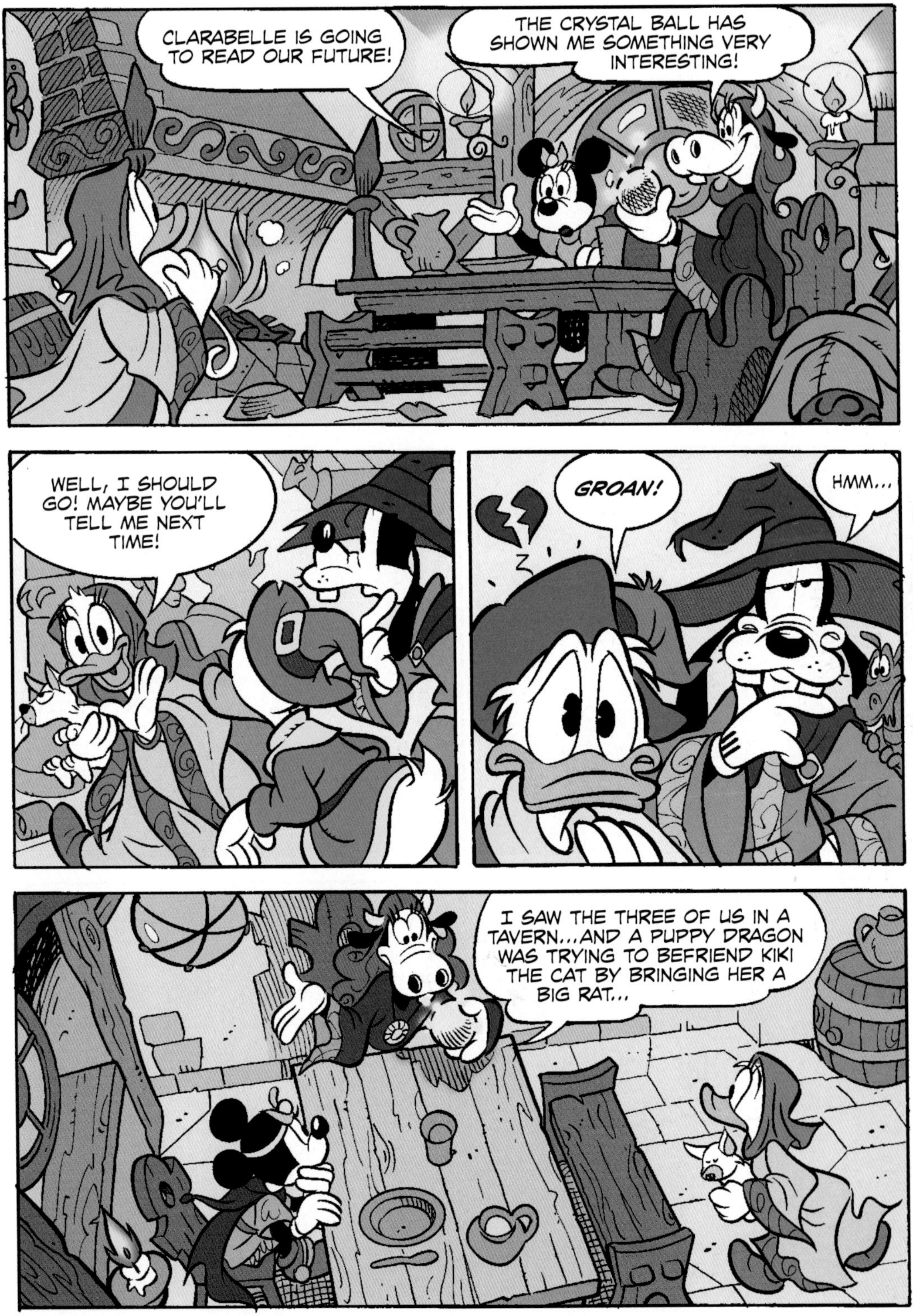
CLARABELLE IS GOING TO READ OUR FUTURE!
THE CRYSTAL BALL HAS SHOWN ME SOMETHING VERY INTERESTING!
WELL, I SHOULD GO! MAYBE YOU'LL TELL ME NEXT TIME!
GROAN!
HMM...
I SAW THE THREE OF US IN A TAVERN...AND A PUPPY DRAGON WAS TRYING TO BEFRIEND KIKI THE CAT BY BRINGING HER A BIG RAT...

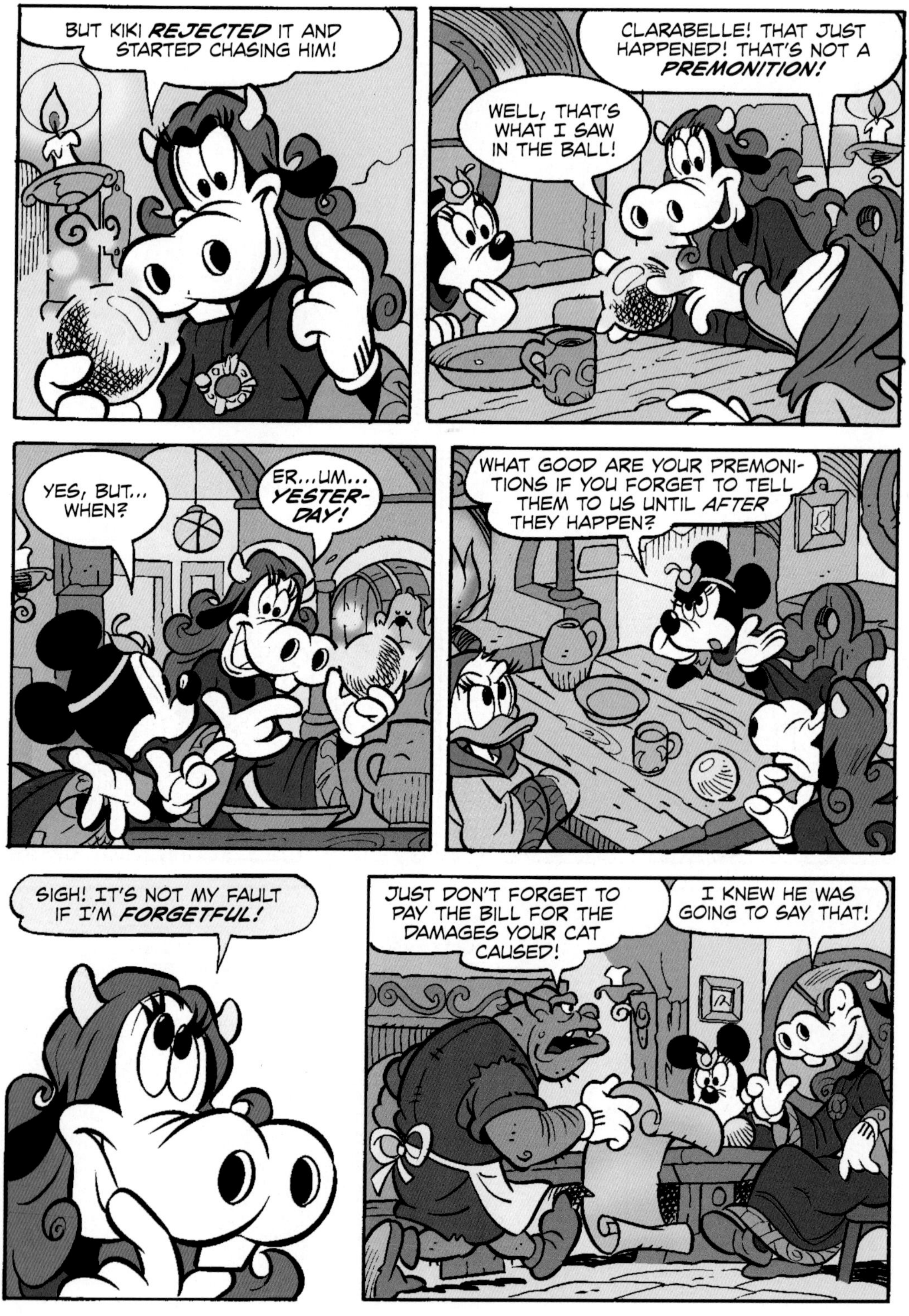
BUT KIKI REJECTED IT AND STARTED CHASING HIM!
CLARABELLE! THAT JUST HAPPENED! THAT'S NOT A PREMONITION!
WELL, THAT'S WHAT I SAW IN THE BALL!
YES, BUT... WHEN?
ER...UM... YESTER-DAY!
WHAT GOOD ARE YOUR PREMONI-TIONS IF YOU FORGET TO TELL THEM TO US UNTIL AFTER THEY HAPPEN?
SIGH! IT'S NOT MY FAULT IF I'M FORGETFUL!
JUST DON'T FORGET TO PAY THE BILL FOR THE DAMAGES YOUR CAT CAUSED!
I KNEW HE WAS GOING TO SAY THAT!

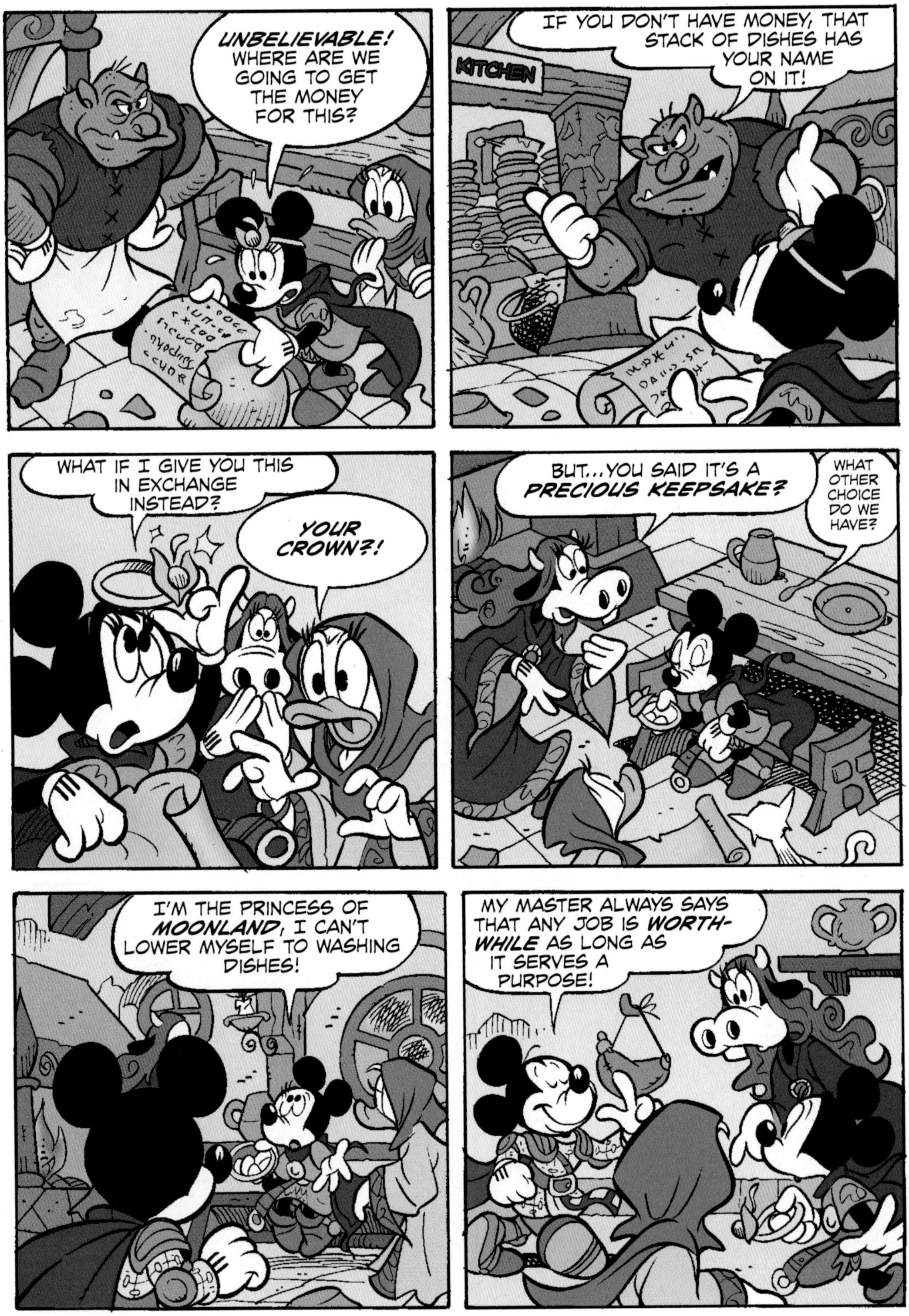
UNBELIEVABLE! WHERE ARE WE GOING TO GET THE MONEY FOR THIS?
KITCHEN
IF YOU DON'T HAVE MONEY, THAT STACK OF DISHES HAS YOUR NAME ON IT!
WHAT IF I GIVE YOU THIS IN EXCHANGE INSTEAD?
YOUR CROWN?!
BUT...YOU SAID IT'S A PRECIOUS KEEPSAKE?
WHAT OTHER CHOICE DO WE HAVE?
I'M THE PRINCESS OF MOONLAND, I CAN'T LOWER MYSELF TO WASHING DISHES!
MY MASTER ALWAYS SAYS THAT ANY JOB IS WORTH-WHILE AS LONG AS IT SERVES A PURPOSE!

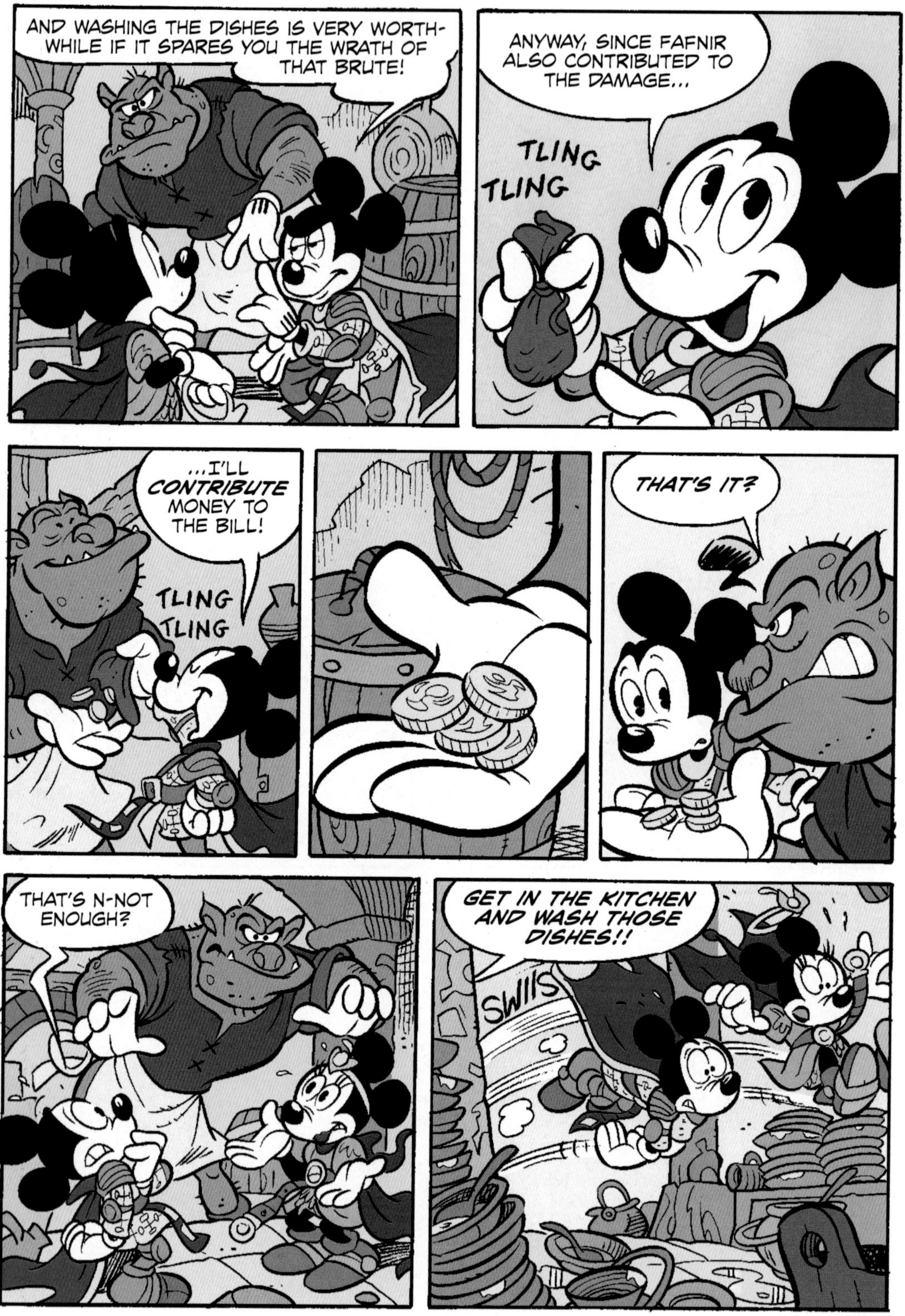
AND WASHING THE DISHES IS VERY WORTH-WHILE IF IT SPARES YOU THE WRATH OF THAT BRUTE!
ANYWAY, SINCE FAFNIR ALSO CONTRIBUTED TO THE DAMAGE...
TLING
TLING
...I'LL *CONTRIBUTE* MONEY TO THE BILL!
TLING
TLING
THAT'S IT?
THAT'S N-NOT ENOUGH?
GET IN THE KITCHEN AND WASH THOSE DISHES!!
SWIIS

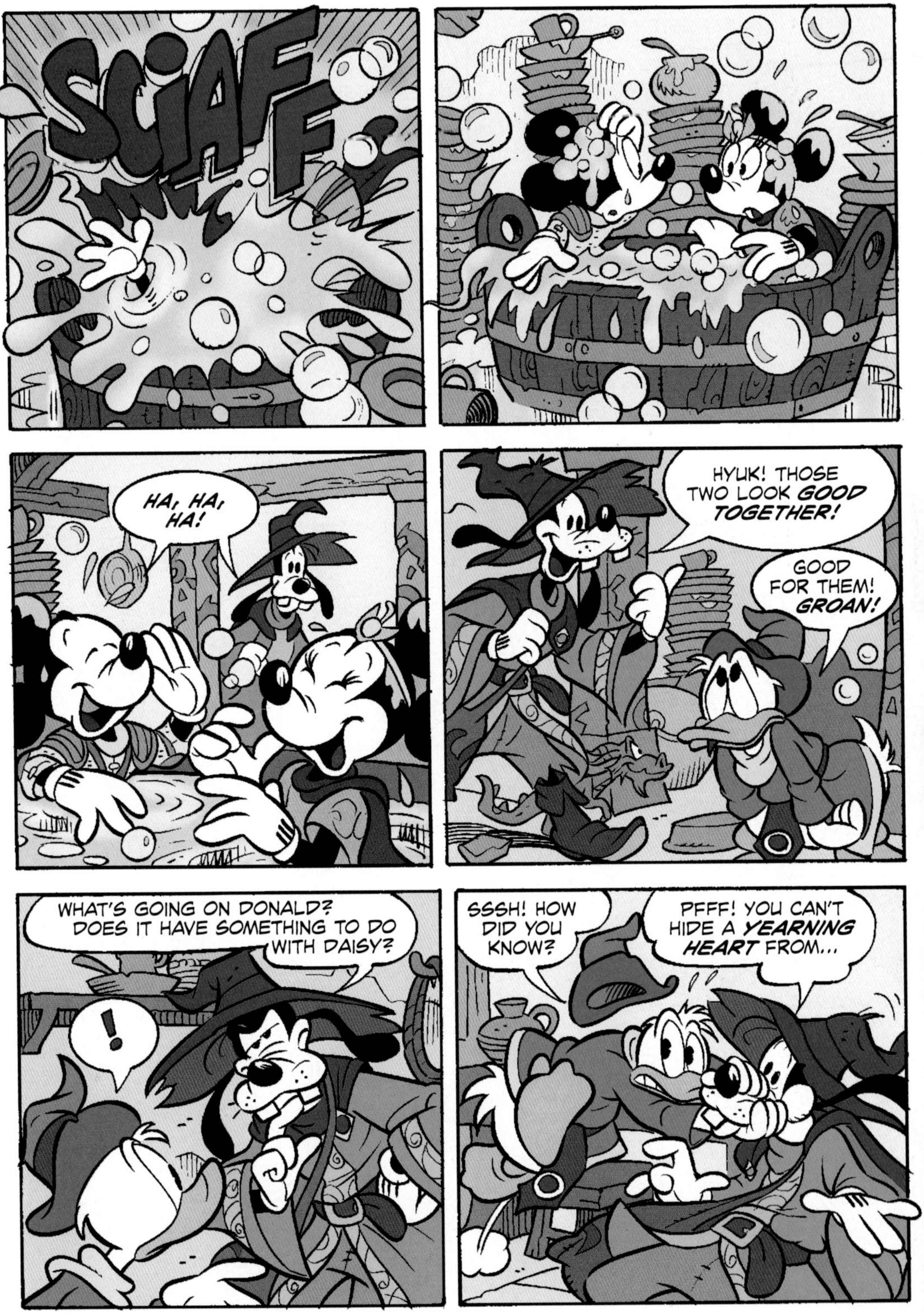
SCIAFF
HA, HA, HA!
HYUK! THOSE TWO LOOK GOOD TOGETHER!
GOOD FOR THEM! GROAN!
WHAT'S GOING ON DONALD? DOES IT HAVE SOMETHING TO DO WITH DAISY?
!
SSSH! HOW DID YOU KNOW?
PFFF! YOU CAN'T HIDE A YEARNING HEART FROM...

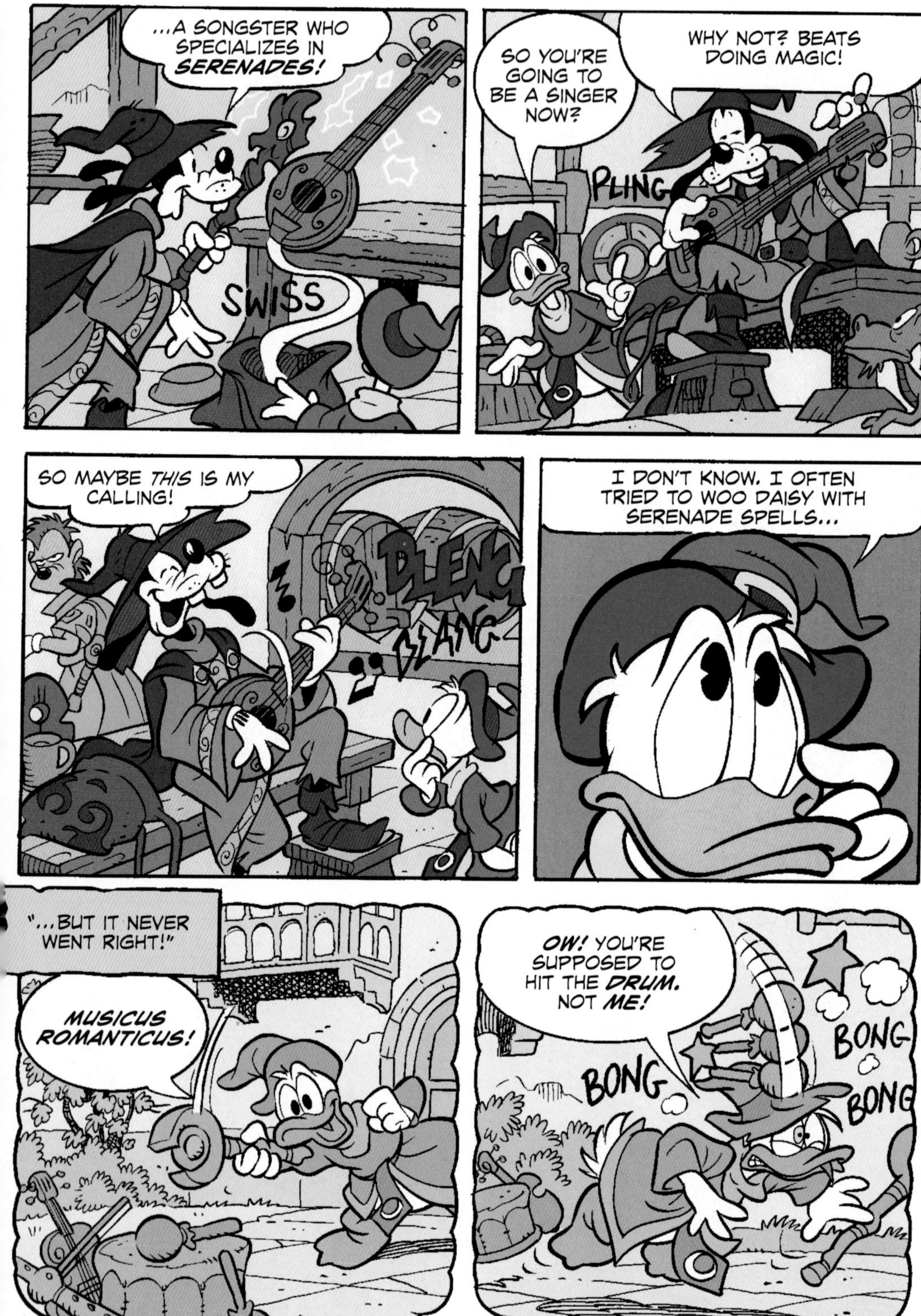
...A SONGSTER WHO SPECIALIZES IN SERENADES!
SWISS
SO YOU'RE GOING TO BE A SINGER NOW?
WHY NOT? BEATS DOING MAGIC!
PLING
SO MAYBE THIS IS MY CALLING!
DLENG
BLANG
I DON'T KNOW. I OFTEN TRIED TO WOO DAISY WITH SERENADE SPELLS...
"...BUT IT NEVER WENT RIGHT!"
MUSICUS ROMANTICUS!
OW! YOU'RE SUPPOSED TO HIT THE DRUM. NOT ME!
BONG
BONG
BONG

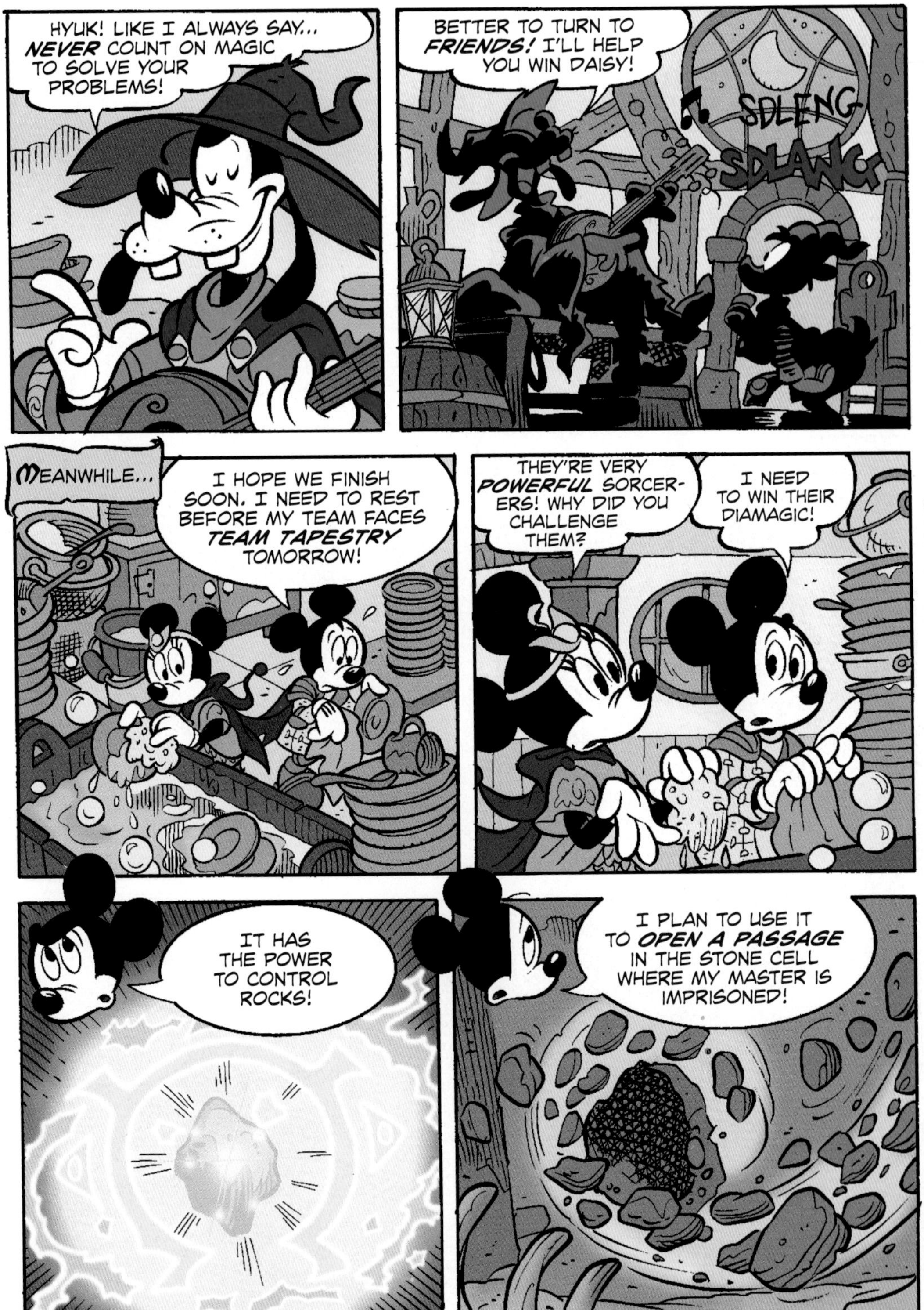

HYUK! LIKE I ALWAYS SAY... NEVER COUNT ON MAGIC TO SOLVE YOUR PROBLEMS!
BETTER TO TURN TO FRIENDS! I'LL HELP YOU WIN DAISY!
SDLENG
SDLANG
MEANWHILE...
I HOPE WE FINISH SOON. I NEED TO REST BEFORE MY TEAM FACES TEAM TAPESTRY TOMORROW!
THEY'RE VERY POWERFUL SORCERERS! WHY DID YOU CHALLENGE THEM?
I NEED TO WIN THEIR DIAMAGIC!
IT HAS THE POWER TO CONTROL ROCKS!
I PLAN TO USE IT TO OPEN A PASSAGE IN THE STONE CELL WHERE MY MASTER IS IMPRISONED!

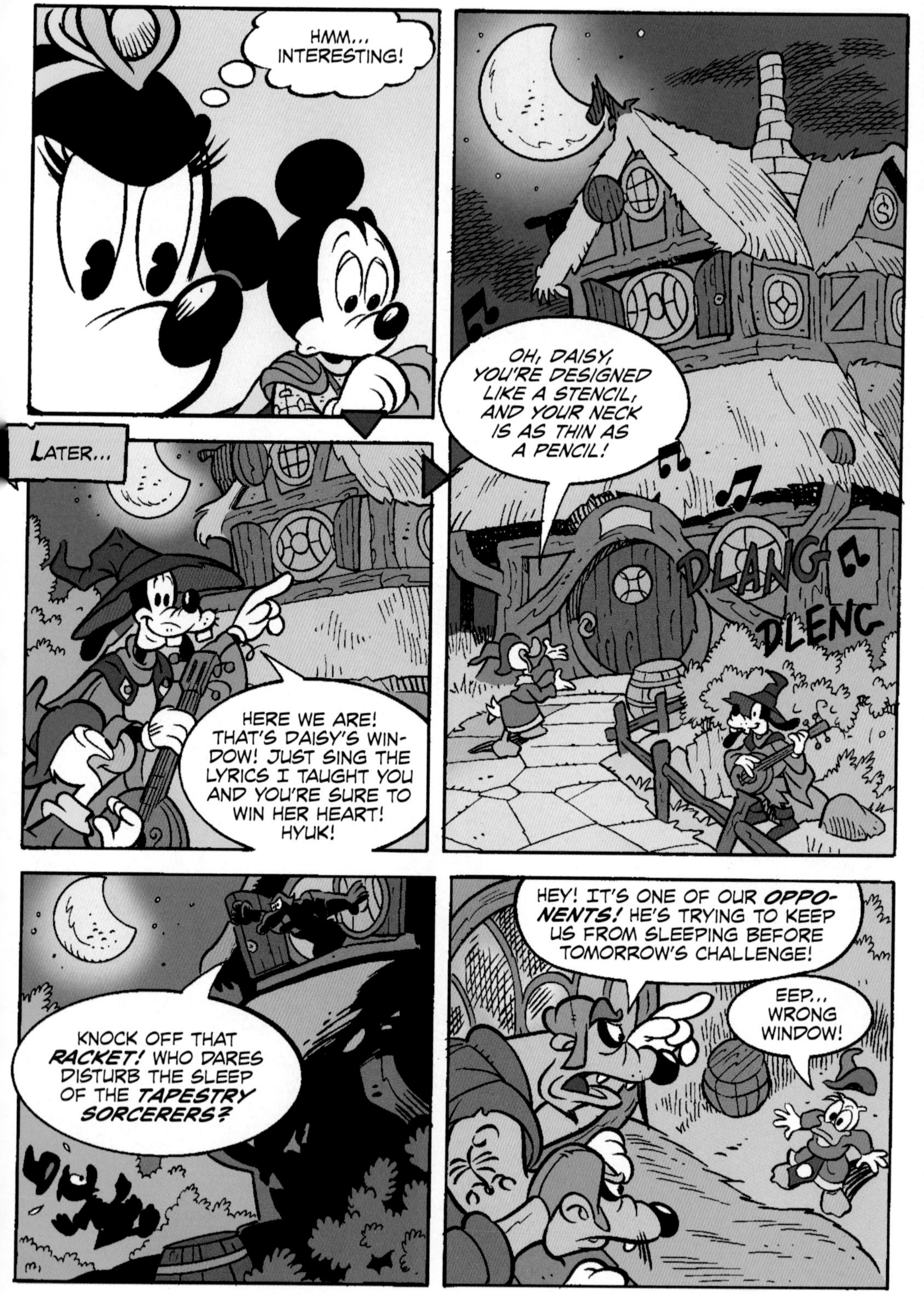
HMM... INTERESTING!
LATER...
HERE WE ARE! THAT'S DAISY'S WIN-DOW! JUST SING THE LYRICS I TAUGHT YOU AND YOU'RE SURE TO WIN HER HEART! HYUK!
OH, DAISY, YOU'RE DESIGNED LIKE A STENCIL, AND YOUR NECK IS AS THIN AS A PENCIL!
DLANG
DLENG
KNOCK OFF THAT RACKET! WHO DARES DISTURB THE SLEEP OF THE TAPESTRY SORCERERS?
HEY! IT'S ONE OF OUR OPPO-NENTS! HE'S TRYING TO KEEP US FROM SLEEPING BEFORE TOMORROW'S CHALLENGE!
EEP... WRONG WINDOW!

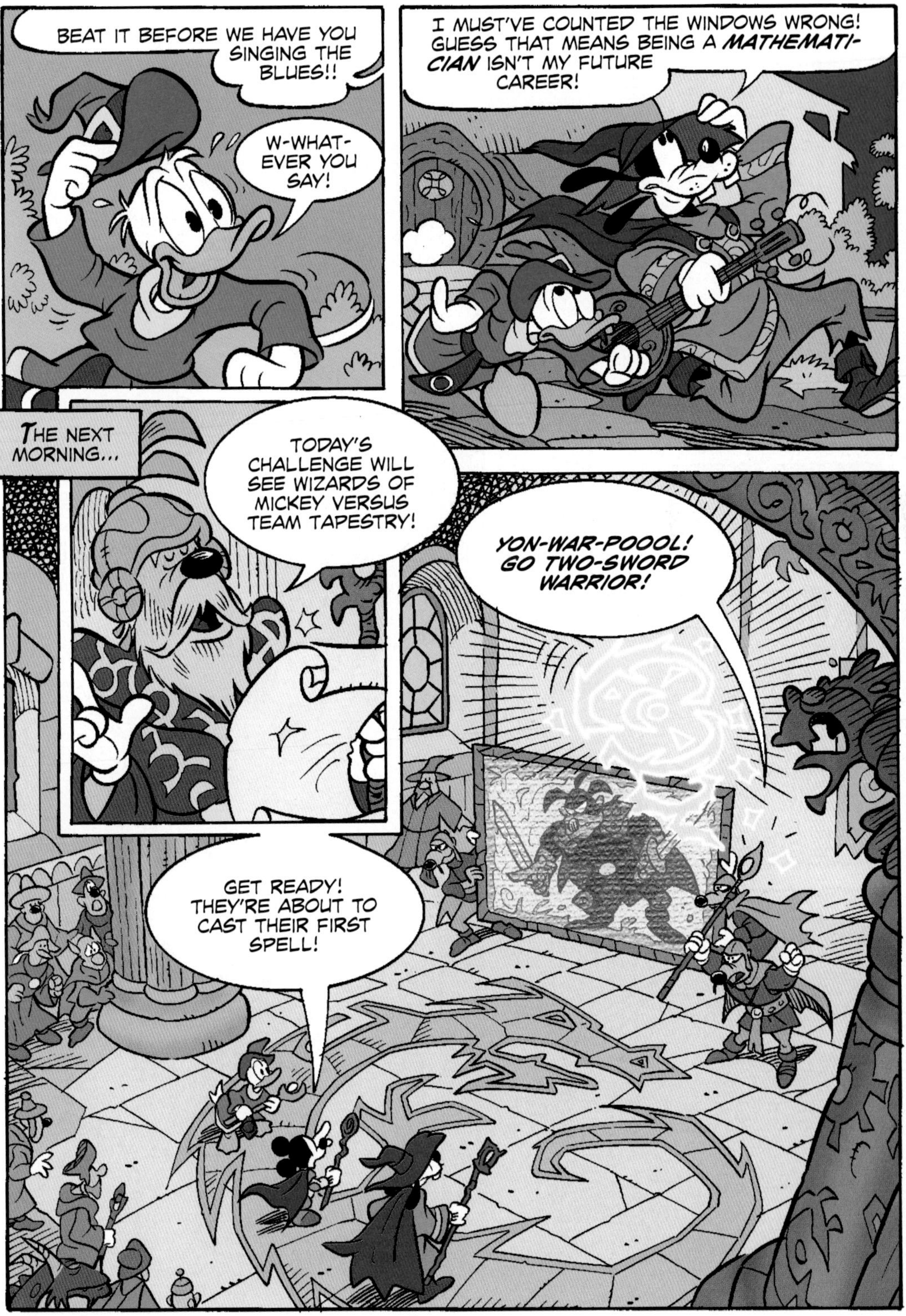
BEAT IT BEFORE WE HAVE YOU SINGING THE BLUES!!
W-WHAT-EVER YOU SAY!
I MUST'VE COUNTED THE WINDOWS WRONG! GUESS THAT MEANS BEING A MATHEMATI-CIAN ISN'T MY FUTURE CAREER!
THE NEXT MORNING...
TODAY'S CHALLENGE WILL SEE WIZARDS OF MICKEY VERSUS TEAM TAPESTRY!
YON-WAR-POOOL! GO TWO-SWORD WARRIOR!
GET READY! THEY'RE ABOUT TO CAST THEIR FIRST SPELL!

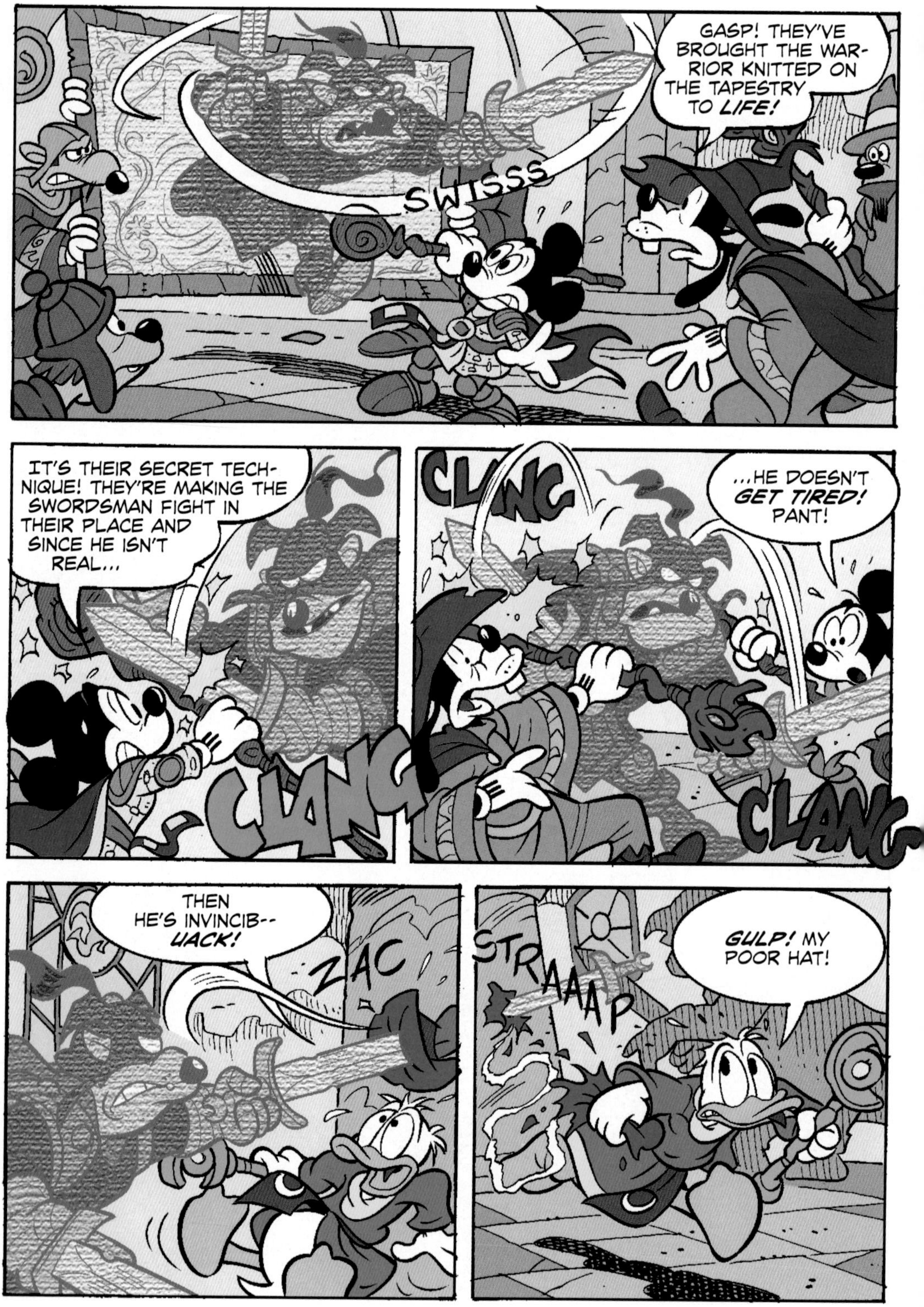
GASP! THEY'VE BROUGHT THE WARRIOR KNITTED ON THE TAPESTRY TO LIFE!
SWISSS
IT'S THEIR SECRET TECHNIQUE! THEY'RE MAKING THE SWORDSMAN FIGHT IN THEIR PLACE AND SINCE HE ISN'T REAL...
CLANG
CLANG
...HE DOESN'T GET TIRED! PANT!
CLANG
THEN HE'S INVINCIB-- UACK!
ZAC
STRAAAAP
GULP! MY POOR HAT!

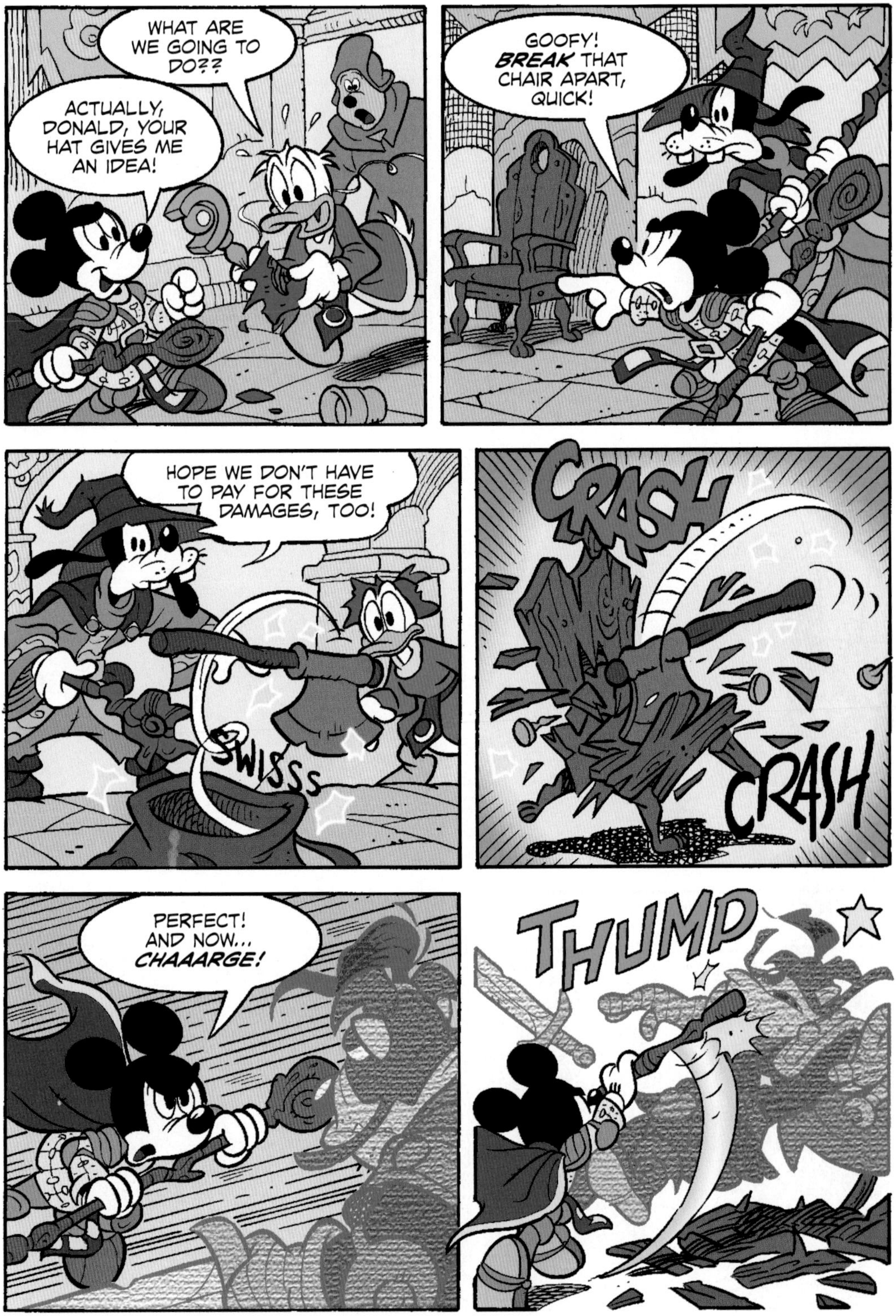
WHAT ARE WE GOING TO DO??
ACTUALLY, DONALD, YOUR HAT GIVES ME AN IDEA!
GOOFY! BREAK THAT CHAIR APART, QUICK!
HOPE WE DON'T HAVE TO PAY FOR THESE DAMAGES, TOO!
SWISSS
CRASH
CRASH
PERFECT! AND NOW... CHAAARGE!
THUMP

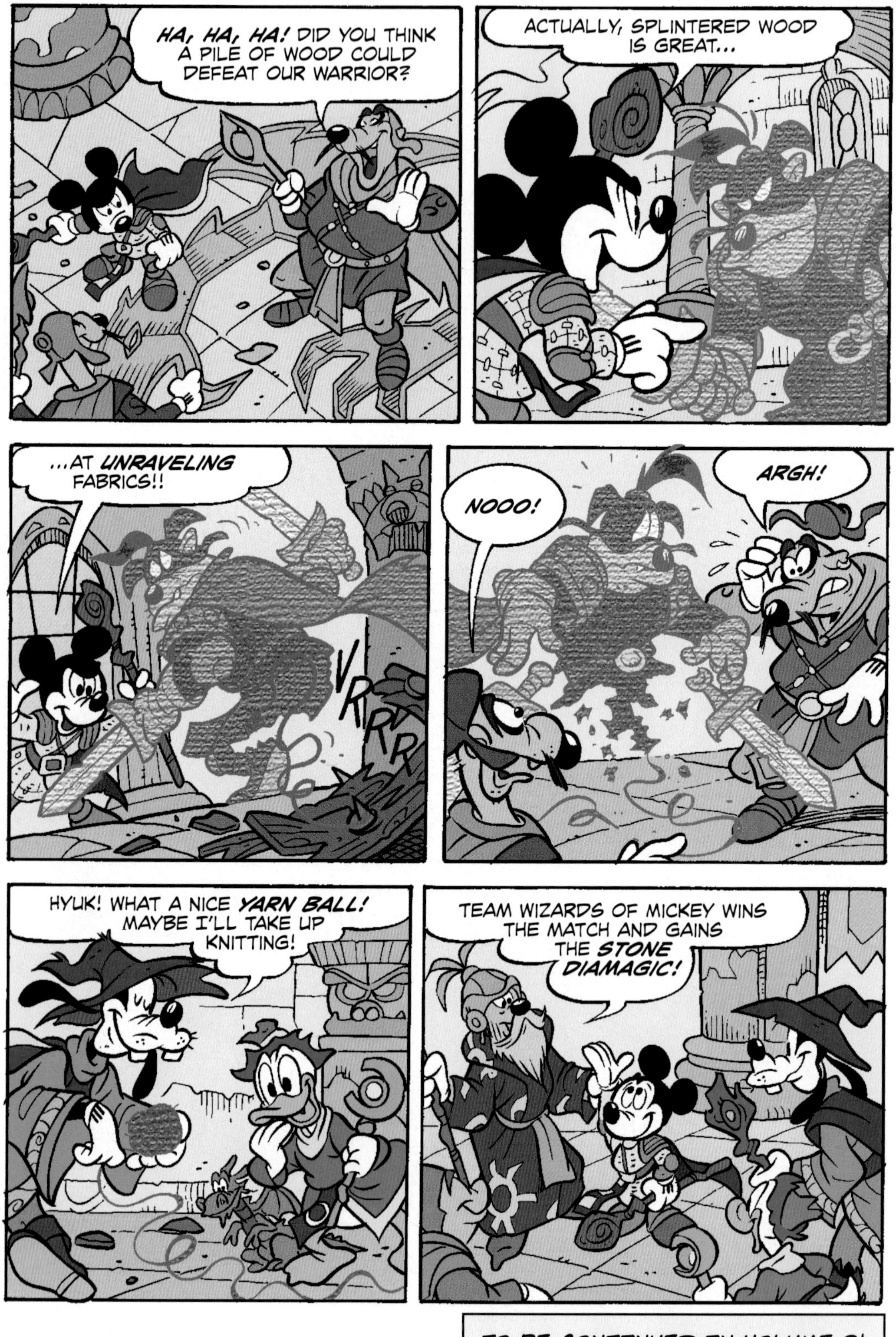
HA, HA, HA! DID YOU THINK A PILE OF WOOD COULD DEFEAT OUR WARRIOR?
ACTUALLY, SPLINTERED WOOD IS GREAT...
...AT UNRAVELING FABRICS!!
VRRRR
NOOO!
ARGH!
HYUK! WHAT A NICE YARN BALL! MAYBE I'LL TAKE UP KNITTING!
TEAM WIZARDS OF MICKEY WINS THE MATCH AND GAINS THE STONE DIAMAGIC!
TO BE CONTINUED IN VOLUME 2!

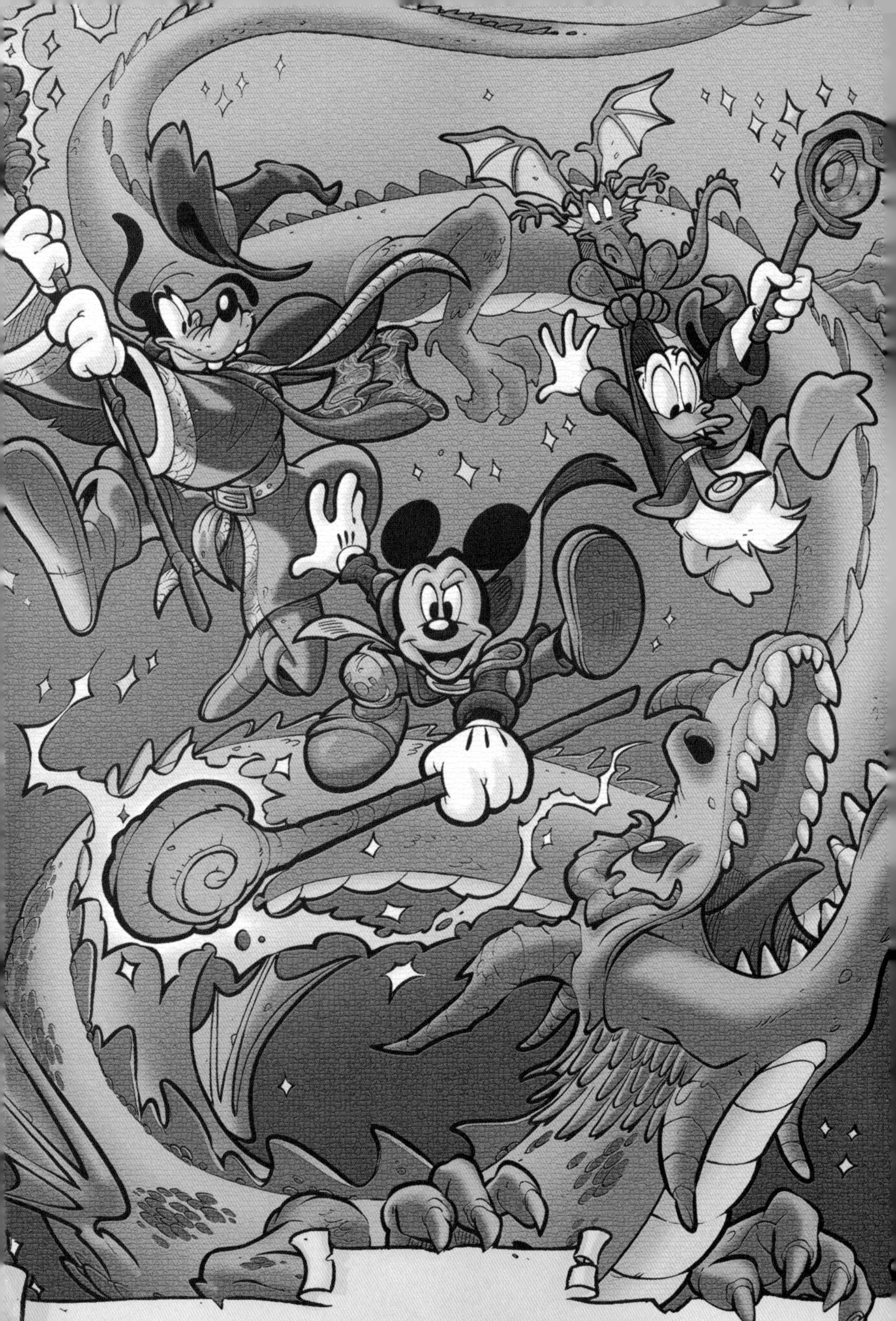

COVER GALLERY

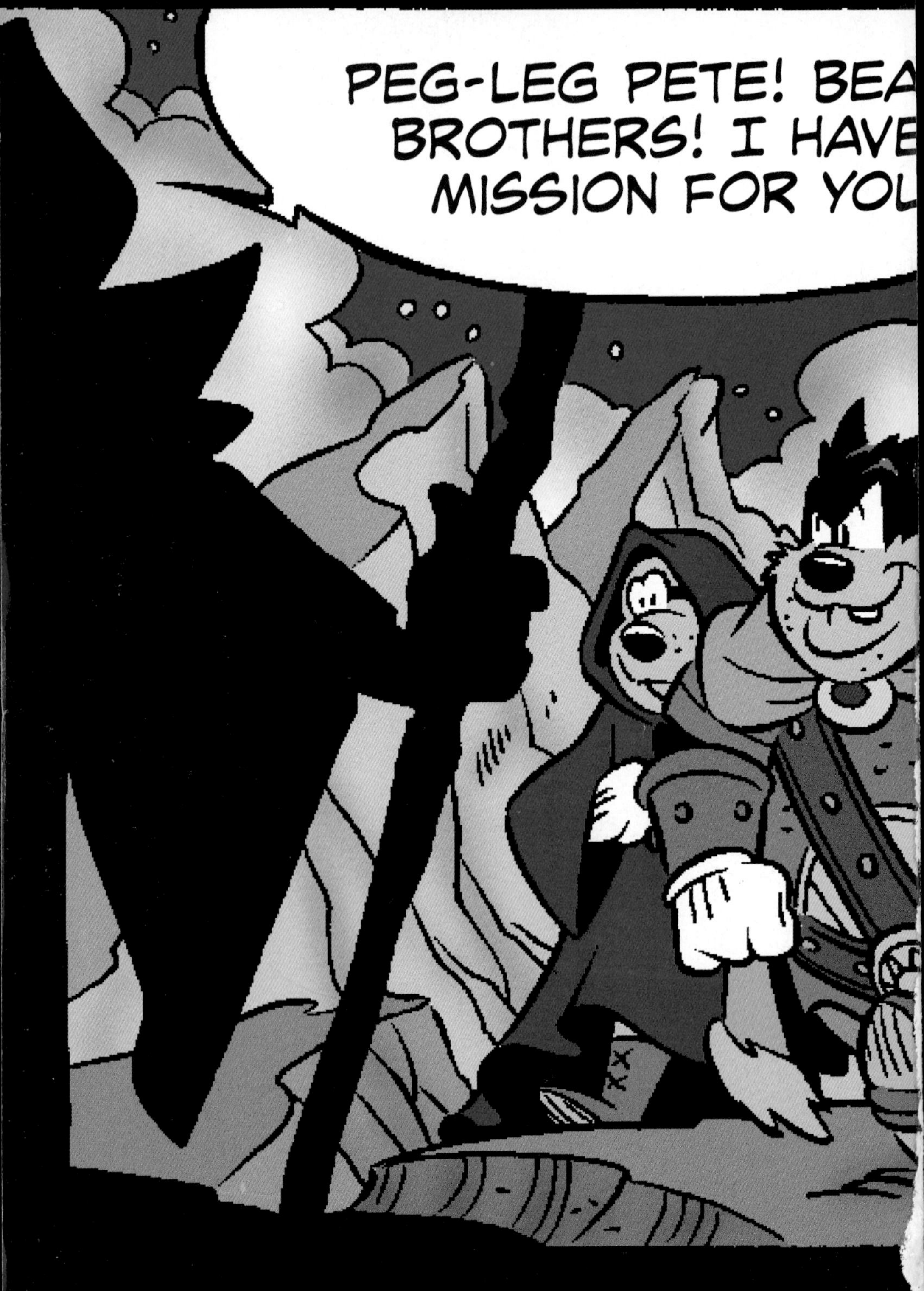
PEG-LEG PETE! BEA
BROTHERS! I HAVE
MISSION FOR YOU